Praise for *Waiting for the Night Song*

"*Waiting for the Night Song* is not just a coming-of-age story, but several coming-of-age stories. It's a novel about how time passes and how time stands still, ties that bind and ties that constrict, place and our place in the world, what keeps us together and what keeps us apart."
—Laurie Frankel, *New York Times* bestselling author of *One Two Three*

"A fresh and engaging tale."
—Kelli Estes, *USA Today* bestselling author of *The Girl Who Wrote in Silk*

"A singular, riveting portrait of persistence and friendship . . . Dalton writes masterfully of an uncertain world."
—Michael Zapata, author of *The Lost Book of Adana Moreau*

"At once timely and timeless . . . It's a novel that burns—figuratively and literally—with sharp prose and uncommon wisdom."
—Peter Geye, award-winning author of *Wintering*

"Deftly constructed, urgent yet slow-burning . . . Reads like a warning from the frontlines of our rapidly deteriorating natural world."
—Omar El Akkad, author of *American War*

"A killer, gorgeous debut . . . Will break your heart, leave you breathless and wanting more."
—Rachel Barenbaum, bestselling author of *A Bend in the Stars*

"A powerful and unforgettable story."
—Erica Ferencik, bestselling author of *The River at Night* and *Into the Jungle*

BOOKS BY JULIE CARRICK DALTON

Waiting for the Night Song

WAITING
FOR THE
NIGHT
SONG

JULIE CARRICK DALTON

A TOM DOHERTY ASSOCIATES BOOK
NEW YORK

WAITING FOR THE NIGHT SONG

Copyright © 2020 by Julie Carrick Dalton

A Forge Book
Published by Tom Doherty Associates
120 Broadway
New York, NY 10271

www.tor-forge.com

Forge® is a registered trademark of Macmillan Publishing Group, LLC.

The Library of Congress Cataloging-in-Publication Data is available upon request.

ISBN 978-1-250-26920-1 (trade paperback)
ISBN 978-1-250-26919-5 (ebook)

Our books may be purchased in bulk for promotional, educational, or business use. Please contact your local bookseller or the Macmillan Corporate and Premium Sales Department at 1-800-221-7945, extension 5442, or by email at MacmillanSpecialMarkets@macmillan.com.

First Edition: January 2021
First Trade Paperback Edition: January 2022

Printed in the United States of America

0 9 8 7 6 5 4 3 2 1

For my husband, Sean,
my true love, my best friend, my perfect coefficient.

And in memory of my grandmother,
Althea Hazel Ross Carrick,
a coal miner's daughter from Appalachia and the boss of
every room she entered. A lifelong educator who taught
countless children to read, she was the source of the ginger
in my hair and the fire in my belly.

Two weeks after my sharp-as-a-tack, fire-haired grand-
mother passed away at age 103, an editor with long red
hair bought Waiting for the Night Song, *my book about*
a little girl with flaming red curls. I refuse to believe that
was a coincidence. I suspect Althea Hazel is still pulling
the strings, just as she always has.

Thanks for continuing to have my back, Grandma. I
miss you.

1

PRESENT DAY

Truth hides in fissures and hollows, in broken places and empty parts. It can be buried, crushed, or burnt, but the truth will always rise. The specific truth Cadie Kessler stalked came in the form of the mountain pine beetle. She pried a strip of bark off a dying pine tree. Her fingers, blistered and raw from hunting the elusive creature, froze as a gush of insects writhed against the exposed wood. They scattered for cover, but not fast enough.

"Got you." Her voice, scratchy and dry from not having been used in days, echoed off granite boulders in the sparse forest. She scraped the beetles into a small envelope and tilted her head up to the morning sun.

Her phone buzzed in her pocket. She braced herself and answered her boss's call.

"What's up, Thea?"

"I looked at the images you sent yesterday. How am I supposed to present this? You're clearly on restricted federal lands."

Cadie didn't respond.

"If we publish your research, we'd have to detail where we got the samples, then you'd get arrested for trespassing."

"This is bullshit and you know it. This is *public* land. I should be able to collect samples on public land." Cadie knew Thea agreed with her, but she needed to yell at someone. "If we don't get control of the infestation now, it's going to get out of control fast. And in this drought, it's all going to burn. Look what happened in California. It's the same beetle."

"Getting yourself arrested isn't going to help prove your case."

Taking advantage of the clear cell signal, Cadie checked her messages as Thea talked on speaker phone.

"I don't like it any more than you do," Thea said.

Cadie scrolled through messages, stopping at a subject heading that grabbed her attention. *Bicknell's Thrush.* The tiny songbird, a favorite from Cadie's childhood, had all but disappeared in the New England woodlands in recent years. The message came from a grad student named Piper. Cadie didn't have time to deal with students. But the thrush.

"Are you listening to me?" Thea said.

"Yeah. I'm here. What do you want me to do? Pretend I don't know the forest is at risk of a devastating fire because of some ridiculous regulation?" Cadie said as she read Piper's message. *Hey Cadence! I'm working on a project to re-create/protect habitat for Bicknell's thrush and found what I think is a bark beetle infestation. Can you confirm?* Piper included a photo dated three days earlier, although Cadie knew the government had closed off that particular forest to environmental research in April.

"Where are you anyway?" Thea said. "Please tell me you aren't anywhere near Mount Griffin. That fire's moving fast."

Uptick in local temps are driving Bicknell's north, plus ski resorts, turbines. Then hurricanes in the DR, Cuba + deforestation in Haiti are eliminating the winter habitat and they aren't surviving to return to New England, Piper wrote. *Same conditions attracting your beetles are driving out my thrush. Can we share data?*

"Cadie, are you there?" Thea sounded annoyed now.

"I'm fine. I'll check in tomorrow." Cadie zoomed in on Piper's photos, which showed the beetle farther north than Cadie realized.

"Don't get yourself arrested." Cadie could hear Thea's fingernails cantering against her desk. "I want to defend your research, but you need to give me irrefutable data and a legal way to prove it."

"There is no legal way. If this forest burns before I establish the beetles are here, I won't have any way to prove my theory." She looked again at Piper's photo. "And it's not just here. They're farther north than I thought."

"How close are you to the fire? This isn't worth getting killed over."

"Exactly my point. People are already dying in these fires. If we can prove they're linked to the beetles, we can get the resources to get ahead of them."

Thea took in a breath as if to say something, but did not speak.

"I'm not planning to get hurt or caught." Cadie paused. "But if I do, I won't bring you into it. As of right now, consider me officially rogue. I have to go."

She hung up before Thea could respond. The idea that defying an executive order to collect insect samples could brand Cadie, a five-foot-two entomologist, as a criminal struck her as funny, despite the potential consequences.

Cadence Kessler: Outlaw Entomologist.

She tried to laugh at herself, but the gnawing worry in her gut reminded her the fire was serious. She needed to get down the mountain by nightfall. If they closed the road, she could be trapped, and since no one knew her location, no one would know to look for her.

When she got home she would storm Thea's office, dump bags of dead beetles on her desk and her lap, and nail poisoned wood samples to the wall. No one who examined her evidence would be able to deny the insects had moved from the Rockies to New England. No one would dare arrest her when they understood the threat. "I told you so" burned sweet on her tongue.

Cadie shook the envelope to the rhythm of a song she couldn't quite remember. The spirited rustle, like seeds anxious to be planted, emboldened her, even as her body ached under the fifty-pound backpack. She trudged on. Only fifty meters to Mount Steady's summit.

She could get a better sense of how much time she had from a higher elevation.

Smoke scratched the back of her throat, confirming the late-summer wind was already pushing the forest fires east. She paused for a sip of water. Working alone in the woods, Cadie marked time in elevation and ounces of water. She was running out of both.

This drought. This spate of fires. This beetle. As the temperature ratcheted up four degrees in less than a century, New Hampshire had practically invited the tiny creature and the fires that came with it. Cadie could slow the wildfires if someone would just believe her. The anticipation of being right, of being the hero, had lulled her to sleep the past several nights under the canopy of stars. Cocooned in her sleeping bag, she'd written the opening to her imagined TED Talk. *When someone says you're overreacting, but you know you're right, keep reacting until it's over.*

Cadie's backpack grew heavier, compressing her knees and spine, as if she might crumble into the rock under her feet. She forced herself up the final incline. If gravity pulled from the dense fist at the center of the Earth, then the higher she pushed herself up the mountain, the farther she removed herself from the core, the looser gravity's grip would be. It tugged at her heels and stole the oxygen from her lungs. Only on the summits did Cadie feel a lightness in her chest. She stood untethered in the rushing wind. Anything seemed possible from the top of a mountain.

Cadie dropped her pack to the ground. A gust whipped her hair across her face, carrying traces of pine and the reedy flute of a distant hermit thrush. Wind stretched the clouds below her like raw cotton on a comb, allowing the rusty tips of dead pine trees to peek through. She pulled samples of tree bark and pine wedges from her backpack and laid them around her in a semicircle. The invasive beetle she had been hunting the last four days had carved lacy lines into the wood. The pea-sized creatures were killing off trees and leaving them as kindling in the parched woodlands. She stroked the delicate destruction with her finger. The beetles' telltale blue fungus—the color of the autumn sky before sunset—stained the wood. That color meant death to a pine. She held a wedge to her face and inhaled the freshly cut wood. The tang of sap should have rushed in. But dead trees don't bleed. They burn.

Smoke blurred the edge of the mountaintops to the west. Mount Griffin rose from the mist, green on the north slope with a slow-burning char on the south. When she finally convinced crews to start thinning the pines, she would salvage a few trunks to mill into floorboards for her home. If she ever stayed still long enough to own a home. The grooves the beetles carved would feel better under bare feet than the slick linoleum in her one-bedroom apartment.

From the mountaintop, home felt distant, as if it might not be there when she came down. Time moved more slowly in the woods, sliding by like the lazy flow of pine sap. As a child, she used to imagine the outside world slipping away as she leapt from rock to rock through the ferny woods surrounding her home. The pine and beech trees had been her friends. They had guarded her, swallowed her secrets whole.

It was her turn to protect the forest.

Silence enveloped the summit, an island of stone floating in the low-hanging clouds. If only time would stop. Right here. Right now. The fires would stall, the beetles would stop their assault, and Cadie would remain at the top of the world, where she could hide from gravity.

She tried to quell the twisting in her gut that reminded her the fires presented an opportunity. If they proved to be a bigger threat than expected, and if Cadie's research stopped an inferno, it would transform her career, her future. She did not want to want that fire, but a small voice inside called out to the flames. *Come if you dare.*

Cadie selected a potato-sized stone from the ledge and dusted it against her thigh. She pressed her tongue to the rock, leaving a wet oval to reveal its hidden mineral life. The dull grays and browns of New Hampshire granite burst into streaks of silver and layers of radiant amber at the touch of her saliva. A creamy, jagged vein glowed in the sunlight. The oval shrank as wind sucked the light from the rock until it reverted to its flat finish. The iridescence of veiled colors fizzed on her tongue. Her mouth watered.

She tucked the stone in the bottom of her backpack, cradling it in the center of the tambourine she carried to scare off bears. *It's just one stone*, she told herself each time. When she built her own house someday, the rocks she'd collected would form the skirt around her hearth. Stolen pieces of every mountain she hiked, markers of time.

The stack of stones—at least thirty by now—formed a cairn in her apartment. She often wondered if the dilapidated building could bear the weight, or if one day it would all come crashing down.

Her cell phone buzzed against the granite slab as a text came through.

It's Daniela. They found him.

The minerals on her tongue turned to acid. She read and reread the words until they became a jumble of illegible letters, and the screen powered down. She hurled a rock off the ledge and held her breath until it struck the slope below, unleashing a torrent of cascading stone. This couldn't be happening.

I'm home. I need you here, Daniela texted again. *They're questioning my dad.*

Cadie imagined the text message in Daniela's childhood voice and didn't restrain the sob that burst out with decades of compressed guilt. More than twenty-five years had passed since she had spoken to Daniela Garcia. If she acknowledged Daniela, Cadie would no longer be able to pretend that long-ago summer had never happened. The fiction of Cadie's childhood, rewritten and edited so she could sleep at night, would come undone. The single gunshot echoed in her mind.

Or she could stay on her mountaintop and turn off her phone. She could hide for a little longer, at least until the fires got too close. She put her head between her knees and stared down at the fissures in the slab. She scratched a rock on the surface of the ledge, leaving white letters next to her wood samples. *Cadie was here.* It felt childish, but she traced over the letters until they stood out in bold blocks. *Cadie was here.*

Horizontal lines in the granite recorded time, a hundred thousand years between lines of crystallized minerals. Climbing her mountains meant traveling through time, treading on scars of each millennia. Unknowable catastrophic events had bent the stone, folding time in on itself. Moments that were never meant to touch, fused together in geological history.

She imagined the panic in Daniela's dark eyes. As much as Cadie wanted to hide in the woods, the ferocity of the bond Cadie once shared with Daniela swelled in her chest, shaming her for wanting to abandon her friend again, as she had done so many years ago.

Her thumbs felt thick and clumsy as she typed a response.

On my way to the cottage. Meet me at 9 tonight? The tacky layer of sap, which felt like part of her skin after four days of climbing trees, stuck to the screen as she typed. She added three rocks to a cairn someone else had built. An offering. A prayer. The chilled morning air telegraphed the metallic peal of mineral against mineral, broadcasting her location into the valley.

Daniela—like the forest—had been her ally, her friend, a keeper of her secrets. Cadie had played everything like a grand adventure back then. Until the game became real. Maybe she had always hoped the truth would rise one day. Or maybe she had convinced herself that the deeper she hid in the woods, the more gently she walked this Earth, the more likely their secret would stay where they left it—where they left him. Buried in the woods.

2

The warped floorboards in the kitchen played like a piano under Cadie's feet. If she maintained her rhythm and bounced from the long board in front of the sink to the short plank behind her father's chair to the narrow strip in the middle of the room, she could coax the melody of "Twinkle, Twinkle, Little Star" out of the moaning, creaking wood.

Standing at the threshold between the kitchen and the hallway, Cadie mapped her route across the kitchen, seeking out the stiff, mute boards that promised silent passage to the door on the other side of the room. Thin light filtered through the muslin curtains at a familiar angle. Six thirty A.M.

Cadie often stole mornings while her parents slept to practice in case she ever needed to escape from something. What she would need to escape from, she did not know yet. Notice your surroundings. Know your escape route. Like Sherlock Holmes. With six leaps, she landed in front of the screen door and eased it open enough to squeeze her torso through. If she opened it one inch too far, the squeak would alert her parents.

Outside, a frothy mist hung over the lake. She tiptoed out to the end of the rickety pier and sat, letting her feet dip into the tepid water. At first Cadie didn't notice the boat, half obscured by the fog. But as it crept closer, the small vessel broke through the gauzy curtain. A yellow rowboat, drifting alone with no captain, no passengers. She stood up to see inside. Maybe someone lay on the bottom. A lost child. Maybe a murderer ready to jump out and grab her. Pressing up on her toes, stretching as far as she dared over the water, she still couldn't see inside.

The boat floated closer, closer, then passed by her pier on the barely noticeable current without pause.

The morning sun infused the mist with a creamy, molten glow. Pressure swelled inside Cadie's rib cage. A longing rippled through her muscles and clung to her bones, pulling her toward the boat as if the universe needed her to act. If she hesitated, if she went inside to ask permission, it would be gone. Disappeared into the clouds, like a dream she would never remember. She peeled off her pajama top and shorts and looked back at the house. Her toes curled around the edge of the warped gray boards, clinging to the rules she always obeyed.

She filled her chest with the misty air, pinched her nose, and jumped.

The lake water caught her as it had a thousand times before, but its embrace felt foreign at this early hour. Her limbs felt dense and stiff as she chopped through the water, trying not to sink too deep, where the water grew cold. From eye level the billowy vapor distorted her depth perception and she lost perspective of where she drifted, where the boat hid. Or the shore. She kept paddling forward. It had to be there. She tried to whistle a low tone to echo off the boat, but humid air absorbed the sound as it escaped her lips.

Finally, her outstretched hand swept the cold aluminum side of the boat.

"Hello?" she whispered, and rapped on the side. Fog muffled the hollow echo of her knuckles on the hull. She pushed the front of the boat and kicked with all her strength. The abandoned craft resisted, but as Cadie fought, the boat slowed, then grudgingly reversed direction. Her labored breath echoed off of the boat with a hush. As she entered the shallows in front of her secluded beach, she lodged the wayward craft in the sand and stood up.

Two oars lay next to a rope coiled on the bottom. Plenty of dings, but no holes. A perfect vessel. As if it had drifted to her, for her. Someone meant for her to find this boat. She would explore the whole lake on her own, discover a place no one knew existed.

Cadie surveyed her house, and, seeing no sign of her parents, she dragged the boat fifty yards around the shoreline and tied it to the drooping birch branches behind the rocks where she used to play pirates. She ducked as a ribbon of starlings curled above her head, their wings murmuring secrets she couldn't understand. The arc of green-black wings swooped toward the water where she stood, wet and naked. She hugged her arms around her waist and hurried through the shallows to get her pajamas from the pier.

Cadie's knees shook as she eased the screen door shut behind her. She snuck back over the creaky kitchen floor, the nighttime chill held firmly in the peg nails securing the warped planks. She pressed her back against the door. Water dripped off the ends of her red ringlets, forming puddles on the floor.

Cadie slipped into the shower to hide her morning swim. She wanted to keep the boat. But even if no one claimed it, her parents would never let her take it out alone. She would be too scared to disobey them. She imagined her boat with no captain and slammed the shower door.

The smell of coffee greeted her as she reentered the kitchen. Her mother blotted a tangle of bacon with a paper towel and offered the plate to Cadie. The salty, chewy bacon exploded in her mouth, filling her nostrils with the bold smell of hickory.

Through the window she spied a glint of gold peeking between the rocks where branches left a sliver of the bow exposed. It glowed, singing a come-hither song only she heard. She squeezed her knees together and prayed her parents wouldn't notice the blaze of anxious yellow.

She *would* take her boat out. No one would ever know.

After breakfast, Cadie wandered around the cottage, bumping into chairs, rereading the titles of books she had read again and again. She fingered the roughly hewn frame around a photo of her parents working on a farm in Canada before Cadie was born. Now her parents painted landscapes and made pottery in the woods of New Hampshire. They canned vegetables and chopped wood. Cadie had never even been outside of New England.

She flopped down on a small rug in front of the fireplace, stroking the woven fibers of dark red and burnt orange set off by flecks of turquoise and fuchsia—colors that did not exist in New Hampshire. She closed her eyes and willed the carpet to soar through the clouds, to take her back to Persia where it came from. Anywhere but the woods that framed her entire life.

"You're making me crazy," her mother said. "Do you want to throw a pot?"

The slip of clay moving through her hands, the sensation of art flowing from the tips of her fingers teased Cadie with possibility every time she sat at her mother's pottery wheel. But Cadie's vessels usually flopped. Despite having two working artists as parents, Cadie had inherited no artistic skills.

"I don't feel like it."

"You could go pick some berries. Then we can make something."

Cadie knew the berries would sit in the fridge and rot, but she grabbed a plastic container from under the counter and slipped on her mud-crusted sneakers.

"Come, Friar," she called to her border collie, and they ducked into the woods. Soggy twigs bent under her weight instead of snapping against the spongy forest floor. Shafts of sunlight broke through the canopy of maple, oak, and pine.

The closest neighbors lived so far through the forest, Cadie imagined herself alone in the world. Mud sucked at her shoes as she approached the swollen creek. According to her father, their creek came from an underground source. The water, filtered through the minerals on its way to the surface, was the purest water anywhere, her dad had told her over and over. She scooped up a mouthful.

Instead of heading toward the blueberries, Cadie followed the creek deeper into the forest in search of the spring she half believed existed. The property along the creek belonged to the state, a wide swath of conservation land dividing her property from that of the neighbors she had never met.

Cloven moose prints and the delicate handprints of raccoons marred the soft mud. Some days she found evidence bears had stopped for a drink. Large trees never took root on the soft banks.

The saplings that tried, tipped and fell as soon as they reached adolescence because the soil turned to soggy cake during the spring thaw and couldn't support their roots. A wide, treeless corridor on either side of the creek let the light pour in.

The Granite State was famous for its thin, rocky topsoil. Farmers pulled stones out of the fields when they cleared the land, but new rocks surfaced every year. The rain came, the freeze, the thaw, shifting the soil so the smaller particles slipped below the stones and pushed rocks up, the way Brazil nuts always rise to the top of a bowl of mixed nuts. The soil shuddered and moaned, heaving new stones up each spring.

But not around Silas Creek, where Cadie could sink up to her ankles in the brownie-batter mud and never hit a rock. The silty mud dried like a dusting of cocoa powder on her ankles whenever she tromped through it.

Countless times, she had tracked the windy waterway deep into the woods where a rusty barbed-wire fence cut through the forest, spanning the creek before she could get to the underground source. The fence created a barrier between her property and protected marshlands on the interior of the peninsula where she lived. She had tried to shimmy under the wire, but dead vines clinging to the fence gave her the creeps. A single rusty scratch could give her lockjaw, according to her mother. She always chickened out.

As she turned a bend in the creek, Cadie halted. A birch tree, reckless enough to take root on the bank, had lost its footing and fallen, buckling part of the fence to expose an opening barely big enough for Cadie to slither under.

She splashed through the icy water and dropped to all fours. First one shoulder, then the other under the treacherous wires. Stones shifted under the slick soles of her sneakers. Friar huffed his disapproval.

The forest on the other side looked similar to hers, but the forbidden woods seemed thicker, denser. She cocked her head to see if the sky looked different from the other side. A stone shifted and she fell to her elbows, her chin hitting the water. Sharp rocks dug into her knees, distracting her so she didn't feel the stabbing in her shoulder at first. An inch-long gash on her upper arm beaded with blood droplets where a rusty barb had torn through her flesh. She crawled backward out from under the fence.

Friar whined and wriggled himself next to Cadie in the water.

"It's okay, boy." The smell of wet dog comforted her.

She splashed the wound, rubbing the cut. If she could have bent her neck only two inches more, she would have sucked the poison out like snake venom. Cadie moved her jaw from left to right and straightened her back as she stood knee-high in the water.

Instead of trying to squeeze under the fence again, she picked up a stone and hurled it at the opening between the wires. The rock passed through without touching a single mangled wire. Kids made fun of Cadie's knobby knees and her clumsiness, but she had perfect aim.

She turned her back to the fence.

The best berries grew on the far bank, flush with a water source, rich soil, and unobstructed morning light. Friar stopped as they approached the clearing where the blueberries grew and growled a low, deep warning. He stiffened his back and pricked his ears up. Cadie froze. She turned the plastic container over and beat on the bottom like a drum.

Bears.

"Come on, Friar. Home." She edged backward. "'Oh, I went down south for to see my Sal, singing Polly Wolly Doodle all the day,'" she sang and backed up, maintaining the steady, hollow rhythm on the plastic tub.

Friar darted toward the noise.

"Friar!" She inched backward. The bushes rustled and parted. "Friar!"

She curled her toes inside her sneakers and fought the urge to run. Never run from a bear. "'For my Sal she is a spunky gal, singing Polly Wolly Doodle all the day.'" She matched her drum to every other beat of her pounding heart.

"Don't stop singing because of me," a voice called.

From behind the bushes stepped Daniela Garcia, a grade ahead of Cadie. They lived in the same small town, went to the same school, but they didn't really know each other.

Daniela wasn't a Girl Scout.

A hot blush slithered up Cadie's neck, her ears, her face.

"You thought I was a bear, didn't you?" Daniela said.

"No." Cadie didn't need another reason for the kids outside the 7-Eleven to laugh at her. Her flaming hair and giant freckles gave them invitation enough. Now she would be the girl who sang to bears in the woods.

Friar ran over to Daniela and jumped up on her, leaving muddy splotches on her shorts. Cadie's stomach lurched.

"Down, Friar." Cadie tried to pull him off Daniela. "Sorry."

"Fryer? Like a fryer hen?"

"His real name is Friar Tuck, from Robin Hood."

"You shouldn't yell for him like that."

"Why not?"

"I thought you were yelling *fire*," Daniela said. "Not what you want to hear in the middle of the woods. I mean, geez. If you lived on a beach, would you name your dog Shark?"

Daniela dropped to her knees, allowing Friar to lick her face.

"You can call him Tuck if you want."

"Nah, Friar's cool. Why'd you sing anyway? I would've run if I saw a bear."

"You don't run from bears. You move slow and make noise. And never look them in the eyes."

"You're a pretty awful singer. Are you picking blueberries?"

"Yeah. My mom wants some."

"Me too." Daniela swept her arm toward the bushes. Cadie took it as an invitation.

Cadie wished she had braided her hair, which had dried into a red puffball. Her pink terry cloth shorts did not match her blue tank top. Daniela wore cutoff denim shorts and a button-down short-sleeved shirt made of red handkerchief fabric. Her black hair hung in a loose ponytail. Although Daniela's parents spoke with thick accents, Daniela had no trace of an accent, unlike the other Mexican kids who transitioned in and out of her school. Other kids moved from farm to farm, there one school year, gone the next. But Daniela had always been there. Cadie often saw her on the porch of her father's hardware store when she walked home from school.

"Why are you in my woods?" Cadie said.

Daniela raised her eyebrows in high, sweeping arches and put a hand on her hip. "Why are *you* in *my* woods?"

Cadie slapped her leg to call Friar closer.

"We just moved here," Daniela said. "The cottage by the water off Woodside. It's my woods."

Although the two properties butted up against each other, their driveways connected to different streets. Cadie had never even seen the cottage, other than glimpses from out on the lake.

A slow grin spread across Daniela's face as she looked Cadie up and down. "Did you fall in the creek?"

Cadie shrugged. Mud clung to her knees. She wiped away the blood on her arm.

"At least it's warm out." Daniela stepped aside to make room for Cadie. "It's sunnier over here. You'll dry off faster."

Daniela paused from picking berries and pointed at the woven bracelet on Cadie's wrist. "What's this?"

"Paracord. The knots unwind to seven feet of rope for, you know, emergencies."

"Are you guys survivalists or something?" Daniela asked.

"No. I just like it."

"Cool."

They picked berries quietly for ten minutes. Daniela surveyed each cluster before picking it, occasionally stepping away, tilting her head up, and swaying her back to look at the sky. She whistled a mournful song Cadie did not recognize. The soft edges of each note rose above the bushes as if they came from a perfectly tuned flute, not Daniela's chapped lips. The drawn-out notes whispered of melancholy, but as Daniela swayed in rhythm with her own music, the corners of her mouth curled up and her eyebrows arched, convincing Cadie the song wasn't meant to be sad.

Cadie paused several times to look through the bushes toward the lake, hoping to catch a flicker of yellow between the branches. Daniela turned and followed Cadie's gaze. Her song drifted into a final note that left Cadie feeling unsatisfied, as if the melody asked a question Cadie could not answer.

"Are you still looking for bears?" Daniela said.

"No." The warm flush crept up her neck as she twisted the bottom edge of her shirt around her finger. "Can you keep a secret?"

"Of course."

"Follow me." Cadie sprinted into the woods, Friar close at her heels.

"If it's the patch of berries down by the water, I already found it," Daniela called.

She heard Daniela running to catch up, but she didn't slow down. The smell of damp pine and stagnant water intensified as they got closer to the lake. Water bugs skittered over pools of still rainwater. Chunks of granite, dropped by glaciers during the Ice Age, ranging in size from a softball to a pickup truck, littered the forest floor, forming crevices that could snap her ankle if she lost focus. She leapt from rock to moss-covered rock, to leaf-strewn patches of forest floor, holding her breath to duck through clouds of mosquitoes. The cheerful trill of a Bicknell's thrush encouraged her to run faster.

As she approached the edge of the lake, she wriggled under a few low-hanging hemlock branches, dripping with the previous night's rain, and stepped out onto a large slab of granite erupting from the woods toward the lake.

Tucked into the nook where the rock met the water, Cadie's boat waited for her.

Daniela emerged from under the hemlock branches and joined Cadie on the rock. "Okay. It's a boat. I don't get it."

"I found it floating in the lake this morning. I swam out and rescued it. My parents weren't even awake yet."

Three inches taller than Cadie, with a confidence Cadie longed for, Daniela turned to Cadie as if seeing her for the first time. She looked at Cadie's muddy sneakers, her bony knees, mismatched clothes, and unruly hair.

Cadie had made a mistake. If Daniela told anyone about the boat, Cadie would lose her chance to explore the lake. Daniela might think Cadie was being childish for hiding the boat, or unethical for not trying to find its owner.

Or, like Cadie, Daniela might be looking for something more than blueberries.

"Whose is it?"

"It's mine now." Cadie pressed up and down on her tiptoes.

Daniela stepped closer to the boat and ran her hand across the rim. Yellow paint flaked off and she flicked it in the water.

Friar sniffed at the boat and growled.

"After my parents go to work tomorrow, I'm taking it out. You can come if you want." Cadie rubbed Friar's ears.

Daniela squinted at Cadie, at the boat, then back at Cadie.

With her shoe, Cadie scratched at a patch of lichen clinging to the rock.

"No one else knows about this?" Daniela said.

"No one else can *ever* know."

Daniela slapped a mosquito on her arm, leaving a bloody smear. "What time should I be here?"

3

Cadie turned down the gnarled road weaving through the woods past the Talbots' ramshackle sugarhouse. Her mother had always called it the James Taylor Road because she liked to listen to his mellow, rolling voice on the twisting, rolling road. Cadie hummed to her mental soundtrack, but sped up the tempo. She wanted to get to the cottage before Daniela.

Her ears popped, as they always did, on the steady incline leading to the "Welcome to Maple Crest" sign. She pressed down on the gas, urging the vehicle to speed up, but the air around her pushed back on the car as if gravity, the mountains, even the road, wanted her to turn around.

A female deer lay on the side of the road, motionless. Its flat eyes stared at oncoming traffic. The fires had been pushing animals out of the deep woods into neighborhoods, parks, and highways for weeks. The number of foxes, deer, and moose struck by vehicles in the past month already surpassed the previous two years combined. The deer looked as if it might peel itself off the sweltering blacktop at any moment and walk away. No blood, no visibly broken bones.

If Daniela came forward with the truth about what they had done, Cadie would never be able to drive back to Concord and reenter her life the way she'd left it. She would become the girl who had covered up a murder, the woman who had harbored the lie.

Even as she considered the ramifications, a yearning simmered in her gut. To tell the truth. The cost of redemption might be her career. Maybe she could live with that. But the New Hampshire woodlands and its inhabitants would pay a much bigger price if no one stepped in to complete her work.

Paint curled off the edges of auction and foreclosure signs slouching in dusty pastures flanked by barns leaning at severe angles. The drought had sucked this land dry, leaving behind stretches of browned cornstalks to stand guard like brittle ghosts.

Towering hemlocks and balsam firs wrapped around the road she and Daniela once soared down on their bikes, focused on the taste of the wind and their next adventure, fixated by maps and secrets. Deep secrets—not the kind that draw heads together in fluttering whispers, but the sort that move between two bodies like shared blood—bind souls closer. Or repel them. She could feel Daniela getting closer as she approached the cottage.

The spice of pine needles and forest decay flooded through the car window as Cadie crept down the driveway of her childhood home. The screen door creaked open weightlessly. Her breath hitched at the familiar scent of musty newspapers, lavender, and oil paint. The year she turned thirteen, after her parents took jobs teaching in Boston, the cottage became a summer place instead of their full-time home. She spent each spring of her teen years trying to find reasons not to join her parents at the cottage that summer. Sleepaway camps, nanny jobs, visiting friends. Anything so she didn't have to bide time in those woods.

She tugged the chain attached to the naked light bulb over the kitchen's butcher-block island. The wrought-iron trivet that read "Kissin' Don't Last, But Cookin' Do" hung, as it had forever, above the sink. She slumped into an oak chair at the table. The seat's caning had cracked with age. Sharp edges pushed through her jeans, enough to notice, but not enough to make her get up.

Tires crunched on the gravel driveway. A string cinched around her heart with a pinch.

Daniela knocked, but didn't wait for a response before walking in. She wore light blue hospital scrubs, her hair swept back in a ponytail. She carried a six-pack of beer and a half gallon of mint chip ice cream.

This woman had Daniela's jawline and dark eyes, but she felt like a stranger. Cadie gripped the countertop, unsure if she wanted to hug Daniela, shake her hand, or run away.

"It's like time stopped in here." Daniela dropped her provisions on the counter and looked around the cottage. She picked up a Mason jar full of pennies from the counter and put it back down.

Cadie brushed a crumble of leaves from the curled-up edge of the shirt she had been wearing for four straight days.

Daniela leaned close to Cadie's face, pulled a dried pine needle from Cadie's hair, and grinned, her head cocked to one side. "Have you seen any bears?"

And there she was. Daniela.

The naked light bulb cast a cozy glow instead of a glare. Daniela softened the sharp edges, as she always had.

"No bears." Cadie picked up a beer and handed one to Daniela.

"Thanks for coming." Daniela's aches had always seemed deeper than Cadie's. She had this way of smiling with her mouth but not her eyes when she wanted people to think she was having fun or interested in a conversation. Seeing the disconnect on Daniela's face caused a lump to rise in Cadie's throat.

"They haven't identified the remains." Daniela twisted the top off a beer bottle. "But there's plenty of speculation."

"And your dad?" The words tasted bitter in Cadie's mouth.

"Right now, they're just talking to him. But he's scared, I can tell. It's the same thing all over again. But it's not going away this time." Daniela put her beer down and leaned on the counter. "He didn't do anything. He knows they can't convict him of anything, but if they start a serious investigation my family's status could be exposed. And I have a kid now."

Cadie choked on a swallow of beer. "You're a mom? I didn't know."

"Sal. She's thirteen."

Cadie coughed harder, laughing, choking.

"Sal? Like *Blueberries*?"

"Exactly."

So much had passed between them in such a short period of time. That one summer took up more space in Cadie's memory than all her other years combined. Each moment lived large and vivid, easily accessible if Cadie allowed herself to remember them.

"You smell terrible." Daniela leaned closer and sniffed.

"Yeah, I can even smell myself." She fanned her hand in front of her face. "I've been out in the woods for four days. I work for the forestry department through UNH, studying insects. How'd you get my number, anyway?"

"I looked up your parents, told them I wanted to reconnect. They gave me your cell."

"What do we do now?"

"We go to the police first thing in the morning." Daniela's words filled the cottage, pressing out against the windows and up against the roof as if the pressure might burst through the walls. "We need to get ahead of this. If they keep looking at my dad for this, they'll start digging. They'll take a second look at our papers," Daniela said. "But you and I can stop the speculation before it gets that far."

"Everyone will know what we did." Consequences. Cadie had set the universe off-kilter by avoiding the natural consequences of her actions. The dark, inevitable shadow chased her in her dreams and woke her in a sweat. For every action there is an equal and opposite reaction. What was equal to and opposite of covering up a murder?

Cadie laced her fingers behind her head and squeezed her elbows together in front of her face. She wanted to run, to sweat, to open her mouth and roar from deep in her gut until she had no breath left to push the sound out, until she lay empty, flat, like a tube of her father's used-up oil paint.

"Let's go get the gun." Cadie surprised herself with the suggestion. The past had grown bigger and twitchier since she read Daniela's text. She could no longer swallow it down and put it back in its hiding place.

"Now?"

"Now." Cadie put her empty beer bottle on the table.

"I've worked two doubles this week. I'm too tired to go traipsing through the woods this late at night." Dark circles framed Daniela's eyes, but more than tired, she looked scared.

"You're the one who called me to rush home, remember?"

"It's been out there for twenty-seven years. It'll wait one more night."

"You're afraid we'll find it," Cadie said.

"I need one more night before explaining to my daughter what we did." Daniela dragged her finger through the dust on the counter. "Besides, it's too dark."

"We'll take flashlights." Urgency simmered up from Cadie's gut like steam looking for release. It hissed and burned. It had to be now. "There's no way I can sleep now. I'm going, with or without you."

A gentle buzz settled over her, stirring a memory she couldn't pull into focus. Not fear or regret, but a reminder of herself, of who she used to be. The Cadie who commandeered lost boats. The girl who rode her bike down hills with her arms over her head. That other Cadie prodded at her from some deep hiding place she had tried to forget.

"Come on." Cadie grabbed two more beers.

Her toes curled in her hiking boots as she remembered the texture of the sun-warped boards beneath her bare feet the day she saw the boat drifting by her pier. Something made her uncurl her toes that day and leap into the unknown. Ever since, she had been walking through life bearing the tension between guilt and consequences unfulfilled. Unbalanced equations.

Using their phones as flashlights, they worked their way through the woods. The path that once squished under her feet now crumbled and crunched. Cadie paused at a tall pine tree and moved her flashlight up and down the trunk, looking for signs of damage. The tree stood strong, healthy, a bubble of sap assuring her the beetles had not found a home in her woods. At least not in this tree.

"How is it, moving back in with your parents?" Cadie said.

"Okay, I guess. It's temporary. I'll let Sal settle into school one more semester before we get our own place. She misses her friends, school, you know. She had a hard time spring semester."

"How about you?" Cadie asked.

Daniela did not answer.

Humidity hung low in the still woods. Stray wisps of hair clung to Cadie's sweaty neck, although her body shivered uncontrollably. The muscles in her shoulders cinched so tight she imagined plucking them like guitar strings.

Cadie didn't need to think about where to put her feet as they wound through the woods. Momentum guided her. The atomic weight of guilt, the incalculable mass accumulated from the compression of energy she left behind, drew her closer. Cadie imagined dirt, stone, and crumbled leaves swirling like a cyclone around the fear she'd left behind in these woods. Faster and tighter, it spun until it forged a pulsing mass with a heartbeat.

She had always been trapped in this forest's gravitational pull.

Not fighting gravity, for once, liberated her. She sprang ahead of Daniela and leapt from rock to rock by the narrow beam of light. Daniela ran behind her. Branches grazed Cadie's head, twigs snapped under her hiking boots. She ran faster, moved more deftly like a child, running to something, from something. Always running.

Moths pollinating night blossoms ruffled among the low-hanging branches near the boulder rising up next to the beech tree. Moonlight sifted down through the sparse clouds casting marbled, shifting shadows on the ground. The dusky silhouette of the beech tree startled Cadie, squashing the hope that her memory had invented the whole story.

Cadie climbed up the boulder beside the old beech and positioned herself next to the deep hollow where a branch had come down decades earlier. She plunged her arm into the hole. Beech nuts, twigs, and crumbled leaves lined the bottom of the otherwise empty cavity. It had to be there. She scratched and clawed at the corners and crevices, driving a splinter under the nail of her index finger with a blinding stab.

"It's not here." She bit her lower lip to distract herself from the pain shooting through her finger. Cadie swatted at gnats swarming around her neck. In the thin light she saw the shadow of a wide spike embedded under her nail.

"Let me see." Daniela grabbed Cadie's hand when she saw the blood.

Cadie pressed her lips together as Daniela probed with her fingernails, finally coaxing the splinter out. Every millimeter Daniela prodded magnified the splinter a thousand times in Cadie's mind. Her brain magnified painful things with exquisite detail.

"Are you sure this is the right tree?" Daniela said.

"I'm positive." Cadie remembered the slope of the rock she had to stand on to reach the hole. She stood inches taller now, and decades had widened the diameter of the trunk, but the dark hollow, the sideways eye, glared back at Cadie with mutual recognition.

"There are thousands of trees out here. We can come back in the daylight and look."

"I'm telling you, this is our tree." Cadie ran her fingers over the smooth bark.

"And you're sure you never moved it?" Daniela said.

"Never. Did you?"

"No. This is bad." Daniela wrapped the edge of her shirt around Cadie's throbbing finger and squeezed. They sat cross-legged at the base of the beech tree, listening to the whispers of the forest. Moonlight melted down Daniela's face. Her round cheeks had grown thinner and a few gray hairs speckled her temples.

The mossy smell of the forest at night—of this particular forest—teased at a memory. A sense of refuge, or of dread. Or maybe both at the same time. She closed her eyes and searched for that slip of time that hovered out of reach, like a color she no longer remembered.

"It's my fault they found him," Cadie said.

Daniela turned her head and waited for Cadie to continue.

"I created models indicating where beetles were most likely to kill off pines so we could dig firebreaks in areas with deadwood. Creeks and riverbeds make natural firebreaks, but sometimes they aren't wide enough. We clear combustible brush so the fire can't jump the waterways. I sent my projections to local fire stations. Most towns ignored me, but not Maple Crest. They cleared the brush."

"On Silas Creek," Daniela said.

"Yeah. On Silas Creek."

"Do you still believe in trees more than people?"

"What's that supposed to mean?" Cadie said.

"When we were kids, I always suspected you talked to trees when I wasn't around. And now you spend all your time alone in the woods. That's the last place I'd want to be."

Cadie pressed her cheek against the beech tree. If she disappeared, maybe only the forest would care. Sweat trickled down her neck. Even with so many years and wounds between them, Daniela still saw Cadie in a way no one else ever had. Daniela squeezed Cadie's throbbing finger, the spike of pain anchoring her in the place she had so long avoided.

"What happens if you prove you're right about the beetles and the fire risk?" Daniela said.

"We can monitor the infestation, predict patterns, and thin the pines to prevent fires before they get out of control." Cadie repeated the line she had recited so many times before.

Daniela took Cadie's hand to examine the finger where the splinter had been. Satisfied the bleeding had stopped, she turned Cadie's hand to inspect the self-inflicted scar on the pad of her thumb.

"Do you still have your scar?" Cadie said.

Daniela opened her hand to show Cadie the faint pink line on her thumb.

"Blood sisters. We were ridiculous, weren't we?" Cadie said.

"More than ridiculous." Daniela's eyes darted around the woods. "Why'd you move back here?"

"I needed work. The hospital here needed a radiology tech, my parents wanted us to move in. Can't argue with free rent." Daniela picked up a small stone and tossed it back and forth between her hands. "All the important decisions I've made in my life were made out of convenience, not because I ever had a real plan." Daniela finished the last of her beer. "I took the first job offer I got after school. I married the first willing guy, then let my parents rescue me when he died. I'm always playing defense."

"I'm sorry. What happened to him? I mean, you don't have to talk about it if you don't want to."

"It's okay. A drunk driver hit him five years ago." Daniela stared into the darkness. "He was a decent guy and a great dad."

Cadie wanted to say something supportive, but she had no right to offer life advice to anyone.

"Think you'll stay here until Sal graduates?"

"I don't know yet." Daniela sat up straighter and faked a smile. "How about you? Are you seeing anyone? Running away from anyone?"

Cadie preferred talking about insects over her love life, but her work problems seemed suddenly insignificant compared to Daniela's situation. And Daniela seemed like she wanted to keep things light.

"I dated this park ranger from Vermont for a while. We talked about moving in together. But, I don't know, it fizzled out a couple years ago. It's been me and the beetles ever since."

"Maybe if you worked on your wardrobe and personal hygiene you'd have better luck."

Humid air wrapped around Cadie like a familiar blanket as she and Daniela slipped into old patterns. When they were kids, Cadie clung to Daniela's tender jabs as evidence of their friendship. Daniela's trust expanded Cadie's capacity to dream out loud. She allowed Cadie to take risks and never judged her. With Daniela, Cadie had felt powerful and explosive and special. Just as she had when she was eleven, Cadie longed to be worthy of that confidence.

Even in the clumsy, surface-level conversation, Cadie felt at ease in a way she did with few people. She imagined friendships still came easily to Daniela, who invited people to like her with her unapologetic posture. She could ask questions that Cadie would never dare, but when they came from Daniela, the inquiries felt endearing and considerate. If Cadie did the same, she suspected she would come off as intrusive or nosy. Daniela attracted closeness, tenderness. She would have no need for a friend like Cadie, and Cadie felt childish and small for wishing otherwise.

Bats circled above their heads, weaving in and out of the trees. Daniela ducked when one dipped low.

"They won't bother us," Cadie said.

Even alone on her research expeditions, Cadie felt at home

among the clicks and chirps of the night forest. The gentle crush of pine needles under her tent as she shifted in her sleeping bag soothed her in a way sheets couldn't. The mossy tang when she unzipped her tent in the chilled morning air mollified Cadie like a drug. But she missed having occasional company in her tent. The park ranger, who used to wake her with pancakes over the campfire on weekends. Fresh coffee by a fire on a fall morning with him had been the one thing that soothed Cadie all the way to her core.

But her reluctance to move into his apartment and give up her cairn pushed him away, and he met someone more willing to play house. She missed him in the mornings. Or maybe she missed the body heat and the pancakes.

Another bat swooped lower than the first. Cadie flinched, and for the first time in a long time, she wanted to go inside.

Cadie stood up and snapped her fingers as they walked back toward her cottage, a habit she had formed over years spent working in the forest. "Remember the tambourine you gave me? I still carry it with me on all my hikes to warn bears off."

"You do not."

"I'm serious. I clip it on my pack every trip. I haven't been eaten by a bear yet."

Daniela stopped walking and looked Cadie straight in the eyes for the first time since she had walked in the door with beer and ice cream.

"You never told anyone?" Her stare pulled Cadie back in time, reminding her of that trust Daniela had placed in her so long ago. The trust Cadie had betrayed. Her chest ached as if a fist squeezed her heart, wringing the blood out of it.

"No one," Cadie whispered.

A loon wail, hollow and wild, echoed in the cove.

"Then who took the gun?"

4

THAT SUMMER

Daniela lay on her back with her eyes closed, playing a wooden flute, when Cadie found her on the rock the morning after they met in the woods. She played the same song she had been whistling the day before. Although her eyes remained closed, her face morphed with each note, her eyes squeezing tight at the high notes and her eyebrows rising as she sustained a long tone. Cadie lingered at the edge of the hemlocks to listen.

Friar nuzzled Daniela's neck. She scrunched her face at the dog's wet nose, but continued playing without missing a note. The breathy melody expanded like an organic part of the forest, fused to the air, the leaves, and the stone.

"Did you see any bears?" Daniela moved the flute from her lips without opening her eyes and put an arm around Friar.

"No. Did you?"

"Nope." Daniela sat up and tucked the flute into her backpack.

Cadie had braided her hair into neat plaits and chosen a pair of frayed cutoff shorts and a red T-shirt, hoping Daniela would forget about her outfit the day before. In school Daniela hung out with the popular, athletic girls, the ones who traveled in clumps. Daniela walked with long, purposeful strides and never looked over her shoulder to see if her friends followed. But they always followed. Cadie suspected Daniela disdained the pack of girls, but tolerated them rather than waste energy evading them.

Cadie untied the rope from the birch branch. There were no seats or benches on the broad, flat bottom covered in leaves, twigs, and dirt. Cadie tossed her backpack in the back corner where about ten curled-up beer tabs huddled in a sandy pile. She inspected the various layers of someone else's history, trapped in coats of paint: Dark green, sky blue, and white hid below the canary yellow.

Friar pawed at the rock and whined as Cadie lowered herself into the boat.

"Go home, boy." Cadie leaned out of the boat and let Friar lick her face. She knew her dog would wait there until they returned.

Cadie imagined the power of digging into the water with her paddle and changing the boat's course with one pull. Her rain slicker shed the misty rain in beads. Her skin prickled with anticipation.

"You can sit in the back, if you want." Cadie offered the captain's seat to Daniela, hoping she would decline.

"If you want me to."

"No big deal." Cadie tried to act casual. She wanted to sit in the back and steer, to control where the boat moved, but even more, she wanted to make this friendship work.

They paddled by Cadie's pier and past a seemingly endless expanse of woods that covered most of the peninsula where they both lived, known as the Hook to everyone in Maple Crest. A vastness spread out in front of her, all around her. Her familiar lake, her backyard, stretched out deep and wide with meandering turns, the surface shimmering with the lure of the unknown. The hugeness of space spread inside her, expanding her pores, her blood vessels, her lungs. Even the sky, which hung low with clouds, gave her the feeling she could reach up, peel away the gray, and see forever up into the deepness of space.

Everything seemed different, silvery, as if she were seeing it in a mirror, through a mirror. They rowed past the remote summer cottages that could only be accessed by boat, until the shoreline opened up to reveal a cove off to the right.

Cadie raised her eyebrows. Daniela answered with a tilt of her head aimed at the cove and guided them toward the opening. Tall evergreens, filled in with a flush of low bushes, lined the shore. Angular rocks rose from the open water of the cove, whether welcoming them or warning them to stay away, Cadie could not determine.

They were the first explorers to enter the hidden cove, Cadie felt certain. Theirs were the first eyes to behold the giant pines draped in sinewy vines. She peeled her slicker off her sweaty arms and dragged one hand through the warm lake water. The rain had tapered off and shafts of morning sunlight sifted through the parting clouds. Everything sparkled—even her skin.

Jagged slabs of granite hid below the surface. If they smashed into a rock or overturned, no one would know where to look for them. She gripped the oar tighter as they paddled deeper and deeper into the basin strewn with islands.

The boat drifted close to the shore, and Daniela grabbed a low-hanging branch.

"Blueberries. They're everywhere." Daniela pulled the boat in closer. She picked off a fistful and opened her hand to Cadie.

As she sucked on a few berries, Cadie inspected the bush, about ten feet tall as it stretched over the water. Almost every bush along the shore hung heavy with berries.

"We have to come back here with a bucket," Daniela said.

They ate handfuls of the berries until they needed to stretch to reach higher branches.

"We should go to another bush," Cadie said.

"There's plenty left on this one."

"We shouldn't take all the berries from any bush. What if a bird eats here and we take them all? Birds fatten up on berries before they go south for the winter, you know. Or what if a weary, lost traveler stops here and is hungry, but we picked all the berries."

"Are you serious? Weary travelers?"

"It could happen," Cadie said.

Before Daniela pushed away from the bush, a brown spider skittered across her foot.

"Get it!" Daniela tried to smash the spider with the end of her paddle.

Cadie grabbed Daniela's wrist. The brown water spider's legs stretched as wide as Cadie's palm. It scuttled to the far side of the boat, dodging Daniela's oar.

"I'm not leaving that thing in our boat. What if it's poisonous?" Daniela said.

Cadie grabbed a few sticks from the bottom of the boat, lifted the creature, and released it on a branch of the blueberry bush.

"Killing that spider could have messed up everything and we would never even know it."

Daniela rolled her eyes. "How could killing one stupid spider ruin everything?"

"What if that spider has thousands of babies, and her babies have thousands of babies. And a crazy, horrible virus carried by mosquitoes comes, *but* because there are so many spiders they keep the mosquitoes under control before the disease mutates into a plague that would wipe out the entire human race. No one dies, or even knows human beings were almost wiped out. All because of *that* spider."

"Yeah, well, what if your spider bites someone and he keels over and dies. But"—she paused, squinting and leaning in toward Cadie—"*that* person was destined to be president one day. And he would have prevented a nuclear war. But because he never got the chance to be president, we elect an idiot who hits the red button and we all die." Daniela swooshed her arms up, emulating a mushroom cloud.

"I'd rather accidentally cause something bad to happen because I did the right thing, than cause a disaster because I did something selfish."

"Fine. No killing spiders," Daniela said.

Cadie smiled and put her oar in the water.

"Do you think we'd get in trouble if we got caught picking berries back here?" Daniela began rowing again.

"No one owns the lake. If we keep at least one foot in the lake all the time, we aren't trespassing, right?"

Stopping periodically to gorge on berries, they paddled around the cove. Several small islands dotted the water, along with clusters of boulders above and below the surface. The cove unfurled into several smaller coves.

"Do you know which way we came in?" Daniela broke their reverie after about half an hour.

Cadie searched for a landmark, but the islands all appeared the same as they blended into the mainland. Every bush looked green. Every rock looked gray. She sank her fingernails into her thigh to fend off the mounting tears.

"I think this is a big island and we've been going around and around it thinking it is the shore. Doesn't that tree look familiar?" Daniela pointed to a birch tree jutting out over the water.

Cadie squeezed the oar. The cut on her arm from the barbed wire ached. Cadie opened her mouth wide and slid her jaw from side to side.

"I'm thirsty," Cadie said.

"Then drink some water." Daniela pointed to the lake. "And we won't starve either. We could survive on blueberries, you know. And live out here in Blueberry Cove like pirates. Plus, we've got your emergency bracelet."

Despite Daniela's teasing, Cadie took comfort in the vision of living on lake water and blueberries.

They stopped rowing and let the boat drift.

Wind shushed through the billowy evergreen branches around her. The breeze from the woods carried the pithy smell of the underside of rotting logs, the breakdown of life into dirt where new life grew. Cadie loved hunting down mushrooms and monitoring the decay of fallen trees in the woods. She sometimes thrust her hands into the rotting wood and rubbed the damp, decomposing pulp between her palms, squeezing it like dough and scattering the crumbs to feed the forest.

The familiar aroma of her woods and lake comforted her. But the longer they drifted, the more unfamiliar the world began to feel.

"What if we sell these berries?" Daniela said. "That guy parks his truck out by the library and sells them for a dollar a box every morning. I've seen Angie buying them for the diner. What if we sell them cheaper and deliver them right to her?"

"I could use the money," Cadie said as she scanned the shoreline. She imagined her boat loaded down with buckets of berries. "I want to buy a new bike seat. The plastic on mine is cracked and it hurts my butt."

"Let's start tomorrow and take them straight to Angie." Daniela bit her lip as she manipulated the rope. "We can say we picked them in the woods so no one finds out about the boat."

"If we ever get out of here," Cadie said. If she didn't call her parents at noon, the designated check-in time, they would worry. They would come home. And Cadie wouldn't be there. They might think she drowned. Or got kidnapped. Or worse, she would get caught with the boat. Her stolen boat. Cadie wrapped the curled end of one braid around her finger, watching as the tip turned purple.

She leaned back on her elbows and chewed on a strand of hair, studying the shore as if she were mapping the cove.

"I don't think it's stealing if no one else is going to pick the berries anyway," Cadie said.

"We're poaching, not stealing," Daniela said.

"What's the difference?"

"Nothing. It just sounds better."

Cadie pulled her sketch pad and a pencil out of her backpack and drew outlines of the shore, the islands, and the rocks surrounding the drifting yellow boat. Daniela watched, her head resting on her arms. Cadie turned the page and started a list:

1. *Never kill spiders.*
2. *Keep one foot in the water.*
3. *Never take all the berries from a single bush.*
4. *Never tell where we pick the berries.*

"If we're going to poach berries, we should have rules," Cadie said. "The Poachers' Code."

"What happens if we break the rules?" Daniela said.

"Terrible, terrible things." Cadie tried to make her voice sound spooky.

"God, you're so weird." Daniela laughed in a way that assured Cadie her new friend would honor the rules.

The boat drifted toward the opening of a smaller cove. If they couldn't find their way out of the cove, they could spend the night on one of the islands, build a shelter out of branches.

The sun emerged from behind a tree and blinded Cadie for a few seconds.

"East! The sun's in the east. We came from the north. We are at the north side of the lake. Right? Go that way." Cadie pointed. Her muscles relaxed, but her hands shook as she paddled. She looked over her shoulder at the blueberry-saturated shore, almost regretting she had discovered a way out.

Cadie longed to be found, but even more, she ached to be lost.

The coves inside of coves twisted and contorted, but by aiming in the right direction, they found the opening where the wide swath of the lake greeted them. A soft rhythm of chirps, flutters, and clicks wound its way in and out of the trees, rising and swooping on the breeze as she rowed, humming in harmony with the forest and the lapping of water against her boat. She inhaled the airy particles glittering in the shafts of light until her lungs felt ready to burst.

The rush of discovery dwarfed her residual panic. As they emerged from the cove, she couldn't contain a triumphant laugh, which burst out in a hiccup and made Daniela laugh, a melodic ripple Cadie grew to cherish that complicated summer.

"Do you want to spend the night?" Daniela asked.

"Sure." Cadie sank her paddle deep, every muscle in her shoulders and back tightening as she drew it through the water. She absorbed the momentum of Daniela behind her and tried to coordinate their strokes in the same rhythm. Her oar cut through towers of light littered with dancing, iridescent particles. The boat—her boat—moved at her will. The lake felt endless. The boat sailed through sky and clouds reflected deep in the rippling water.

They were flying.

✳

Cadie skipped the entire quarter-mile path through the woods from her house to Daniela's, her sleeping bag and a backpack bouncing against her back. She balanced with sure feet over the log bridge spanning the creek separating her family's property and Daniela's.

A spicy aroma wafting through the woods prompted Cadie to sprint the last few yards. The smell grew stronger as she climbed the porch stairs. Through the open kitchen window, she watched Daniela and her mother dancing with wooden spoons as pretend microphones. They sang along to the Beatles' "I Want to Hold Your Hand" playing on a boom box on the counter.

Daniela sang a line, her mother sang the next, and back to Daniela. Dolores Garcia danced in place, flipping something on the stove, turning sideways every few seconds to smile at her daughter as they sang. She wore jeans and a polo shirt with the Garcia's Hardware logo. From behind, she looked like she could be a teenager.

Daniela's father, Raúl Garcia, saw Cadie looking in through the window. Cadie knew him from the hardware store. He smiled and twirled his finger at his temple to indicate his wife and daughter had lost their minds. He waved Cadie inside and greeted her by handing her a wooden spoon to sing into.

"You like the Beatles?" She accepted the spoon from him.

"Doesn't everyone?" His eyes crinkled in the corners as he smiled.

Pockets of stuffed dough sizzled on the stove, filling the room with the elusive sensation of Christmas morning. Cadie's stomach churned at the earthy, savory aroma. A prickly eagerness stirred in her feet.

Cadie knew the words, but her feet remained glued to the floor as Daniela and her mother danced. Raúl took Cadie's hand and spun her around and around until she felt dizzy and her body forgot she didn't know how to dance. Waning light outside made everything in the small kitchen glow with a golden sheen. Sunlight glinted off a set of rosary beads dangling from the curtain rod in front of the sink.

Cadie sang loudly, not caring her voice was off-key. She danced with flailing arms, although she knew how uncoordinated she looked. Daniela laughed at Cadie, so Cadie sang louder and Daniela smiled in approval.

Daniela dropped to her knees and leaned back like a rock star as she belted out the final *I want to hold your ha-a-a-a-and.* Daniela pulled Cadie's arm so she fell next to her on the linoleum. Sweat plastered Daniela's hair to her face as she panted to catch her breath.

"Are you hungry?" Daniela asked.

"I am now."

"Can we have some?" Daniela looked up at her mother and batted her eyes with her lower lip pouting out.

"One each." Dolores wagged her spoon at the girls, smiling to reveal a deep dimple in each cheek. "Just one."

Daniela grinned and whispered in Cadie's ear, "She's only letting me have one because you're here. She never lets Dad and me have any."

"Who are they for?"

"She makes dinner for the kids of some of the farm workers every Monday night while their parents take English classes. Dad and I have to eat spaghetti." Daniela pulled Cadie up. "You should come over every Monday so I can have one."

Dolores handed each girl a plate with a sizzling bundle. "Have you ever had a pupusa?" she asked Cadie. "These are exactly like the ones my mother used to make me."

Cadie shook her head.

Raúl came up behind Daniela and snuck a bite off his daughter's plate. "My wife makes the best pupusas in all of New Hampshire."

"You mean the only pupusas in New Hampshire," Daniela said with her mouth full.

"No más." Mrs. Garcia slapped her husband's hand away as he reached for his own pupusa. "Son para los niños."

Melted cheese and spiced meat she could not identify burnt Cadie's tongue as she bit into the crusty dough. The pepper made her eyes water, but she couldn't stop eating until she scarfed down the last bite.

"Thank you, Mrs. Garcia," Cadie mumbled, her mouth still full.

"Mrs. Garcia sounds like someone else's name. Like an old lady." Dolores tapped the straight end of her spatula playfully on Cadie's head. "Tía. In this house you call me Tía.

"Tía," Cadie repeated, the word crisp and light on her tongue. Cadie had never seen Dolores Garcia act playful when she worked in the store, or when she volunteered in the school library. She usually seemed quiet and reserved, although her tone could turn sharp without warning. Cadie acted extra polite on days Dolores ran the library so she wouldn't get scolded for talking too loudly.

Dolores hummed as she layered the steamy pupusas between paper towels in a large, flat box.

"I'll carry them to the car for you." Raúl tried to pick up the box, but Dolores nudged him away.

"Ha. You'll eat them. I can carry them myself."

"Stop being stubborn. You'll hurt your back again," he said.

"What's wrong with her back?" Cadie whispered.

Daniela shrugged. "It always hurts. Doctor said she might need surgery."

Raúl stood in the doorway watching Dolores drive away. He stayed with his hand on the doorknob, unmoving long after her car disappeared. Daniela's eyes darkened as she watched her father stare out the window. Cadie pressed up on her toes to look over his shoulder to see what he stared at. Dusk tinted the woods with a gray-green light. Nothing moved outside.

Raúl's shoulders drooped and Cadie realized he was no longer in the room with them. Whatever he was watching—or thinking—had taken him far away from the kitchen.

5

The first time they saw the Summer Kid, he sat in an aluminum lawn chair with a sagging mesh seat on the end of a spindly gray pier. His fine, blond hair reminded Cadie of a baby shampoo commercial as it flopped over his eyes. He sat curled up in the chair, one knee bent up, leaning against the aluminum armrest. About their age, maybe a couple years older, he looked wispy, like the wind might blow him away.

Daniela and Cadie slowed their paddles to quiet the splashing as they approached. "No witnesses," Daniela whispered as they glided past.

The boy sighed and puffed his long bangs out of his face. Out of the corner of his eye he found the boat and turned his head to meet Cadie's stare. He startled in his chair and almost tipped over. Cadie waved, or tried to, but she held the oar in both hands and the attempted greeting ended up more like a convulsive splash of the paddle.

"Keep going!" Daniela hissed. "Don't let him see your face."

Cadie lowered her head and paddled faster. But the boy's frantic stare gripped her. He pushed his hair out of his face and looked back over his shoulders at the shore, then back at Cadie, then back at the woods behind him, then back again at Cadie.

His pier stuck out from a peninsula between two large natural rock ledges. The rock wall to the right of the pier loomed about twelve feet above the water. A tackle box and a fishing pole lay on top of the ledge next to a second lawn chair that matched the one he sat in.

The boy, with wide, panicked eyes, frantically waved his arms, as if he were trying to move the wind and push them away. The distance between the boy and the boat widened as he swooped his arms. A red-tailed hawk rode an air current above them in a tightening downward spiral. Cadie's breath quickened. The boy's urgency pressed Cadie to paddle harder, faster, until they rounded the bend in the shoreline and paddled out of his sight.

"What a weirdo," Daniela said. "Must be some rich summer kid afraid of townies."

"What if he's in trouble? What if he was kidnapped or being held hostage and he's afraid the kidnappers might see us and kidnap us too?"

Daniela rolled her eyes.

The bubbly anticipation Cadie usually experienced as she approached their cove fell flat, like a soda left open overnight. She kept seeing the Summer Kid's eyes. The panic. The girls resumed a silent, steady pace, not talking for several minutes. They both paused when they spotted a loon with two fuzzy babies swimming about twenty yards offshore. Cadie searched for the other parent.

She tilted her face up to the sky, not caring that she had forgotten to put on sunscreen.

The boat twisted in the gentle current, and Cadie craned her neck, turning to find a break in the water's surface where the other loon parent might be swimming. A plume of sudsy clouds reflected off the water, revealing the height of the sky trapped in the depths of the lake. As Cadie adjusted her eyes, shifting her focus from the reflection above to the contours below, the mother loon burst through the clouds and the water and stared straight at her. The precision of her fine white collar on the shiny black neck, the bloodred eyes, stole Cadie's breath.

The loon's howl bounced across the water. Her mate answered with the same ethereal note, so close it echoed in Cadie's chest. Two ashen chicks hustled to keep up. The family regrouped and swam away, their wake leaving an expanding triangle aimed like an arrow back toward the Summer Kid on his pier.

"I bet Angie would double the order if we offered to pick more berries," Daniela said after they settled into their normal blueberry-picking routine.

Cadie didn't respond.

"Don't you want to make more money?"

"Yeah, but I want to go swimming too. And explore stuff."

Daniela stopped paddling. "Okay. We increase by fifty percent. Not double it."

Cadie didn't answer. She wanted a pirate ship, not a merchant vessel. She wanted to climb the rocks and slash through the dense interiors of the dozens of unexplored islands in the cove.

"Do you think that Summer Kid's in trouble?" Cadie said.

"I don't know. You're picking really slow. I have almost twice as many as you."

Cadie put her bucket down and reached into her backpack. She scribbled a note in her pad, tore the page out.

Are you okay? Do you need help? Leave us a signal.

"I'm going to climb the rock wall and leave it there. It's so far around the bend there's no way he will be able to see us or the boat from there," Cadie said.

"What if someone else sees us?" Daniela cocked her head to one side and chewed on a strand of hair. "It could ruin our whole business if someone finds out we're stealing berries."

"Poaching."

"Whatever. We should sell Angie more berries."

Only one year older than Cadie, Daniela seemed a thousand times more sophisticated. Even the way she chewed her hair made her look older. Her black hair fell thick and wavy, almost curly, but not frizzy. Most days she wore it back in a ponytail, but that morning it hung loose, skimming her tan shoulders.

Cadie's own deep red curls stuck out in every direction when they got the chance. After painful years of growing it out, her hair hung almost to her shoulder blades. Every morning she woke up, parted it down the middle, wet it, wrestled the knots out, and braided it into two tight plaits. The bottom two inches stuck out below the elastic and wound into tight springs. She liked the way the coils sprang back when she stretched them out. On hot days like this one, short wisps of hair above her temples frizzed into tiny ringlets framing her face. Cadie pressed down the childish curls as she watched Daniela.

As they paddled past the Summer Kid on the way home, neither Cadie nor Daniela looked up at the boy, but his fear sizzled in the air. They rounded the bend out of his line of vision and aimed for the shore, where they tucked the boat in below the rock ledge. Cadie put the note in her pocket and stepped out of the boat into the shallows. She scrambled for footholds as she scaled the wall, which looked much higher up close.

Cadie clawed her way up high enough to see over the top of the ledge and found a copy of *The Swiss Family Robinson* on the ground near the lawn chair. She opened the book to the bookmark, and scanned the familiar words, brushing her fingers over the damp linen cover. The same salty smell as her own copy of the book wafted up from the worn pages, although she owned a much older edition. She tucked the note next to the bookmark and placed the book back where she found it.

Her knees trembled as she shimmied down the rock face. Blindly seeking a solid ledge below her, she lost her footing and slipped. She smacked her face on the top of the ledge as she came down. She grabbed at a tree root and balanced there, her mouth and nose pressed against the granite, afraid to move. She turned her head to Daniela, who splashed through the water toward Cadie. The empty boat drifted behind her.

The dirt on Cadie's lips mixed with blood pooling from a gash on her lip. As she made her way back toward the boat, Cadie scooped a handful of water into her mouth and swished it around to soothe the cut. Lake water could heal anything. She spit out the blood and watched the lake absorb the crimson swirl.

The next day, as she paddled close to the Summer Kid's ledge, the cut on Cadie's lip throbbed in rhythm with her oar strokes. A rock the size of a cantaloupe perched where the book had sat the day before. A brown piece of paper stuck out from underneath.

Daniela raised her eyebrows and paddled closer, trying hard not to splash. "I'll do it this time."

"No. I got it." Cadie didn't give Daniela a chance to argue as she stood up in the wobbling boat and stepped into the water. Daniela leapt to her feet, poised to jump in if Cadie fell. When Cadie's head cleared the ledge, she found a note written on a torn piece of a paper grocery bag folded under the rock. She forced herself to put it in her pocket so she and Daniela could read the message together.

"Go," she instructed Daniela as soon as she got one foot in the boat. They paddled hard for several minutes until they were out of sight, then let the boat drift while they read the note. *I'm so bored. Can you bring me a book? I'll give it back.*

"That's it? Don't his kidnappers let him read?" Daniela said, turning the note upside down to search for clues or hidden messages. Cadie had moved on to the reading list. If he liked *Swiss Family Robinson*, he would love *Robinson Crusoe* or *Treasure Island*.

"Let's give him *Are You There God? It's Me, Margaret*," Daniela said. "Can you imagine?"

"No way." Cadie squirmed, setting the boat off-balance.

"I'm calling Angie when we get home to see if she wants more berries tomorrow."

"*Kidnapped*! We have to give him *Kidnapped*. Get it? *Kidnapped*? Then *Treasure Island*. Or, oh my God, *The Dark Is Rising*? I love that one." Cadie bounced on her knees, rocking the boat.

"Geez, calm down."

"This is important." The magnitude of her power shivered up Cadie's spine. She gripped the sides of the boat and scooted closer to Daniela. "We get to shape someone's brain."

"I thought you wanted to rescue him."

"Maybe we *are* rescuing him."

6

Cadie slept fitfully the night after she and Daniela failed to find the gun. Forest noises that had been her childhood lullaby jarred her awake. Lying in bed by an open window, she licked her lips and attempted to mimic the night song of the Bicknell's thrush. She called out to the bird again and again, as she tried to purge the image of the Summer Kid's terrified eyes from her mind.

She should have helped him. She should have been braver.

She held her breath and waited, but the thrush did not answer.

At 5 A.M., she stopped fighting the insomnia and watched the sun rise from the back porch while wrapped in her grandmother's afghan. A reminder of the previous night's failed expedition throbbed under her fingernail where Daniela had extracted the splinter.

A row of empty beer cans sat on the kitchen counter next to a puddle of melted ice cream shaped like a fist giving her the finger. The pounding in her head and thumb clashed in uncoordinated rhythms. She had several hours until she had promised to meet Daniela in the parking lot outside the police station.

She flipped through a stack of her old comic books, a mix of *Wonder Woman*, *Spider-Man*, and all twelve issues of *Captain Planet and the Planeteers*. She winced remembering the Planeteers Club she had tried to organize. No one showed up at the inaugural—and only—meeting.

If her parents had been home, her dad would have been rousing soon to fry up some eggs and bacon. Her dad looked like a cartoon character in the morning. His hair—redder and curlier even than Cadie's—stuck out in every direction. He would be wearing a Campbell's Soup apron.

"Morning, angel," he would have said.

Her mother would have crawled out of bed to read the paper with a cup of coffee on the porch.

But the cottage sat empty.

Out of desperation, she made a cup of stale instant coffee. Three cans of tuna, two cans of lentil soup, and a few half-full spice jars sat on the otherwise empty pantry shelves. Above the fridge she found an unopened box of saltines. She tore a sleeve open with her teeth and carried the coffee and crackers out to the back porch. Steamy heat from the previous day already asserted itself.

Cadie walked barefoot into the forest toward the clearing about a hundred yards behind her house. She treaded gently on crackling twigs and pine cones, the tender soles of her feet no longer seasoned the way they had been in her youth. Small trees had sprouted, older ones had slumped and melted away. But the unmistakable silhouette of a familiar hemlock remained unchanged. The thick trunk had hidden her pocketknife, the matches, their hand-drawn map of the cove and the woods, and The Poachers' Code inside a slim hollow near the base of the tree.

Cadie crouched down and eased her hand into the dark opening. Although the exterior of the pine looked the same, the opening, which once barely held a jelly jar, had expanded so wide it could have swallowed a football. Other than Cadie's old pocketknife, now rusted closed, the hollow was empty, their laminated map and The Poachers' Code carried away by squirrels, weather, and time.

The code of ethics she and Daniela had sworn an oath to had become a guidepost for Cadie even into adulthood. A measure of right and wrong. What she should do and what she should never do. *Never kill a bug*, she had written on the inside cover of her first entomology textbook in college.

The Code had given her a compass when she needed direction. Maybe more than afraid of defying her rules, she had been terrified of betraying Daniela.

She knelt on the forest floor, unmoored.

Cadie squeezed a fistful of decay from inside the hollow. The tree, it seemed, was rotting, digesting itself from the inside out. She swallowed the last of her bitter coffee, and walked back toward the beach.

The surface of the lake reflected the morning rays, making it hard to look directly at the water. Bobbing white lilies peeled open toward the morning light, exposing their saffron centers.

The diving rock peeked out through the glassy surface, stirring in Cadie an urge to jump in. She couldn't see any fishing boats, or even another house, from her beach nestled in its quiet cove. She shimmied out of her sweatpants. Pulling her arms into her T-shirt, she undid her bra and tossed it on the pier with her pants. After a quick scan for fishermen, she yanked off her shirt and slipped into the water.

Free and aimless, she drifted. She sank until the chill enveloped the crown of her head. Lake water lived inside her. She had swallowed and inhaled it in gulps and gasps. Flecks of eroded granite boulders and millennia-old secrets had settled in her cells. She had always been made of these mountains. This lake. This forest. She had reciprocated with sacrifices of her own blood, tears, sweat, and urine, which circulated among the fish, feeding the lilies and the roots of blueberry bushes.

Could the forest have absorbed that gun? Her younger self would have imagined roots and tendrils pulling the ugly memories deep below the surface. She longed to believe in the magic of the forest again, instead of the indisputable reality that only a person could have removed the gun.

Cadie pulled with fierce strokes away from the shore toward the tanning rock. Happy memories lived here too. The rough, uneven surface had been their favorite spot to soak up the sun. Daniela always sat on the flat side, her feet dangling in the water. Cadie preferred the higher, sloping side.

"Do you think I'll ever get boobs?" Cadie had asked Daniela as they lay on the rock, Daniela, with her newly rounded breasts in a bikini, next to Cadie in her red racing-back one-piece suit.

"Nope. I think you'll be a pancake forever," Daniela had said, yanking on Cadie's braid. "Just kidding. You'll get boobs. I got my period last week."

"What?" Cadie rolled over on her side to see if Daniela looked different. "I can't even grow boobs." Cadie flopped onto her back, a sharp protrusion in the rock jabbing her under her left shoulder blade. It left a tender bruise that lasted weeks, reminding Cadie she had no breasts every time she raised her arm.

Rings of white, tan, and green now circled the rock, marking decades of rising and falling water levels. Cadie had never seen the lake water this low. Tips of rocks, normally hidden under the surface, reached up ready to snag cocky boaters who thought they knew this lake. Cadie knew better than to trust a smooth surface.

She closed her eyes as she floated on her back and let the lake rock her. The increasing amplitude of the waves confirmed that boaters were awake. She rolled her shoulders forward and let her whole body sink, keeping her eyes wide open. Morning sun broke through the surface in blurry shafts of orange highlighting the outline of her feet.

She longed to stay under, to be the weightless mermaid she imagined herself at eight years old. She had trained herself to draw in a deep breath, then release it, emptying her lungs so she wouldn't float, to see how long she could sit cross-legged on the throne she had built herself out of rocks below the surface.

The minerality of the lake, the same water she ingested by the gallon as a child, filled her mouth. Every particle in the water felt familiar on her tongue, stirring the dormant granite racing through her, the tug she had tried to ignore for twenty-seven years. Swimming back toward shore she once again felt like part of the lake, the water so temperate she couldn't feel where she ended and it began.

A chorus of birds chirped and twittered around her. Cadie tried to isolate the sounds and distinguish the morning chirrup of a Bicknell's thrush, but it did not rise. As the tiny bird had pushed north out of central New Hampshire, it left the high-elevation orchestra without their piccolo. The gray-cheeked bird never should have settled in these woods, which made its absence an even greater loss.

We live at the wrong elevation, her father had told her as they swung in the hammock, practicing bird calls. *Bicknell's prefer mountaintops and dense balsam forests.*

Yet every year they returned to Cadie's woods. Like magic. There had been so much magic in the forest of her childhood.

She reminded herself to write back to Piper, the grad student, and ask about her research into the Bicknell's disappearance even in the northern elevations. Thinking about the daytime forest without the Bicknell's melody seemed unfortunate, but imagining that she might never hear its night song again made her eyes sting with unexpected tears.

A twig snapped on shore. The distortion of sound moving over water made it difficult for Cadie to guess where the noise came from. Probably a deer. She slowed her movements and scanned the water's edge, hoping for a glimpse of a timid black nose dipping into the lake.

Another crack erupted from the trees, then a burst of movement along the shoreline. Deer wouldn't be so careless. Bears wouldn't be so light-footed. Footsteps. Human footsteps, erratic and hurried, crashed through the forest.

A cold current swirled around Cadie's feet and a strand of lake grass grabbed her ankle.

She yanked her leg free and pulled up a handful of a feathery green boa of a plant that had infiltrated the lake. She sculled in place, trying not to attract attention to herself. Her teeth chattered.

The woods, again, fell silent.

Cadie swam toward shore and ran naked to the house, not pausing as sharp pebbles and acorns jabbed at her bare feet. She locked the door and pulled the kitchen curtains closed, immediately feeling foolish. Deer, fox, moose, and bears tromped through these woods every day. Not people.

The balm of lake water lingered on her skin, but a chill she couldn't shed sank deep into her bones.

7

THAT SUMMER

The morning after the Summer Kid requested a book, Cadie and Daniela delivered *Kidnapped* to the rock ledge. The sun beat down from a cloudless sky, watching her like a giant eye as she bided time picking berries. She sucked on the end of her braid and tried to focus on filling her bucket. In a few days she would have enough money to buy a new bike seat.

"You ready?" Daniela said from her position a few bushes away.

"Yeah," Cadie said, although she had room for another pint in her bucket. The boy must have found her book by now.

Cadie gripped the end of her paddle tighter than necessary to control the shaking in her hands. The water felt thick and resistant as she pulled the boat forward, toward the boy's pier. The Summer Kid hunched over a book. *Her* book. The shush of a single page turning skittered across the water. His posture stiffened, but he did not look up at them.

Cadie squirmed, unable to contain her delight. What chapter was he reading? Was a book enough to distract him from whatever—or whoever—made him so jittery?

In bed that night she watched the shadow creatures sway on her bedroom wall and wondered what page of her book the boy read at that exact moment. What if he did not like her taste in books? Did he lick his finger to turn pages the way she did? Maybe he burrowed under the covers with a flashlight to hide the book from his captors. Cadie pulled her sheet up to her chin and scrunched her eyes closed.

A lonely thrush called out and Cadie wondered if the Summer Kid heard it too.

On the second day after they left the book, a red T-shirt hung from a branch on the ledge.

"It's a sign," Cadie shouted.

"Shhh. No kidding. I'm going up this time."

Cadie folded her arms across her chest, wanting to protest, but unable to conjure a reason she should go instead.

Daniela slipped Cadie's copy of *The Dark Is Rising* into the back of her waistband and splashed through the shallow water toward the rock wall. The gilded lettering on the spine of *Kidnapped* glinted in the sunlight below the T-shirt flag.

Cadie twisted her pigtail until it hurt, as Daniela swapped the books and slid down the rock face, a folded note clenched between her teeth.

Daniela wagged the paper over her head as she splashed toward the boat. Cadie almost fell in the water trying to grab it.

Thanks. I loved the book. Please bring another. I will get in BIG TROUBLE if you ever come to my dock. And so will you. No one can EVER see you. I'm serious. It's dangerous.

He liked her book. She bit the inside of her cheek to suppress a smile.

"Do you think he's in trouble? Like, for real?" Daniela pushed off from the shore and paddled toward home.

Cadie shrugged, already planning the next book she would bring after *The Dark Is Rising.* Two days later Cadie scrambled up the rock and left *The Outsiders,* then later that week replaced it with *Are You There God? It's Me, Margaret,* at Daniela's insistence, although Cadie had argued against it.

Days later Cadie felt a twinge of dread as they approached the drop-off spot, where she expected to see a flag indicating he had finished *Are You There God.* Such a quick read. Unless he hated it.

Along the shoreline the patchwork of maples, oaks, and birch trees glowed with a near-neon green, except for a single maple branch whose leaves had turned prematurely. Cadie scanned the ledge for the red shirt, but it wasn't there. He should have finished the book by now.

As they rounded the peninsula, Cadie braced herself for the rush of fear and anticipation she always felt as they approached the Summer Kid's pier. The pages of *Are You There God* fluttered open on the dock next to his empty chair.

Cadie thrust her oar down into the water, breaking their forward momentum.

"Why are you stopping? He didn't leave a signal," Daniela said.

"He needs a new book." They never should have left him a Judy Blume book. It felt as if Daniela had been mocking Cadie by suggesting it. Daniela leaned back on her elbows while Cadie guided the boat to shore by herself.

Cadie scrambled up the rocks with a paperback *Tuck Everlasting* clenched between her teeth. She almost fell backward when she cleared the top of the ledge and found the boy sitting cross-legged a few feet away. She froze, afraid to breathe. Until that moment, the Summer Kid had been a character whose story she controlled in her mind. To be so close to him that she could see his chest rise and fall felt like stepping into someone else's story.

Cadie looked over her shoulder at Daniela, lying on her back in the boat with her eyes closed. The boy crawled toward her on his knees and extended a hand to pull her up. "Thanks for the books."

Her throat clamped shut at the shock of his voice. Cadie accepted his hand and pulled her torso onto the warm rock ledge. She swung her legs over the top and sat next to him, her feet dangling over the water. It looked higher than she expected, and she wondered if he admired her bravery for scaling the wall to deliver his books.

"Is it safe?" Cadie found her voice although it came out raspy. She looked around at the towering pines, identical to those in her own yard.

"Yeah. I'm alone, for now." The boy fidgeted, unable to make eye contact for more than a few seconds. "They're your books, aren't they?"

"How can you tell?

"I just can."

"Sorry about that last one."

The boy blushed but didn't respond.

The warmth of where his hand had touched hers lingered, rushing up her forearm. His eyes seemed slightly asymmetrical, the corner of his left eye drooping a bit lower than his right. It gave him a vulnerable appearance, like a puppy.

He looked over his shoulder and chewed on his cuticle.

Cadie wanted to speak but couldn't think of anything to say to the boy she had imagined so many conversations with. A squirrel jumped from a branch overhead. The boy startled and looked back at the cabin again.

"What's wrong?" Cadie asked.

"You should go. He'll be back soon."

"Who? Are you in danger?" Cadie felt like a character in one of her books.

"My uncle. I live with him."

A chipmunk poked its head out from under a rock next to the boy's leg. He slipped his hand into his pocket and pulled out a plastic bag with bread crumbs.

"What about your parents?" Cadie watched as he placed a pile of crumbs a few inches away. The chipmunk twitched its nose, bobbed back under the rock, then popped out and scooped the morsels into its cheeks.

He looked past her at the lake. "They died in a car crash when I was eight."

"Oh." Cadie scooted back away from the edge. The chipmunk sat back on its hind legs with its head cocked to one side, as if listening to their conversation. The animal didn't flinch when the boy placed another pile of bread inches away.

"What's so scary about your uncle?"

"He's mean. I don't want him being, well, mean to you." The boy turned away from the animal to look at Cadie. "I don't want him to see you."

She squirmed under the weight of his stare and turned to look him in the eye. "Why don't you tell someone if he's that bad? I could help you."

"No," he said. The chipmunk jumped at the change of tone and scurried away with bulging cheeks. The boy turned in the direction the chipmunk had fled and tossed a handful of crumbs. He made a low *tut tut* with his tongue against the roof of his mouth. But the animal did not reappear. The boy's shoulders slumped. "I'd get sent back to foster care. And I'm *never* going back there."

"Wouldn't it be better than living here, if he's that bad?"

The boy turned his head and lifted his shaggy hair off his collar, revealing a circle of purple scars. He dropped his hair down to cover them.

"Cigarette burns. And that's not the worst of it. Not even close." He narrowed his eyes and leaned his face closer to Cadie's. "I'll *never* go back there."

Cadie shuddered, in part at the sight of the scars, but mostly because of the way his voice lowered to a tone that sounded like an adult as he said *never*.

"It's just you and him?" She regretted all the times she had wiped her mother's kisses away.

"I moved in with him two years ago. He can be a jerk, but it's way better than my foster dad."

"How come you don't go to school?"

"Cadie!" Daniela called.

"I'll be right down." Cadie squirmed, not wanting to leave, not wanting to keep Daniela waiting.

"I go to boarding school. My dad went there, and my grandad. I'm their charity case since my parents died. But in the summer, I have to live here with him."

She picked up a small rock and hurled it into the woods. A sharp squawk rose from the bushes and several crows rushed from the bush where Cadie's stone landed.

"Why'd you do that?" The boy flinched.

"I didn't mean to. I'd never hurt an animal on purpose." Cadie felt nauseous. Her aim never failed, even when she didn't try to hit anything. She silently vowed never to throw a rock unless she could see where it would land.

"I know. It's okay," he said. "I'm glad you came."

"Me too," she whispered. "But I should go."

He put his hand on top of hers before she turned to lower herself down the ledge. His face was so close to hers. His eyes were the shocking blue of the ocean in movies. The color seemed to churn like water as he stared at her. Cadie held her breath, afraid she smelled like the peanut butter she had spread on an English muffin that morning.

"Wait." He leaned closer and kissed her, right on the mouth. Not a long movie kiss, but a feathery touch that lingered for just a few seconds. Cadie felt the blush burn under her skin, through her torso and chest. When he pulled his head back Cadie grinned more than she would have liked. She wished she had been cooler, but the smile burst with a small laugh before she thought to contain it.

The boy smiled back and wrinkled his nose, as if a little embarrassed, but pleased at Cadie's reaction.

"Do you want anything besides books? Do you have food?" She blushed. Of course he had food.

He smiled a half-formed, crooked smile. "He feeds me. Just books." He leaned forward and looked down toward the water. "But you could write back."

"Back to what?"

"The notes."

"Cadie! Come on."

"Coming." Cadie stood up and brushed the dirt off her shorts. "What notes?"

"In the books. They're for you."

"I have to go."

"I'm Garrett."

"Cadie."

Garrett stood about three inches taller than Cadie. He stood so close she had to tilt her head back to look at him.

"You'll come back?"

She nodded, wondering if he could hear the pounding of her heart.

"But you can't ever come near unless you see me on the dock, okay?"

"Okay."

"Will you still bring books?"

"For as long as you need me." She felt a blush rise up her neck. "I mean as long as you want books."

That night Cadie waited until her parents had gone to bed before she pulled *Kidnapped, The Dark Is Rising,* and *The Outsiders* under the covers with a flashlight. She shook the books, fanned through all the pages, but she didn't find any notes. Maybe Daniela had intercepted them and thought they were for her.

Cadie's face grew hot. Of course Daniela would assume the notes were for her. Boys noticed Daniela. She carried an easy confidence that made everyone want to sit next to her. She didn't flip her hair or look up through fluttering eyelashes. She slouched and looked you straight in the eye when she talked. If she didn't know something, she would ask without shame, which somehow made her seem even smarter.

But Garrett chose Cadie.

She opened *Kidnapped* to the first page and read the opening sentence, imagining what Garrett had been thinking as he read her first book. Did he think about her? Did he get lost in the story the way she did? She stuck her nose into the crease between the pages and inhaled. The pages smelled vaguely of cinnamon gum and the metallic edge of lake water.

Sitting cross-legged under the tent of her covers she aimed the flashlight on the opening page. Halfway down, a dull pencil line underscored the letter *I.* Cadie's heart thumped so hard it hurt. She turned the page and found a faintly underlined *L.* The air under the covers felt muggy and hot, but she kept turning the pages. *I. K. E. Y. O.* She couldn't hold the letters in her racing mind, so she grabbed her journal and pen from her nightstand.

I like your braids. If you find this note, wear ribbons on your braids so I know you read this.

She pulled the book in tight to her chest and hugged it. She didn't bother pulling the covers over her head. She picked up *The Dark Is Rising* and held the musty cover to her lips as she wriggled back against her headboard. With her flashlight in her mouth aimed at the book, she opened to the first page. And there she saw it—a faint line, barely more than a smear, under the letter A. She transcribed Garrett's second message.

Are your eyes green? I'd like to see them close up.

8

Cadie tripped on a rock pushing its way up through the gravel parking lot of the Maple Crest Police Department. The edge of granite rose a few inches above the ground, but Cadie suspected the block extended deep below the surface. Ice heaves had forced it skyward, despite the construction crew's best efforts to grade the gravel. Next spring it would thrust itself even higher. There was no stopping it. No ignoring it.

Daniela caught Cadie's elbow to steady her.

"Anything we say in there, we can't take it back." Cadie stopped walking as they approached the stairs to the police station. "Maybe we should talk to your dad first."

"No. We're doing this. Now." Daniela drew her shoulders back.

Daniela had shaken the truth, dislodged it so that it no longer settled in place when Cadie stopped moving. It swelled uncomfortably in her chest, barely leaving room for her to breathe.

The thermometer outside the door read eighty-eight degrees. Too hot for 9 A.M. Sweating made people look guilty. Cadie wiped her forehead with her hand and peeled her shirt from the damp skin on her lower back where it had been pressed against the vinyl car seat.

The heavy metal door resisted as Cadie pushed it open to a lobby filled with the smell of fresh paint, printer ink, and coffee. The burst of air-conditioning sharpened the throbbing in her temples.

"We have information about a crime." Daniela didn't bother introducing herself to the woman sitting behind the desk wearing bright pink lipstick and a lime cardigan. Cadie paced behind Daniela.

"What kind of crime are we talking about?" the woman said without looking up.

"We'd like to talk to an officer. In private," Daniela said.

The woman wrinkled her brow. She looked offended.

"There's no one available but the deputy chief. If this is a traffic thing, or missing wallet, you're better off filling out an incident report and letting us follow up, okay, dear?"

"It's not an incident. It's a crime," Daniela said.

"Okay, okay." The woman looked at the clock. "But he has to be over at the middle school in less than an hour, so don't make him late."

"We'd like to talk to him." Daniela put a hand on her hip, the way she did when they were kids.

Cadie had to turn around so the receptionist wouldn't see her smile.

The woman shook her head as she walked down the hall. "I've got a couple of women out here who insist on talking to you about some crime. I tried to get them to fill out a report."

"What's the problem?" a man's voice said.

"They won't say." She sighed. "I'll come interrupt you so you won't be late."

Daniela rolled her eyes at Cadie. "Does she think we can't hear her?"

The sweat on Cadie's skin grew clammy in the air-conditioning. The clock above the receptionist's desk ticked loudly.

"Follow me." The woman gestured to them.

Cadie had spent twenty-seven years pushing the story down, training her brain not to think about it. She had bitten the inside of her cheek, dug her nails into the palms of her hands so often her nerves were numb to the distractions. As she walked down the corridor in the police station, the past clawed its way up her throat, demanding to be spoken.

The door to the deputy chief's office stood open. A tall man dressed in street clothes stood up and extended a hand to Daniela. "Come on in. I'm Deputy Chief Tierney."

Daniela shook his hand. "I'm Daniela."

Cadie hung in the doorway. One more step and there would be no going back.

"Can we close the door?" Daniela said.

Daniela looked at Cadie and tilted her head, urging her to come in. The receptionist hovered in the doorway.

"Whatever makes you comfortable," the officer said.

The receptionist shrugged and closed the door, forcing Cadie inside the room.

"We have information about the remains the fire crews uncovered," Daniela said before Cadie had a chance to sit down.

Officer Tierney shifted in his squeaky chair. The air conditioner whirred with dogged determination. Dried sweat pulled Cadie's skin tight.

"It's probably not what you think." He picked up a pen and twisted the two ends apart until the spring popped out and bounced to the floor. He leaned over to pick it up.

Daniela motioned for Cadie to sit down next to her. Cadie walked over to the chair, but remained standing. She squeezed her throbbing fingertip, searching for a spike of pain to distract her.

"There've been a lot of rumors," he said, his head still under the desk searching for the spring. "The remains have been out there a long time, decades it looks like, so I'm not sure what information you could have."

"We lived here then. We remember it," Daniela said. "And we know—"

The officer bumped his head on the desk.

Daniela prodded at the truth, she tugged on it, but froze. She pinched the bridge of her nose as if her head ached unbearably. Like the splinter in Cadie's finger, the truth needed to come out, no matter how painful the extraction.

"We were there," Cadie said. The words tore at her throat, although her voice barely rose above a whisper. "We know what happened, where it happened, and who did it."

The officer sat upright and looked at Cadie. He leaned forward. Sweat glistened on his upper lip. The air conditioner cycled off, filling the room with a sudden silence, but for the tick, tick, tick of the wall clock.

"You were there." He spoke so quietly, he could have been talking to himself. "Cadie."

"You know each other?" Daniela said.

Cadie looked at his face, searching for the porcelain cheekbones under the scruff, the slight asymmetry of his face. His eyes gripped her, just as they had decades earlier.

"Garrett."

The clock on the wall cranked out long seconds.

"Are you fucking kidding me?" Daniela broke the silence. "Why are you interrogating my father if you already know what happened? You know damn well my dad didn't do it."

"Raúl's your father?"

"Yeah, he's my father." Daniela crossed her arms and narrowed her eyes. "This is bullshit. I want to talk to the real chief. Not you."

"Wait. I can help you," he said. "I can make sure your dad won't get in any trouble."

"Of course he won't, because we're going to tell the truth," Daniela said.

Cadie's knees felt like rubber. She lowered herself into the chair. He survived. The Summer Kid. Garrett. All the nights Cadie had sat up worrying about him living with that monster crashed together in her mind.

Tierney—Garrett—stood up.

"You're okay." Cadie squeezed the armrests on her chair.

"No way. You are not doing this again." Daniela looked at Cadie.

Cadie could feel the accusation in Daniela's eyes, but she couldn't look away from Garrett.

"Of course he's fine," Daniela said. "He's got this comfy office and spends his time investigating innocent people so he doesn't get his asshole uncle in trouble."

"It's not like that," Garrett said.

"Really? I think people would be interested to know their deputy police chief covered up a murder," Daniela said.

"Your father has not been accused of anything. Chief Schmidt talked to him a few times for background info. The record from back then indicates he was the last person seen talking to a person matching this victim's basic description. We had to interview him. It's protocol." Garrett gripped the front edge of his desk. "The body hasn't been officially identified yet. Coming forward now—it would destroy everything. For all of us."

"I'm not too worried about my reputation." Daniela's nostrils flared. "I'm worried about my father."

Cadie imagined having to explain to Thea and her research team that she had covered up a murder. How would she tell her parents?

"There isn't any evidence against Raúl."

"Then stop it now. We know your uncle killed him, then dragged him into the woods, and buried him. You probably helped him bury the body, didn't you?" Daniela said.

Garrett looked at Cadie with a confused expression. He started to say something, then stopped.

Cadie's heart pounded in her throat, boomed in her ears.

Daniela drummed her fingernails on the arm of her chair.

"Give me a few days to convince the chief to back off."

"What about your uncle?" Cadie forced herself to look up. Garrett's eyes were the same exact color she remembered. She fought the urge to press down the ringlets on her temples. "He just gets away with it?"

Garrett stood up again. His once-scrawny frame had filled out to a lanky lean. Broad shoulders pulled on his plaid button-down shirt. He moved with a familiar awkwardness, as if he felt unsure of the space around him. Images of the day he jumped up, moving his arms through the air as if pushing them away from his pier, flashed through Cadie's mind.

He had moved the wind for her.

As a child, Cadie had thought sending Garrett back to abusive foster care was the most imminent threat. But as an adult she wondered if helping Garrett had condemned him. She had lain awake countless nights wondering if he was alive.

"The argument got out of control and the gun just went off," Garrett said. "It was an accident. You couldn't see what happened."

"I heard everything," Cadie said, the gunshot echoing, yet again, in her mind.

"Your uncle protected himself," Daniela said. "And I sure as hell don't owe him—or you—anything."

"He knew if he went to jail, I'd go back in the system. He took care of me the best he could." Garrett squeezed two handfuls of his hair, still long and shaggy, but a few shades darker.

"By killing someone? And letting my dad take the blame?" Daniela's face reddened.

A firm rapping on the door startled Cadie. The receptionist stuck her head inside. "You don't want to be late. I can help these ladies with any paperwork." She looked at Cadie and Daniela as if they were being a nuisance.

"Thanks. Can you call the school and tell them I'll be a few minutes late? They can start without me."

"I'm sure you can finish this business later." Her smug smile made Cadie want to slap her. "You don't want to make the kids wait."

"Call the school and tell them I'll be late."

The receptionist gave Cadie a disapproving look and left.

"The medical examiner's report will come back in three days. I expect we'll get a positive ID. That's when we need to worry. I mean, people are already speculating about the identity, but until there's a positive ID, it would be impossible to bring any charges," Garrett said. "In the meantime, I can intervene with the chief and convince him to back off Raúl. Nothing's going to happen to your dad."

"People are already talking, and we don't need people in our business," Daniela said.

"Look, I know what you're worried about. I don't give a shit about whether your dad's illegal."

Daniela's lips turned white as she pressed them together.

"I don't care. No one cares. He's been running a business here in town as long as I can remember. Your family's safe as long as we stay quiet."

"Is that supposed to be a threat?" Daniela leaned closer to Garrett.

"Geez, no. I'm just saying that I already know, and I don't care. I mean, not that I don't care. I care." Garrett closed his eyes for a second and started again. "I just mean there's no way he's getting in any trouble about, well, what happened, as long as we're smart."

"Are you for real?" Daniela uncrossed and recrossed her arms, then looked from Cadie to Garrett. "You don't think a bunch of bored hicks will turn on my dad when those rumors start up again?"

"I'm not the enemy here," he said. "There would be consequences for coming forward now. We covered up a murder, for God's sake."

"We were kids. Scared kids, stupid kids," Cadie said. "They can't charge us with anything."

"But any adults involved could still be charged. There's no statute of limitations on murder," he said, staring at Cadie. "Or on being an accessory to murder after the fact."

Cadie focused her eyes on the linoleum squares on the floor. Fourteen across, twelve deep. *Don't look up. Do not make eye contact.* She could feel Garrett's eyes bearing down on her.

"I don't give a shit that your uncle could get charged," Daniela said. "He deserves to be charged."

Garrett ignored Daniela and continued staring at Cadie. "Do you understand that being an adult accessory to murder after the fact can carry the same sentence as the murder itself?" He paused. "No statute of limitations. Any adult who helped cover up a murder."

Sweat dripped down Cadie's neck.

"Great trivia question, but it's irrelevant," Daniela said. "Maybe we were accessories, but we were kids. We can't be charged."

"Three days," Cadie said.

"This is not your call." Daniela glared at Cadie.

"Give him three days. If this doesn't go away, we tell everything."

"I love how both of you want to gamble with my family's safety," Daniela said.

"Will you promise to call if anything comes up, or if you are worried about anything in the meantime?" Garrett said.

Cadie turned to Daniela, who nodded grudgingly.

"I need to know how to contact you." Garrett handed them each a blank paper and they wrote down their numbers. "Maybe some-day, later I mean, we can talk. There's a lot I'd like to know about that summer, the books, the boat."

"I don't think so," Daniela said.

Garrett stood awkwardly in his office doorway as Cadie and Daniela walked down the corridor to the lobby.

"I need to stop at the post office," Cadie said as they walked out. A blast of steamy air greeted them as they opened the door. "Call me after work?"

"I'm working late." Daniela didn't look at Cadie as she spoke.

"I'm not caving in to him," Cadie said. "Maybe it will work out better this way. And it will be less risky for all of us."

"Risky? Are you kidding me? Cadie, you mean well, but you've never had one damn thing to lose."

9

The sun peeked in and out of the clouds as Cadie pedaled up her long, steep driveway. She thrust all her weight into each rotation. Pine needles and gravel churned under her tires.

"This is the day, Cadie Brady," Daniela shouted as they approached the incline.

Cadie squeezed the rubber handlebar grips and pedaled harder. Daniela's nickname for her, with its nerdy Brady Bunch connotations, chafed, despite the flutter of pride that Daniela had bothered to give her a nickname at all.

Daniela, with her sleek ten-speed, always made it to the top. Cadie, with her secondhand banana-seat bike, usually sputtered out at the two-thirds mark.

She thought of Garrett. Of his eyes. The kiss. She licked her dry lips and panted in a steady rhythm to propel herself forward. Her thighs ached. Sweat gathered on her brow. Had Daniela ever kissed a boy? Cadie wondered as she watched her friend's ponytail swing from side to side ahead of her.

They pedaled nearly a mile up the dirt lane from Cadie's house, over the rickety wooden bridge spanning Silas Creek, and passed by the road that led to Daniela's house. Several long driveways branched off in both directions as they approached the base of the peninsula and turned onto the main road toward town. Fifteen homes, mostly vacation cottages, were situated on the peninsula, but in Cadie's mind the entire peninsula belonged to her and Daniela. Cadie was pretty sure her house was the only one accessible by road on her side of Silas Creek, where bogs and wetlands fortified the natural moat. The homes on Daniela's side of the Hook were year-round homes and much closer together than on Cadie's side of the creek.

Cadie approached the stone wall, the farthest she had ever made it up the hill. Had anyone ever written Daniela secret love notes? She stood up to bear down on the pedals.

"Go, Cadie Brady, go!" Daniela screamed.

Cadie passed the stone wall. Her lungs burned. She passed the downed pine that had fallen the previous winter. She could barely feel her legs by the time she reached Daniela, who waited for her at the top of the hill, straddling her bike.

"I knew you could do it." Daniela beamed as if Cadie had won Olympic gold.

Cadie folded her arms across her handlebars and put her head down. She turned sideways to see Daniela smiling so broadly Cadie could count every tooth in her mouth. Tufts of pollen hung in slices of sunlight breaking through the trees.

If only this summer could last forever.

Cadie whooped as they soared downhill and powered up the inclines on the dirt road. On an average day, it took them forty-five minutes to get to Angie's by bike, but on this day, they flew. Sweat poured down Cadie's face and neck as they entered the town center, made up of a spattering of municipal buildings, restaurants, and shops. On one side of the street sat the 7-Eleven, a Five n Dime, Angie's Diner, and the fire station, with the hardware store, pharmacy, and a pizza place on the opposite side. Beyond the firehouse, at the only intersection in town with a stop sign, sat the rec center, the middle school, the post office, police station, the library, a few small shops, and the art studio Cadie's parents owned.

Cadie estimated she had read at least one hundred books while sitting on the studio porch during the endless summer vacations of her youth. From the rocker on the porch, Cadie placed bets with herself every August on which day she would see the first flicker of red in the changing maple leaves on Crier Hill, which rose up behind the police station. But not this year. She didn't want to wish away a single day.

Cadie and Daniela parked their bikes in front of Angie's Diner and unloaded their blueberries. The sun cast elongated shadows, morphing Cadie's banana seat and ape-hanger handlebars into a distorted cartoon on the brand-new concrete sidewalk. Flyers advertising a car wash, babysitters, and dog walkers covered the wall outside the diner. Wedged between a notice for a math tutor and housekeeper, a pale blue flyer caught Cadie's eye.

Missing: Yellow rowboat with two oars. Last seen drifting near Anchor Harbor. 555–3002. Reward.

Cadie grabbed Daniela's elbow and nodded toward the sign.

Daniela read the handwritten note, shrugged, and continued walking toward their usual seats at the breakfast bar.

"It must be some other boat," Daniela whispered with such conviction that Cadie allowed herself to almost believe it.

Cadie squeezed the cracked leather bar stool with her knees as she spun in circles, sweeping her hand across Angie's lunch counter every other rotation to maintain her speed. On the stool next to her, Daniela spun in the opposite direction. Their timing had to be perfect. If either of them miscalculated, even by a fraction of a second, their knees would collide.

Cadie kept her eyes focused on a rusty tractor seat hanging on the wall behind the counter. She whipped her head around like a pirouetting ballerina so she wouldn't get dizzy.

"I wish we could have watched his face while he read *Are You There God? It's Me, Margaret*," Daniela said.

"I still think that was kind of mean. He probably had no idea what he was reading about." Cadie took her eye off the tractor seat to catch Daniela's smirk.

"I'm picking out the books from now on." Cadie pushed off so fast she had to drag her hand on the aluminum counter to avoid a crash.

"Can I borrow *The Outsiders*?" Daniela said.

"You can read any of my books you want." Cadie sucked her cheeks in to hold back a smile.

A group of guys in their late teens and twenties talked in Spanish at a booth in the corner. Workers from the farms outside town, Cadie guessed. Angie pushed the swinging kitchen door open with her hip and carried plates of blueberry pie over to the young men.

"It's on the house today." Angie placed a slice of pie in front of each of them.

Angie skipped over to Cadie and Daniela. Cadie didn't know any other adults who skipped. Angie also played cat's cradle with the girls on slow days.

"Hello, ladies. Looky over there." She pointed to the men. "Your blueberries at work."

"Why'd you give them free pie?" Daniela stopped spinning. Cadie crashed into her.

"Why not? I give you free soda." Angie placed two glasses on the counter. She squeezed the trigger on a soda gun to fill the glasses almost to the point of bubbling above the rim.

"But we bring you blueberries," Daniela said.

Angie leaned toward the girls and lowered her voice. "They come in here, and sometimes they don't order anything. Sometimes they get a soda. But that's it. See the blond guy with them, Clyde something or other. He's a manager or something out at Crittenden Farm. He and his dad used to live on the property. His dad died, but he still works there, I think."

The group laughed as they shoved forkfuls of berries—Cadie and Daniela's berries—into their mouths.

"The local kids always gave Clyde a hard time. I used to hear them in here making fun of him for hanging out with the farm workers. I don't think he had many local friends back in high school." Angie piled her curly brown hair on her head in a loose bun with a pen sticking out of it. She glanced over at the table and bit her lower lip.

"I know him." Daniela wrinkled her nose. "He works for my dad on weekends. I don't know why my parents are nice to him."

"Why shouldn't they be nice?" Angie said.

"He's super creepy," Daniela said.

"He doesn't always know how to act around folks," Angie said.

"Anyways, sometimes it's just nice to give people free pie. They love your berries, look."

Cadie and Daniela swiveled around on their stools. Four empty plates, stained purple with blueberry ink, sat on the table.

"I'm always extra nice to folks who eat my pies. We are bound together forever because I put a lot of love into those pies. And it keeps them coming back. It's the same for you girls, you know. If someone eats my blueberry pie, they're bound to you, too. So always be extra nice to them."

"Be kind to anyone who eats our berries," Cadie repeated. She would add it to her list of rules.

"Speaking of pies, I've got three in the oven. Enjoy your sodas." Angie disappeared into the kitchen.

Cadie watched Clyde, the older blond one, lick blueberries off his fingers. He laughed with his friends and collected the plates, scraped the remnants onto a single plate, and stacked them at the edge of the table for Angie. Cadie's parents would have been proud of her for doing that in a restaurant without even being asked.

He caught Cadie's eye, stopped laughing, and narrowed his eyes at her. His skin, pocked with acne scars, looked rough like sandpaper as he wrinkled his brow.

Cadie spun back around. She fought the blush rising up from her chest, consuming her face. Even her forearms turned red, and the translucent hairs from her neck all the way down to her wrist stood on end.

She stared at a puddle forming around her Coke from the beads of condensation sliding down the glass. She twisted a paper straw wrapper with her berry-stained fingers.

Daniela straightened her back as the group of young men walked toward the counter on their way to the door.

"Hola, chula," one of the younger guys, who looked about seventeen, said to Daniela. He leaned on the counter next to her, putting his face close to hers.

Daniela had perfect skin and soft brown eyes. She looked fifteen, even though she wouldn't turn thirteen for months. None of them acknowledged Cadie. Despite her flaming hair, she often imagined her translucent skin made her invisible to most boys. But not to Garrett.

Daniela swiveled her seat and turned her back to them. Clyde walked past them, not acknowledging them, toward the door.

Cadie focused on the puddle of water expanding around her glass, getting closer and closer to the scrunched-up straw wrapper. With a few more drops of water, the pool would overtake the paper.

"Not worth your time," said a tall skinny boy in a plaid shirt. "This one might look Mexican, but she's white as her friend."

Another drop, then two more, slunk down the hourglass-shaped glass.

Daniela spun around. "I'm not Mexican."

The skinny guy threw his hands up in mock apology. "Oh, okay. Two white girls having lunch."

"Leave us alone," Daniela said through clenched teeth.

"I see you, coconut," the skinny boy said.

"*Basta*," said the fourth man, in his mid-twenties, short and stocky. He pulled two crumpled bills from his pocket and slipped them under the edge of the blueberry-stained plates for Angie.

The stocky man stepped between his friends and Daniela, blocking her from their snickers as they headed for the door. He had a square face and wide-set eyes. He turned back to Daniela when his friends weren't looking and wagged his fingers at her as if he were casting a spell. She copied his motion and held her fingers up to touch the tips of his.

"See you," he said with a heavy accent and gentle lisp that made him sound younger than he looked.

"What was that?" Cadie spun around on her stool to face Daniela.

"Secret handshake." Daniela sipped her Coke, not looking back at Cadie.

"Why do you have a secret handshake with that guy?"

"Juan."

"With Juan."

"He works in my dad's store sometimes too. Whenever my dad starts bossing me around, which is, like, all the time, Juan hides where my dad can't see him and waves like that. He tries to make me laugh."

"That's weird."

"He's funny, I guess. He comes to the house for dinner a lot with some of the older guys who work on Crittenden Farm. Mom likes him because he eats a lot. Dad says he doesn't have any family or anything. That blond guy gives me the creeps, though. I don't care how nice Angie thinks he is."

"Why'd you tell them you aren't Mexican?"

Daniela's jaw dropped open. She curled the left side of her upper lip into an angry Elvis. "Cuz I'm not Mexican."

Another bead of water rolled down Cadie's Coke glass, testing the surface tension of the anxious puddle. It looked ready to spill across the counter at any second.

"But, I thought you said—" Cadie stammered. "I mean, your parents speak Spanish."

"We're from El Salvador." Daniela took a sip of her Coke and slammed the sweaty glass on the counter. "There's a big difference."

The vibration of her glass shook the counter, and the puddle of condensation forming around Cadie's Coke spilled over, enveloping the scrunched-up straw wrapper, which twisted and writhed as it absorbed the water.

Cadie watched the men cross the road and disperse. Juan stayed behind as the others turned toward the rec center. Clyde picked up a stone and hurled it at a cluster of birds bathing in a puddle.

"What an asshole," Daniela said.

"Yeah, but, I guess we have to be nice to those guys now," Cadie said.

"Why?"

"The berries. We're bound to them for life."

"You are the most gullible person I have ever met."

Through the large open window in the front of the diner, Cadie and Daniela watched Juan walk toward the hardware store Daniela's family owned. He kicked a small stone, rolling his foot over it, around it, with perfect control.

Daniela's father stood in the doorway wearing the faded Garcia's Hardware baseball cap he always wore in the store. His face turned red and he kicked at the welcome mat outside the door as the conversation with Juan escalated into an argument. Juan gestured wildly, his hands pumping in the air.

"Why are your dad and Juan yelling at each other?"

Daniela shrugged.

"Don't you understand Spanish?"

"Geez, will you stop it. I'm American. I speak English. Just like you." Daniela spun to face away from Cadie.

Angie pushed through the swinging door. "Refills?"

"No thanks," Cadie said without looking up.

"I'll take one." Daniela pushed her empty glass toward Angie. "Cadie and I were thinking we could double how many berries we pick. If you want to buy them."

Cadie opened her mouth, but no words came.

"Fantastic. You've got a deal, ladies."

Daniela stuck her jaw out and raised her eyebrows, daring Cadie to challenge her.

10

"No matches in the woods," Cadie said as Daniela laid her supplies out on the rock the following morning. "We don't want to start a fire."

"I know. I know. We'll do it in the lake."

Friar paced on the rock instead of lying down to wait for them as he usually did. He forced his head under Cadie's arm as she untied the boat. He barked twice as the girls stepped into the boat.

"Quiet, boy."

"Maybe we should take him with us," Daniela said.

"He'd bark at every loon that swam by. We don't want to attract attention," Cadie said.

"Sorry, boy. We'll be back soon." Cadie rubbed Friar's ears. He lay down on the rock, rested his head on his crossed front paws, and waited.

As they made their way inside the mouth of the biggest part of the cove, Daniela dropped her oar inside the boat.

"If we're going to do this, we have to mean it," Daniela said. "First, we each need to share a deep, dark secret, something no one else knows."

Cadie dug into her sheltered life searching for a secret, mining her memories for something worthy of the oath they were about to take.

"I peed in my sleeping bag at Girl Scout camp in third grade?"

"Nope."

"I've never been outside of New Hampshire?"

"Nope. It has to be something big," Daniela said.

She considered telling Daniela about Garrett's notes and the kiss, but she wanted to keep those secrets a little longer. She liked replaying everything he had said to her, how he had looked at her.

Reading and rereading his notes. They were meant for her alone. And, she suspected, Daniela wanted something darker.

"Well, there's one thing." Cadie hesitated. Clouds churned over themselves, casting a shadow over the mountains behind Cadie's home. "You'd never tell? Like, ever?"

"That's the whole point. If you break a blood oath, you are cursed for the rest of your life."

Cadie sat up straight and planted her palms on her knees. The boat rolled gently with a hypnotic rise and fall. Daniela leaned closer with eyebrows arched high.

"My grandparents are Quakers, which means they hate war."

"That's your big secret?"

"No. My parents aren't religious at all, but when Dad got drafted for Vietnam, my parents told everyone they were Quakers so Dad wouldn't have to go fight, but the government didn't believe him." An uncomfortable feeling brewed in her stomach. "So they ran away to Canada and worked on some farm, a commune or something, for three years, so my dad wouldn't have to go fight in a war he didn't believe in."

"Wow."

"But that's not everything." Cadie sucked in a deep breath and leaned closer to Daniela. "When he came back to the US, he went to jail for dodging the draft."

Daniela nodded approvingly and they floated silently for a few minutes. Woolly clouds that had been gathering over the mountains edged their way toward the lake, stirring a breeze.

"My turn," Daniela said. "This is really serious."

"More serious than jail?"

"A lot more serious." Daniela's pupils, dark and deep, sucked the light from the sky and reflected nothing back.

Hairs prickled up on Cadie's arms and neck.

Daniela sat cross-legged and leaned forward toward Cadie. Her fingertips pushed against the bottom of the boat as she balanced on arched claws.

"My family's here illegally."

"What'd you do that's illegal?"

Daniela rolled her eyes. "We didn't do anything. We just aren't supposed to be here. If the police find out, they could make us leave. We'd lose the store, my parents could go to jail, and I don't even know what would happen to me."

"Why would they make you leave?"

"You can't just come here from another country and walk in like 'Hi, I'm here.' You have to go through the court or the government or something."

"Then why didn't you do that?"

"We just couldn't. But it would be really bad if people found out." Daniela pulled her knees up to her chest. "I'd have to leave and never come back."

Cadie couldn't imagine being separated from her family, forced to move to another country. The weight of Daniela's secret fell heavy on Cadie. The boat spun gently on an invisible current, shifting Cadie's perspective of the familiar shoreline. Her own worries shriveled and sank to the bottom of the lake.

"I'll never tell anyone for as long as I live," Cadie whispered, and pulled Daniela into an embrace.

"Are you crying?" Daniela asked after Cadie sat back and wiped her face.

"I don't want you to leave." Cadie felt the blush rising up her chest and neck. "Why'd you trust me with something like that?"

"Because you're my best friend," Daniela said.

Cadie wiped her face and sat up straight.

"Are you ready?" Daniela opened her backpack and pulled out a pocketknife, a bottle of rubbing alcohol, cotton balls, matches stolen from the hardware store, and two Band-Aids. She spread them out on the bottom of the boat.

"And The Poachers' Code." Daniela pulled out a sheet of paper with the list of rules Cadie had been working on all summer. Daniela had copied them with a calligraphy pen. Around the edges Daniela had drawn a frame of delicate blueberry clusters.

"Did you trace those?" Cadie admired the details.

"Nope." Daniela pressed her lips together to hide her smile.

Daniela opened her father's Swiss Army knife and placed the blade on her thigh. She handed Cadie the matches. "Light the match and hold it under the knife."

Although Cadie had watched her father light thousands matches for his pipe, she had never struck one herself. She didn't know how to hold the matchstick or how hard to strike it. The first attempt left a gray smudge on the red strip on the end of the matchbox, emitting a weak puff of sulfur.

With sweaty palms and clumsy fingers, Cadie adjusted her grip. The second time, moving her thumb closer to the head of the match, she swiped it across the red strip with conviction. The matchstick erupted.

"Hold it still." Daniela guided the tip of the knife under the flame. When it fizzled, Cadie struck another match and continued blackening the tip of the knife.

"Alcohol," Daniela said. Cadie poured alcohol on two cotton balls, wiped the blade clean, and dumped a splash over the knife. Daniela folded a paper towel and rested it on her knee. "Want me to do yours first?" she said.

"I guess." Cadie handed the knife back to Daniela.

"Put your thumb facing up on the paper towel."

Cadie rubbed alcohol on her thumb and put it on Daniela's knee. Daniela gripped the hilt and stared at Cadie's hand.

"Shit. I can't do it," Daniela said.

"Give me your hand."

Daniela let Cadie grab her limp hand and wash her thumb with alcohol.

"Are you ready?" Cadie said.

"Yeah." Daniela gritted her teeth and squeezed her eyes shut. "Do it."

She knew Daniela expected her to chicken out. The knife cut through Daniela's skin more easily than she expected. The gash opened and a bubble of blood burst out and flowed down Daniela's hand and wrist.

"Shit, Cadie. You actually did it."

Cadie doused her own left thumb with alcohol and sliced into her flesh. Dark red oozed down her thumb, but it didn't hurt.

Supporting her cut hand with her other hand, Daniela held up her thumb to face Cadie, who did likewise. They pressed their wounds together.

"Repeat after me," Daniela said. "I do solemnly swear."

"I do solemnly swear."

"To uphold The Poachers' Code."

"To uphold The Poachers' Code."

"To never tell."

"To never tell."

"And to take *all* our secrets to the grave."

"And to take *all* our secrets to the grave."

Cadie pressed her bloody thumb harder against Daniela's until the beating of their hearts synched. On shore, the tall pines nodded, complicit in their oath. The tightness in Cadie's chest loosened so that, for the first time since they left shore, she could draw in a full breath.

They pressed bloody thumbprints on the bottom of The Poachers' Code and each signed the paper below the oath. Daniela waved the document in the air to dry the ink and the blood.

"You okay?" Daniela said.

"Yeah." Cadie put her thumb into her mouth and bit down to calm the sting.

"You have more guts than I give you credit for," Daniela said.

Daniela lay on her back on the bottom of the boat, her knees bent. Cadie lay down next to her in the opposite direction so their faces were inches apart, their feet at opposing ends of the boat. The clouds stretched thin above them. Cadie sucked on her throbbing thumb, swallowing her own heartbeat.

The boat had drifted into pebbly shallows of a small cove.

"Do you want to swim?" Daniela said.

Cadie wriggled out of her jean shorts and lowered herself into the lake. She scooped up a mouthful of water and spit most of it out. She swallowed a cool sip and let it slide down her throat.

"Nice Wonder Woman undies." Daniela leaned over the edge of the boat, looking down at Cadie in her tank top and underwear.

"You're jealous because your mom buys you boring underwear." Daniela took her shorts off and jumped in.

Cadie lay back against the surface of the water, letting the lake bear all of her weight. As she floated on her back with her eyes closed, she heard the muted sound of Daniela sloshing toward her. Cadie stretched her limbs out wide and thrust her chest toward the sky like an open water lily praying to the morning sun. She reached with the tips of her toes and fingers, imagining herself unfolding.

Daniela's hair billowed against her shoulder. When Cadie stretched her arms behind her head to make sure they didn't collide, Daniela grabbed Cadie's hands and they held on to each other, floating head to head like a raft. The loose curl of Daniela's fingers around her own anchored Cadie as her legs melted into the lake. If she didn't move, it felt as if her legs weren't even there, as though her body had merged with the lake. The air, thick with honeysuckle, breezed over Cadie's lips and open mouth.

"Cadie." Daniela's voice sounded far away to Cadie's submerged ears.

"Yeah?"

"I won't ever tell either." Daniela squeezed Cadie's fingers.

The cadence of water, the quiet pulse in the rise and fall, lulled Cadie into a trancelike drift. The shush of blood in her ears harmonized with the swells, syncopated by the warbling one can only hear below the surface of the lake.

Cadie tried to imagine where they drifted, which direction she faced, whether Daniela's eyes were closed too. She opened her eyes to see the leaves of a river birch dangling a foot above her face and jerked up just in time to stop Daniela from smashing her head on a rock poking through the surface.

Curled up in a sleeping bag on the floor of Daniela's bedroom that night, Cadie fingered long strands on the shag rug as she listened to Daniela toss and turn in her bed. Moonlight through the window scattered dancing shards of light on the wall opposite the window. The light bounced off of two rings that hung on the wall. Cadie crawled out of her sleeping bag and walked over to touch the wooden hoops.

"They're tambourines." Daniela sat up. "My dad hung them up when I was little. He told me fairies lived in the flashes of light and they would watch over me when I slept."

Cadie touched one of the hoops and the rustle of the tiny cymbals startled her.

"The katydids are so loud tonight," Cadie said.

"The what?"

"Katydids. Crickets, but their chirp is higher. Listen. It sounds like they're saying *katydid, katydid.*"

"*Cadie* did, *Cadie* did, *Cadie* did," Daniela enunciated. "What did Cadie do?"

"I didn't do anything."

"Do you think The Poachers' Code is good or evil?" Daniela said.

"It's just words."

"Anything can be good or evil. Depends on how you use it," Daniela said.

"Then I say we only use The Poachers' Code for good for the rest of our lives."

Daniela turned on her desk lamp and pulled The Code from her nightstand drawer. The gloss of their two perfect thumbprints glistened below Daniela's calligraphy. Sealed in blood, The Code seemed powerful. Upholding the rules felt like a noble calling, bigger than Cadie or Daniela, weightier than the secrets it guarded. Cadie could believe in The Code.

"We need to make a tablet, like Moses. You know, in the Bible," Daniela said.

"You go to church?"

"I watched the movie. We should make a tablet. Something that'll last forever."

After dismissing several options, they decided to carve The Poachers' Code into the underside of a shelf in Daniela's closet.

They took turns scooting on their backs into the closet and wrote the words on the underside of the lowest shelf. Using the same knife they'd sliced their thumbs with hours earlier, they etched over the penciled letters.

Flakes of white paint and slivers of pine peppered Cadie's curls. She closed her eyes and ran her fingers over the lettering, trying to read the words by touch.

"Move over. Let me in." Daniela tapped on Cadie's knee.

As Cadie rolled on her side to make room for Daniela, a Bicknell's thrush song curled through the woods and drifted through the window to nestle into Cadie's chest. The resonance swelled with vibrations that tingled in her fingertips and cheeks. Wriggling up until she was even with Cadie's face, Daniela put her hand in the small space between their heads and The Poachers' Code on the shelf above them. Cadie raised her hand to meet Daniela's. They laced their fingers together and squeezed until it hurt.

The Poachers' Code

1. *Keep one foot in the water.*
2. *Never take all the berries.*
3. *Don't kill bugs.*
4. *No witnesses.*
5. *Be kind to people who eat our berries.*
6. *No evidence.*
7. *Don't throw a rock if you can't see the target.*
8. *Lake water heals anything.*
9. *No matches in the woods.*
10. *Never tell.*

11

Cadie stood in the police station parking lot and allowed Daniela's accusation to gnaw at her. *You've never had one damn thing to lose.* Maybe Cadie didn't have a child, a home, or a stable job. But she had everything to lose.

She pulled her research samples out of her car and slammed the door.

Carrying a box full of dead insects felt silly, unimportant, as Cadie made her way from the police station parking lot to the post office so she could mail the package to Thea. The dead bodies rustled in their envelopes as she shifted her grip.

A day earlier, her research had been the only thing that mattered to her. Now, her past felt more urgent—and more dangerous—than her future. The mythology of the Summer Kid had assumed a misty sepia in her mind, which often made her question her memory. Encountering Garrett Tierney confirmed all the things she longed to unremember.

He had survived, which dulled the edge of guilt she had been carrying. But his reemergence introduced more problems. Did Garrett take the gun? If he did, why hadn't he told them? And if hadn't taken it, then who did?

It could have been any August day from Cadie's childhood. Three men leaned on the railing outside Garcia's Hardware, talking, spitting. A cracked cinderblock propped the post office door open, as it always had.

The post office smelled like her high school yearbook room. Adhesive, ballpoint pens, and expectation. Cadie filled out an overnight label and stuffed the box with crumpled-up newspaper from the recycling bin to protect her samples.

Human Remains Found Near Silas Creek read the banner headline from the morning paper. Cadie smashed the words into a tight ball, then unwound the story. The remains had not been identified. Speculation about a young farm worker who had disappeared decades earlier. A mention that police had questioned Raúl Garcia, the well-liked hardware store owner, in the young man's disappearance decades earlier.

Cadie wadded up the news story, threw it back in a recycling bin, and used sports pages to fill in the gaps between her bark and wood samples, the packets of beetles, and her field notes. Her fingertips ached from days spent prying back pine bark.

Call me as soon as you get this, she wrote in thick black marker next to the label. The tang of solvent stung her nose as the frayed felt tip squeaked out the words. She pressed down hard to seal the adhesive and held her hands in place, praying that her report would be enough to convince Thea, even though she had been trespassing when she collected samples.

"Whatcha got in there? The answer to world peace?" The postal worker tapped her pink fingernails on the counter, waiting for Cadie to let go of the package.

"Sorry." Cadie started to hand over the box but paused. "Are there any same-day courier services around here?"

"Where to?"

"Concord."

"For a hundred bucks, my son'll drive it there right now." She thumbed toward a skinny twenty-something sitting in a lawn chair outside. "He's out of work and could use the money. You got cash?"

"It's important." Cadie looked at the man, long hair pulled up in a knot on top of his head, drinking bottled organic iced tea.

"It'll get there or I'll kick his ass," the woman said.

Cadie exchanged phone numbers with the man, gave him the address, and left. As soon as she saw him pull out of the parking lot, she regretted her decision. She should have driven it herself. Nothing prevented him from taking off with her money and dumping the package by the side of the road.

She looked back inside at his mother behind the counter. The woman smiled and waved, flashing her pink nails. The makeshift courier's beat-up Honda disappeared over a rise in the road, carrying Cadie's future with it.

Cadie walked past the newly constructed Dunkin' Donuts in the place where a sandwich shop once stood. The bright pink-and-orange logo stood out like a gaudy bauble against the other sleepy storefronts on Main Street. Cadie felt an unexpected flicker of anger at the audacity of the colors and the smell of mass-produced pastries.

Three firefighters sat in lawn chairs in front of the fire station next to a life-sized Smokey Bear carved out of a tree trunk. The day her Girl Scout troop finished their Fire Safety badge, they had posed for a photo with the bear. A placard hung around the statue's neck reading *Fire hazard extremely high*. Cadie looked over the treetops toward the mountains to the west. To another eye the green-gray smear might look like smog or a low-hanging storm cloud, but Cadie knew better.

"Holy shit, it's Cadie Kessler," called a firefighter named Ryan, who Cadie had gone to middle school with. "Haven't seen you around here in years."

Cadie waved, then turned her gaze back to the smudge of smoke on the horizon.

"I saw your name on that letter about those beetles. That why you're here?" he said, following Cadie's eyes to the horizon. "The chief didn't want to do it, but I talked him into clearing the firebreaks, like you recommended. You were the smartest girl in class. I figured it would be stupid to ignore you."

Cadie walked toward Ryan. The paint on Smokey's blue jeans had peeled off in strips, making the weathered figure itself look like a fire hazard. The three men on the lawn represented a full third of Maple Crest's paid fire department.

"Have you noticed pine trees dying around here, the needles turning rusty orange?"

"No. But there's a drought," said an older firefighter sitting next to Ryan.

"Yeah. I heard." Cadie fought the urge to add *dipshit* under her breath. "There's this beetle, I've been seeing it up in higher elevations. It's killing off the pines. It's adding more dry wood, and in this drought—"

"We're keeping an eye on it," Ryan said. "Don't worry."

"The state might start thinning affected pines." Cadie tried to sound confident in her wishful thinking. "I can help tag them, if you've seen any."

"You seen any killer beetles?" the older man asked Ryan.

"I'm being serious," Cadie said. "You haven't noticed any pines turning orange? There's already so much dry wood."

"Thanks for the tip," the older man said, and winked at Cadie as a group of men in work clothes passed by on the sidewalk, talking in Spanish and laughing.

"Maybe you're looking for the wrong invasive species," one of the other firefighters said, eliciting laughs from his coworkers.

Cadie paused, unsure if she had heard him correctly. She didn't want to be there. She should be in the woods, or in the lab. She should be writing up her findings. Not there. Not in this town where decades of decay hid under freshly painted clapboard.

"What the hell is wrong with you?" she said to the man, who looked to be her father's age.

The firefighter stood up and took a step forward. Cadie recognized him as Chester Talbot, one of the Talbot brothers who owned and operated Talbot's Sugarhouse, a small maple farm on the edge of town.

"Cadie, back off. He's kidding." Ryan stepped between them.

"Good thing Canadians are more evolved than you." Cadie glared at Chester.

"What's that supposed to mean?"

"Your maples are creeping north as the temperatures increase.

If you want to keep making syrup, your family'll be the invasive species in Canada soon, following the maples."

"My family's been tapping New Hampshire maples for generations." Chester mopped his brow with a bandana folded in a perfect square. "We aren't going anywhere."

"Sugar maples are pretty particular. Time-lapsed maps show they're edging farther north at a fast clip. Some models predict there won't be any left in New Hampshire in fifty years. That's if the forest fires don't kill them first."

"Good grief." Chester swatted his arm at Cadie. "A couple hot summers and you kids run around like the world's going to end."

"We're monitoring the fires," Ryan said. "Besides, you know what we call a few extra fires? Job security."

Chester and the other firefighter laughed.

"You're hilarious." Cadie turned her back on the men and walked away. Ryan followed.

"I'm sorry about those guys. They're just messing around," he said.

"Maybe they should stop spouting racist crap and do something productive, like get ahead of the fires."

"Don't stress about the fires. We got an update thirty minutes ago."

"And?"

"Six hot spots reported today, but they're all under control. None near us. We've been through dry spells before."

Cadie sped up, wishing Ryan would go back to his lawn chair.

"You staying in town long?" Ryan stopped walking, but didn't turn back. "A bunch of us are shooting pool at the Deer Park tomorrow if you're around."

"I don't think so." Cadie continued toward the diner.

"Cadie, wait." Ryan ran to catch up. "You can see some browning pines up the east face of Crier Hill, behind the police station." Ryan shoved his hands in his pockets. When he smiled, his mouth turned down in the corners, making it hard to tell if he was being sincere or smug. "Is that what you're looking for? Are these bugs for real?"

"Why would I make that up? Of course they're real. It's the same beetle that devastated Colorado and caused some of the biggest fires in decades."

"Check Crier Hill. If I notice anything else, I'll let you know."

"Thanks."

"How do I get in touch with you?" Ryan pulled his cell phone out. "Give me your number."

Cadie typed her information into Ryan's phone.

Ryan turned back toward the firehouse and shouted, "I told you she'd give me her number. Women can't resist me."

Cadie turned her back on Ryan and raised a hand with her middle finger extended.

"See you at the Deer Park," Ryan called after her.

When her family left Maple Crest and moved to Boston her eighth-grade year, Cadie couldn't get out fast enough. The paved streets of Boston drowned out the noise in her head that the quiet of the forest amplified.

But the forest always pulled her back. College in Colorado lured her to forestry, entomology, and the chatter that happened in the dark, under the soil in the woods. She belonged among the trees.

But the trees in Maple Crest were different than anywhere else. Despite her longing to hate her hometown, the particular flavor of her lake water and the smell of decaying leaves specific to the area surrounding the cottage always drew her in with a comfort that teased her like a drug she knew she shouldn't take. Every forest has a personality. Although similar to the mountains in New England, the Colorado woods did not speak to Cadie. While working on her dissertation, she spent weeks hiking and camping out west. With her ear pressed against stone, her hands flattened against the soil, she waited for the subtle vibrations that rose from the earth. But they never came. She, and all the molecules that coursed through her body, had been fine-tuned to the frequency of the granite in New Hampshire.

She'd shared her theory over a joint under a wide-open Colorado sky with a fellow doctoral candidate. Three shooting stars slashed the sky as they smoked, but her wish had not come true. In the morning, her friend laughed at her drug-induced pontifications, and from then on, she had kept the theory to herself. The low-grade vibrations in her bones eventually drew her back east where her desires synched with the needs of the soil and stone of New Hampshire.

She looked over her shoulder at the firefighters laughing in their lawn chairs. Ryan slunk into his seat, just as he always had, just as he always would, with a comfort in his own skin and hometown that Cadie could never capture.

12

Garrett's lawn chair sat empty on the end of the pier as Cadie and Daniela rounded the point. Frayed strands of the nylon seat flapped in the unsteady breeze. Cadie looked over her shoulder at Daniela, who shrugged and continued paddling.

"I'll leave the berries and the book real quick," Cadie said. He always sat in his chair at this time every day. Cadie scanned the shore, the house, but didn't see him.

"He said not to stop unless we saw him on the pier."

"I'll be quick." Cadie paddled hard toward the ledge.

"I know what you're doing." A lopsided smirk spread across Daniela's face. "You want to leave the berries for him so you'll be bound to him forever."

Cadie's ears flared with heat.

"I do not. I just thought it would be nice. And he needs a new book."

"Sure." Daniela whistled to the tune of "Cadie and Garrett sitting in a tree" while eyeing Cadie. "I didn't know a person's neck could turn so red."

They pulled the boat up onto the sand and Cadie climbed out with the bag of berries between her teeth and *The Call of the Wild* tucked in the waistband of her shorts.

Daniela made kissing noises at Cadie as she climbed.

Footsteps and two voices approached the top of the wall right before Cadie reached up to put the book on the regular spot. Cadie froze. Daniela beckoned her to come down, but Cadie couldn't move. She wrapped a tree root around her wrist to hold herself steady and pressed her body against the rough stone, trying to become invisible.

"So this is my fault?" a man, probably Garrett's uncle, said. "I was trying to get back *your* fifty dollars that guy stole."

"I never asked you to do that," a second voice with a thick accent answered. "If they catch you, I got nothing to do with this."

"He's a racist bastard. He can't just steal your money," the uncle said. "That guy sits on his white ass all day while you work hard. He can't just steal your fucking money."

"That's all nice and shit, but I don't have rights in this country." His long, feathery s-s-s sounds layered under the accent reminded Cadie of Juan, the man Daniela shared a secret handshake with. Daniela's eyes widened as she recognized his voice too.

"I know." The uncle paused for a few seconds. "That's why I tried to help you."

They were so close Cadie could feel their footsteps above her.

No one ever looked out for Cadie when she got picked on. No one stepped in on her behalf when the eighth-grade boys called her Little Orphan Annie because of her hair. Maybe the uncle wasn't as mean as Garrett claimed.

"Help me? You *shot* the guy," Juan said.

Cadie's knees locked. Her wrist curled tight around the slippery bark of the tree root, which cut into her skin. Her elbow cramped from holding her body tight to the rock.

The footsteps moved closer to the edge.

"Look, I know you didn't mean to, but, man, you still shot the guy. Don't get me involved. I wasn't even there."

"Why do you have a gun?" A third, smaller voice came from farther away. Garrett's voice. "Who'd you shoot?"

When no one answered, Garrett yelled, "Who did you shoot? They're not sending me back to that place if you get arrested. I won't go."

Cadie clenched her jaw on the plastic of the Ziploc bag of berries clamped between her teeth. The plastic started to tear, but she didn't have a free hand to grab it. She sucked a corner of the bag farther into her mouth and held on. A drip of berry juice seeped through the torn bag, quickly turning from sweet to acidic before it hit the back of her tongue.

"Tell him, tell him he should go to the police," Juan said. Waves nudged the rowboat off the sandy perch below Cadie. To pull the boat back onto the sand would make too much noise. Cadie watched the boat with Daniela inside slip away from the shore out of sight from the men on the ledge. With small, slow strokes, Daniela guided the boat to hide behind a cluster of boulders just off the shoreline. Daniela disappeared from view.

Cadie was alone.

"Get back in the house. Anyone finds out and you'll go right back to that foster guy. You want him to break your other arm? You want one more concussion?" Garrett's uncle paused.

Cadie's wrist throbbed as she squeezed the tree root tighter. She pressed her cheek against the stone wall to steady herself. Her breath rustled the plastic.

"Don't be stupid," Juan said. "Tell the cops you didn't mean to do it. The guy's not hurt so bad."

"I'm not going back," Garrett whimpered.

"Don't worry, little man, Juan's not telling anyone anything, right?"

"This is messed up," Juan said. "Just turn yourself in now. Better than getting busted later. I'm out of here. I'm going to go stay with my cousin in Vermont."

Gravel crunched and feet shuffled above Cadie's head. She squeezed her eyes closed.

"Put that thing down," Juan said. Everyone stopped moving.

"Garrett, go inside." The uncle's voice remained calm and slow. "Now."

"Okay, okay, I won't say anything," Juan said. "I don't know anything. Don't point that at me."

"How do I know you aren't going to turn me in to protect yourself?" the uncle said.

Don't let go. Don't let go. Don't let go. Cadie shifted her weight from one foot to the other on the narrow, gravelly perch. She could no longer feel her hand, tangled with the tree root.

The air above Cadie exploded. The gunshot reverberated in the stone against her cheek. She stared fiercely at the bowing veins in the rock wall and summoned strength from the granite particles coursing through her. Her fingers locked around the tree root. Her muscles stiffened, her joints froze.

The stench of sulfur stung her sinuses. She swallowed hard to suppress a dry heave.

Silence. Stretched-out silence. So long and deep Cadie worried they might hear her breathe.

She looked across the lake but couldn't see the boat or Daniela.

She wanted to call out to Garrett. She tried to swallow but her throat tightened and she gagged on the plastic bag and the ooze of smashed blueberries. She tried bending her knees, but her muscles would not respond. If anyone saw her, she wouldn't be able to escape. She would fall into the lake like a rock and sink to the bottom.

"You do everything I tell you, got it?" the uncle whispered. "And don't you fucking cry."

Was Garrett crying? Please let Garrett be okay.

"We'll be okay." The uncle's voice softened. "I'm going to take care of everything. Stay here." Cadie listened as footsteps trailed off toward the house.

Her knees hurt where sharp edges of rock pressed into her flesh. She clenched her teeth, tearing the corner of the baggie, which fell against the rock and tumbled into the water with a splash. Cadie held her breath.

Gravel and sand fell from the ledge above into Cadie's hair. She looked up, expecting to see Garrett's uncle pointing a gun at her.

13

Cadie looked up to see Garrett peering down from the rock ledge. He looked back over his shoulder and flicked his wrist with a short jerk.

"You need to get out of here." His chin trembled as he spoke. "You can't talk to anyone about this. I'll get sent back to that place."

"Come with us. You can't stay with him. He just—" Cadie tried to calm her voice. "He shot someone. I heard everything."

"You don't understand. If he goes to jail, I go to foster care." Garrett's bony shoulders curled forward and inward as if he might collapse in on himself. "You can't say anything. I'll run away."

Cadie's arms burned from clinging to the tree root. She moved up a step and held on to the top of the ledge, warm from the sun.

Garrett dropped to all fours so they were almost at eye level. He put his hand on top of hers. "Please help me." Garrett scooted closer to Cadie, his breath warming her cheek.

She fought the urge to back away from him.

He squeezed her hand. *Jump. Run. Do something.* Garrett's pulse beat against her skin.

A surgical scar ran up the inside of his forearm, with round purple scars where pins must have held him together. Cadie shuddered, trying not to imagine the abuse Garrett had endured.

"I need you to do something. It's important." He crawled a few feet backward and returned with a white plastic grocery bag, stretched tight by the weight of its compact but heavy package. "Take this into the middle of the lake where it's deep, and dump it."

He put the bag on the ledge in front of Cadie. Metal clinked against the stone. She picked the bag up. It weighed more than she expected. She dropped the bag back on the ground with a clang.

"No way." Her heart thumped wildly.

"Drop it in the lake. That's all." Garrett leaned his head inches from Cadie's. The smell of fear and sweat and dust swirled around her as he whispered. "Please help me."

Garrett had the reddest lips, almost purple against his pale skin.

Cadie picked up the bag again and wrapped the plastic around the item inside several times. It looked like a shapeless blob.

"Garrett. Where the hell are you?" his uncle shouted from the driveway.

Garrett jerked upright and grabbed a fistful of his sweaty hair. "Don't let him see you. Go!"

Cadie slid down the rock face, scraping the skin off her knees. She huddled at the bottom of the ledge until she heard Garrett and his uncle climb the porch stairs and slam the door.

She waded silently into the lake and swam with one arm holding the plastic bag above water, kicking with both legs and pulling with her other arm. The rocks looked so close from shore, but they seemed to get farther away as she swam toward Daniela's hiding spot.

The weight of her denim shorts and T-shirt dragged as she pulled forward. Water grass wrapped around her ankles. As she closed the distance between the shore and the rocks, the tip of the rowboat emerged. Daniela's face peered through a gap in the rocks.

Daniela crawled to the end of the boat where Cadie climbed in. Daniela put her hands on Cadie's knees and leaned forward until her forehead rested against Cadie's; neither of them blinked. Daniela cupped her hand under one of Cadie's braids to catch the water dripping off.

Through the opening between the rocks, Cadie watched Garrett walk out to the ledge and crane his neck to look for her. She couldn't see anyone else on shore. Cadie picked up an oar to push off the rocks, but Daniela grabbed her wrist.

"Not yet," Daniela said.

Through the gap in the rocks, Garrett spotted Cadie. He locked his eyes on her. She lifted a finger to her lips. He mirrored her gesture. Finger to lips. Lips to finger.

In the distance behind Garrett, a lanky male figure stepped out of the woods. The slight cheekbones, the stringy yellow hair. Clyde, the blond guy from the diner, was Garrett's uncle.

Garrett turned away from Cadie and walked toward the house. Clyde put his arm around Garrett's shoulder, and they disappeared.

Neither of the girls spoke as they paddled home.

"Are you going to tell me what happened?" Daniela said as she tied the boat to the birch tree.

"I don't know." Cadie picked at her cuticles. "But if we tell anyone, Garrett will go back to foster care. They broke his arm and burned him. He can't go back there."

"Yeah, well isn't that better than living with—with him?"

"We don't really know what happened anyway. It's not like we saw anything," Cadie said. Visions of the frail boy being locked in a basement, whipped, and starved flooded Cadie's mind as she tried to imagine how foster care could be worse than living with that uncle.

"But we heard it. Did they hurt Juan?"

Echoes of the blast resounded in her head. "I promised him I wouldn't tell the police, but—"

"No police," Daniela hissed in a voice that did not sound like her. "We can *not* go to the police. You aren't going to tell your parents, are you? Because they'll definitely call the cops."

Cadie shook her head.

"Are you going to tell me what's in there?" Daniela pointed to the bag as they tied off the boat at the rock.

"I didn't look inside." Cadie picked at a scrape on her knee. Friar jumped up on Cadie's thighs, barking and sniffing her as if she hadn't been home in weeks. Cadie pushed him away.

"What are you going to do with it?" Daniela said.

"I don't know. He told me to throw it in the lake."

"But you didn't."

"What if we need it for evidence one day?" Cadie let Daniela tie off the boat, although it was usually her job. She cradled the bag and paced. If she tossed the gun in the lake it would be there forever, every time she jumped in the water. Every touch of water to her lips would taste of sulfur and fear.

"Follow me." Cadie walked into the woods toward the creek. Daniela did not follow right away. After about twenty paces, Cadie could hear her friend's reluctant footsteps.

Friar circled around Cadie's feet, whining for attention. Cadie shooed him away. Friar fell back and walked in step with Daniela. Mud sucked at Cadie's feet along the wide-open swath on the bank of the creek. Cadie stopped in front of the beech tree.

"If we hide it, no one else gets hurt." Cadie placed the bag on the ground. She pulled a wad of large Ziploc bags from her backpack, the ones she used for berries when the buckets got full. She wrapped the grocery bag as tight as she could and put it in the Ziploc. Then she placed that Ziploc inside another one, and then one more. She pressed out the air and sealed it tight.

"Why'd you do all that?" Daniela said.

"We can preserve the evidence. You know, just in case." The longer she held the bag, the heavier it became. Cadie looked up at the tall beech tree at the edge of the clearing. She had been saving the hiding spot to stash her diary when she was older and had secrets worth hiding. Cadie climbed up the boulder next to the beech. The hollow, shaped like a sideways eye, made a perfect hiding spot, only visible from on top of the boulder.

She imagined the tree growing around the bag until the hole closed over. In two hundred years maybe the tree would rot, and someone would find the fossilized package and wonder what had happened in those woods all those years ago.

Daniela handed the bag up to Cadie. She tried not to touch the shape so it wouldn't imprint on her brain. Maybe she was wrong about what was inside. But as she lowered it, she felt the bumpy texture of the grip panel, the arch of a trigger. She took a deep breath. With slow movements, she lowered it until she hit the bottom of the hole. She covered the bag with bits of broken branches and leaves and willed the tree, the forest, to absorb it.

The tall trees around her swayed. Cadie pressed her palms flat against the smooth beech bark and closed her eyes. Her wet clothes clung to her body. She stamped her feet to bring circulation into her cold toes.

They couldn't leave Garrett with that man. They had to help him. She paced in a circle at the base of the tree. What was she doing? Why should she protect this boy she hardly knew? Her teeth chattered uncontrollably. She closed her eyes. The air in the forest felt thick, gelatinous, as if she were underwater. Underwater where she could hold her breath, and sink deeper and deeper, away from the surface, the woods, the gun. Shafts of light broke through blurry green-gold water and warbled noises slurred in the background.

"Cadie." Daniela shook her shoulder. "I'm talking to you. Can you even hear me?"

"What?" Cadie jerked her eyes open as Daniela's voice pulled her back into the forest.

"Stop it." Daniela grabbed Cadie by the arm and held tight. "You need to get control of yourself."

The trees around her rushed into focus. Nothing appeared different, but it somehow felt completely unfamiliar.

"We need to act normal. Can you act normal?"

Cadie nodded.

"We can't tell, you understand that, right?"

"What about Juan?"

"No police." Daniela's eyes widened so far, the whites completely encircled her dark irises like a ring on a bull's eye. "I'm taking you back to my house." Daniela walked toward her house, but Cadie's feet felt stuck to the ground, as if she would never again have control over anything, over her limbs or even her mind.

"Come on. I'll make you a milkshake." Daniela let her shoulders droop, softened her glare, and extended a hand to Cadie.

Cadie followed Daniela through the woods, the gunshot echoing in her head over and over.

Dolores startled them when they walked into the kitchen.

"Why are you home?" Daniela said.

"I'm playing hooky. Your father's at a meeting in Concord, so I asked Agnes to watch the store for a few hours. I'm going to sit outside and read a book." Dolores pulled Daniela in for a quick hug. "Don't tell your father."

Daniela stiffened in her mother's arms and Dolores pulled back. "What's wrong?"

"Nothing." Daniela glared at Cadie, warning her to act normal.

Cadie tried to shove her trembling hands into her shorts pockets, but the wet fabric wouldn't give, so she clasped her hands behind her back.

"Girls? What happened?" Dolores fingered Cadie's shirt. "Why are you wet?"

"She fell off the pier. It just scared her," Daniela said. "She's fine."

Cadie clamped her jaw shut.

"You're crying." Dolores touched Cadie's cheek.

The gentleness of Dolores's fingers broke Cadie. She shook her head, although two hot tears slid down her cheeks.

Dolores looked back at Daniela, who stood stone-faced.

"There's this boy," Cadie said. Garrett needed her.

"Cadie, don't."

Dolores put her hand up to silence Daniela and nodded at Cadie to continue. "A boy?"

"Okay, so I pushed her into the water. I'm sorry I pushed you off the pier, Cadie," Daniela said with sharp, deliberate syllables.

"He's in trouble. Someone got shot, maybe." Cadie felt as if her body had been ripped open and all her secrets spilled out onto the floor. "We were there."

"What do you mean shot?" Dolores said.

"She's making stuff up. We were making up stories, you know, like we always do. Right, Cadie?" Daniela glared at her.

"His name's Garrett and he's in trouble." She couldn't bring herself to look at Daniela as the words tumbled out.

The phone rang, but Dolores ignored it.

"Tell her it's a game." Daniela pulled hard on Cadie's arm and turned to her mother. "It's just a stupid game."

"In trouble how? Do you mean shot with a gun?"

Cadie nodded. "We have to help him." Cadie felt Daniela's eyes burning into her.

The phone stopped ringing, then immediately started again.

"You're shaking," Dolores said to Cadie, and guided her to a seat at the kitchen table.

Cadie couldn't quiet her limbs. She clasped her arms across her chest, which made her shoulders shake. Dolores pulled one of Raúl's jackets from a hook and wrapped it around Cadie. Dolores beckoned Daniela to join them at the table, but Daniela did not move.

As soon as the phone stopped ringing it started for a third time. Dolores sighed and picked up the receiver.

"He's not home. Can you call back later?"

Daniela squinted fiercely at Cadie and pressed her body into the far corner of the kitchen. Cadie watched Daniela's chest heave as the anger in her eyes morphed into an icy fear that Cadie felt in her gut, but didn't quite understand.

A muffled voice yelled on the other end of the phone, but Cadie couldn't decipher the words.

"I don't know when he'll be home."

Dolores held the phone away from her ear as the caller shouted.

"Calm down," Dolores said. "What happened?"

A muffled ramble of indecipherable syllables poured through the line.

The caller hung up.

"There's an emergency at the store. I need to go in. We need to finish this conversation, though. I want you to wait here until I get back, both of you." Dolores did not look at either girl as she spoke. "I don't want you to talk to anyone else about this."

When Dolores put her hand on Cadie's shoulder, Cadie felt her trembling too. "Not even your parents. I'll help you when I get home, and we can discuss what happened."

Dolores grabbed her keys and paused in the doorway. "I'm sure this is all a misunderstanding. We'll sort it out as soon as I get things straightened out at the store."

Cadie watched Dolores's car until it disappeared.

"How could you do that?" Daniela broke the silence in the kitchen. "You swore a blood oath to always keep our secrets. Do you know what happens to people who break blood oaths?"

Cadie nodded.

"They're cursed forever." Daniela pointed to the door.

"But your mom said—"

"I don't care what she said. I want you to leave." Daniela narrowed her eyes. "We're going to tell her you made the whole thing up and you were upset because you fell in the lake. Tell her I pushed you in and you're mad and that's why you're acting so weird."

Cadie stood up. Her knees felt unstable and she gripped the edge of the table.

"You put my entire family in danger." Daniela's look of disdain burned Cadie's skin. "We cannot be witnesses. We cannot be involved. My mother cannot know anything. Do you understand?"

A wave of nausea rose up and Cadie ran for the door. She sprinted through the woods toward her house. Branches whipped across her thighs and her face. Tears clouded her vision and she caught her toe on a root. She landed prone on the path with her arms stretched out. The thud to her chest knocked the wind out of her.

She couldn't go home. If her parents saw her they would know something was wrong, and she didn't trust herself not to tell them everything. She lay on her stomach and swallowed down the dirt that had kicked up on her face when she fell.

Her fear bubbled into anger. Daniela wasn't the only person who needed protecting. Someone had to look out for Garrett.

The fall knocked the soggy copy of *The Call of the Wild* from the back of Cadie's waistband. In all the commotion she had forgotten to leave it for Garrett. She hadn't even felt it as she swam to the rocks where Daniela hid. Cadie thumbed through the fragile, wet pages, imagining what kind of message Garrett would have coded for her in the words.

If Daniela was too selfish to rescue him, Cadie would do it herself.

14

Cadie closed her eyes, imagining how Garrett's property connected to the wooded path where she sat. She visualized rowing past several homes and the long swath of woods. Around the tip of the Hook. She imagined herself a bird, flying over the lake and the forest. She could find his house from the woods.

She picked up a large stick and headed for Silas Creek.

Cadie thrashed through the icy water until she came to the barbed-wire fence. She rubbed the pink scar on her shoulder from where she cut herself the day she met Daniela in the woods. She lay on her belly in the water and slithered under the wire. With her walking stick for support, she navigated the slippery stones until the water became too deep to walk in.

She crawled up the bank and continued through the woods, unsure what she hoped to find. Maybe she could find Garrett and convince him to come home with her. Or what if the uncle saw her first? Gooseflesh crawled across her wet skin.

You know what happens to people who break blood oaths?

The look on Daniela's face when she pointed to the door stung like a fresh wound. Cadie squeezed her walking stick tighter.

Cadie froze at a crackling sound followed by huffing, dragging. Her well-practiced instinct told her to make noise if she heard a bear, but a deeper intuition pleaded with her to stay silent. The noise came closer and Cadie crouched behind a bush. A sniffling, a scraping, like something being dragged through the underbrush. A pause followed by an unbearable silence. Cadie shrank into the bush and pressed her back against a tree. She could disappear into the branches.

The movement started again, inching closer. A grunt. Twigs cracking. Two people moved into view, struggling to drag something heavy. She craned her neck to see better. Not some*thing*. They dragged some*one*.

The lump in her throat swelled again. *Don't move. You are invisible. You are part of the forest.*

The figures were too far away to distinguish faces, but she recognized the skinny arms and stooped shoulders. The silhouette from the pier. Garrett. He struggled to support the feet of a man's body, while the other person gripped under the armpits and staggered backward.

They moved so slowly. One shuffled step after another. Garrett ran back to retrieve a long-handled shovel, tossed it ahead of them, and resumed. Cadie's feet started to fall asleep as she crouched low for what seemed like hours as they dragged the body a painful twenty feet. Thorns stabbed at her ankles, but she didn't dare move.

As they drew closer, the adult stood up and stretched. Cadie held her breath, expecting to see the face of the uncle. She clamped her hand over her mouth to hold in a gasp when Dolores stood up and stretched her back.

The phone call, the harried voice. Why wasn't Dolores at the store?

Cadie wanted to scream, to run.

Garrett and Dolores struggled, one step and a pause; Garrett lost his grip on one leg and a heavy work boot thudded against a rock. Every sound in the forest seemed amplified. A squirrel scampered overhead and Cadie held her breath, hoping Garrett and Dolores wouldn't look in the direction of the animal and see Cadie cowering.

"I can't do it." Garrett dropped a lifeless leg and crumpled to the ground. His face looked cold as granite, his lips as pale as his skin. "He's too heavy."

"We don't have a choice," Dolores said.

"Can't we do it here?"

"It's too rocky. We need to get closer to the creek bank." Dolores held her gaze up high, not looking at Garrett, or the body. As Garrett sat on the ground, Dolores straightened her back and began pulling him without Garrett's assistance. She barely moved the body an inch before stumbling and falling.

Cadie crept backward, sharp stones and twigs digging into her palms and knees. If she could get behind the large boulder fifteen feet away, she would be able to sneak off without being seen.

Dolores stood up and tried to lift the body again. She pulled the man by his armpits and heaved with all of her body weight. She lost her grip and the man's head fell against a rock with a crack.

Dolores cried out at the impact and rushed to cradle the man's head. She brushed the floppy black hair from his forehead, exposing the face.

"Oh, Juan." She held his head on her lap and leaned over until her forehead touched his. "Oh, Juan."

Cadie stopped moving, the crack of skull on granite reverberating through her joints. No longer caring if they saw her, she wanted to run, to get far away from Garrett and Dolores, far away from that body.

Run, Cadie screamed inside her head. *Run*. But her body refused to move. She could not breathe as she thought of Juan's fingertip fluttering against Daniela's, his slippery *S* sounds, and broad smile.

After a few long minutes, Dolores stood up and groaned, covering her mouth with her hand to suppress a sharp cry. Her other hand moved to her lower back. She froze, stuck halfway between standing and bending over. Her shoulders shook, just slightly, but enough for Cadie to know Dolores was crying.

"What's wrong?" Garrett asked.

"I'm fine." Her voice quivered. She stood up slowly, both hands pressing into the small of her back.

"Please, can't we just leave him here," Garrett said.

"It's too late for that." Dolores bent over and tried again to drag Juan. She breathed in deep rasps as if trying to blow through the pain. Her chin trembled.

Dolores's ache swelled inside Cadie's chest. She thought of the fear in Daniela's eyes as she had pressed herself into the corner in the kitchen. The air in Cadie's lungs burned.

She was only a few feet from the boulder. She could get away.

Dolores's pained breath grew louder, filling Cadie's head until she could no longer hear her own thoughts. Dolores moaned again and Cadie jumped up.

"I'll help you," she said.

"What are you doing here?" Dolores grimaced as she tried to stand up straight. She scanned the woods behind Cadie.

Garrett took off running.

"It's me. It's Cadie." She couldn't see him among the thick trees, but she heard his footsteps stop abruptly.

Dolores grabbed Cadie's shoulder so hard it hurt. "Why are you here? Who is with you?"

Garrett peeked out from behind a tree.

"I'm alone. She's not with me." Cadie chewed the inside of her cheek.

Dolores looked gray. Her dimples had disappeared and Cadie wondered if they would ever return. Could fear wipe away a lifetime of smiles?

"You need to leave," she said.

Cadie stepped next to Dolores and put her hands under the man's armpits. Through his work shirt the body felt soft, not stiff like she expected. She strained, digging her heels into the ground, but she barely budged him. She slipped and fell onto her backside, got up and tried again.

Dolores stepped next to her and took one arm while Cadie took the other. Garrett picked up the legs and they moved slowly toward the creek. Cadie felt as if she were watching herself from high up in the tree. She was in a movie. In a book. The trembling calmed. None of it was real.

They worked together, but each of them walked alone in that forest. Cadie stole sideways glances at Dolores, but Dolores would not make eye contact. She could feel Garrett looking at her, but could not meet his stare.

When they found a place near the creek with soil deep enough to dig in, they laid Juan down gently. His eyes were closed, a sliver of white showing between his lids. His jaw lay slack and she could see his soft tongue. He could have been asleep. One side of his collar stuck up higher than the other because his buttons were off by one. Cadie felt the urge to correct the buttons, but quickly forgot when her eyes drifted to the dark red stain covering his abdomen and spreading down one pants leg.

Cadie moved away from the body. She no longer watched the scene from high up in the trees. On the ground, in her own skin, and surrounded by the smell of blood and decaying leaves, the weight of the moment choked her. She leaned against a tree and vomited.

The leaves and soil absorbed her sick nearly as fast as it burst out of her. A timid hand touched her back. She turned, expecting to see Dolores ready to comfort her. Instead, she found Garrett, looking as terrified as she felt.

The touch of his skin, which had once exhilarated her, now repulsed her. She jumped up, fetched the shovel, and started digging. The three took turns shoveling, prying rocks out, and untangling tree roots from the damp earth. As the sun climbed, Cadie dug faster, clawing at the earth with bloodied fingertips. The forest grudgingly gave up three feet of soil, deep enough to produce a dull thud when they rolled the body in.

They did not speak. The scratch of the rusty shovel on the wet, sandy soil followed by the gentle thump of loose earth landing on Juan Hernández filled the forest. *Chush, thud. Chush, thud. Chush, thud.*

They piled heavy rocks on top of the soil to keep animals away. When they had finished, Dolores formed a rough, almost imperceptible cross out of tiny stones and walked to the creek to wash her hands. Cadie and Garrett did the same.

"We will never speak of this. Ever." Dolores looked at Garrett, then at Cadie. She splashed water on her legs and rubbed at her muddy shins. "Not to Daniela. Not to your parents."

Cadie nodded, blinking back tears.

"What happened today is terrible. Unspeakable." Dolores's voice cracked as she looked back at the mound of stones. "Telling anyone about it will make the situation worse."

Dolores took Cadie's hands in hers. A warmth radiated from Dolores. A silent assurance. An apology for this moment that she must have known would twist and contort inside Cadie for the rest of her life.

"Mr. Garcia does not need to know about this. Not your mom and dad. No one. Do you understand what's at stake if my family gets caught up in this?"

Cadie had to focus on each individual muscle in her head and neck to make herself nod, as if her body knew better than to comply.

"And you know what would happen to you and your uncle?" Dolores said to Garrett.

"I know," he whispered.

"Why isn't he here?" Cadie whispered to Garrett. "Why did he leave you to do this?"

"That's not important now," Dolores said.

"But how could he—"

"We won't talk to anyone, especially not the police." Dolores ignored Cadie and turned again to the pile of stones. Cadie didn't know what prayer looked like or felt like, but when Dolores closed her eyes, so did Cadie. What would someone pray for in a moment like this? Protection from the police? To keep your family safe? To stay out of foster care? For Juan's soul?

Cadie prayed for forgiveness. Not so much from God, if there was one, but from Daniela. She scrunched her eyes so tight it hurt as she pleaded to whomever or whatever listened. *Please let Daniela forgive me. Please let her be my friend again.*

She squeezed her eyes tighter, waiting for a sense of comfort she hoped praying might deliver. But nothing changed. *I'm so sorry,* she pleaded silently to Juan. *I'm sorry this happened to you. I'm sorry I'm not standing up for you.* If only she could wind back time and warn Juan when he spoke to Daniela at Angie's. She would whisper something in his ear and change the course of everything that followed. She would wind back further and let that yellow boat drift right past her in the mist. *Don't jump,* she would tell herself. Her stomach tightened. Without the boat, would she have become friends with Daniela?

Cadie shifted her weight from foot to foot, her soles sinking deeper into the damp earth until she felt rooted. She was a tree. A boulder. Affixed to this forest, this place forever. Garrett scuffled around her, adding rocks to the pile. The tick of granite on top of granite settling in Cadie's bones.

Cadie opened her eyes. Dolores's lips moved slightly as if she were talking, but no sound emerged. The numbness that had possessed Cadie while moving Juan and digging the hole began to fade. Blisters stung her palms. Her shoulders ached.

"Tía," Cadie said softly, the breath barely escaping her lips. The endearment that once floated on her tongue now weighed heavy like a stone in her throat.

Dolores squeezed Cadie's hand and opened her eyes.

"Go home and clean up," Dolores said to Garrett.

He looked younger, frailer. Color had returned to his lips. Mud smeared his cheek and forehead. Cadie wanted to talk to him, to say something profound, maybe comforting, but the lump in her throat blocked her words.

"I'm sorry. I'll make this right," Garrett said in a low monotone. But his eyes told Cadie he was thinking the same thing she was—that nothing would ever make this right. "I don't know how, but one day I'll—"

Garrett let his sentence hang in the air. No words could finish that sentence.

Syllables crashed around inside Cadie's head, desperate to get out, but words would not form.

"Cadie," he whispered.

She would never see him again, she knew. She would never hear him say her name.

"We will never discuss what happened here." Dolores repeated her command. "Ever."

Her voice sounded like Daniela's. *We can never tell. Ever.*

Cadie nodded. This time, she would keep her promise.

A muggy breeze poured through the oaks and maples and pines, carrying the iridescent taste of fear across the shallows of the cove, beyond the vastness of the lake, and up into the mountains where the broken fragments of Cadie's childhood took refuge in the fissures—and waited.

15

As Cadie walked away from Ryan and the firefighters, the entire town seemed to press in on her, wringing out the sharp memories and scattering them across the uneven sidewalk. She yearned for the comfort in Ryan's annoying posture.

Hers should have been a fairy-tale childhood. Two loving parents. A cottage in the woods. But fairy tales always turn dark, especially the ones that take place in a forest. She wanted to remember the Girl Scout, the scrawny girl fighting her way up hills on a rusty bike. Not the scared child cowering in the woods.

A staccato of bouncing balls and whoops from a group of teenage boys echoed off the cinderblock wall at the far end of the middle school basketball court.

"Cadie!" a voice called.

Garrett, now wearing a Maple Crest Police Department T-shirt and athletic shorts, left the group of boys and jogged toward her. Sweat glistened on his brow as he clung to the chain-link fence separating them.

He wiped his forehead with his arm. His splotchy cheeks glowed red from exertion and he smiled the first real smile Cadie had ever seen on his face. As a boy he always looked scared. In the police station he'd appeared nervous, uncomfortable.

"Who's your lady friend?" one of the boys called. Garrett ignored him.

"Police work?" Cadie looked over his shoulder at the boys.

"I'm part of a mentor program." He squeezed the links in the fence. "I'm getting too old to keep up with them."

Garrett didn't look out of shape. Long, lean arms and chiseled calves. Cadie had never imagined the skinny boy in the lawn chair filling out. A basketball rolled toward him. He stopped it with his foot and picked it up. A boy sprinted over to get the ball.

"Who's your friend?" The boy punched Garrett in the shoulder.

"None of your business, Fernando."

"You know, he is, like, totally available." Fernando grinned. "I tried to get him to ask my aunt out, but he's too shy."

Cadie felt her face reddening.

Garrett put a hand on Fernando's shoulder and pushed him back toward the other boys, who were all watching them.

Fernando winked at Cadie and nodded his head encouragingly as he walked backward toward the basketball court.

"Sorry." Garrett wiped his face again and rocked back on his heels.

"Should you get back to your game?" Cadie put a hand in her pocket to stop herself from twisting a strand of hair.

"Yeah, but they have to be back in class in five minutes. Do you have time for a coffee?"

"I'm going to the diner for lunch. You can come if you want." Cadie knew Daniela would be annoyed if she met with Garrett alone, but she needed to know more about the boy imprinted in her memory.

Cadie felt like a schoolgirl as she gripped the fence, watching boys playing ball. When she was their age, none of the boys had looked back.

"I need to finish up with these characters." He nodded toward the boys, who were now making kissing noises directed at him.

"See you at the diner?"

"I'll be there in ten minutes." He joined the boys and they walked toward the gymnasium door.

"You ask her out?" a boy yelled, holding his fist up to Garrett.

Garrett answered with a fist bump and all the boys roared with approval.

Time folded in on itself. The Summer Kid. Officer Tierney. Garrett. Cadie couldn't suppress a smile as she walked toward the diner.

Angie's had closed years earlier. In its place stood a new lunch and breakfast spot with the same table configuration and breakfast bar. Colorless walls and furniture replaced the warm, earthy tones she remembered. The view from the picture window, however, had not changed.

She walked past the lunch counter and spun a black leather bar stool. Instead of the easy glide she remembered, the seat creaked with rusty resistance.

A huddle of elderly women drank coffee at the counter. A couple with twin toddlers wrestled eggs into their kids' mouths. The group of men who had passed her at the fire station sat at a table in the corner, reading menus.

No one recognized her as the girl who had picked the blueberries for Angie's famous blueberry pies. She had become a stranger in her hometown, a ghost of the carefree girl who spun herself dizzy at the counter.

Cadie took a table by the window. Within seconds a waitress greeted her with a pot of coffee and a stoneware mug. The men in the corner burst out laughing as the waitress poured. Their laughter drowned out her greeting.

The waitress scowled. "I don't even know why they're still here, since Crittenden went under. It's not like we have a bunch of extra jobs around here for them." The waitress leaned in and lowered her voice as if taking Cadie into her confidence. "I'm pretty sure one day they'll walk out without paying."

Cadie clenched her jaw, not wanting to get into another argument. This town wasn't worth it.

"You know they found a body in the woods? Folks think it might be this kid who disappeared like thirty years ago. They're looking at the guy who owns the hardware store across the street." She leaned in to whisper again. "The day that kid went missing, people saw the hardware guy fighting with him, then, boom. No one ever saw him again."

"Can I order?"

The waitress stiffened with offense. "I'll be back with a menu."

A rusty cowbell over the door clattered as Garrett, back in street clothes, walked in. He slouched as he stood next to the table, rocking back on his heels.

"You can sit." Cadie motioned to the empty side of the booth.

"Right."

"How was basketball?"

"Great. Sorry if they were a little, well, embarrassing?"

"They're middle schoolers. They're supposed to be embarrassing." Cadie picked up a menu and pretended to read it. "So what's the mentor program about?"

"I shoot baskets with them once or twice a week during free blocks and meet them after school to work on homework sometimes. But mostly, we shoot the shit. They talk about girls, baseball. We have lots of volunteers."

Garrett looked like he spent a lot of time outdoors. A pale raccoon mask framed his eyes in the shape of the sunglasses sticking out of his shirt pocket.

"Ryan Stevens told me the pines on Crier Hill are turning brown. Have you noticed it?" Cadie said.

"Why would they turn brown?"

"I think it's a beetle infestation tied to the drought. If I'm right, it's a huge fire hazard."

"I haven't noticed anything." Garrett picked up the water and took a sip. With the glass still at his lips, he looked around the table and put the glass down. "This is your water, isn't it? Sorry. I'll get you another one." He wiped his hands on his pants and squirmed in his seat.

A tall man with short-cropped hair walked over and slapped Garrett on the shoulder. "What time tomorrow morning?"

"My place at six forty-five."

"Ouch. That's early."

"Tino and I run a wakeboarding business together," Garrett said. "You know the smart aleck you met at the basketball court, Fernando? That's Tino's brother."

"Watch out for this clown." Tino nodded his head in Garrett's direction.

"I'll be careful," Cadie said.

Silverware rattled on the table as Tino's friends passed Cadie and Garrett on their way to the door. Cadie looked back at the table where they had been sitting. A tip stuck out from under a plate, at least five dollars in ones. The waitress walked by the table, carrying Garrett's and Cadie's lunch. She noticed Cadie looking at the cash and scowled, as if to say, *But I bet they'll stiff me next time.*

"There's something I should tell you," Garrett said after Tino left. "Your boat, the flat-bottom, you remember?"

"What about it?"

"It was mine," he said.

Cadie felt her toes curl around the warped boards as the boat tore through the curtain of mist. Cold fingers of morning water reaching up for her legs as she splashed through the surface. Cadie traced everything back to that moment, that boat.

"Why didn't you tell us? We would've given it back." She could feel the grit of sand grinding into her skin as she knelt on the bottom of the boat to paddle, the grainy wood of the oar in her hand, the paint flakes embedded in the treads of her sneakers. "It appeared at the end of my dock one morning. I never knew where it came from."

"I didn't want it back. Clyde and his buddies used to take that boat out fishing and drinking. Mostly drinking. They'd go out on the boat, eat all our food, and we didn't have much."

"You're not making a strong case for protecting him."

"Clyde seemed like my best chance at a normal life. That foster placement, right after my parents died, scared the shit out of me."

Garrett's hair hung below his collar, covering the cigarette burns. Faded pink scars marked the screws that had held his broken forearm together.

"One night after Clyde and his friends came up from the dock, all hammered as usual, I snuck down to the beach and untied the boat. I pushed it off and prayed it would never come back." Garrett mimed pushing the boat away, reminding Cadie of the way he used to swoop his arms when they got too close to his dock. "Then a couple days later, you came by in the boat and I panicked. I didn't want Clyde to see you guys and recognize the boat. That's why I warned you guys not to come near my pier. I was afraid Clyde would recognize the boat and take it back. And I did *not* want that boat and all of Clyde's friends back at our house."

"That's why you acted so crazy when we came close? I used to feel guilty for not saving you from your kidnappers."

"You didn't really think that, did you?"

"I guess not. But we did make up all sorts of stories about you."

"Like what?" He leaned across the table.

"That you were being held for ransom, or you were a foreign prince in exile. That was before I met you."

"Sorry to disappoint you."

"So, are you married or living with anyone?" Cadie blushed. "I mean, do you live here alone?"

"I thought Fernando made my situation pretty clear." He grinned. "I knew my love letters would win you over eventually."

"You were a real poet."

"I live in the same cottage. It was held in trust for me until I turned eighteen. Clyde rented it out while I went to boarding school in Minnesota. He lived over on Crittenden Farm for a while, then bounced around from friends' couches to cheap rentals. He's always stayed in the area, but never in the same place too long."

"Minnesota. Figures." Cadie refused to react to Garrett's attempt to humanize Clyde.

"Why?"

"I tried to find you by tracking down yearbooks from all the New England boarding schools I could find online. I almost called Daniela's mother once to ask her how to find you, but I couldn't bring myself to talk to her."

"I used to leave notes in library books thinking that one day you would check out the books and find them." Garrett leaned back in the booth.

Cadie felt a lump rise in her throat. Scores of unanswered love letters. Letters for her. So many what-ifs lingered in the cracks and crevices of Maple Crest.

"I need to get back to work," Garrett said after they finished their lunch. "But if you aren't in a rush, we can take a quick look for those browning pines on Crier Hill, if you want."

He shuffled his feet as they walked down Main Street, his untied laces skittering across the pavement. She tried to push back the memory of his mud-streaked face, his ghost-white lips, but seeing him again made the memory feel present. And dangerous.

Footsteps behind them hurried closer. Cadie instinctively picked up her pace.

"Cadie, is that you?" a voice called.

She didn't need to turn around to recognize Raúl's voice. She didn't need to look to know he wore a Garcia's Hardware polo and wrinkled khakis. The faint scent of turpentine found her before he caught up.

"I'd recognize those fireball curls anywhere," Raúl said. His chest looked a bit broader, his hair more salt than pepper, but his huge smile looked exactly the same, the creases around his eyes a little deeper as a result of his ever-present smile.

Garrett clasped Raúl's hand like an old friend and gave Cadie an uncomfortable sideways glance.

"You know Garrett?" Raúl said as Cadie sank into his hug the way she had as a girl. He rocked sideways from foot to foot as he lifted her off the ground. "Does Daniela know you're in town?"

"Yeah, I just saw her."

"Come for dinner tonight. Dolores would love to see you. You too, Garrett. We'll make a party of it."

"Thanks, but I don't want to spring that on her." Cadie imagined Dolores's face if Cadie walked into her house with Garrett. "Next time I'm in town, I'll give you some advance warning."

"I won't take no for an answer." Raúl turned to Garrett.

"I appreciate the invitation," Garrett said. "But I don't think Dolores would be too happy to see me, you know, considering—"

"She understands the chief has to interview me. It's part of his job. We've got nothing to hide." Raúl tilted his head and raised his eyebrows as if daring them to refuse his invitation.

"I guess I could stop by," Garrett said. "Cadie?"

"Great. I'll see you both at six thirty. I need to get back to the store," Raúl said before Cadie could answer.

"Wait, I can't—" Cadie started.

"I'll see you at six thirty." Raúl waved as he headed back toward the store.

"Why'd you say yes? We can't go over there." Cadie paused at a stone wall in front of the post office. A rock the size of a tangerine had tumbled from the face of the wall, leaving a hole. She tried to replace it in the cavity, but it no longer fit. She put it in the pocket of the shirt she had borrowed from her father's closet. She would add it to her cairn when she returned to her apartment.

"He didn't give me a choice." Garrett walked backward down the sidewalk in front of Cadie.

"I don't know who's going to be angrier, Daniela or her mom," Cadie said.

"So we're going?" Garrett walked across the parking lot of the police station toward the edge of the woods about a hundred yards behind the building. Main Street was mostly flat, but behind the library, post office, and police station, the ground swelled upward, gently at first, then burst forth with granite peaks in the near and far distance. A mix of old pine and hardwoods covered all but the fiercest eruptions of stone.

Every photo advertising leaf-peeping season in Maple Crest featured an image of orange and red leaves framing the old-fashioned library and post office. The town's identity was tied to these trees. She hadn't appreciated the iconic beauty until long after she moved away. The library, which had seemed enormous in her memory, looked small against the backdrop of the mountains surrounding the town.

Cadie followed Garrett into the woods leading up Crier Hill. Stepping off pavement into the forest usually calmed Cadie, but as she tromped behind Garrett, soggy memories of their last walk in the woods together prodded at her. Wet shoes, mud in her hair, under her fingernails, in her mouth. The chush of the shovel cracking the ground open.

The ground now crunched underfoot; twigs snapped instead of bending. The town felt dangerously brittle.

"Do you really think you can protect Raúl?" Cadie caught up to Garrett.

"Definitely. Everyone respects him. No one wants to see him in trouble."

"Daniela's going to want more than assurances."

"She doesn't know you and Dolores were there, does she?"

"No."

"I get it that she's upset and worried about her dad. But we can *not* come forward with the truth. It's not Raúl we need to worry about. It's Dolores," Garrett said. "You and I were minors. We'd have to deal with the public fallout of admitting we covered up Juan's death. I'd probably lose my job. *We* wouldn't face any actual legal problems. But Dolores could get charged with being an accessory after the fact to a murder, which can carry the same sentence as murder itself. There's no statute of limitations."

Cadie stopped walking. A soft breeze moved through the mixed-wood forest. The air tasted like the crush of leaves on a fall night, although an August sun blazed above the canopy.

"If Raúl gets charged, which he won't, the charges would never stick. There's no evidence tying him to Juan's death," Garrett said. "We could step in and clear his name if it came down to it. But if we come forward now and tell the truth to clear Raúl, Dolores is the one who could get in real trouble."

"We just ride it out and hope Raúl doesn't get charged?"

Garrett nodded and continued up the incline.

"This feels wrong."

"I know. Look, Dolores saved me. I don't know what would have happened if she hadn't come over that day. Clyde probably would have gone to jail and I would have gone back into the system. He was—he is—the only family I've got."

"Was state care really such a bad option? Not that it matters now."

"Looking back, I don't know why anyone would have let Clyde have custody in the first place. He was twenty-three and could barely take care of himself. But I didn't see it that way then. I just wanted to make sure I never had to smell my own skin burning again while my foster dad used me as an ashtray." Garrett shuddered as if trying to release the memory.

Cadie remembered the desperation in his eyes the day he showed her his burns. The filter of time and perspective couldn't mute the aching solidarity they had shared. She had so desperately wanted to believe she was saving him.

"I'm so sorry that happened. I am," Cadie said. "But it makes me sick letting Clyde get away with it, while people point fingers at Raúl."

"I know this doesn't make it any better, but it was an accident. The gun was just supposed to scare Juan so he wouldn't turn Clyde in for robbing that store. But it, it just went off."

"Sorry, but it's pretty cut and dry to me. If you knowingly pick up a loaded gun, point it at someone, and the gun goes off, you should be held accountable."

Garrett picked up his pace and walked ahead of Cadie.

"We should at least tell Daniela the truth so she'll stop pushing for us to go public," Cadie said.

"That should be Dolores's decision. I owe her that much."

"Three days. That's it."

"They haven't officially identified him, but there's already plenty of speculation about who it is," he said. "There've been a few fights between locals and some of the farm workers over the past few weeks since the layoffs started. Now there's a bunch of locals throwing around accusations that if it's Juan, another farm worker must have killed him. And, yeah, some folks are dragging Raúl's name into it."

"So Clyde walks away? No rumors, no harassment," Cadie said. "He made you and Dolores bury a body for him. And me too. I will never outrun those woods. No matter what I do, I will never not be in those woods. How can we not hold him accountable?"

"There's nothing tying him to any evidence. I mean, the gun was registered to him, but it's at the bottom of the lake."

"What if someone found it?" Cadie couldn't look at him as she spoke. Her voice felt shaky. Why hadn't she thrown the gun in the lake like she promised? How could she have been so stupid?

"Impossible. It's been in the water so long, it's under a foot of sediment and rocks by now."

Cadie met his eyes. Was he testing her to see if she would admit she hadn't thrown the gun in the lake? He didn't flinch under her stare.

"What are we looking for out here, anyway?" he said.

"Evidence of a beetle that's causing a die-off among pines." Cadie continued up the slope. She stopped in front of an old-growth pine mottled with resin tubes. "There. That's their calling card."

Cadie squatted in front of the tree, steadying herself with one hand against the broad trunk. The doomed pine tree offered Cadie a way forward. She could prove her theory about the beetles without relying on illegally obtained samples. But the tree also suggested her worst-case scenario might be playing out in her own hometown.

She snapped a picture on her phone and tried to text it to Thea, but she couldn't get a cell signal.

"What can we do about it?" Garrett touched a bubbled glob on the trunk.

"It's still early. We can get ahead of it if we thin the affected trees before someone throws a cigarette out the window and the whole forest lights up."

"This patch of woods backs up to Ryan's father's place. There's no way he'll cut down old growth. These trees are over a hundred years old."

"Then he'd better get ready for a fire."

Cadie pulled a small handsaw out of her day pack and sliced

a thin wedge out of the tree. She held it out to Garrett. "See the blue stain? It's a fungus the beetles inject into the tree to cut off the resin flow and starve the tree to death. They move in when there's a drought and attack the already-stressed trees."

Garrett put his hand under Cadie's and brought the wood sample close to his face. His breath grazed her palm as a humid breeze shushed the leaves overhead, lifting Cadie's hair off her neck.

"It's incredible that a tiny creature could bring down such a huge tree," Garrett said with a reverence that sent a shiver up Cadie's spine. "It's terrible. But it's also kind of amazing."

"They're incredible creatures," Cadie said in a near whisper.

Garrett examined the blue stain on the wood for several seconds, his head so close to Cadie's that she could feel the unsteadiness of his heartbeat.

"Where are they?" He looked up at her, his hand still cupped under her hand.

The crisp blue of his eyes unnerved her. She looked away as she placed the piece of wood in his hand. She pulled a pocket knife from her bag, eased the blade open with her teeth, and peeled a stretch of bark off the dead tree to reveal a tangle of crisscrossing burrows the insects had carved into the wood.

"They've already moved on to another tree," she said.

"It looks like writing. Almost graceful." Garrett floated his fingers over the lacy lines, as if trying to extract meaning from the markings.

Cadie squinted to see the carved lines through his eyes. Her heart rate fluttered at the intricacies, delicate curves, and wild arches etched into the wood. Garrett's eyes widened. Cadie swallowed hard to quiet her breath.

A *rat-a-tat-tat* rose above the chirps and clicks in the forest. Cadie held a finger to her lips. Garrett froze, not even moving his eyes.

Rat-a-tat-tat. Rat-a-tat-tat resounded through the treetops.

"The forest is fighting back," Cadie said. "Woodpeckers devour beetles."

"So how do we encourage more woodpeckers to show up?"

"The scale makes it unfeasible, and they'd cause too much other damage if we tried to relocate them here in large numbers. Everything's a delicate balance." The woodpecker paused, clearing the air for a melodic *pit-pit-pit chirrup*.

"A wood thrush," Garrett whispered.

The fluted call lifted high above the chatter of forest noises. The rustle of leaves, the crush of squirrel paws, the hum of insects drove a breathy crescendo that only the lilt of a Bicknell's thrush could complete.

A melancholy silence hung at the end of the song. Cadie cleared her throat to break the tension of the unfulfilled melody.

"They didn't thin trees in time in Colorado or California. And look what happened there." Cadie palmed the broad pine trunk like a mother taking a child's temperature. Maple leaves drooped in the steamy air. Premature brown tinged the tips of oak leaves. The forest felt unstable, on edge.

"You can't cut down the entire forest," Garrett said.

"We have to do something. I feel like I've been screaming 'fire' in a theater and no one is running out. It's going to take a significant fire before people will believe how serious this is," Cadie said.

"I believe you. Tell me what I can do to help," Garrett said.

"Don't you have to get back to work?" Cadie turned her back to Garrett to hide her smile and walked back down the rocky slope. Cadie felt the urge to jump from rock to moss-covered rock the way she had as a girl. To skip. To bounce. To fly.

Garrett hustled to catch up.

The precise perfume of the crushed leaves and pine needles in Maple Crest, a sweeter, mushroomier aroma than that in the forests where she worked, stirred in Cadie a fierce desire to protect the home she had long ago forsaken and the people she had come back for.

16

Fear can generate a fever, Cadie discovered the day after she helped Garrett and Dolores in the woods. She tried to force the images of misaligned buttons, the rusty shovel, and Garrett's mud-streaked face out of her mind. She visualized the molecules in her brain rubbing together in panic until they generated enough heat that her mother could feel it when she touched her forehead.

Her mother stayed home and made her tea and soup. Cadie's stomach hurt if she ate. It hurt if she didn't eat. She waited until Raúl and Dolores would be at the store and called Daniela, but the answering machine picked up again and again.

Cadie's mother went back to work the second day, and Cadie finished the last of her library books.

The cottage felt too small, the air too stale. She paced. She tried to draw. She sat on the porch with Friar. She waited for the phone to ring. By the time her parents got home, she needed to get out of the house.

"I'm going to the library," Cadie said as she cleared her plate after dinner.

"I'll drive you," her dad said.

"I'm taking my bike. I need some air." Cadie wanted to bike up the hill, to cry and rage and sweat and scream.

"Be back before dark." Her mom kissed her forehead, letting her lips linger on Cadie's skin to gauge her temperature. "You sure you're feeling better?"

"I'm fine." She loaded her backpack with books to return.

Cadie took longer than planned picking out six new books. By the time the librarian flickered the lights to indicate it was closing time, the sun touched the mountain ridge, threatening to set.

Her mom would be worried.

Cadie looked down at her feet as she walked around the back of the library to get her bike. She would read *The Hobbit* when she got home and disappear into that other world.

Magic lived in her forest too, Cadie had been certain. But now the magic felt dark and Cadie wanted to get home. She jogged toward her bike, her bag of books thumping against her hip. When she turned the corner of the building, her feet turned to lead.

Clyde waited for her, sitting on her bike. She turned to run, but Clyde jumped up. "Don't be an idiot. You know I can catch you. I just want to talk."

Her heart racing, she backed up until she hit a large maple tree.

He put his hand on her shoulder and pressed her body against the maple. She tried to scream, but it emerged as a high-pitched yelp.

"No one can hear you."

No one would come to the back courtyard at this time of night.

"I don't know what you *think* you know, but you better keep your mouth shut," he hissed in her ear. "You want your little friend to get sent back to Mexico?"

Cadie stiffened. *El Salvador*, she corrected him in her mind.

"I hear stuff on the farm." He growled against her cheek. "That whole family's illegal, you know. And I'll make sure they get sent back if you talk."

She clung to the tree, the spongy bark giving way as her nails dug deep, slivers driving up under her fingernails.

"You want your friend to disappear?"

Like Juan? she wanted to scream. Cadie fixed her gaze on the trio of birch trees behind Clyde and let his words slide over her, around her. She breathed in his sour body odor mixed with stale cigarette smoke.

Cadie shook her head.

"Then you keep your mouth shut."

Cadie bit the side of her tongue.

A sharp breeze stirred behind him, swirling prematurely fallen leaves into a loose funnel that crept toward them. She imagined Garrett standing on his pier, sweeping his arms to control the air. Clyde spun around as the leaves and the wind hit him, choking him with dust. The cloud moved over her, through her, leaving dirt in her mouth and eyes. The wind tugged on her braid then dissipated to nothing.

Clyde released the pressure on her shoulder and pushed her to the ground as he choked on the dust.

"You understand me?" His eyes darted across the parking lot, at the woods, then back at Cadie. He almost looked ashamed. His narrow eyes opened wide to show a flash of the same blue in Garrett's eyes.

He stepped back from Cadie, kicked her bike over, and sprinted toward the woods.

The humid air, saturated with the lingering hopes of summer, teased of fall. Pressing her back against the warmth of the tree, she sucked the bark out from under her nails. She scooped up a handful of the leaves that had interrupted Clyde and saved her. "Thank you," she whispered to the forest behind her, and shoved the leaves in her pocket.

Her own sinewy shadow chased her home as the sun sank in the sky. By the time she reached the long driveway to her house, Cadie couldn't make out the dips and divots in the dark, bumpy road. She squeezed the well-worn, rubbery handlebar grips. The torn plastic of the seat chafed her thighs. Holding her breath between patches of light on the gravel road, she strained to see far enough ahead of her to maintain her speed. A long stretch of darkness lay before her.

She hit a bump. Not a pothole, but something rising up above the road. A soft object, yet heavy enough to slow the momentum of her bike and throw her over the handlebars. Gravel tore at her shoulder as she slid across the rocks and sand.

Cadie saw the outline of a dead opossum lying on the road behind her. She shivered at the glistening, splayed intestines feet from her rear tire. Its eyes glowed in the dark. Shaking, she got back on her bike and pedaled hard the rest of the way home, grateful for the fresh cuts and bruises that gave her permission to cry in her mother's arms without raising questions she didn't want to answer.

Before going to bed Cadie fished the crumpled leaves out of her pocket and flattened them on her lap. Magic still lived in her woods. She pressed the leaves into the pages of *Kidnapped* as a reminder.

17

Three days after the shooting, Cadie lay in bed staring at the ceiling until the sun crept to its 6 A.M. position. She hadn't slept. Instead, she had watched shadows on her wall shift with the rise and fall of the moon and the sun.

The warped glass of the antique window panes morphed the tree branches into grotesque distortions of faces and bodies against her wall. She startled at the thump of the local newspaper landing on the porch. The first edition printed since the shooting.

"Morning, sunshine," her father greeted her as she shuffled into the kitchen.

She collected the newspaper from the porch, careful not to look at the front page as she extracted the comics. She tried to position herself so she couldn't read the headlines her father held up in front of his face as he drank his coffee. Friar nuzzled his head under Cadie's arm and put his front paws on Cadie's lap to help distract her. Cadie dug her hands into Friar's long fur and buried her face in her dog's back. But her eyes kept drifting up.

Once she saw the headline, she couldn't stop herself from reading.

Someone had held up a convenience store two towns over and shot the store owner. The bullet passed through the shopkeeper's shoulder. He would recover. The shooter wore a mask, so the man could not ID him. He only took fifty dollars, although the register drawer held over three hundred at the time of the robbery.

The police were looking for Clyde, but they didn't know it.

Cadie's mother walked into the kitchen. She sat on a chair behind Cadie and stroked her back.

"You okay?"

Cadie nodded. She was not okay.

"Let me braid your hair. You never let me do your hair anymore."

Her mother returned with a comb, which she dipped in water to calm Cadie's unruly curls.

"It's grown out so beautifully." The comb jerked Cadie's head back as it hit snarl after snarl. The pain from each yank distracted Cadie from the noise in her head. "I wish you would have sat this still when you were little. You used to scream and cry every time I picked up a brush."

Cadie wanted to scream and cry right then. She wanted to tell her parents about the boy on the pier, the gunshot, Juan. The rustle of newsprint in her father's hands crackled in the air like static.

"I can do my own hair." Cadie pulled her hair from her mother's hand and went to her room.

"We're leaving for work, hon." Her mom tapped on Cadie's door a few minutes later. "Why don't you come in with us today? I miss having you around the studio."

"Fine," Cadie grumbled, grateful not to have to stay home alone. She quickly tossed on some clothes and grabbed a book. Friar jumped into the backseat next to her. The ten-minute ride to town went by too quickly. She would have liked to ride in the car with her parents and dog for hours, drive far away, and never look back.

The studio, flooded with sunlight, seemed overly cheerful as Cadie settled into a cushy chair near her mother's pottery wheel. Cadie had always been afraid to watch the spinning of her mother's wheel for too long because she believed it might hypnotize her. The spinning, spinning, spinning made her dizzy.

But on this day, Cadie longed for the world to disappear. She perched next to her mother and stared at the clay. It oozed between her mother's fingers as she centered a mound and coaxed it up into a cylinder. Slippery mud dripped down her wrist all the way to her elbow.

Cadie chewed on her thumbnail, trying to pry out the stubborn mud that hid under her nails since digging in the woods. She dislodged a grain of sand and rolled it around on her tongue as her mother pulled the vessel taller, mud thinning out between her fingers.

So much mud.

She hadn't felt the retch coming, but just as her mother finished the first cup, Cadie swallowed the grain of sand and dry heaved. She squeezed her eyes closed, trying not to think about vomiting in the woods days earlier.

"Are you going to be sick?" Her mother slowed the wheel and put the back of her muddy hand on Cadie's forehead. Cadie leaned against her mother's shoulder but the smell of clay and earth made her gag again.

"I'm taking you home," her mother said. "Give me a sec to wash my hands."

"I'll wait on the porch." Cadie walked out to the front steps of the studio. Across the street she saw Raúl taping papers up in the windows of the post office. He saw Cadie and waved.

Cadie buried her face in her knees, hoping he wouldn't come over, but within a few seconds she heard his footsteps approaching.

"I thought Daniela said you two were picking berries this morning." He looked worried.

"I'm going home in a few minutes." Cadie's pulse sped up. Maybe Daniela had forgiven her.

"Can I put this in the shop window?" He held up a flyer with a large picture of Juan's face under bold letters spelling out *Have you seen this man?* Under the picture and a description of Juan, it listed the Garcias' home number to call with any information. "One of my employees is missing. It's been a few days, but the police won't look into it yet. But I know him. He wouldn't run off without telling me."

Cadie took the paper and pretended to look concerned. Juan, with the gap between his front teeth, smiled up at her from the grainy black-and-white image. The page trembled as she handed it back.

"Will your parents mind if I put this up?"

Cadie shook her head and watched as he taped the paper to the door of the studio.

"Someone's seen him, I'm sure of it," Raúl said. "He's a great kid. If he isn't found by tomorrow, the police promised to organize a search of the woods near the farm where he works. You and your parents can help if you want."

Unable to locate her voice, Cadie nodded.

"You girls be careful in the woods today," he said as he walked away to hang more flyers.

After she got home, Cadie waited until she heard her mother's car leave to go back to the studio before jumping off the couch where her mother had tucked her in with a can of ginger ale, saltines, and a bucket in case she got sick. She sprinted through the woods toward the rock, hoping Daniela might be waiting for her, as Raúl had suggested.

Her heart skipped a beat when she saw her friend's silhouette. Daniela sat with her arms wrapped around her shins and her head buried in her knees. Cadie sat next to Daniela for several moments, neither of them speaking.

"Clyde knows we were there," Cadie finally blurted out when the silence became too much.

"I guess your boyfriend can't keep his mouth shut either." Daniela lifted her head so her eyes showed. The skin on her forehead furrowed so deeply it looked like she might crack. Purple half-moons hung under her eyes.

"He followed me to the library. He said if I—if we—told anyone, he'd tell everyone your family's illegal."

Daniela ducked her head back into her knees. Crickets chirped loudly, so loudly Cadie could barely think. *Katydid, katydid. Cadie did, Cadie did.*

Cadie picked up a small stone and skipped it across the lake surface, smacking the water three times before the pebble sank.

"The police came to my house last night." Daniela's voice sounded far away, muffled by her knees.

"What'd you tell them?"

"They didn't want to talk to me. They wanted my dad. They were asking him questions about Juan. The farm where he lives reported him missing. Remember when my dad argued with him outside the store the other day? When we were in the diner? That was the last time anyone saw Juan. Fighting with my dad in front of the hardware store."

"What did your mom say?" Cadie rubbed the jagged edge of a fingernail on the coarse granite slab. Tender scratches, scabs, and blisters covered the tips of her fingers.

"Nothing. She seemed fine when she came home. I think she believes me that you and I were fighting and you were making stuff up."

Cadie longed to tell Daniela the truth about finding Dolores in the woods. She wanted to tell her friend about the nightmares she had. Nightmares about Clyde, nightmares about Juan, nightmares about Daniela never speaking to her again.

"We messed up bad." Daniela turned to face Cadie.

"There's no way they will believe your dad did anything. I mean, he didn't do anything." A scab on her finger reopened as she rubbed it on the rock. She put her finger in her mouth. The blood tasted like damp soil.

"God, Cadie, you don't get it." Daniela buried her face in her knees again.

"Get what?"

"This isn't some adventure in one of your stupid books. The worst that could happen to you is you'd get grounded." Daniela drew in a long, stuttered breath. "We're not from here. Juan wasn't from here. We will *never* be from here."

Waves lapped up against the rock in a slow rhythm that stretched out the silence between the girls. How many thousands of years would it take for the water to erode the boulder they sat on? Eating away at it, one lick at a time. Swollen seconds slipped into the waves. Cadie wanted to dive into the lake and scream underwater where her breath would split open the fractured rocks, thrusting themselves up from the lake bottom until they exploded where no one could see or hear.

"Maybe we'd all be safer if we told the police," Cadie said.

"It's too late. If we tell, they'll figure out *I'm* not supposed to be here, and they'll know my parents aren't either. We could get sent away. If you're here illegally and commit a crime, you get sent back no matter what. We hid evidence. We committed a crime. I ruined everything for my parents." Daniela pounded her fist on the gray-and-white-speckled granite over and over. "I'm trapped."

"What if we sent an anonymous letter telling the police what we heard?"

"What are you going to do, cut letters out of a magazine and paste them down like on TV? We do that and the police will have evidence of a murder *and* my dad will be the last person who saw Juan before he disappeared. You think they won't investigate us then?"

They could both disappear. Daniela and Garrett. Gone.

Daniela beat her fist on the rock harder and faster. Friar circled around Daniela, licking her ear and trying to shimmy into her lap.

Cadie grabbed Daniela's balled-up hand midstrike. "You're going to hurt yourself."

Daniela wrenched her arm free from Cadie's grip and slammed her fist down even harder. "I already did."

Cadie scooted closer and put her arm around Daniela's shoulder. Daniela continued pounding the granite. Cadie didn't stop her.

"What if I go to the police alone and make them swear not to reveal my name? I'll keep you out of it and never even mention you," Cadie whispered. "No one would bother your father."

"You're going to tell them about the boat and the blueberries and the gun? No one would believe that in a million years. You're such a Girl Scout."

"I'm quitting Scouts."

"Besides, our parents know we spend every day together. I'll get dragged in somehow."

"I could have done it alone."

"All by yourself, you just *happened* to be paddling by in a boat you stole, while stealing blueberries—" Daniela paused. "And then you heard a noise that sounded like a gunshot but decided not to tell anyone? Aren't you on the Safety Patrol at school? No one would ever believe you did that."

"But I *did* do it." Cadie looked down at her translucent, noodley arms, splattered with splotchy freckles. Arms that had dragged a body, buried a body. Saliva gathered around her words, the way it always did right before she vomited. She plucked a handful of trumpet honeysuckle blossoms from a bush behind her. One by one, she bit the tender ends off, unthreaded the delicate interior, and sucked out the nectar in an attempt to displace the acid in her mouth. She tossed each empty flower into the lake until a small flotilla of red petals gathered in the water.

"You take it for granite that everything will always be fine in the end," Daniela said.

"Granted."

"What?"

"Granted. You take it for granted. Not granite."

"No, it's granite. Like, things you assume will always be the same." Daniela picked up a stone and smashed it against the rock they sat on. She held up the stone, unmarred by the impact. "Like granite, like a rock that won't ever break."

Cadie fingered a speckled rock in her hand. Light glinted off the iridescent flakes. Daniela was wrong, but as Cadie scratched a rough edge of fingernail over the stone, she felt certain that Daniela was actually right.

"Yeah, okay. Granite makes more sense."

"If you tell anyone, Clyde will know you did it. He'll tell the cops about my family. End of story." Daniela stood up and brushed pine needles from her shorts. She ducked under the hemlock branches and disappeared into the woods without saying good-bye.

Cadie lay in bed that night, staring up at the bony shadows dancing on her bedroom walls. They pointed at her, wagging like witch fingers, until she could no longer bear their accusations. She tiptoed into the family room and curled up on Friar's bed next to her warm dog. She pulled the afghan her grandmother made from the back of the couch and tugged it over their heads.

In the darkness Friar licked the dried salt off her cheeks. Gaps in the yarn allowed moonlight to sift through the weave of the blanket. Last summer she had nestled on the couch with her father, watching *The Amityville Horror* with the afghan draped over her head so the familiar yarn patterns could screen out the scary parts.

Her protective shroud couldn't filter out the dangerous bits anymore. What she feared most huddled under the blanket with her, inside her. Friar whimpered in solidarity and curled into a ball against Cadie's chest. The bed smelled of damp dog and urine. Cadie panted in rhythm with Friar, filling their stagnant bubble with heat, humidity, and dread until the sun rose.

18

Why had she agreed to this dinner? she berated herself as she walked through the woods toward the Garcias' house. Sitting around a table with Garrett, Daniela, Raúl, and Dolores felt reckless. Dangerous, maybe. Daniela would sense the tension between Cadie and Garrett and Dolores.

Her phone buzzed. *We're short-staffed again. Be there soon. Eat without me,* Daniela wrote.

Daniela would probably make sure her emergency lasted long enough to avoid dinner, to avoid Cadie. She relaxed slightly. But part of her had hoped that being together in that same, familiar space would bridge the distance between them.

Cadie stopped walking. She could turn back and skip dinner, avoid having to face Raúl and Dolores. But Garrett. He would already be on his way to the Garcias'.

Her phone buzzed again. *Don't even think about skipping dinner. Dad will be disappointed.*

Garrett pulled up in the driveway right before Cadie knocked on the door. She smoothed down the curls on her temple and waited for him. Cadie tried to act casual, as if this were any other dinner with friends. Garrett lifted his hand to ring the doorbell, but Cadie grabbed his wrist. "Give me a minute. I can't go in there and act like everything's fine."

Before Garrett could respond, Raúl opened the door.

"You made it," Raúl said, pulling her into a booming embrace. "Daniela's going to be late, but Sal will be home any minute."

"Come, come. Dolores will be so happy to see you. How many years has it been?"

"Dinner's almost ready," Dolores said without looking up from a pan on the stove. Unlike Raúl, Dolores seemed smaller than Cadie remembered, leaner, stronger. More tightly coiled. She wore her dark hair pulled back in a tight knot on the back of her neck, not a single strand escaping. Her arms and shoulders still looked capable of carrying a heavy load.

The dinners at the Garcias' Cadie had attended as a girl had been full of belly laughs and smells that made Cadie's stomach hunger for more food than she could eat. No matter who Raúl brought home unannounced—usually men from the farm or employees from the store—Dolores always magically had enough food. Cadie had imagined how annoyed her own mother would have been if her father brought guests home for a meal without warning. But Dolores always greeted them with fierce embraces as if she had been expecting them all along.

Tonight Cadie was the unexpected guest foisted on Dolores by Raúl. Or maybe Dolores had always known Cadie would return to her kitchen one day too.

"Smells great." Cadie kissed Dolores on the cheek. "It's nice to see you."

Dolores flickered an unconvincing smile. Garrett extended a formal hand to Dolores, who hesitated before accepting it. Vegetables on the stovetop hissed.

Raúl pulled two bottles of beer from the refrigerator and held them up to Garrett and Cadie. Cadie nodded. A little alcohol might make the dinner easier to get through.

"Did you see the new wakeboard ropes I got in?" Raúl handed Garrett a beer.

"No, but Tino told me they're better than ours. How much?"

"Seventy-nine dollars."

"For a rope? That's criminal," Dolores said. "Come by when I'm running the register. We'll work out a deal."

"If I let you run the business we'd be broke." Raúl threw his hands up in the air. "You want to give everything away."

Dolores stirred vegetables with rapid, short strokes, her lips pressed into a tight line.

"Can I help?" Cadie stepped up next to Dolores and looked out the window, where the rosary beads still hung. Instead of dangling down the center of the window catching light as they once had, the beads hung in the corner of the window, all but the bottom inch hidden by the floral fabric.

Dolores stopped stirring, closed her eyes, and took in a deep breath. She laid the spoon on the counter. Up close Dolores's gray roots showed in a chalky line framing her face. Tiny wrinkles radiated out from her mouth after years of pursing her lips.

"I don't need any help, thanks," Dolores said. She put one hand on top of Cadie's and both women looked out the window toward the lake. "How have you been?"

"I'm fine," Cadie said. Dolores's hand felt small, the skin loose over the wiry muscles and tiny bones.

"What brought you home?"

Before Cadie could answer, a young girl burst through the door in a navy blue one-piece bathing suit with a striped beach towel wrapped around her. "I jumped the wake. Well, almost the whole wake, but I landed strong. Tori said I got really big air."

The girl stood as tall as Cadie. She had lanky, lean arms, short black hair, and thick lashes framing dark eyes. Daniela's eyes. Cadie looked at the girl, who she assumed to be Sal, half expecting her to recognize Cadie through those familiar eyes. Sal did not react to Cadie's presence.

"We have company for dinner. Why don't you go get dressed?" Dolores said.

"You jumped the wake?" Garrett said.

"*Almost* jumped it." Her eyes widened as she recognized him. "Why's there a cop here again?"

"He's having dinner with us," Dolores said, her lips barely parting as she spoke.

"Are you drinking a beer?" Sal put a hand on her hip, exactly like

Daniela. Cadie tried to stifle a laugh, but the girl turned and looked at her without saying anything, then looked back at Garrett.

"I'm not on duty," Garrett said.

"Then why are you here?"

"Sal," Dolores said. "These are friends of your mom's."

"Where's Mom? I need to talk to her."

"She's stuck at the hospital."

"Of course she is." Sal turned to Cadie and looked her up and down.

A jolt of memory prompted Cadie to smooth the curls on her temples as she imagined Sal seeing her the way Daniela had the day they first met in the woods. Wild frizzy hair, mismatched clothes, muddy from having fallen in the creek.

"This is Ms. Kessler. She grew up with your mom," Dolores said in a flat voice.

"Hi." Cadie extended her hand.

Sal offered a limp hand and turned back to her grandmother. "What's for dinner?"

"Stir fry."

"Don't forget I don't eat meat anymore," Sal called as she disappeared down the hall.

The phone rang and Raúl answered. He paced in short strides as he listened to the voice on the other end. Dolores stood still, straining to hear.

"Is this necessary?" He shook his head at Dolores, then closed his eyes for a few seconds. "I don't have anything new to tell you."

Dolores straightened her back and turned to the stove with a spoon suspended in the air above the vegetables as she listened. Onions and peppers sizzled and squirmed until a curl of smoke rose from the pan. Dolores did not move. Cadie stepped up beside her and took the spoon from her hand. She turned the heat down and stirred from behind Dolores, who did not step away from the stove, her eyes locked with Raúl's.

"Okay. I'll be there in the morning." Raúl hung up. "Friends of yours," he said under his breath to Garrett.

"You know they have to go through the process." Garrett placed a hand on Raúl's shoulder. "It'll be fine. I promise."

"Good grief, I'm getting old." Dolores forced a smile and took the spoon back from Cadie. "I almost ruined dinner."

Raúl pulled a handkerchief out of his pocket and wiped it across his brow and the back of his neck. Dolores twisted a small gold pendant necklace around her finger. Her fingertip turned dark red and she loosened the charm for a few seconds, then began twisting it again. Twist and release. Twist and release.

The stew of heat and the tension, seeing Garrett next to Raúl, and watching Dolores's agitation made Cadie dizzy. She tried to take in long, slow breaths, but her tense muscles cut them short, leaving her gasping for air.

"I'll be right back." Cadie hurried down the hall toward the bathroom where Daniela had taught her to shave her legs decades earlier. The walls swayed as she walked the dark corridor. Inside, she bent over and put her head between her knees, trying to clear her vision. The pattern of familiar floor tiles grounded her. She leaned one arm on the cool porcelain of the bathtub and lowered herself to the floor. She dragged her jagged fingernail along the grout to smooth the rough edge of the nail where she'd caught the splinter the night before. The pressure hurt, but she welcomed the distraction.

Cadie held on to the counter with both hands and pulled herself up. Her reflection in the mirror looked pale, even for her. Dark circles hung under her eyes. She let cold water run over her wrists and splashed her face, practicing a calm smile.

The bathroom door gave way when she pushed it open as Sal yanked on the other side at the exact same time.

"Sorry. I didn't know you were in there," Sal said.

"It's fine. I'm done."

"Are you sick? You look kind of green," Sal said.

"It's just strange being in this house after all these years. I used to hang out here as a kid." She paused, trying to shake off her pathetic tone. "I can't believe she named you Sal."

"It's from a book."

"*Blueberries for Sal,*" they said simultaneously. Sal rolled her eyes, making it clear she had heard the joke too many times.

"I was with her the first time she read it. I couldn't believe she had never heard of it, so I dragged her to the library and—"

"You're Cadie?" Sal cut her off.

Before she answered, Sal spun Cadie around and ran her hand across Cadie's shoulder blades. "She said you had fairy wings, but they were invisible to everyone but her."

"What?"

"I didn't think you were real."

"Why wouldn't I be real?"

"She used to make up stories about stuff you did when you were little. I always thought you were an imaginary friend, but then . . ." Sal paused. "I read The Poachers' Code, and I know it's stupid, but I started wondering if it was all true."

A single tear spilled over Sal's cheek and she wiped it away with her forearm. "It's like, all the fairy tales she made up were real. She used to tell me Cadie Brady stories when I couldn't sleep." Sal scuffed her bare foot back and forth over the threshold. "After Dad died. I used to think Mom was trying to magic my father back with her stories. You always did something amazing and saved someone. I think Mom wanted something magic to happen and make everything okay again."

"I didn't mean to upset you." Cadie wanted to reach out and put her arm on Sal's shoulder or hug the girl, but she stood frozen. She imagined Sal lying on her back under the shelf in Daniela's room in the dark, reading The Poachers' Code with a flashlight.

"She said you could taste sunlight and read every book ever written." Sal leaned closer. "And she said you could control the wind and the lake and the trees with your mind."

"I was a pretty strange kid." Cadie couldn't suppress a smile, knowing that despite their silence all those years, Daniela had been thinking of her too. "Did she ever tell you about our blueberry business?"

"Don't be mad." Sal lowered her voice. "But she took me there.

She's never told anyone else in the world about Blueberry Cove. She didn't want to betray you, but she said you'd understand."

"You're *Sal*, for God's sake. Of course it's okay."

"Do you wear braids anymore?" Sal asked.

"Sometimes."

"You're Cadie Brady. You have to wear braids, or you aren't Cadie *Braidy*."

"I don't think that's where the nickname came from. She called me Cadie Brady after *The Brady Bunch* TV show."

"No. She told me you were Cadie Braidy because of your braids. She said you kept your magic powers in your braids."

A lump in Cadie's chest loosened. The nickname she both loved and hated. She had always resented the goody-goody connotation she thought Brady implied. The dizziness and nausea that possessed her minutes earlier dissipated.

"You two ready for dinner?" Dolores called.

"I'm starved," Cadie said.

"Mom said you had superpowers," Sal said as they sat down at the table. "Like, you could hold your breath longer than anyone she ever knew. And you could scare off bears with your terrible singing."

Garrett raised his eyebrows. "Do you still have these superpowers?"

"No comment." Cadie wished she could be that brave girl Sal believed her to be.

The front door opened and Daniela walked in. "Did you save any for me?"

"I found Cadie Braidy." Sal jumped up. "Now I can hear all the stories of her badassery from her."

"Sal." Daniela wrinkled her brow at her daughter exactly the way Dolores used to wrinkle hers at Daniela.

"What?" Sal smiled innocently at her mom. "Badassery is a word."

"First, it's not a word. Second, even if it was a word, it's not one you use at the dinner table." Daniela kissed Sal on top of her head.

Raúl's shoulders shook as he held in a laugh.

"Mom said you wore Wonder Woman underwear."

"I didn't make that part up, and you know it," Daniela said. Her expression darkened as she looked at Garrett, nodding to acknowledge him but not saying hello.

"You know he's a cop, right?" Sal balanced her chair on the back two legs and crossed her arms.

Dolores pulled her lips into a tight line.

"Garrett's our guest tonight. Not a police officer," Raúl said.

"Mom, is it true you want to build a house on one of the Crittenden Farm lots?" Sal said.

Daniela's face froze.

"Tori's mom's a real estate agent. She said you looked at a lot the other day."

"I just looked. They're really cheap." Daniela looked flustered. "Don't you want to get our own house?"

"You know why they're so cheap? The bank foreclosed on the farm and kicked all the farmers and workers out," Sal said. "People like *you* are the reason the farms are failing."

"No. The drought is the reason farms are failing," Daniela said.

"Actually, it is climate change's fault," Sal said. "The oil companies' fault. And it's our fault too, I mean, it's like, everybody's fault. But if no one buys the cheap real estate from the bank, maybe they wouldn't take the land next time. Maybe they'd try to help the farmers keep their farms."

"I didn't know you were thinking of moving out," Dolores said.

"Let her look if she wants to," Raúl said. "In the meantime, Sal, maybe you should run for mayor."

"Did you know that because it keeps getting warmer, the growing season in New Hampshire is twenty-two days longer now than a century ago? Twenty-two days. It affects water resources and what crops can grow here. But let's all keep pretending it's not a problem," Sal said. "If you buy that lot, you are taking advantage of a global disaster that hurts vulnerable people so you can build a cheap house."

Daniela rolled her eyes.

"Hey, Cadie Braidy, will you take me blueberry picking tomorrow? Mom keeps saying she will, but she's never home."

"Cadie doesn't want to take you blueberry picking," Daniela said.

"I want to see her magic powers." Sal turned to Cadie and batted her thick lashes in an exaggerated plea.

"I'd love to," Cadie said, although the idea of being alone with Sal terrified her. She hadn't been comfortable with thirteen-year-old girls when she had been one herself. "I can come by in the morning."

Sal turned to her mother with an I-told-you-so smile.

Cadie forced a smile when Dolores brought out a warm blueberry pie. The first tart bite stung her saliva glands. She looked up at Garrett. But she saw the Summer Kid. Her throat constricted before she could swallow the berries. Her fingers tightened around her fork at the memory of sucking on the plastic bag full of blueberries while she clung to the tree root listening to Juan and Clyde arguing.

She tried to swallow, but gagged on the fruit. Behind her, Sal dropped a serving spoon on the hardwood floor with a crash. But Cadie heard a gunshot.

She choked on the pie and gulped down her water.

"Are you okay?" Dolores asked.

Cadie glared at her. The memory dislodged a rage she had long tried to ignore. Dolores should have helped Cadie. She should have checked on her, reached out to her. Cadie swished the water around her mouth, between her teeth, but the acid lingered and burned.

After dessert, Raúl and Garrett went outside on the deck. Sal watched them through the glass, then disappeared into her room, leaving Cadie, Daniela, and Dolores in the kitchen.

"You girls go catch up. I'll do the dishes," Dolores said, holding Cadie's eye for a second.

Daniela grabbed two beers from the fridge. Cadie followed her into the family room.

"Are you really buying a house?"

"Probably not. But God, I'd like something of my own for once.

Not my parents' house. Not the house that belonged to my husband's parents. My house." She put her feet on the coffee table and yawned. "That's why I'm working so many shifts. They're short-staffed, and I'm taking advantage of it. In a few months I'll have enough for a down payment."

"You don't sound too enthused about it."

"Would you be excited about building a house in Maple Crest?"

"Probably not."

"Just once, I'd like to feel in control of my life, decide where I'm going instead of always being on the defense," Daniela said. "When we were kids, I thought about challenging you so I could sit in the front of that stupid boat. I wanted to control where we went, just once. But I couldn't do it. It felt safer to let you steer. I've done that my whole life."

"You do know that the person in the back of the boat is the captain, right? You steer from the back." Cadie laughed. Daniela, the strong one, the popular one. Daniela, who had made Cadie feel brave, had been as insecure as Cadie. "You were steering the whole time."

"Great. My one shot. And I didn't even recognize it." Daniela pressed her temples as if trying to fend off a headache. She squeezed her eyes shut and Cadie thought she might be about to cry.

"Or, maybe you've always been in control, you know, school, job, family stuff. You were always steering. From the back of your boat," Cadie said. "Look at Sal. She's amazing. I mean, maybe a little too smart for her own good. But generally you raised a spectacular kid."

Daniela smiled weakly.

Cadie picked up a photo in a birch-bark frame from the end table. Daniela and Sal, who looked about five years old, sang into wooden spoons. In a hula skirt and a bikini top, Sal cocked one hip out and sang with her mouth wide open.

"What are you grinning at?" Daniela asked.

Cadie held up the picture. "Reminds me of us singing in your kitchen when we were kids."

Daniela took the picture from Cadie and put it back on the table. "What's going on with you and the Summer Kid?"

"It's not like that."

"It's always been like that. He's not some Prince Charming from one of your books. He's just a guy." Daniela took a swallow of beer. "Who's investigating my father for a murder he knows he didn't commit."

"And it's all my fault. Go ahead, say it."

Daniela refused to give Cadie the satisfaction.

"Garrett and I will come forward. We'll leave your family out of it." Cadie doubted Garrett would agree to this plan, but she would push him.

"Jesus, Cadie, you don't get to swoop in and play hero now. It will all come back on my family no matter what. Just stay out of it." Daniela pressed her palms against her temples and closed her eyes again. "I don't want to be your project. Saving that Summer Kid from kidnappers, his murderous uncle, or eternal boredom, or whatever we pretended we were doing. It was always a game for you." Daniela's voice strained to maintain a whisper. "You wrote us all into a book. And I let you. I wanted to be in your stories."

"You were never a project." Cadie's skin felt tight, as if it was shrinking around her, compressing her. "You were my best friend."

"You thought you were so tough and rebellious because we stole a boat and didn't tell our parents. We were playing two entirely different games."

"I didn't know."

"That's what made me feel safe. Nothing bad ever happens to girls like you." Daniela's eyes were angry, but the fierceness in her voice did not seem directed at Cadie. "Just sleep with him. Get it out of your system and go back to Concord. At least when you were a kid, you believed all your save-the-world-by-never-killing-a-bug bullshit. Now, you're just pretending, and you don't even recognize the difference."

If Daniela hadn't promised Angie to double the blueberry order, they would have already been home when Clyde and Juan argued that day. But they had stayed late to fill an extra order Cadie never wanted to fill in the first place. Daniela bore at least some of the blame, but Cadie felt petty to point out the grudge she still carried.

Raúl's laugh drifted in through the screen. Garrett stood next to him; their backs were to the window. Cadie searched his posture, his profile, for hints of the boy who had haunted her for so long. Their laughter felt irreverent, disrespectful to the threats and questions hanging over all of them.

"Your dad doesn't know anything, does he?" Cadie said.

"Neither of them do."

Dolores's stir fry churned in Cadie's stomach.

More laughter came from the deck. Dolores slammed a cabinet door in the kitchen.

"I shouldn't have gotten so mad at you back then. You were scared. We both were." Daniela tilted her head back and stared up at the ceiling.

"Maybe, but I should have kept my mouth shut. I should have kept our pact."

"God, that oath." Daniela laughed and bumped her shoulder against Cadie's. "The Poachers' Code. We were such fucking idiots."

Daniela let her head rest against Cadie's, their shoulders pressing together. The tightness in Cadie's chest loosened. She allowed herself to inhale a deep breath that stretched her lungs until they hurt, and oxygen rushed into the hidden spaces she had closed off for decades.

19

"Is everything okay between you and Daniela?" Garrett said as he drove Cadie home after dinner at the Garcias'. Waning light of an unsettled sunset caught on his stubble. "Things seemed kind of tense at dinner."

"We're fine. She's just worried." Cadie forced a smile. She had no idea if things were okay between her and Daniela. How could they be? They didn't even know each other anymore.

You've never had one damn thing to lose. Daniela's words from earlier that afternoon stung, partly because Daniela had no idea what Cadie had sacrificed for her. But mostly because Daniela was right.

"You believe me that I'll protect Raúl, don't you?" Garrett said.

"I hope you will." She wanted to believe him, to trust him. She also wished she had bothered to put mascara on her translucent red eyelashes.

"Do you want to come in?" Cadie said as they pulled in her driveway. The roof shingles, covered in slick moss, looked like scales in the silvery light.

He followed her up the porch steps and into the kitchen.

"Sorry it's so dusty." Cadie avoided the creaky boards as she stepped into the kitchen. "No one lives here right now. It's kind of a mess."

Cadie opened a window and looked out over the weed-covered beach.

"What do you think would have happened if we had become friends, real friends, back then?" Garrett stepped beside her at the window.

"I don't know." Cadie had played out all the scenarios in her head.

"We wouldn't be standing here right now." He picked up *The Outsiders* from the bookshelf and thumbed through the pages until he found the letters he had underlined decades earlier.

You are prettier than Cherry Valance, he had written in code all those years ago. Cadie knew the message in each book by heart. Her face burned as she watched him read his own words.

"You were my first kiss, you know," he said. The silence at the end of his sentence filled the room, like an explosion about to go off.

The Summer Kid had always had shape and color in her mind, but now he had dimension and heat too. His footsteps rattled ceramic plates hanging on the wall. He paused in front of the plates until they quieted.

"My mom made them. She only keeps the imperfect pieces." Cadie ran her fingers over weepy pockmarks in the glaze, the same broken bubbles she rubbed against her lip as she sipped tea from her mother's imperfect mugs.

"And my father painted these." She turned to the oil paintings. Her father's rough brush strokes pulled in the possibilities of a fall afternoon, all the things that could happen, but might not. An image of the woodpile, a stack of kinetic energy that could either burn or rot, made her sad and hopeful at the same time.

"Why did you stay here?" Cadie said.

"I don't know. I guess I felt like I should do something meaningful with my life. I had a lot to atone for. And to look after Clyde."

Cadie wanted to argue with him that Clyde was a monster who did not deserve his loyalty, but the tenderness in Garrett's voice and his dedication to his uncle stirred an unwanted pang of admiration.

"Don't you think, at some point, a person can earn forgiveness?" he said. "I mean if they try to live a good life, to make up for their past?"

Cadie had spent long nights lying awake, alone, trying to convince herself that she was living a better life, a more intentional life, because she had something to prove to the Universe. She had been a scared child who made a bad decision. Her adult conscience always interrupted to remind her she could have come forward any time since. But she never did. She could forgive the child. But could she ever forgive her adult self for never being brave enough to take responsibility for what her younger self had done?

"It'll be okay." He stood so close beside her she could feel the heat of his arm millimeters from her bare shoulder.

"How does any possible outcome seem okay?" She wanted to touch him, to confirm he was real. She let her cheek rest against his shoulder and listened to the thump of his heart. His fingertips glanced her lower back, barely skimming her skin through the thin cotton of her shirt. His touch felt dangerous, as if it invited the past and present to collide and undo everything she wanted to hold together.

Her phone buzzed in her pocket. She pulled it out, hoping to see a message from Daniela. Instead, a message from Thea popped up. *Call me ASAP.*

"It's my boss. This'll just take a minute."

"That was a crappy field report. It looked like a kindergartener did it," Thea said, although her tone did not sound angry. "But it doesn't matter."

Thea let the loaded sentence hang in the air.

"Why doesn't it matter?" Cadie braced for Thea to fire her.

"I showed your work—well, I neatened it up first—to the administration. Shit, Cadie, after I read it, how could I not tell someone? You're right. You're fucking right about the beetle and fire risk." Thea said words that should have made Cadie feel better, but her tone told Cadie something wasn't right.

"But the dean went ballistic when he saw where you collected data. You collected samples on land specifically declared off-limits months ago. He knows you understand the new laws. And he knows I do. He flipped out on me for supporting your work, said it threatened our program, the whole university." Thea paused for a second. "And said he wanted to terminate your fellowship. Immediately."

"This is bullshit. Does he understand how much environmental research is at risk if they restrict scientists' access to federal land? I pay taxes. It's *my* land. There are projects that have been going on for decades. This data can never be replaced."

"He knows that. But what's he supposed to do? It's the law."

Cadie paced in front of the window, her feet leaving prints in the long-settled dust. Her fellowship took funding from the state Forestry Service, and Cadie knew they would side with the federal government if it came down to it. Hadn't she known the risk when she climbed Mount Steady? But she had trusted that the university would stand with her. Truth. Knowledge. Justice. Bullshit.

"So that's it? You're just letting them push me out the door?" Musty air burned hot in her lungs. "Did they even read my findings?"

"I fought for you. Maybe too much." Thea took a deep breath and waited a few seconds before continuing. "He threatened to fire me too."

"You aren't responsible for my actions. You told me not to do it. I did it anyway." Rage simmered in her chest. Now she not only lost her job, but she bore the burden of possibly getting her mentor fired as well.

"I thought you were acting like a spoiled brat. All the projections say the beetles shouldn't be here yet. But I read your report. And, shit. I'm in this too now. I'm not going to ignore evidence because a bunch of close-minded bureaucrats don't believe in science."

"We can fight this, right?"

Garrett furrowed his brow and mouthed, *"Everything okay?"*

Cadie shook her head.

"We can try. But, FYI. Everyone knows," Thea said.

"What do you mean everyone? I'm the last one to find out I got fired?"

Garrett raised his eyebrows and put a hand on her wrist. Cadie pulled away.

"Maybe if you checked your messages. I've being texting you for hours. Remember that Piper person? Ornithology, I think? I don't even know how she found out about it, but she organized a bunch of grad students and within an hour, they occupied the dean's office, demanding he reinstate us."

"Why does ornithology care about my beetles?"

"It's not about your research. It's the underlying principle that politicians shouldn't be restricting scientific research on federal lands. Eventually, it will affect them too. Brace yourself before you look it up online. I think they turned you into a hashtag."

Over the years, Cadie had grown comfortable with her ability to become invisible. To disappear into the background, into the woods. The idea of purple-haired grad students turning her into a cause made her feel vulnerable and exposed at a time when she didn't need anyone looking at her.

"It's not all bad news. After six hours of grad students chanting outside his office, the dean caved and agreed to read your report. I think he agrees with you, but he feels backed into a corner. There's going to be an ethics committee review. You have a chance to make your case. Everyone's watching us. Other schools and foundations are already calling because they're up against the same regulatory crap."

"I don't want to be anyone's poster child. I just want to get ahead of the fires. I found the beetle here in Maple Crest. I don't even need the samples I sent you. I can stick with my original thesis, but gather new data on land that's not off-limits." She felt a flicker of hope that she could hang on to her job and still prove the beetles had arrived.

"This thing's taken on a life of its own. It's not about the beetles anymore. It's about government interference in science. Your hearing's scheduled for tomorrow at three. It's going to come down to how bold the committee members are. Will they choose the safe path and throw you under the bus to protect their own jobs, or will they side with science?"

Cadie felt a flush of shame at her own instinct to take the easy path.

"I hear you."

"Even I thought you were exaggerating at first. But, the beetles.

They're real. Your projections are shocking. Maybe a bit of a stretch, but it will get their attention."

"It's not a stretch. I drove by Morningside and Hobson. I haven't collected samples there, but I'm positive the forest in between them is already affected. Seriously. It's so dry. If there's as much dead wood in there as I think, it's just going to take one match and that forest is going to burn. It's probably the most vulnerable place in the state right now. A swath of dead trees abutting a campground and a populated area in the middle of a drought. One stray match and it will be out of control."

"Try to contain the drama. We can't get apocalyptic if we want them to take us seriously," Thea said.

"Drama? Do we need a wildfire to drive people from their homes before anyone believes me how serious this is?"

"I believe you. But I'm just advising to keep your shit together during the presentation."

"What presentation?" Cadie said.

Garrett walked out onto the back porch.

"The ethics committee wants you to defend your position tomorrow and explain why you were on federal land. Maybe if they understand the stakes."

Garrett stood on the deck, framed by an orange glow settling behind the mountains. He took an imaginary bat in his hands, choked up, and took a few practice swings. He planted his feet shoulder width apart, bent his knees, and took the bat to his shoulder.

"Tomorrow?" Cadie said loudly. Garrett looked in through the screened window and raised his eyebrows. She nodded that everything was fine. "I don't have a presentation prepared. And I'm two hours away."

Leaning forward and wagging his hips, Garrett waited for an imaginary pitch. He smacked an invisible ball with the full force of his broad, angular shoulders. Cadie found herself following its trajectory as it arched gracefully over the dusky lake.

"We can do this." Thea sounded uncharacteristically excited.

"And, for God's sake, please check your messages. I've been cleaning up your mess all day because no one can get in touch with you."

"I'll try. The woods up here are a cell signal dead zone." She looked out the window, but Garrett was gone. "I'll talk to you tomorrow."

She tucked her phone into her pocket and went outside. Maybe Garrett got tired of waiting for her and left. She found him behind the door, standing on an upside-down paint bucket, detaching the spring on top of the screen door.

"It's pretty rusty. Do you mind if I take it with me so I can measure it up when I'm in town? I can grab a new one at the hardware store for a few bucks." He reached up over his head to release the spring, exposing a few inches of tan skin between his board shorts and shirt.

Cadie tried not to stare at his obliques.

"Thanks. It's creaked for as long as I can remember," she said. "I don't even hear it anymore."

"What happened? That sounded serious."

"Nothing much. Except I knowingly collected samples on restricted federal land. My research has the potential to head off forest fires, but instead of backing my work, the university might fire me for violating these asinine regulations."

Garrett jumped down from the paint bucket and released the screen door, which hung open without the spring to pull it closed.

"This is such bullshit." Cadie slammed the door shut with so much force the windows rattled. "And to top it off, a bunch of do-gooder grad students turned me into a hashtag, and now I need to prepare a presentation for the ethics committee for tomorrow afternoon."

"Why would they restrict the research? I mean, they must have a reason."

"Because they don't want to believe climate change is real. They don't want more data proving temperature increases are killing their darling maples. Their donors want to keep on drilling and fracking. If we don't do the research, we can't prove species are disappearing or that invasive ones are moving in. They just stick their heads in their fucking sand and cash checks from Big Oil." She kicked the paint bucket Garrett had been standing on and walked over to the porch rail. "They don't want to believe my research because it's inconvenient."

Garrett stepped up behind her and put one hand on each of her shoulders.

"I believe you," he whispered. She could feel his breath through her hair.

Goosebumps rushed down her shoulder until the hairs on her arm stood straight up. Cadie's body betrayed her emotions too often. Her eyes always darted where they shouldn't. Like her merciless blush, her skin divulged her intimate desires. But, for once, Cadie didn't feel like she had anything to hide. Garrett already knew her secrets, her shame, her rage. She could never extricate herself from him now, as if they had been tangled up together all along. Sharing guilt eased her burden a degree.

She turned around to face him. The eyes that terrified and intrigued her as a child now evoked a raw, disarming hunger.

"Can you be ready by tomorrow afternoon?" he asked.

"Yeah. I'll terrify them with the truth."

"I'm going to go so you can work," Garrett said, but he didn't move.

Cadie felt emboldened by a long-dormant, yet familiar recklessness. The events of the last twenty-four hours had yanked her out of her carefully constructed sanctuary. She had so much to fear—losing her job, getting arrested, facing her past—that she felt numb to the panic.

"Is there anything I can do to help?" he whispered, the hush of lake water on his breath. His skin smelled like the wind over the shallows, wet granite, and honeysuckle.

"Stay a little longer." She pressed up on her toes and kissed him. She almost laughed, remembering her reaction to Garrett's unexpected first kiss all those years ago.

"You have work to do." His fingers touched the skin on her back between her shirt and her waistband as he pulled her closer. Heat moved up her back, and she lost her breath for a second.

"I don't want to be responsible for a forest fire because you couldn't get your presentation finished. Can you come over after the presentation tomorrow? We can eat dinner on my boat."

Cadie nodded. "If I convince them to support me, this could change everything. It could be my chance. There's also an outside chance I could get arrested."

"I believe in you," Garret said.

The idea of going out on the boat with Garrett suddenly felt more important than stopping the fires.

"I'm really leaving now." He pulled away. "If there's anything I can do, call me. Otherwise, I'll see you tomorrow night. Does six thirty work?"

"I'll be there."

He kissed her lightly on the lips and backed toward the door.

Watching the screen open and close without the squeak of the rusty spring disoriented Cadie, like watching a TV show with sound that did not sync to the video. She startled when the door slammed shut and Garrett was gone.

She hopped across the kitchen floorboards in her old familiar patterns, trying to extract out-of-tune childhood melodies, and poured a glass of her father's bourbon over a few ice cubes.

She highlighted the vulnerable areas with flames superimposed over the map of New Hampshire as the first slide, which she knew Thea would think was too dramatic. But Cadie was feeling dramatic. By 2 A.M., she had finished putting the slides and maps into her presentation software, which she e-mailed to Thea to review.

She needed sleep, but this silent hour of the night felt like a gift. The rest of the world had stopped moving. She rummaged through her bookshelf until she found the water-warped copy of *The Call of the Wild*, the book she had never delivered to Garrett.

How had that wispy boy summoned the courage to send her those notes? Did he act out of desperation, boredom, or sincere admiration? Had she ever been that bold in her life? Could she ever be that brave?

She pressed open the paperback and underlined letters, spelling out a note for Garrett. *I think I've been waiting for you my whole life.* She hugged the book to her chest and tucked it and *Kidnapped,* the first book she had shared with Garrett, into her backpack.

20

The morning chill had dissipated by the time Cadie stepped into the woods and headed to the Garcias' house the following morning. Why had she agreed to take Sal blueberry picking? She had six hours before delivering the presentation that could possibly change the trajectory of her career. Or get her arrested. She should be rehearsing. But something about the way Sal looked at her, imagining fairy wings, made Cadie want to be that person Sal imagined her to be.

Cadie picked up her pace as she made her way down the overgrown path, leaping up onto the granite stones and launching off to the next one. She moved faster, skipping, running, careful to avoid twisting her ankle in hidden crevices.

Cadie misjudged the traction of dried moss, parched from the drought. Instead of finding a spongey landing pad, her boot slipped over the slick moss and she fell, banging her shin on a rock. The cut was small, the bruise inconsequential, but the tiny burst of adrenaline made her fingers and toes buzz.

By the time she reached the clearing, sweat dripped down her back. She put her hands on her knees and leaned forward to catch her breath.

The outline of that boat stood out against the forest floor. The ghost of a ship formed from rocks Cadie had arranged to elevate the boat where she had stored it in the winter. Time had tried to pull the rock outline down under the forest floor. Curling vines and tufts of moss covered some stones, but the resilient skeleton of the boat held fast.

The forest breathed around her. She closed her eyes and inhaled the succulent exhale of the woods.

Instead of heading straight to the Garcias', Cadie stepped off the trail and walked toward the beech tree where she had hidden the gun. Maybe she and Daniela had missed something. It had been dark. They'd been drinking.

She climbed the boulder next to the tree and sank her arm inside the eyehole. She moved her fingers more carefully this time, avoiding another splinter. Amid the dried leaves and acorns, her finger touched the edge of what felt like a plastic bag. She recoiled, afraid of what might be inside. She put her hand back in and pulled out a small Ziploc bag with a folded piece of paper sealed inside.

Go Home. Or someone will get hurt.

She dropped the note and jumped off the rock. A rustling in the woods behind her, the swoosh of a blackbird overhead. Cadie picked up the note, which appeared to have been written recently, shoved it into her shorts pocket, and ran back toward the path.

Had the note been there the night she and Daniela went looking for the gun? Had Cadie missed it because of the splinter? Garrett believed the gun sank to the bottom of the lake. And if Garrett wanted her to leave, why would he have kissed her? Daniela had called Cadie back to the cottage in the first place, so it couldn't be her. Could it? Dolores never even knew Garrett gave the gun to Cadie.

That left Clyde.

Go Home. The message burned in her pocket. Threatening the Garcias was still Clyde's only weapon. Would he really expose them after all this time?

Raúl met Cadie at the door, his hair neatly combed. Instead of his Garcia's Hardware logo shirt, he wore a freshly pressed button-down and a tie. Sal hung back in the darkened hallway behind her grandmother.

"I want to take the canoe out instead of going into the woods." Sal fidgeted and picked at her cuticles as she spoke from the shadow.

"Sure," Cadie said.

Sal pointed to the blood on Cadie's shin and wrinkled her brow.

Cadie stepped behind a chair so Raúl and Dolores wouldn't notice and touched her finger to her lips so Sal wouldn't say anything.

"I'm going now." Raúl kissed Dolores on the cheek.

"Are you sure you don't want me to come?" Dolores's knuckles whitened as she squeezed the handle on her coffee mug.

Sal's eyes moved back and forth from her grandmother to her grandfather.

"Bring some berries back for me?" Raúl's hard face broke into a smile so unnatural that Cadie couldn't look at him.

Sal nodded and walked outside, her hair sticking up in messy spikes around her crown. Cadie followed her outside.

"Were you rock jumping?" Sal pointed at Cadie's cut. "Mom said you always bounced from rock to rock instead of staying on the path."

"Apparently, I'm out of practice." Cadie touched the tender bruise forming around the scrape.

Cadie took a seat in the front of the Garcias' canoe. With a running start, Sal pushed the boat into the shallow water and leapt into the rear seat.

"Where do you want to go?" Cadie said.

"Blueberry Cove." Sal's words sounded like a challenge.

Cadie wanted to ask Sal how she liked her new school, if she had made any new friends, but the questions sounded trite and cliché as she tossed them around in her head. She strangled the heel of her paddle, smiling too much whenever Sal looked at her.

"Why were you and Mom fighting last night?"

"We weren't fighting." Cadie looked over her shoulder at Sal.

"Right," Sal said.

"Look, there's a loon family." Cadie pointed toward a pair and a chick.

"She can be a real bitch sometimes."

"Your mom's not a bitch. We disagreed about something. It's not a big deal," Cadie said. "How do you like the new school?"

"It sucks. It's a bunch of hicks."

"That's not true. Your mom and I grew up here."

"And you both couldn't wait to move away. The only reason we came back is because Mom needed a job."

"People here are nice. You should give them a chance."

"Like the kids who spray-painted 'Build the Wall' on the back of the gym? You want me to give them a chance?"

"Someone did that?"

"Yeah. Someone did that." Sal paddled harder on her side of the boat, forcing Cadie to compensate on the other side in order to keep the boat moving straight.

Cadie tried to think of something else to talk about, but she had nothing in common with this girl.

"Why'd you bring that cop over last night?" Sal said.

"Garrett wasn't being a cop last night. He's a friend."

"Ummm-hmmm." Sal laughed. "A friend."

Heat rushed to Cadie's cheeks. She squeezed the paddle tighter to calm the rush that burst forward when she thought about Garrett.

Sal threw her head back and laughed out loud. "Oh, my God. Mom's so right. She said you blushed redder than anyone she'd ever met."

Although the joke came at her expense, Cadie laughed. The storm in Sal's eyes lightened.

"Thanks. Pointing out that I'm blushing really helps." Cadie splashed water at Sal.

"Mom says you're into trees and forestry."

"I'm a professional tree hugger."

"Did you know that only two percent of El Salvador's forests remain standing because of all the logging and irresponsible agriculture? A lot of it's local farmers clearing land, but US companies bought up a ton of land and clear-cut it to grow bananas and stuff."

"Really?" Cadie already knew about the deforestation in Central America but she wanted to keep Sal talking about climate disasters instead of Cadie's love life.

"And the drought there is *way* worse than the one everyone's freaking out about in New Hampshire."

"Conditions here are pretty bad, too."

"But not like there." Sal's playful demeanor when she had teased Cadie about Garrett morphed into a serious, weighty stare.

"True. How do you know all this?"

"The Internet." Sal paddled with slow, even strokes. "I had to do a summer research project. I did it on the effects of climate change in El Salvador."

"That seems kind of cruel. We never had summer work."

"It's our fault, you know."

"Summer work?" Cadie tried to swallow a yawn. She hadn't slept much the previous night.

"No, geez. The drought in El Salvador. Countries like the US pump so much CO_2 into the air with all our air-conditioning and giant SUVs. We're doing most of the damage, but poor countries— it's *always* the poor countries—are feeling climate change first and worst. And then when their crops fail and no one has any money, crime goes up, and the gang stuff gets worse."

Cadie stopped paddling, took a swallow of water from her water bottle, and offered it to Sal. Sal drank down a few gulps and wiped her mouth with the back of her hand.

"And then when people want to save their families from, like, starvation or violence, they cross into the US, but Americans get all like 'Build the Wall.' 'Latinos are all rapists.' It's bullshit." Sal knitted her thick eyebrows as she spoke.

"Maybe you should skip running for mayor and head straight to Congress."

"I'm being serious. It's wrong. We can't go around screwing up the whole world, then turn our backs on the people who get hurt by it."

"There are efforts to replant forests in Central America, and they're trying to work with farmers to stop them from clear-cutting and burning land," Cadie said.

"Tell that to the people starving right now." Sal looked across the mountains flanking the lake.

"You're right. It's not helping them, is it?"

"There're kids in my school who came here alone. Not even with their parents. Completely alone. Can you even imagine? I know one kid who held on underneath a moving train to get here. *Underneath.* Is that even possible? But I know he's telling the truth because he has all these scars on his back and legs from stones kicking up and hitting him. But he didn't let go. He still has pebbles embedded in his scalp. I felt them."

"Geez. That's awful. Is he okay now?"

"I guess. He lives with his brother, Tino, who has been here like eight years, I think."

"Wait. You mean Fernando?"

"You know Fernando?" Sal stopped paddling and she bit down on her lower lip. Her eyes widened with panic. "I shouldn't have said that. I mean, I don't even know if it's true. He probably made it all up. Besides, I think he probably has papers now."

"I would never say anything." Cadie tried to imagine the wiry boy on the basketball court clinging to the undercarriage of a train. "Things would have to be pretty desperate for a kid to make that journey."

"I shouldn't have told you." Sal started paddling again. "Do you think the drought here will get worse?"

"Maybe. I'm working on a project to try to head off forest fires related to the drought right now."

"I know what you do. Internet, remember? It sounds pretty cool, the bugs and all. It's important."

"Right." Cadie smiled. At least Sal and Garrett believed in her. If the ethics committee agreed, maybe they would forgive her for trespassing on federal lands. Cadie looked down at her watch, gripped her paddle tighter, and pulled harder through the water, as if quickening their pace might hasten the movement of time.

As they approached Garrett's pier, Cadie dragged her paddle to slow down. The dock had the same gray-green mossy patina as the one at her own cottage, but Garrett had replaced several planks with new boards, giving the structure an unsettled, irregular appearance. New, yet still weighed down with the past.

The stone ledge, however, did not look the way she remembered. Taller, more severe. How had she scaled that wall as a girl? The foothold looked impossibly small. The house sat much closer to the ledge than she remembered. Maybe she had the wrong place.

But even from dozens of yards away, she could make out the white mineral vein arching through the granite. Her fingers curled tighter around her oar and her pulse sped up. The rush of her first kiss had become intertwined with the crack of the gunshot and smell of smoke. It had become impossible to revisit one memory without wading through the other.

"Why are you stopping?" Sal said.

"I need to drop something off at Garrett's real quick."

She pulled *The Call of the Wild* from her bag and sucked her cheeks in to suppress the schoolgirl flutter in her stomach. Sal cocked her head to one side and looked from the book to the pier to the rock wall and back to Cadie.

"This is Garrett's house?" A slow grin spread across Sal's face, and she pointed to the rock wall.

"What?"

"He's that weird Summer Kid, isn't he?" Sal's eyes, which had looked so gloomy minutes earlier, sparkled in the sun.

"She told you about that?" Through Sal's eyes, Cadie and Daniela were always the heroines of the story. Maybe Daniela had been trying to overwrite the truth, disentangle the terror from the moments of pure exhilaration.

"I wasn't sure if that part was real either, but it's him, isn't it?" Sal stomped her feet on the bottom of the boat like a drum roll. "And you're leaving him another book."

"I will neither confirm nor deny that," Cadie said, allowing the memory of adventure to flutter in.

"I knew it." Sal squirmed like a child waiting to open a Christmas gift.

"Let's drop this off on his pier." Cadie tapped the cover of *The Call of the Wild*.

"Oh, no. There's no way we are leaving the book on the pier," Sal said. "It has to be on the rock ledge."

"No."

"Why not?"

"I'm too old to climb that wall," Cadie said, although the surging adrenaline made her feel like she could scale a mountain without pausing.

"I'll do it." Sal guided the boat toward the rock wall.

Sweat soaked the back of Cadie's shirt by the time they approached the shore. Thin white veins marred the granite face with jagged lines and deep fissures, simultaneously drawing Cadie close and pushing her away.

Sal jumped to her feet as they drifted into the shallows, causing the canoe to rock. She took *The Call of the Wild* from Cadie, tucked it into the waistband of her shorts, and splashed through the water. She grabbed at tree roots and found footholds with greater dexterity than young Cadie had.

The gentle arch in Sal's back tugged on Cadie's memory. "You're just like her."

Sal whipped her head around with a stern glare. "I am *nothing* like her."

Cadie's heart pounded in her throat, in her stomach, as Sal climbed higher, almost even with the white vein in the rock. Cadie saw her younger self scrambling up the rock wall with a wildness, a thirst, for something. An adventure. As she watched Sal, the sound of Cadie's own heart grew so loud it seemed to come from outside her body, as if the heartbeat she heard belonged to someone else.

"Come down," Cadie called to Sal. "I changed my mind. Please don't go up there."

"I'm fine." Sal climbed higher.

"It's not safe." *Please don't go up there,* Cadie begged her eleven-year-old self in a desperate hope that she could go back and undo it all. *Please don't go up there.*

"Of course it's safe." Sal pulled the book from her shorts, left it on the ledge, and eased her way down backward, searching blindly for footholds.

Loose stones crunched and Sal slipped. Both feet lost their hold as she dangled from a tree root.

"Hold on. I'm coming." Cadie stood up in the wobbly canoe.

"Geez, relax. I'm fine." Sal clawed at the rock with her feet. She found a stable perch and eased herself back down.

"You're bleeding," Cadie said as Sal sloshed through the shallow water.

"It's a scratch. Besides, lake water heals everything." Sal splashed water on her knee and stood in the shallows with her feet apart, hands on her hips. "Now I'm in the story too."

Cadie forced a smile. She did not want Sal to have any part in her nightmare.

"Can I read your research paper?" Cadie changed the subject after Sal got back in the boat.

"Maybe," Sal said. "Let's go to Blueberry Cove."

As they approached the cove, Sal tilted her head back and breathed deeply through her open mouth with her tongue out.

"How does it taste?" Cadie said.

"Peach, maybe?"

"We should slow down a little." Cadie looked for rocks lurking below the surface, but the sharp angle of the sun turned the water opaque.

"I'm right, you know," Sal said.

"About what?"

"He likes you."

Cadie dipped her hand into the water to splash Sal just as the boat lurched and tilted to one side. Cadie's hip slammed into the wall of the boat. The bow, lodged on a submerged boulder that lifted it out of the water, wobbled and threatened to tip over.

"He watched you with googly eyes the whole dinner."

"Are you going to help me?" Cadie pushed her paddle against the rock and the boat tilted precariously to one side.

"If you admit I'm right." Sal tried to paddle backward, but the boat teetered.

"You should mind your own business." Cadie inched toward the back of the boat to shift weight from the bow.

"God, you are *so* blushing."

"I just met him yesterday." Cadie wedged her oar against the rock and pushed hard. The boat broke free from the rock and Cadie fell backward on top of Sal.

"That's not true. You've known him your whole life. It's the most romantic story I've ever heard." The rise and fall of Sal's voice, her self-satisfied innuendos, sounded exactly like a young Daniela.

"But." Sal's voice turned sharp and she pulled away from Cadie. A cloud darkened the sky. "You better make sure he leaves my grandfather alone."

21

Sal remained silent as they paddled back to the Garcias' house. More clouds amassed, but no rain would come of them.

"I told your mom I'd drive you to your tutoring thing at the rec center," Cadie said as they pulled the canoe up onto the Garcias' beach. "Do you need to change or anything?"

Sal looked down at her tank top and shorts. "What's wrong with my clothes?"

"Nothing," Cadie stammered. "You look great. So, are you ready to go? Or do you want to eat first?"

"I'll eat later." Sal walked past Cadie and up the stairs to the house.

"What are you getting tutored in? Math was always my worst subject," Cadie said.

"I'm not getting tutored. I'm helping this kid who's learning English as a second language. We have to do community service hours every semester." Sal filled a water bottle in the kitchen and slipped on a pair of flip-flops. "But I'd do it even if I didn't have to."

Sal followed Cadie into the woods and down the path toward Cadie's cottage. She hurried through the clearing, her skin prickling as she passed the flattened grass where she had ducked off-trail earlier that morning.

Sal slumped into the passenger seat and remained quiet as they drove toward town.

"I'll walk you in," Cadie said as she parked in front of the rec center.

"I don't need a babysitter."

"I know. I'll walk you in anyway."

"Whatever."

Inside the main room several men and women sat at tables working with teens and a few adults. Cadie ran toward a small boy, maybe nine years old, sitting alone at a table. He smiled when he saw Sal, who ruffled his hair and sat next to him.

"Cadie?" A woman's voice startled her.

"Is that you, Claire?" Cadie gave Ryan's younger sister an awkward wave.

Claire jogged a few steps with exaggerated enthusiasm. "Cadie Kessler, what on earth are you doing here?"

"Just visiting. I'm dropping Daniela's daughter off for her."

"Right. I forgot you two were friends. You never come home anymore."

"What's going on in here?"

"It's an English as a second language program. We teach classes on weekends and the middle schoolers volunteer to practice reading with our students."

"You run this?"

"No. A few families who used to work at Crittenden started this years ago. I just help." Claire placed both hands on her hips and smiled broadly while she surveyed the room.

Last time Cadie had seen Claire she had been making out with some boy in the back of a pickup truck when they were teenagers. This Claire looked so together now, her hair in a neat ponytail, wearing a perfect pencil skirt and a tank top.

Cadie watched Sal, who smiled with animation as the boy read to her. A tall man with thinning hair stood behind Sal. A chill of familiarity shot up Cadie's spine before she consciously recognized the figure.

Clyde.

The door to the rec center slammed and Cadie dropped her bag.

She looked around the room to see if anyone else noticed him there, to see if she could report him to anyone. But his presence didn't seem to bother anyone. Surely Claire would notice him. Cadie looked back at Claire, who continued monitoring the room, unbothered that a murderer stood a few inches from Sal.

Clyde leaned over Sal's shoulder and said something that made her laugh.

Cadie had always imagined Clyde lurking in shadows, hiding in dark alleys and empty parking lots. Not working a community center. How could he have stayed here? How could he get up each morning and walk down the streets of Cadie's hometown? Arrogance. Lack of conscience. Maybe he was a sociopath. What other crimes had he committed while hiding in plain sight? The thought sent a chill up Cadie's spine. If he had committed other crimes, Cadie was, in part, responsible. She could have turned him in years ago.

"Are your parents here too?" Claire said.

"What?" Cadie didn't take her eyes off Clyde. "Excuse me for a minute."

Clyde looked up and caught Cadie staring at him. His expression looked casual, and he nodded a greeting toward her, but within half a second, he recognized her and his demeanor changed. He froze. He didn't blink. Even the muscles in his face didn't twitch.

Cadie was clinging to the rock wall, falling, underwater, being pulled down. She couldn't breathe. Or move. Her legs locked in place. Run toward him. Or run away. She couldn't do either.

Sweat beaded up on Clyde's forehead as he withdrew his hand from Sal's chair and straightened his back.

As soon as he moved, Cadie's legs unlocked and she walked, half running, toward Sal. Her footsteps on the linoleum echoed inside the metal-roofed building. Clyde moved quickly toward the back of the room. Cadie's heart pounded so hard it felt like it might bruise her ribs.

"Cadie?" Sal called as she ran by.

She followed Clyde down a back hallway toward the bathrooms. The shadow in her dreams, the monster she feared most, stood in front of her. She felt outside of herself, as if this moment were part of a dream she would wake up from.

"You stay away from her," she said to Clyde's back as he moved toward the rear exit.

"I just work here. I don't want any trouble," he said.

The back door burst open and a middle-aged woman walked through. Clyde stepped to the side and nodded at her without making eye contact.

"Oh, Clyde." The woman grabbed his elbow. "I'm so glad I caught you. You did such a great job with the landscaping out front. You spoil us."

"Happy to help." He looked down at his shoes.

The woman looked at Cadie, the anger and fear on Cadie's face registering. The woman turned back to Clyde. "Everything okay here?"

Neither Cadie or Clyde answered.

"Holler if you need anything." She patted his arm and looked sideways at Cadie.

"You're a coward." Cadie held her car key so it stuck out from between her fingers. The memory of Clyde pressing her up against the tree still dominated her nightmares. But in person, his scraggly hair and pasty skin gave him the appearance of someone she should pity, not fear.

Clyde nodded toward the key she clutched in a ready position and scowled at her.

The note she found in the tree, folded into a sharp square, pressed against her hip bone from her front pocket.

"Your threats don't scare me anymore," she said.

He shrugged as if her opinion of him did not matter in the slightest. His indifference seemed impossible. How could he change the course of her life, yet not fear the depth of her hate? The single overhead light in the otherwise dark hall cast shadows down Clyde's face, darkening the pockmarks in his cheeks. Clyde coughed a wheezy hack, shuffled toward the exit, and let the door clang shut behind him.

Cadie's hands shook as she powered up her phone to call Daniela. A stream of text messages, missed calls, and voicemails scrolled across the screen, but she didn't look at any of them. She didn't want to read any more about the grad students who had signed a petition in support of her access to public lands.

She dialed Daniela, but the call went straight to voicemail.

She walked back to Sal's table with a fake smile. "Hey, something's come up. I need to take you home early."

"I'm not allowed to leave once I sign in. School rule. Plus, this is for community service credit. It's not like I can just skip out."

"I'll talk to Claire. She knows me. It'll be fine."

"You don't have the authority to sign me out, even if I wanted you to." Sal turned to her reading partner and smiled. "Let's do another chapter. We have plenty of time."

Cadie called Daniela, but again went to voicemail. "Hey, call me. I'm at the rec center with Sal." Cadie paused. "Clyde's here. I'm not leaving Sal. Please call me. If you can't get here, can you call to give Sal permission to leave with me?"

Cadie gnawed on her thumbnail, watching for Clyde, waiting for Daniela to call. She couldn't be late to her committee review. If she left after dropping Sal off at home, she wouldn't have time to meet with Thea before her presentation, but she could still make the hearing. Maybe.

Daniela texted a few minutes before Sal's shift ended. *I can't leave the hospital. I emailed permission for you to pick her up when she's done. Can you drive her home? Please don't let her leave alone!*

"You in town long?" Claire walked over to Cadie.

"Just a couple of days. Do you know that man who was talking to Sal?"

"You know Fieldstone Landscaping? Best landscapers in town. He's the owner. President of the Rotary too."

"What's he doing here?"

"He's one of our biggest donors. He's the only one who actually shows up in person. The rest just write checks. He's kind of crusty on the outside. Not the greatest people skills, but he means well. And he speaks fluent Spanish, which is a help," Claire said. "Are you looking for a landscaper? He did my parents' place if you want a reference. They were real happy with the job."

Clyde had a lot more at stake than she did. He must know why Cadie had returned to Maple Crest. He must know she wanted to expose him. And that made him dangerous.

"Hey, have you seen what's happening in Hobson?" Claire said.

"Hobson? No, what?" Cadie didn't have the mental energy for small talk. She kept her eye on Sal.

"A fire broke out last night. From what I hear it's getting close to a housing development. They had to evacuate dozens of families."

"Where's the fire?" The news jolted thoughts of Clyde out of Cadie's mind and filled her with a rush of hope that sprang from the soles of her feet straight to her chest. She predicted this. Her models. She had warned them.

"Over by the campground in the national forest. A campfire got out of control or something last night, and poof. What with this drought and all. It's already partially contained, but still." Claire made an exaggerated shudder. "That's thirty miles from here. Way too close for comfort."

Cadie swallowed the hope she felt stirring. *Stop it*, she chastised herself. But yet, there it was. Her chance.

"Wow, that's too bad." Cadie tried to sound concerned. The university couldn't deny that Cadie had predicted this fire. The urgency of her findings had to outweigh the means by which she had acquired the data.

"I need to get back to work, but it was great seeing you. Tell your folks I said hi," Claire said.

After Claire walked away, Cadie sifted through the barrage of texts and calls—all of them from Thea.

Fire in Hobson, JUST like you predicted!

Are you watching Hobson?

Holy shit. This fire underscores every point in your presentation.

WHERE ARE YOU? Call asap.

The fire was small, but the ramifications could be huge.

Cadie paced in front of the door, watching Sal and scanning the room for Clyde as the clock over the exit ticked off each long, slow second.

22

"I'm still not sure why we're doing this," Cadie's mother said as they drove over to Crittenden Farm to join in the search for Juan.

"The kid's been missing for days," her father said.

Cadie slumped down in the backseat.

"He's not a kid. It says he's twenty-two," her mom said.

"But he's still missing. I talked to Raúl about it yesterday and he's pretty upset. Says Juan is really reliable, and apparently, he didn't take anything with him. Not his money or family photos. He didn't even cash his last paycheck from the farm or say good-bye to anyone."

"There're thousands of acres of woods around here," her mother said. "What do they think we can accomplish?"

Cadie dug her fingernails into her thigh, trying to push out images of Juan's misaligned buttons.

"I doubt this will do much good, but Raúl went through a lot of effort to organize this. He's even putting up a reward and Dolores is making lunch for everyone who shows up to help."

"Mrs. Garcia is helping?" Cadie bolted upright in her seat. Dolores knew as well as Cadie did that they weren't going to find anything near Crittenden's.

"Turns out he works at the hardware store, and I guess they really like him."

"It feels like too much of a coincidence that he disappeared the same day as the convenience store robbery and shooting," her mother said.

"Juan didn't shoot anyone," Cadie said.

Both of her parents whipped their heads around. The car veered onto the shoulder and her father jerked the steering wheel to right the car.

"Oh, honey. I didn't realize you knew him," her mother said.

"I don't really. He was, he is Daniela's friend. He wouldn't shoot anyone."

Her parents exchanged a concerned-parent look.

"If you don't want to go, we can take you home," her father said. "It never occurred to us you might know him. I'm sure Juan is fine. I think it would mean a lot to the Garcias if one of us showed up, but we don't both need to be there."

"I'm fine. I'll go with you," Cadie said.

Dozens of cars lined the driveway to the farm. Why had all these people showed up to look for someone most of them probably didn't even know? Cadie sloshed through the muddy ruts in the driveway and made her way to one of the barns where people had gathered. Raúl distributed whistles and gave people instructions on where to go.

"Blow your whistle if you find anything," he told everyone as he handed out maps. The smell of pupusas wafted over to where Cadie stood. She let go of her mother's hand and walked toward the smell.

Dolores stood at a folding table to the side of the barn, handing out pupusas wrapped in paper towels. Cadie's stomach churned, but not with hunger. Dolores's shoulders were hunched and she moved in tight, jerking motions, slapping away hands that tried to grab second helpings.

Her skin looked almost gray against the backdrop of the weathered barn. Cadie stood in the driveway watching Dolores flicker smiles and accept compliments on her cooking. She paced behind the table during the breaks between hungry people.

Mud seeped through Cadie's sneakers.

Dolores stared up at the sky and twisted her necklace around her finger, released it, and twisted it again. When she lowered her eyes, she caught Cadie watching her. She scrunched her forehead up and seemed to be asking Cadie a thousand questions at one time. *Are you okay? Are you going to keep our secret? Will you protect my family?*

Cadie shoved her shaking hands into her shorts pockets and nodded at Dolores.

Two men walked by munching on Dolores's cooking. "You know what they're saying, don't you," one man said to the other. "Garcia arranged this whole fake search party to cover his own ass. Heard he and Hernández got into it the day he disappeared. Punches thrown, shouting. Then the guy disappears, and all of a sudden Garcia's his best friend?"

"I just came for the food," the other man said.

Cadie wanted to scream at them. Raúl had nothing to do with Juan's disappearance. Cadie had witnessed the argument. Yelling, yes, but no one threw any punches. How dare they eat the Garcias' food while accusing him of murder?

Dolores, out of earshot of the men, picked up a pupusa and extended it toward Cadie. She gestured for Cadie to come get it. Cadie could not go near Dolores. Not now, maybe not ever. She could still feel the pressure of Dolores squeezing her hand as they prayed on the banks of Silas Creek. She had felt Dolores's sorrow and fear in the sinewy muscles of her hand. Cadie had enough ache of her own now. She didn't want any more of Dolores's.

Cadie felt trapped in Dolores's stare, afraid to keep staring at her, but afraid to look away. She didn't notice a man step up to Dolores's table and help himself to lunch. The man followed Dolores's stare and Cadie felt him watching her. She shifted her gaze and found herself staring at Clyde.

A fierce pain gripped her chest and she couldn't breathe. She wanted to run, but her feet seemed stuck in the mud. Clyde looked at Dolores, then back at Cadie, as if to remind her of his threat. *You don't want your friend to disappear, do you?* He lifted his pupusa to his mouth and took a bite, chewing slowly with his mouth open. He wiped his mouth with his hand and tossed the paper towel on the ground. Clyde pointed a finger at Cadie, stabbing at the air as if he could hurt her from yards away.

Cadie turned and ran. Dolores yelled after her, but she didn't stop. She bumped into someone, but she didn't see who, then someone else, but she kept running down the driveway. Mud slapped against her legs, and the farm blurred into a swath of trees and bodies. Voices called out to her and she heard his heavy footsteps thumping behind her.

She leapt over a low stone wall at the edge of the woods and hurled herself into the forest. Thorns whipped across her legs, branches smacked her in the face. Feet thrashed through the underbrush, getting closer, closer. She could smell the stale tobacco on his breath. Her lungs burned as she plowed blindly between trees. Just when she felt she couldn't keep going, two large hands grabbed her and pulled her to the ground.

"No, no," she yelled, and thrashed against the arms pinning her. "Let me go."

"Cadie."

"Don't touch me." Tears blurred her eyes as she pounded her fists against Clyde.

"Cadie, it's me. It's Dad."

Cadie wriggled free to see her father sitting next to her in the mud. "What happened? Who did you think was chasing you?"

"The person who killed Juan," she blurted out without thinking.

"No one said anything about Juan being killed. We don't know where he is, that's all." Her father pulled her close and she sat on his lap, sobbing. "I had no idea this would scare you so much. I'm so sorry. I'm going to take you home. You're okay. No one is going to hurt you."

They sat in silence for several minutes, her father rocking her back and forth until her breath calmed. Beyond the edge of the woods, cars rolled down the driveway as more people arrived to join the search efforts. Her chest ached with a hurt deeper than guilt, a pain greater than loss. An overwhelming premonition that nothing would ever feel normal again.

A chorus of chirping crickets filled the forest. She picked up a small rock and squeezed it with all her might. She didn't know how to pray to whatever Dolores believed in, so instead she called on the highest power she knew—the forest—to keep her and her secrets safe.

23

"The question is not whether the mountain pine beetle has migrated to New England forests. The question isn't even what are we going to do now that we know it's here." Cadie practiced her opening remarks as she sped toward the ethics committee hearing. After driving Sal home from tutoring at the rec center, Cadie had zero margin of error if she was going to make it to the hearing. "The question is whether *you* are going to suppress research that you know is solid to appease Washington. Science or politics? Which one are you going to side with?

"We have a responsibility to act, to head off a disaster on the scale of what we've seen in Colorado and California." She mentally flipped to a dramatic slide of a forest fire. "It will be our fault when the fires get out of control, our fault when more homes burn or people die. If we don't act, *we* will bear the guilt because *we* are the ones who saw it coming and did nothing because we caved to political pressure."

Maybe she should tone down the melodrama, like Thea said. No. She needed to scare them. She wanted to scare them. The thin haze of smoke thickened from a barely noticeable veil when she got on the highway to a denser fog sliding in from the west where a shroud blurred the mountains.

A pickup truck going forty-five miles an hour held up the traffic in front of her. "Get out of the fast lane," she muttered as she swerved past the line of vehicles and sped up.

She put the window down and let her hair blow in the wind. A stagnant cloud of smoke hovered over the mountain separating the highway from Hobson. At least the wind had calmed, which would help contain the fire thirty miles from Maple Crest.

"We've seen a four-degree change in the temps in New Hampshire in less than a century. That's wildly disproportionate to the average increase in the rest of the world. We are the canary in the coal mine. Vegetation is migrating. Habitats are shifting. Warming temperatures have disrupted the equilibrium in our ecosystem. *That* is the permanent situation no one wants to talk about."

The committee would agree with her recommendations to thin trees ahead of the beetles. How could they ignore the facts? Even if they were obtained illegally.

"When they closed off public lands for environmental research they sent a clear message: They don't want to know the truth. But truth lasts longer than fear or ignorance. I refuse to play by false rules when I know the risk we face."

The air blasting through the car window tasted like the remnants of a barbeque. If not for the smear of smoke on the horizon, it would have been a perfect late-summer day.

The black bear on the side of the road could have been a boulder or a stump, camouflaged against the woods.

The thick mass of fur and limbs went from motionless to flying in half a second.

The black blur lunged from the woods, interrupting Cadie's speech rehearsal. She slammed on her brakes and fishtailed, narrowly missing a car next to her. She nicked the bear's hindquarters, and the animal ricocheted into the pickup truck behind her. The truck hit the animal broadside with a hollow, wet thud. The forest spun past Cadie; around her, brakes screeched as she fought to right her car.

She skidded sideways and saw the bear tumble and roll and get hit again. She felt herself scream, but did not hear her voice over the squealing of brakes and crunching of metal around her.

She missed the guardrail by less than a foot, but the three cars behind her collided into a tangle that spanned the road. Everything fell silent around her. She peeled her fingers from the steering wheel and took inventory. No pain. No injury. Outside, car doors opened. Car doors slammed. She became aware of blurred bodies moving outside. A man knocked on her window to see if she was hurt and she waved him off.

With the mess of vehicles blocking the road in front of her and traffic quickly piling up behind, Cadie's car was blocked in.

The ethics committee would be convening in twenty-five minutes. Cadie beat her fist on the steering wheel. She stepped out of her car to a silence that swelled from a murmur to a collective panic. A child wailed. People talked into cell phones, yelled at one another. No one appeared injured, as far as she could tell. She walked around her car to survey the damage. Her blood-smeared driver's side fender had crumpled, but not enough to prevent her from driving—if she could get around the pileup.

The bear, sprawled out and bloodied on the ground in front of an SUV, looked across the macadam at Cadie. Its wet eyes pleaded with her.

A man circled the bear, inching closer, then jumping back when the animal groaned.

The bear blinked twice at Cadie, drawing her close. *Never look a bear in the eyes*, she cautioned herself. But she couldn't turn away. With slow steps, she crept toward the animal, keeping her body low, her arms at her sides to appear small and unthreatening. The bear did not react as she crouched twenty feet away.

"Are you crazy? Move back," a voice shouted at her.

The bear's right front leg twisted at an unnatural angle. Blood from a wide gash on its belly pooled on the road. She repositioned herself so she wouldn't have to look at its intestines spilling onto the street. The smell of blood and offal overpowered the smoke in the air.

The bear did not appear able to move, but its eyes followed Cadie. Blood and mucus trickled from one nostril.

"It's okay, friend," Cadie whispered, still several feet away from the animal. The bear's hind legs twitched and it let out a low, guttural groan. The lament reverberated inside Cadie until it blocked out the clatter swirling around her. The pool of blood expanded into a river on the sloped pavement, running toward the edge of the highway. Toward the woods.

Cars on the opposite side of the highway median flew by, unaware that a bear was dying and that they had all collectively killed it. Timbering forests, cutting paths for power lines, polluting the air. Corporations burying science. All creating the conditions for a fire that would drive this bear into moving traffic.

Stones dug into Cadie's palms as she crawled over the hot pavement.

Everyone should have to face the things they kill.

The animal let out a low, wet moan, followed by several stuttered, shallow breaths, and closed its eyes. People milling around in Cadie's peripheral vision blended into a smear of color and muted sounds. She crept closer on all fours, ready to spring back if the bear moved. The gamey air hung hot with grease and blood, mixed with spent fuel and desperation rising off the asphalt.

The raspy breath sounds from the unconscious animal slowed, then stopped.

Cadie inhaled deeply, holding the bear's final breath in her lungs until it burned. She sank her fingers into the coarse fur on the animal's neck.

"I'm so sorry," she whispered close to its ear, and stroked its fur.

She increased the pressure on the bear's neck, seeking out contact with its skin, sticky with blood. A weak pulse fluttered against her fingertips. Thick neck muscles stiffened and fell slack under her hand. A gentle warmth moved up Cadie's arm and torso, uncoiling the knots in her own neck and back as the bear slipped away.

Approaching sirens and stranded drivers yelling at cell phones spun into a background hum. A thick wood flanked the highway, arching down into a valley where countless deer, moose, bear, and foxes took refuge from the fires pushing them from their homes. Motionless cars lined up behind them as far as she could see.

Cadie got back in her car, and inched her way back and forth until she found a narrow path around the pileup.

"Hey, you can't leave the scene." A teenager banged his hand on the hood of her car as she maneuvered toward the shoulder. Cadie ignored him and drove off as the first emergency vehicle lights flashed in her rearview mirror. The rumble strips on the side of the road rattled her teeth. She clenched her jaw and accelerated toward the university.

※

Cadie sprinted up the stairs and burst through the stairwell doors into the third-floor hallway. Bodies lined the dark corridor, some standing, some seated with their backs up against the wall. She stopped, confused by the crowd. A young woman with faded purple hair stood up and started a slow, rhythmic clap as Cadie walked down the hall. Students wearing shirts from colleges all over New England joined the steady beat, clapping, stomping, pounding on doors as if they were marching her off to battle.

A lump rose up in Cadie's throat as she tried to maintain her composure. Who were all these people who had shown up for her? She nodded awkwardly at the crowd as she made her way to the assigned room. The slow, steady beat continued as she opened the door, and persisted after she closed it behind her.

Thea stood in front of the committee, pointing to one of Cadie's slides projected on the wall.

"Nice timing," Thea said without looking at Cadie. "We started without you."

"Did you get my message? There was an accident. They closed the highway." She brushed her hair out of her face and tried to compose herself. Her hands smelled of bear and death.

"We've been reviewing your research," said Dr. Larry Spencer, a professor Cadie had worked for years earlier.

"Then you understand the beetles are responsible for much of the die-off." Cadie tried to catch her breath and sound calm. "You saw the data. Forget my slides and look out the window." Cadie gestured to the windows facing out toward the highway. "I'm sorry I'm late, but you need to understand why."

Thea gave Cadie a cautionary look.

"I hit a bear on the way here. A black bear. It ran out of the woods onto the highway. The entire southbound lane of 93 is closed because I hit a bear. My right front fender is a crumpled mess and I think I broke a bunch of laws by leaving the scene of the accident to get here. But this is important.

"I'm the one who hit the bear, but why did it run onto the highway? Because its home was on fire," Cadie said. "It's going to happen again and again, but it's not just the animals that will be displaced or injured. It's us. No one got hurt in Hobson. That might not be the case next time."

Thea nodded to Cadie to continue.

"We can prevent some of these fires if we can predict where they will happen and head them off. I prepared this presentation for you, but you can read my slides on your own if you want. Look out the window. That cloud of smoke you see, that's all the evidence you need." Her voice no longer shook. She stared above the heads of the committee members at the smoke as it stretched out over the mountains. "Hobson is burning right now. People are evacuating. Tomorrow it will be another town. Then another. Washington can tell you to look away. But I'm begging you, look out that window."

Cadie switched the screen to a map of areas she suspected might be vulnerable, and areas she had not been able to assess yet. "I could tell you about the potential loss of trees, the deer, moose, and bear populations at risk. I could tell you how many homes might be at risk. But if I'm honest with you, those are not the things that keep me awake at night.

"This is my childhood about to burn." She pointed at Maple Crest on the map. "The forts I built in the woods, my hammock, the chipmunks I tried to capture, the hollow trees where I hid my secrets." Cadie swallowed to keep her voice from cracking. "This is a disaster for the state of New Hampshire. But for me, it's personal, and I know it is for each of you, too."

Cadie moved her hands as she spoke, the smell of the bear wafting closer with each gesture. She paused, afraid the smell might make her gag.

"Politicians don't want facts. But the people do." Cadie flipped to the next slide. Muffled sounds of the pounding in the hall rose up through the floor. Fists beat on the door, the walls. Cadie's presentation notes trembled as the vibrations climbed the table and shook the pages. Each beat resounded in the soles of Cadie's feet.

The committee members fixed their eyes on the map, assessing their own personal risk.

"You can tell me I'm restricted from doing research on federal lands, but that doesn't change the fact that the bark beetles are already here. I know the models say they shouldn't be here. Screw those projections. They're here. We can protect some of these communities if we collect enough data to predict patterns and thin affected areas. But it's not just my research in jeopardy." Cadie pointed to the door separating them from the students waiting, clapping, stomping in the hallway. "I can't even guess how many environmental research projects this ban impacts. What you decide here today has broader implications than stopping a few fires. Other institutions will look at this decision as a precedent."

"The research is compelling." Thea jumped up to distribute copies of Cadie's map.

"This meeting isn't about the validity or even the quality of your research. It's about the fact that you broke the law and violated our ethics standards by illegally collecting samples," Dr. Spencer said.

"The forests are burning. I'm not going to look away. And neither should you. People are going to die. You want that on your conscience?"

"Cadie," Thea said.

"I'm willing to put my career on the line because I know I'm right. I'm pretty sure all of you know I'm right too." Cadie slapped the packet down on a table. "Are you willing to pretend this doesn't matter because you don't want to cross a line that shouldn't exist in the first place?"

Cadie stood in front of the silent room and prayed that she hadn't destroyed her career.

"This isn't the most professional presentation, Ms. Kessler,"

Dr. Spencer said as he flipped through the pages Thea had handed out. "But I can't argue with your evidence. I'm from California. I've seen what these beetles leave behind."

"Ms. Kessler, are you hurt?" another committee member asked Cadie. "You're bleeding."

Thea pointed to Cadie's temple. Cadie touched her face to find a crusted smear of bear blood.

"I'm fine."

"Give us some time to review your materials and we'll get back to you," the chairwoman said.

"Thank you," Thea said. "We—"

"No," Cadie interrupted. "We can't give you time. There isn't any time."

"I'm inclined to agree," Dr. Spencer said.

"We cannot sit here and publicly condone breaking the law," the chairwoman said.

"Then fire me now," Cadie said. "If scientists rolled over every time we encountered some inane obstacle, we'd all still believe the world was flat. Looking back, no one will give a damn about this university's protocols. They might not remember my bark beetles. But they will remember that we had a chance to stand up for something and we chose not to."

"You are putting us in an awkward position," the chairwoman said.

"*I'm* putting *you* in an awkward position? I'm the one climbing mountains in ninety-five-degree weather to hunt these beetles. I'm the one risking my career to do the right thing. I'm sorry that's uncomfortable for you." Cadie began gathering up her papers. She had not intended to resign when she walked in the room. Her intention had been to fight for her job, but as she addressed the committee she understood it wasn't her job she needed to safeguard, it was her research. She needed to protect the truth. The bark beetles were in New Hampshire. The beetles would lead to increased fire risk. She might work for the university, but her loyalty remained with the forest, the animals, and the communities at risk.

"Fire me. Report me. Do what you need to do. I'm not sitting on this. I have the data. I'll publish it without the university's backing."

"If she goes, I go." Thea stood up and looked at Cadie with a furrowed brow offset by a reluctant smile. "If we aren't willing to fight for the access to do legitimate research, then what are we doing?"

"You don't have to do this, Thea," Cadie said.

Thea remained standing.

Dr. Spencer stood up and cleared his throat. "I think I speak for the committee that we cannot officially condone breaking the law. But my house is on that map, and so are the houses of everyone in this room, along with thousands of other residences and businesses. I would rather risk punishment for doing the right thing than have regrets for being a coward."

Cadie bit on the inside of her lip to keep from smiling. She was winning him over.

The professor made deliberate eye contact with the four other committee members, each of whom nodded their heads in agreement.

"I look forward to reading your full report," the chairwoman said with a slight smile. "After you finish collecting your data."

Cadie wanted to scream. No, she wanted to roar from deep in her gut. For the bear, for Juan, for her missing thrush. *Do this thing right*, she told herself. *Don't be afraid.*

"Thank you." Cadie nodded at each committee member as they shook her hand before leaving.

"God help us if this goes bad," the chairwoman said to Cadie's professor as they filed out of the room. "I was hoping to retire in a few years."

Cadie tried to maintain a professional demeanor until Thea closed the door and they were alone in the room.

"What the hell just happened?" Cadie threw the stack of papers in the air and let them rain down around herself and Thea. "I was half expecting to be led away in handcuffs."

Thea shook her head. "One suggestion: before your next hearing, wash the blood off your face."

"I think it added to the urgency of my presentation." Cadie wondered if Thea could smell the bear on her.

"We need to get serious now. I don't know what's up with you, but you need to get your shit together." Thea's gray-streaked braid hung over her shoulder, swinging like a pendulum as she bent over to organize her bag. "Your lack of professionalism reflects poorly on me too."

"I know. I'll get it together. I promise."

"Are you okay?" Thea asked.

"I'm fine." Cadie squeezed her eyes shut, trying to push out the image of the bear's eyes staring at her. "No. I'm actually not fine. But I will be."

Thea pulled a bottle of water from her backpack, handed it to Cadie, and gestured for her to sit down.

"It just darted out in front of me." Cadie put her hands up to her face. "I can't get the smell off of me. And my car—"

"But you're not hurt. And your research is safe." Thea pressed Cadie's hands between her own to calm the shaking. "I know you well enough to tell something else is eating at you. Something that doesn't have anything to do with fires or bears. I also know you well enough to know you won't want to talk about it."

"I'm that transparent?" Unpacking the past in recent days had sharpened the edges of compressed memories, making it harder to force them down when they threatened to consume her.

"I'm here if you want to talk, you know." Thea refused to break eye contact, giving Cadie the feeling that Thea knew exactly how uncomfortable she was making Cadie feel.

Cadie didn't know how to put the whirl of emotions into words, in part because she couldn't distinguish between them. Guilt over killing the bear felt less acute than a broader regret about having contributed to the big-picture circumstance that led to the drought, the fire, the bear's loss of home. She was as guilty as anyone, maybe more so, because she had seen it coming. Indignation at the government's attempts to squash her research stirred an urgent rage in her belly. And under all of it, Cadie suppressed a low-grade terror at what awaited her when she returned to Maple Crest, what awaited Raúl if an investigation revealed his immigration status, what would happen to Dolores if she were charged as an accessory to murder. And Garrett. She couldn't allow the flutter in her stomach to disarm her when she needed to remain focused.

Thea smiled gently, letting Cadie know she did not need to respond. For a brief moment, none of Cadie's regrets or fears seemed quite as threatening now that Thea had put her life's work on the line because she believed in Cadie.

"Are you one hundred percent engaged in this?" Thea pointed to the map behind her. Thea had bumped the projector, shifting the angle of the image and distorting the map of New Hampshire. The eastern edge of the state swelled with a cartoonish bulge emphasizing the locations where Cadie had predicted fires were most likely to occur. "This is your chance to do something important. If I'm going to risk losing tenure, getting fired, and possibly arrested, I need to know you're all in."

"I'm all in." Cadie threw her arms around Thea. After four years of working together, Cadie had never hugged Thea. They had never gone out for a beer or shared anything personal. For the first time, Cadie wondered why.

24

After the hallway cleared of cheering grad students, Cadie went to the restroom to clean up. She washed her hands four times and doused them in lemon-scented lotion. But the smell of the bear permeated her skin, her hair, her clothes.

It would be easy to go back to her apartment, less than half an hour away from the university, and immerse herself in her work. She could sink into her bed, hide behind her cairn. Never return to Maple Crest. Easy. Safe. She could disappear. Yet something in that town refused to release her. The cord she had worked so hard to sever now felt stitched into her soul in a way that made her insides ache when she thought of breaking it.

She owed it to Daniela to go back.

I'm home. I need you here.

The space Daniela occupied in her mind had swelled from a child-shaped hiding place in the woods to a fortress Cadie could not ignore.

I need you here.

She leaned close to the bathroom mirror and wiped the smear of bear blood from her forehead and smoothed her messy hair. Although she wanted to believe her instinct to return to Maple Crest grew from her commitment to help Daniela, the strongest pull came from the surge of adrenaline that flooded her body every time she thought of Garrett. The Summer Kid. He believed in her work, which fueled her ambition to be right. To protect the forest and the people she loved. To protect the town that wouldn't let her go.

She crumpled the paper towel covered in the bear's blood and threw it in the trash.

Cadie had to be all in.

On the two-hour trip back to Maple Crest she drove slowly, watching the shoulders for anything that moved. The smoke had stretched to a thin band, billowing like a slow-motion banner over the mountains ahead of her. Halfway through the drive, she rolled down the windows and let her hair whip around her face. She turned on the radio and sang quietly to a string of familiar songs. The rattle of her loose fender, which she and Thea had duct-taped in place, changed pitch as she sped up.

Maybe she could work the incident with the bear into her future TED Talk. She could tell the story of storming into the meeting late with bear blood on her face and demanding the committee support her work. *When someone says you're overreacting, but you know you're right, keep reacting until it's over.*

Her ears popped as the road climbed toward Maple Crest. By the time she turned down Garrett's bumpy dirt road, a sliver of optimism had taken hold. Maybe Garrett was right. Maybe this one truth did not need to rise. Raúl and Dolores would be safe if they could all stay quiet. Maybe no one needed to know what happened in those woods.

Garrett's driveway crossed over the creek on a wooden bridge similar to the one on Cadie's driveway. The acres of marshlands that separated her home from Garrett's had dried up over the last three years, leaving a crusty swath of brown in the aerial photos Cadie monitored. The wetland vegetation had died off, rendering it a tinderbox.

Cadie, I'm down on the dock. A yellow sticky note, curling in the heat, clung to the front door of the small cabin. She took the sticky note with her and pushed the door open.

She expected to feel a prickle of foreboding as she crossed the threshold into the cottage that had once been Clyde's home. In her imagination, the run-down, windowless house leaned to one side and likely had a dungeon in the basement. Instead, she found herself in a cozy cabin that smelled of aged pine.

Large windows framed a bright kitchen. Cabinets with door

hinges but no doors held canisters of coffee, cereal, rice, and pasta in clear containers. Carved into the pantry door frame, etchings marked Garrett's childhood growth. She ran her fingers over the markings that stopped when Garrett was eight, the year his parents died.

Sun-bleached silhouettes on a yellow pegboard wall memorialized pots and pans that had long since been displaced by mesh baskets full of rubber bands, calculators, duct tape, and fishing tackle. The worn floorboards in the house did not creak as she walked. The lack of feedback made her feel uneasy.

Cadie pressed the sticky note flat on the counter and pulled out the note she'd found inside the beech tree. The handwriting looked completely different. Garrett wrote his sticky-note message in felt tip with tight, neat letters that swished up slightly at the end of each word. The note from the beech tree was written by a heavier hand, with strong, decisive letters that slanted a bit to the left. She folded both notes and slipped them into her wallet.

An open window gave her a clear view of the rock ledge she used to climb to deliver Garrett books. The flat area at the top of the rock had grown over with low, scraggly brush. She forced herself to remember. The lawn chair, the box of fishing tackle. The smell of a gunshot.

Juan died there. Right there. Where exactly had he fallen? How close had Cadie been to him as she clung to the tree root? Her pulse quickened, but she couldn't look away from the space where she imagined the body must have lain.

A hummingbird crashed into the window overlooking the porch. Cadie jumped away from the glass and froze as she waited for the bird to rise and fly off. When it didn't get up, Cadie ran outside. The hummingbird lay motionless in a puddle of sunlight below the window. She squatted over the tiny creature and touched a finger to its iridescent wing. It sprang up, almost touching her cheek, and disappeared into the woods.

Cadie fell backward against the porch rail, breathless. She held her hands to her face and inhaled the lingering lemon lotion to calm her racing heart.

Garrett's property rose from the water at a steep angle, large boulders and a rock face climbing out of the water to the left of a small, pebbly beach. His boat looked too big for the rickety pier, as if the boat held the pier steady instead of the other way around.

Garrett waved as Cadie descended the deck stairs. He stood chest-deep in the water, no shirt. He wore a diving mask and held a wrench in one hand. No longer the pinched boy with a nearly concave chest, Garrett had grown into a chiseled leanness that revealed every twitching muscle in his shoulders and torso as he shook water from his hair like a puppy.

"Give me two minutes," he said. "I hit a rock this morning during the wakeboard lesson. I've never seen the lake water so low. I'm almost finished replacing the prop."

"No rush. I'm early," Cadie said.

Garrett drew in a deep breath and disappeared under the boat. After a minute, he burst through the surface with a big smile. He grabbed a towel and dried his face before pulling himself up to sit on the pier.

"Good lesson?" she said. "Other than hitting a rock."

"We didn't lose anyone, so it was a stellar day." Garrett examined the ruined prop. "I was mostly worried about fixing the boat in time to take you out."

The tips of Cadie's ears burned.

Garrett put a T-shirt on. "I need to change before we head out. Want to come up?" He walked backward, his wispy hair already drying in spiked tufts that looked like corn silk. He swung his arms as he walked, reminding Cadie of a scarecrow.

The thin cotton of his shirt clung to his damp body. Water dripped off his swim trunks, leaving a trail on the sunbaked boards leading to the kitchen door.

Cadie followed him, training her eyes on each wet footprint so she wouldn't inadvertently look toward the rock ledge.

"I'll be right out. Make yourself at home," Garrett said as they entered the kitchen.

The rusty spring from her door lay on his kitchen counter.

"How'd the meeting go?" Garrett emerged in a fresh T-shirt and khaki shorts. His cheeks glowed pink under his tan.

"Not the way I expected. I hit a—" Cadie paused at the memory of the bear's blinking eyes. Witnessing the animal's death felt suddenly intimate, not something she was ready to share. "I hit a roadblock and almost missed the meeting."

He slouched as he leaned on the counter with one hand. His outline, although bigger and broader now, followed the same angles Cadie remembered from the boy on the pier. She doubted she would ever be able to look at him without seeing both versions—the boy and the man.

"I still have a job. For now, at least. All these grad students, I don't even know where the hell they came from, showed up to support me. I think they're all looking at my situation as a test case on whether or not research institutions are going to push back against the restrictions cutting off access to public land," Cadie said, keeping her back to the window overlooking the ledge. "They think I'm some martyr, but honestly, I just want to prove I'm right about these beetles. They can fight for their own research." Sharing her news with Garrett felt comfortable, something she could get used to.

"Sorry to keep you waiting so long," he said.

"I was early," Cadie said.

"But you've been waiting for me your whole life." The corners of his mouth turned up.

"You found the book."

"It's about time you wrote back." He put a bottle of wine, two glasses, and several plastic food containers in a cooler and they walked back down to the pier.

Clouds cast a patchwork of shadows across the mountains as they motored toward the center of the lake. They cruised by the marina where Garrett and Tino taught wakeboard lessons, and by the landing where the high school crew team launched their boats. A velvety breeze gathered as they moved into the opening of the bay. Cadie closed her eyes. The spray of the lake, the tenderness of the evening, stirred a longing for something she couldn't name. Escape, maybe? A respite from her fear, a break from fires and guilt.

Garrett slowed down and cut the engine.

"Any updates on that fire?" Garrett said.

"No major damage. Not that I wanted to see the Hobson fire happen, but I have to admit the timing helped make my case."

"We should celebrate." He brushed a strand of hair out of Cadie's face, leaned close, and squinted. "I knew it. Your eyes *are* green."

Her whole life had been moored to the distant specter of that summer. Tethered to Garrett.

"I hope white's okay?" He poured two glasses of Chardonnay. He reached into a cooler and lifted out carefully prepared containers of cheese, olives, grapes, smoked salmon, and a baguette, already sliced. He arranged the food on a cutting board.

The horizon bloomed with an apricot glow that seemed as thoughtfully planned as the meal Garrett laid out. She sucked on a briny olive as he arranged separate knives for a hard cheese and Brie, her favorite. Condensation slid down the wine bottle, leaving warped trails on the label.

The unmoored boat rolled with the swells.

Cadie swallowed a sip of wine. She wanted to feel calm and re-laxed, focused on the present moment. But the itch and gnaw of unease wouldn't release her as her mind drifted from the sunset to the bear to her encounter with Clyde at the rec center.

"You look like him," Cadie said. The patchy gray scruff on Gar-rett's chin blended in with the rest of his three-day-old beard, a shade or two darker than the lemon-yellow hair she remembered.

Garrett stared at the chalky smear of sunset blanketing the mountains. Cadie thought for a moment he hadn't heard her. He took a long swallow of wine. "He's my mother's half brother."

"I saw him today." A gust of wind stirred the silvery leaves of a birch tree extending over the lake. Tightly curled tips of young lily shafts pierced the surface under the willowy birch branches. The swift breeze skimmed the surface of the lake, lifting the edges of mature lily pads to reveal their red underbellies.

Garrett shifted in his seat and cracked his neck.

"He was lurking around Sal at the rec center, leaning over her, putting his hand on her shoulder like they were old friends. I think he did it on purpose to threaten me, or send me a message or something."

"He volunteers there." Garrett offered Cadie a piece of bread.

"It wouldn't be the first time he tried to scare me. He found me, alone outside the library one night after the shooting." Cadie had never told anyone but Daniela about the encounter. "He said he'd expose Daniela's family if I told anyone."

Garrett looked down at his sneakers and chewed on his lip for a few seconds. "He won't hurt Sal. He wouldn't have hurt you back then either. Or the Garcias. He was scared."

"Are you kidding? I had every right to be afraid of him. Then and now." Cadie stood up and walked to the back of the boat.

"No, I get it. I'm sorry. I'm sorry he scared you." Garrett followed her. He looked agitated as he combed his fingers through his hair. "I'm not saying he's a fantastic guy or anything. He never knew what was the right thing to do. He made a lot of mistakes, but he never gave up on me."

"He made sure you didn't starve, so now I'm supposed to just forget that he killed someone?" The humidity of late summer wobbled between warmth and chill.

"He set up a college account for me right after the incident. Instead of living here, we moved a couple of miles away and he rented the cottage out. He banked all the rental income for my tuition. He said that's what my mom would have wanted. We moved away the summer after I met you and lived in a one-bedroom dive a few towns over. He started landscaping, then eventually started his own business."

"None of that makes what he did any better. Isn't there any part of you aching to tell the truth?" Cadie said.

"There would be a lot of fallout, you know. Just because we can't be charged, doesn't mean there won't be serious ramifications for all of us. The hospital could fire Daniela. You could lose that job you're fighting to keep. And me? How could I keep my job as a police officer?" He took a swallow of wine. "I'm meeting with the chief tomorrow. I can convince him to back off Raúl. You promised me two more days to figure this out."

Cadie had been trying to evade the natural order of conse-quences for nearly thirty years. The cloak she hid behind felt thin and worn, but she clung to it like an old friend. She could wait two more days.

Time seemed to be moving slower and faster simultaneously since her past had begun seeping out in wisps and torrents. Floating in the middle of the lake offered a respite, as if she and Garrett had stepped outside of time.

She folded bits of smoked salmon on the bread. It had been a long time since someone had made her dinner. She smiled remem-bering the kissy noises Daniela used to make whenever Cadie men-tioned the Summer Kid.

"What are you grinning about?" Garrett said.

"It feels like this conversation was a long time coming. Like we're supposed to be here together right now."

Mountains cresting in the distance appeared crisp, as if Cadie could reach out and crush them in her fist. Green leaves tempered with prematurely brown edges. She closed her eyes so she didn't have to look at the warming of her forest or the exposed watermarks on the rocks near shore. She wanted the lake and the mountains to look and feel the way they had before it all turned dark. Before the boat, before Garrett, before Clyde.

Cadie wrapped her arms around her waist against the cooling air. Garrett pulled a fleece blanket from under a seat cushion and put it over her shoulders. A wave rocked the boat and she allowed her body to fall against him. Nothing could touch them in the mid-dle of the lake. Not the fires, not Clyde.

She closed her eyes and breathed in the mist, the clouds, and the linger of honeysuckle.

Garrett's phone rang. Cadie willed him not to answer it.

The voice on the other end shouted, but Cadie couldn't make out the words.

"There's another fire," Garrett said after he hung up. "We need to go back. I'm really sorry."

"Where? Is it bad?"

"It sounds pretty minor. Just a brush fire. We need to set up some detours outside of town near Talbot's Sugarhouse. It sounds like it's mostly under control, no buildings involved. It shouldn't take longer than an hour or two to reroute traffic. I don't suppose you want to meet me at the Deer Park later?"

"Yeah, maybe. I'll see if Daniela's up for shooting some pool. We could meet you there."

Garrett scrunched his nose up and raked his hand through his hair.

"What?"

"Daniela doesn't like me much."

"Can you blame her?"

"Not really, I guess," he said. "I was looking forward to a quiet night with you."

"We've got all the time in the world." Cadie tried not to let the disappointment seep into her voice as he turned the boat around.

25

The morning after the search party at Crittenden Farm, Cadie lay in bed as her parents hustled around the house getting ready to go into the studio. "I'm going back to bed." Cadie tried to make her voice sound sleepy when her mom came to say good-bye. "I'll call you at lunch."

After her parents' car drove out of the driveway, Cadie sat up in her bed. Garrett's unfinished reading list stared at her. She moved the stack of *A Connecticut Yankee in King Arthur's Court*, *Great Expectations*, *To Kill a Mockingbird*, and *A Wrinkle in Time* to the other side of the room, but the melancholy of unread books accumulated like a raincloud.

A rapid pounding on the door startled her.

Clyde could have changed his mind about trusting Cadie to stay quiet. He could have watched to see when her parents left.

Friar leapt off Cadie's bed and ran toward the kitchen.

"Friar, come back," Cadie hissed.

The pounding grew more furious, then stopped abruptly. Cadie crawled across the floor and locked her bedroom door. Footsteps marched around the porch, crunched on the gravel driveway. She ducked inside her closet and pulled the door closed. She wriggled behind her long winter coat in the back corner and tried to make herself small, invisible.

A pebble crashed against her window. Then another.

"Cadie, I know you're in there," Daniela yelled. "I saw your parents and they told me."

She felt silly sitting on the closet floor, but she didn't come out right away. It was easier to avoid Daniela than to face her accusing eyes.

Friar barked loudly from the hall and scratched at the outside of Cadie's door.

"Cadie Kessler, you can't hide forever," Daniela yelled. "Open the door."

Cadie pulled herself up and opened the kitchen door.

"We need to talk." Daniela pressed her face inches from the opening. Instead of her usual ponytail, Daniela wore her hair loose and unbrushed.

"About what?" Cadie opened the door.

"What do you think?"

Maybe Daniela was pushing Cadie to see if she would keep Dolores's secret. It felt like a trap. Cadie's insides went cold as if her blood had stopped moving.

"I trusted you," Daniela said.

Cadie walked into the family room, lowered herself onto the couch, and squeezed a fistful of her grandmother's afghan.

"Did your mom ask you about the kid? About Garrett?"

"I think she forgot about that part. I'm only here because I need to know what happened to Juan. We have to go back and ask that kid."

"No way. It's too dangerous." Cadie couldn't let Daniela talk to Garrett. He might tell her that Cadie and Dolores had helped him.

"What if Juan's fine and we're worrying for nothing?" Cadie pulled the afghan over her head. The pilled wool smelled like everything that had ever happened in her life. Her mother's beef stroganoff, the lake, Friar's breath. But instead of comforting her, it amplified her unease.

"Maybe he's hurt," Daniela said. "Maybe he is still at that kid's house. Maybe we could still save him."

"He's not okay!" Cadie yelled, and pulled the blanket tighter around her head.

"How do you know?"

"I know." Friar licked her toes, trying to comfort her. She pulled her feet under the blanket with her. Her breath came fast and heavy and she felt dizzy. Her insides felt like they were going to explode from the pressure of all the truths and untruths battling inside her.

"Tell me what you know." Daniela yanked the blanket off.

Daniela deserved to know what happened to Juan. "After I left your house, I ran into the woods. I couldn't go home. My parents would have known something was wrong."

Daniela sat down next to Cadie.

"I followed the creek back along the easement toward Garrett's property. I don't know why I went. It was stupid. Then I heard them." Letting a half-truth out might relieve some of the pressure.

"Heard who?"

"Who do you think? They were dragging something. I hid in a bush. At first, I couldn't tell what, but they got closer." Cadie looked up to assess if Daniela believed her story. "It was Juan. They were dragging him through the woods."

Daniela squeezed her eyes shut as Cadie squashed her last bit of hope that Juan had survived. "Was he . . . ?"

"Yeah. He was dead." Saying the words made Cadie feel sick.

"What did you do?"

"They started digging a hole and I snuck away." Lying to Daniela made her feel sicker.

Daniela got up and walked around the room. Her chin trembled, but she did not cry. "He was my friend."

"I know. I'm sorry." Cadie was sorry for breaking her promise and telling Dolores about Garrett, sorry about lying to Daniela.

"Take me there." Daniela stood with a balled-up fist on each hip.

"No way. I'm not going back there. Ever."

Daniela pulled at Cadie's arms, but Cadie let her body go limp.

"Cadie Kessler, you are going to take me to that grave."

Inside her head Cadie screamed an apology. She wanted to throw herself on the ground and beg Daniela to forgive her. *You are the best friend I've ever had. I would do anything to take it all back.* But Cadie couldn't speak the words crushing her from the inside. Her tongue felt swollen. Her thoughts jumbled.

Cadie squeezed her eyes shut, pushing out the echo of the shovel in the dirt that played over and over in her mind. *Chush, thud. Chush, thud.*

"Please." Daniela didn't look mad as much as she did desperate. She dropped to her knees in front of the couch. "I need to see it."

Cadie didn't know how seeing the grave would help anything, but maybe if Cadie helped her find it, Daniela would forgive Cadie for having told Dolores in the first place.

They walked through the woods without speaking. Friar stayed close to her legs. Everything looked normal, which made her want to yell at the gurgling waters of Silas Creek, scream at the trees, and shake Daniela. Nothing should ever be normal again. The sunshine, the squeak of her sneakers, it all felt wrong. She wished she were back in her closet, hiding behind her winter coat.

She paused at the cluster of bushes where she and Daniela first met that day in the woods. Blueberries were scattered farther apart on the August branches, no longer slipping off in lush clusters of eight or ten at a time. Some bushes had already given up and begun transitioning to a subtle flush of red leaves.

Cadie pulled off a leaf and turned it over. Lines of purplish red spiked up the underside of the leaf, defining the exact place where the bush had declared summer over. Maybe that's how summer always ended. A moment that turned one leaf from green to red, a moment no one noticed unless they were looking for it.

The young birch tree still lay across the buckled barbed-wire fence. Brown leaves curled on the ends of the branches chattered in the breeze.

"We have to crawl under." Cadie stretched her jaw open and shut.

She waded into the water and dropped to her hands and knees. She crawled under the opening, shimmying so low her stomach and chest were half submerged. Careful not to catch her hair on a barb, she ducked through the small space, twisted sideways to get one shoulder, then the next through the opening. As Cadie shimmied under the fence, a barb snagged the back of her shorts. She tugged, but it wouldn't release. Daniela splashed over to Cadie and stood in the water above her.

"Are you going to help me?"

"You look pretty funny. Like a fish on a hook," Daniela said.

Cadie's hands and lower legs felt numb from the cold water. Sharp rocks poked into her knees. She tugged harder, shaking the fence. "Unhook it!" she yelled. Tears burned her eyes. "Now!"

Daniela untangled the barb and Cadie slithered through.

Cadie sat in the cold water staring at Daniela on the other side of the fence.

"It wasn't funny. I'm sorry," Daniela said. "We can go back if you want."

Cadie shook her head. "Are you coming?"

Daniela crawled under the fence. Friar followed.

It seemed darker on that side. The trees stood taller and huddled closer to block out the light. The girls walked through the water where they wouldn't leave any footprints.

"You know I wouldn't have left you there, right?" Daniela whispered.

Cadie stopped in the middle of the creek after they had walked about fifteen minutes. Cadie guided them toward the burial site, but let Daniela find it first.

Daniela touched Cadie's shoulder and pointed to the mound of freshly turned earth covered in rocks about twenty feet from the creek.

"Can we go now?" Cadie whispered. "What if someone comes back?"

Daniela climbed the bank.

Cadie tried to grab Friar's collar to stop him from following Daniela, but he pulled free of Cadie's grip.

Daniela knelt in the loose soil in front of the oval-shaped mound. She looked so small among the tall trees. Daniela squeezed a fistful of mud until it oozed from between her fingers. Her knuckles blanched, then burned red. Her shoulders rocked with small heaves that mounted into silent, convulsive spasms.

Cadie climbed the bank and stood beside her. She ached to hug her friend, to apologize, and tell her the whole truth. That she had been there. That she had dug up the soil Daniela now held in her fist. Instead, Cadie put a hand on the bare skin of Daniela's shoulder. She wanted to say something to comfort her, but her mouth felt too dry to speak. Daniela looked up with eyes so wide with fear that Cadie's knees buckled and she dropped down beside her friend. The mud sucked both girls down until their knees all but disappeared into the earth.

"We should say something. Like a funeral or a prayer." Daniela straightened her back and jutted her chin forward. "Juan made me laugh. He could do these stupid faces. And he could lift anything. My dad always waited for Juan to help carry heavy stuff. He liked my mom's cooking a lot. She used to bring him leftovers all the time. But mostly, Juan was my friend. I don't know anything else about him." Daniela looked at Cadie with desperation in her eyes. "No one knows what happened. No one's going to be sad."

"Juan was brave," Cadie said. "He stuck up for you when those guys teased you at Angie's. And he wanted Clyde to go to the police and confess about robbing that store, so he was honest, right? And he left Angie a tip after she gave them free pie. He didn't have to do that." The wound on her thumb from where she had sliced her skin days earlier throbbed like a drumbeat, pulsing in her hand, pounding in her chest.

"That's not enough," Daniela said. "Even if someone finds him someday, no one will even remember his name or be sad."

"We'll remember," Cadie said. "We will be sad."

Daniela scooped up a handful of dirt from the mound and let it fall between her fingers. She wiped her mud-smeared face. Her eyelids hung heavy as if she hadn't slept in days.

Cadie's shirt clung to her skin, her wet denim shorts hung heavy and chafed her legs when she moved. Sand in her wet sneakers had rubbed blisters on her heels. Cadie felt certain she would never smile again, never feel happy again.

Daniela stared at a mosquito on her arm, but didn't swat it away. She didn't flinch as it bit her and sucked her blood. Cadie plucked a stone out of the mud and added it to the bottom of the cross Dolores had formed. She slipped another small stone into her pocket.

She couldn't look at Daniela as they trudged back through the creek. They shimmied silently under the barbed fence. Daniela walked several paces in front of her until they got to the path splitting off to their respective homes.

"See ya," Cadie said.

"Maybe." Daniela walked into the forest toward her house without looking back.

Cadie felt as if her insides had turned to cardboard. She couldn't feel anything. Not hunger, although she hadn't eaten since breakfast. She didn't feel cold anymore, although her clothes were drenched. She stood motionless in the woods listening to Daniela's footsteps until she couldn't hear them anymore.

From the lake she heard the flapping wings and slapping feet of a loon running across the lake's surface as it tried to lift off into the air. It failed and tried again, but never got into the air. She wondered where the loon had been planning to go, and if any of the other loons would notice if it didn't show up.

Daniela sat on the steps of the hardware store the Saturday before school started. Cadie's mother dragged her into Angie's for breakfast. Daniela leaned up against the wooden railing and picked at her cuticles.

"We should invite Daniela to eat with us," Cadie's mom said as she stopped to wave.

Daniela looked up through stormy eyes.

"Let's eat by ourselves." Cadie pulled on her mother's elbow.

"Is everything okay with you girls?"

"God, Mom. We're fine. I just want to have breakfast with you."

Cadie had called three times the day after she and Daniela had gone to the grave. And twice the following day. But Daniela never called back.

The hollow space in Cadie's gut echoed with shared loneliness as she watched Daniela's shoulders slump. Daniela tapped a foot in a muddy puddle below the bottom step, not caring—maybe not noticing—as the brown spray splattered up her calf.

Cadie wanted to run across the street and throw her arms around Daniela so they could squeeze each other until they had wrung all the ugly memories out. She took a hesitant step toward Daniela.

"Go ahead." Her mother rubbed her shoulder.

Daniela stood up and turned her back. From across the street Cadie felt the creak of each bowed wooden step as Daniela climbed the stairs and disappeared inside the store. The door slammed shut.

26

How many times had Cadie sworn to herself that she would never become one of those locals who hung out at the Deer Park shooting pool? Yet, there she stood, with a beer in one hand and a cue stick in the other. Peanut shells crunched under her feet as she lined up a shot. She closed one eye and wrinkled her nose at the stale beer infused in the felt of the grungy pool table. The white ball glanced off the closest ball and ricocheted into a corner.

"I guess you don't get much practice living in a hut in the mountains." Daniela set up her shot after Cadie's failed break.

"I don't live in a hut." Cadie looked over toward the door for the third time.

"So where was this fire Prince Charming ditched you for?" Daniela said.

"Over near Talbot's. But he said it's under control." Cadie wiped her sweaty palms on her jeans. "He should be here soon."

Music blared on the speaker above Cadie's head. She adjusted the low braid that hung down her back and looked at the door again.

Cadie ached to tell Daniela the whole story.

I buried him, Cadie wanted to scream. The weight that had been pressing on her for twenty-seven years contorted and twisted. *I was there. I dragged his body through the woods. I dug his grave and shoveled the dirt over his body, his eyes still open a sliver. It was me. And your mother.*

"I know you don't trust Garrett, but—"

"But what?" Daniela ground a peanut shell into the cement floor with the heel of her boot. "He has dreamy eyes?"

"He's got your family's best interests in mind. We both do."

"Are you kidding me? The only thing he cares about is protecting himself and his uncle."

"You have no idea what you're talking about."

"Then tell me. I feel like you two are conspiring behind my back, gambling with my family's safety." Daniela slid the pool cue back and forth over her fist as she lined up a shot. She squinted at the ball so fiercely it looked like she was trying to make it explode with the heat from her eyes.

The crack of colliding balls exploded in Cadie's chest. Her pulse leapt. She squeezed her pool stick until her hand hurt and her fingers felt numb. *Don't let go.* She imagined herself clinging to the vine on the stone wall at Garrett's house, the reek of gunpowder burning her nose as she locked her eyes on the arcing white vein that bent through the granite.

"Cadie? Hey, you okay?"

"I'm fine, why?" Cadie said. The gunpowder faded into the smell of beer-soaked peanut shells.

"It's your shot." Daniela tapped Cadie's pool stick with hers. "You're solid."

"Right."

Cadie squeezed the stick to hide her trembling fingers and lined up an easy shot, which she missed. The cue ball dropped into the corner pocket.

"Where were you just now? You ghosted on me for a minute." Daniela bounced her cue stick on its rubber heel.

"I remembered this thing I forgot to finish at work." Cadie retrieved the white ball and held it in her palm for Daniela to take.

We will never speak of this day. Ever. Cadie heard Dolores's voice in her mind.

The air in the room felt hotter than it had a few minutes earlier. Firefighters from a nearby town took a table behind them.

"You ask me, that Hobson fire looked a little too neat." A firefighter in his fifties waved his hand toward a waitress who didn't notice him. "They're blaming it on a campfire. But I don't know."

Cadie took a step backward toward the firefighters so she could hear better.

"So now you're a fire investigator?" his friend laughed.

"Maybe I should be. Something felt off."

Cadie wanted to grab the man by his collar and yell, *It's the fucking beetles, you imbecile! They shouldn't be here. They aren't supposed to be here.*

A man with worn construction boots leaned over the pool table, about to rack up the balls Cadie and Daniela were playing. He reeked of cement dust and sweat.

"Excuse me?" Daniela grabbed the rack from his hand. "Do you need something?"

"You done here? We're waiting for a table," the man said.

"We're going to be here awhile." Daniela moved to the other end of the table and sank the ten ball.

The guy looked like he was trying to think of something clever to say to Daniela, but Daniela flicked her wrist at him like a pest. "You're blocking my shot."

The guy, in his thirties with a work shirt from a construction company Cadie did not recognize, walked back to a group of men with similar logo shirts and hovered near a different table.

Cadie fingered the folded note in her pocket. *Go Home. Or someone will get hurt.* She had been planning on showing the note to Daniela, but this wasn't the place. The bar was getting too crowded. The crowd had doubled in size since they arrived. She looked at the Budweiser clock on the wall. Garrett should have been there by now. Maybe the fire was more involved than he had expected. She checked her phone, but, again, couldn't get a signal.

"Do you really like him?" Daniela said.

"I don't know. We have history." Cadie dropped the eight ball into the corner pocket. "Shit."

"Bad history."

"I need another drink," Cadie said. "Rack 'em up and I'll get us another round."

"Keep an eye out for my dad. He's finishing up inventory and said he might meet us for a beer."

Cadie pushed through the crowd toward the bar and ordered two more drinks.

Daniela stood next to the pool table, guarding it from interlopers. She swayed to David Bowie's voice as if in a trance. Her knees, hips, and shoulders moved in a subtle, continuous wave as she tilted her head back. Daniela looked lost in herself as she stepped around her cue stick like a dance partner. Cadie longed for Daniela's lack of inhibition. Even the cue looked graceful as it moved with her.

Ryan approached Daniela. His long, narrow face looked pinched, as it always had. In elementary school Cadie once told him he reminded her of Beaker from the Muppets, which made him cry, although she hadn't meant it as an insult. Cadie willed him to walk past Daniela, let her dance, let her drift away from all that weighed on her.

Wearing a Maple Crest Fire Department work shirt, Ryan leaned in too close to Daniela and whispered in her ear. Daniela pulled back when she saw Ryan so close to her face.

A hand moved across the small of Cadie's back and settled on her hip. Garrett pressed his lips against her ear. Not a kiss, but a breathy hello. She spun around and he kept his hand on her waist. He wore a plaid button-down shirt, jeans, and untied sneakers. He smelled like cinnamon gum. His lips were bright red like those of a child who had been running in the cold.

"Everything okay?" she said.

"They got it under control pretty easily."

"We have a table in the back." Cadie tried to sound casual. She walked slowly so his hand wouldn't break contact with her hip as they made their way through the crowd.

Still talking to Daniela, Ryan's eye went straight to Garrett's hand on Cadie. He slapped Garrett on the shoulder, sloshing his beer. "You and Cadie Kessler? Damn, Tierney."

"You know each other?" Daniela said to Ryan.

"Everybody knows Garrett." Ryan extended his hand, staring Garrett in the eyes, as if daring him not to accept.

Garrett lifted his chin and nodded in Ryan's direction, patted him on the shoulder, and walked past him.

"What was that?" Daniela said after Ryan walked away.

"We've had our moments," Garrett said. "He's a nasty drunk."

Raised voices at a pool table behind them morphed into shouting. The men from the construction crew were trying to take over a table where Tino and a friend were playing.

"This isn't the best place to be tonight." Garrett scanned the room. "The bank foreclosed on the Welker farm this morning. A bunch of folks got laid off, people who'll be drunk and angry tonight. And those assholes working on the condo site are here dumping salt into an open wound. They won't even hire local crews; brought these hacks in from Massachusetts instead."

Daniela turned to Garrett. "So, did you figure out your magic plan to protect my father?" She leaned her cue stick against the wall and put one hand on her hip.

"I met with the chief today." Garrett walked toward the corner, away from the gathering clusters of people. Cadie and Daniela followed. "He knows Raúl didn't have anything to do with it. He's just checking all the boxes."

Garrett paused, waiting for Daniela to acknowledge his update, but she appeared unimpressed. "Look, you should know, they ID'd the body earlier than expected. We got confirmation this afternoon."

"You said we had more time," Daniela said.

"I thought we did. I convinced the chief to hold off on releasing the name until after the dust from the foreclosure settles."

"So what? That buys time. It's not a solution," Daniela said.

A construction worker stumbled backward and bumped into their table, sloshing beer on the felt.

"Let's go somewhere else. We can't talk here." Cadie walked toward the door, expecting Garrett and Daniela to follow. But when she turned to talk to Daniela, she found a drunk construction worker behind her. Still standing by the pool table, Daniela spoke with wild gestures at Garrett, who sank his hands deeper into his pockets.

Cadie needed to get outside. The packed bar was sloppy with tension. The hum of a baseball game and the wail of music competed from opposite ends of the bar. A body sat on every bar stool, two rows of people behind them jockeying to get the bartender's attention.

At the far end of the bar, hunched over the counter, Clyde stared at Cadie.

She gasped out loud, although no one could hear her over the noise. She felt eleven years old again. Scared and small. The memory of Clyde's hand on her shoulder, pushing her up against the tree, burned on her skin. The taste of dust and dried leaves filled her mouth and she coughed. Had he been there on that bar stool watching her all night? She had imagined him in dark corners and under rocks, not in plain sight doing the things that normal people do. But now Clyde, the monster in her dreams, sat comfortably on a bar stool less than twenty feet away, drinking the same brand of beer she held in her hand.

His lack of surprise when she saw him told her he had been watching her for a while. Clyde did not avert his glassy eyes, did not acknowledge her.

Someone bumped Cadie from behind and she jumped. When she turned back to Clyde, he looked down at the half-empty beer he drank alone.

The music grew louder but could not drown out the thrum of discontent rising up from the crushed peanut shells. The colors in the room seemed off, as if someone had altered the filter on a camera lens.

Ryan yelled at two men who were angling for his pool table. "I said, I'm not done. Comprende?" Ryan's voice rose over the noise. He stumbled backward and bumped into Daniela, knocking her on the ground, spilling beer down the front of her shirt.

Tino reached down to give Daniela a hand up, but Ryan shoved

Tino away from Daniela. Cadie swam through the crowd toward them.

"Ryan, you need to walk away." Garrett switched into police mode. His posture straighter, his shoulders broader.

"We don't need you here," Ryan yelled over Garrett's shoulder at Tino. "I know one of you people buried that body in the woods. It's only a matter of time before we find out who."

"What the fuck, Ryan. I'm standing right here." Daniela backed away from him. "You know you're saying that to me too, right?"

"I'm not talking about you, Daniela." Ryan slurred his words as he tried to push past Garrett. "You're one of us."

"Are you fucking kidding me?" Daniela said.

Garrett took Ryan by the elbow and forcibly maneuvered him toward the door.

Cadie and Daniela tried to follow them toward the exit, but a crowd pushed back, hungry for something or someone to snap and break the tension choking the bar.

"Sal's right," Daniela said. "This town is full of hicks."

"It's not you. It's the goddamn illegals," Ryan shouted over his shoulder to Daniela, as Garrett pushed him through the exit.

A group of farm workers got up from a table in the corner and gathered behind Tino. The room seemed to shrink around them. The smell of bodies and beer stewed in the tight space. The bass from the sound system thumped in Cadie's chest, although the melody and words dissolved into the chaos. Everyone moved either toward her or away, in opposing currents.

A crowd followed Garrett and Ryan out onto the street.

Beneath the undulating hum of angry voices, tension rose off the cracked pavement. Strobe lights from two approaching police cars distorted faces to melted wax.

Raúl marched toward them from the direction of the hardware store. His long stride, his arms swinging at his sides, gave Raúl the appearance of a soldier headed into battle. Cadie turned to tell Daniela that Raúl was coming, but Daniela was already making her way toward her father.

"Time to move on," Garrett yelled as two uniformed officers joined him.

But no one moved on.

Raúl now stood across the street, his feet set wide apart and his hands clasped behind his back. He stared forward over the heads of the crowd.

"Go the fuck home," a voice yelled at a group of farm workers, walking away from the mob.

"This is their home." Raúl's voice boomed over the scraps of quarreling. "And my home." The crowd turned toward Raúl. A small stone hit his chest, and he flinched. His eyes darted around the parking lot with a flicker of panic.

"Raúl's got nothing to do with this." Chester Talbot grabbed the arm of a twenty-something lobbing rocks.

"I have everything to do with this." Raúl licked his dry lips and swallowed hard.

"Dad, don't," Daniela yelled as she pushed through the crowd.

"This is my home as much as it is anyone's." Raúl's voice quivered. He drew in a deep breath and opened his mouth to speak.

"Dad," Daniela called out.

Raúl caught Daniela's eye and swallowed hard.

"You're legal, Raúl." Ryan, still in Garrett's grip on the periphery of the crowd, slurred his words. "There's a big difference."

Cadie wedged her shoulders between strangers as she tried to get to Raúl before he spoke words he could never take back. She felt them expanding in his chest the way the truth about Juan was clawing its way up her own throat.

Inside the bar the crowd had felt thick and soupy with the accusations and economic angst of a small town coming undone at the seams. But as they regrouped on the street, the bodies numbered less than fifty. What had felt crowded and oppressive moments earlier looked sad and desperate under the open sky.

The law of entropy said the tangle of bodies should disperse in the open air, take up more space, and dissipate. But in the street, the residents of Maple Crest wound themselves into a tighter knot, with Raúl in the center.

The crew of construction workers from Massachusetts stood in the doorway of the bar, then went back inside, probably congratulating themselves on the chance to take over the abandoned pool tables, Cadie thought.

Ryan ducked and twisted out of Garrett's grip. Garrett let him go without a fight.

"Everybody knows who they found in those woods," another voice yelled at Raúl. "What were you and Hernández really fighting about that day?"

The accusation landed like a stone in Cadie's gut. Raúl's vulnerability splayed out in front of everyone. Truths unspoken sizzled in the air.

Daniela froze. The battle between her desire to run to Raúl and her fear of unmasking her family lay exposed in every tense muscle. She appeared paralyzed, trapped in the space between fear and action. Only her eyes moved.

If folks were this willing to blame Raúl now, how would they react when the ID was made public?

"We're all feeling the drought and the foreclosures. All of us," Raúl shouted. His fingers twitched as if he were squeezing the trigger on the Windex bottle he always carried in the store. Cadie moved around the outskirts of the crowd to get to Raúl from behind.

"We've got no problem with you, Raúl." Ryan moved closer to Raúl.

"If you have a problem with my friends, you have a problem with me." Raúl's voice remained steady but his eyes skipped around the crowd nervously.

Tino put himself between Ryan and Raúl.

"You." Ryan placed a palm on Tino's chest and shoved him. "You, I do have a problem with."

Tino pushed Ryan back and something snapped in the crowd. A roar rose up in front of Cadie, around her. She couldn't see Daniela anymore. The hairs on Cadie's neck pricked up with an icy feeling that what was about to happen could never be undone.

Ryan cocked his arm back and landed a sloppy fist on Tino's cheek. Tino stumbled backward and Ryan hit him again. Tino leaned over and spit blood on the ground. Cadie pushed through unfamiliar shoulders, trying to get closer to Raúl as he coiled his arm back like the slow-motion draw of a bow and slammed his fist into Ryan's jaw before Ryan had a chance to hit Tino a third time.

Flashing police lights disoriented Cadie as she pushed against the bodies separating her from Raúl. The pavement trembled, or maybe it was Cadie's own knees shaking or the vibrations of Daniela's fear rising up through the ground. Cadie lunged between Raúl and Ryan, who was already pumping his drunk fist and raising it in Raúl's direction.

Cadie's knuckles stung as her fist smashed into the side of Ryan's face. He turned from Raúl to Cadie and stepped back, confused as to where the punch came from. The impact sent a sharp pain through Cadie's shoulder and set her off-balance. She fell backward, and the side of her face slammed against a crumbling stone wall.

Raúl pulled Cadie up and wrapped his arms around her shoulders, pinning her arms to her sides. Her back rose and fell against Raúl's heaving chest.

"Enough," he whispered.

A buzz of indistinguishable voices swelled into a single, desperate lament. Sweat, or maybe blood, dripped down the side of Cadie's face.

She scanned the faces, searching for Garrett and Daniela. Instead, she found Clyde. The streetlight behind him cast shadows across the pasty, mottled skin hanging in pouches around his jowls.

Cadie tried to break free from Raúl's restraint, but he clamped his arms tighter around her. Heat emanated from Raúl, a calm resolve that hushed the dagger-edged voices flying around her. Garrett grabbed Tino by the elbow and dragged him over to the edge of the crowd where Clyde stood, his eyes still fixed on Cadie. Watching the urgency in Garrett's gait, the tenderness in the drape of his arm across Clyde's shoulders, Cadie felt a disconnect. Garrett was protecting Clyde while Raúl stood vulnerable in front of the whole town. How did everyone not see the evil in Clyde's face?

Garrett ushered Tino and Clyde into his police car, and drove off. Cadie slipped her hand into Raúl's warm palm. He squeezed her hand until an officer dragged them both to the police station.

27

Other than the trees, which wore prematurely crisp edges on their green leaves, everything in downtown Maple Crest was white. The post office, the police station, the library. Stark clapboard buildings, storefronts, and houses with saggy front porches.

The royal blue words spray-painted on the front of Garcia's Hardware Store screamed against the starchy palette. *Go Home.* No one could look away, even if they didn't want to read the words. The fuzzy edges of the imprecise lettering blurred into the flaking paint as if the pigment wanted to claw its way into the wood and infiltrate the framing.

Cadie walked past the darkened hardware store, fighting the urge to inspect the vandalism. Raúl should have been inside wiping down the previous day's fingerprints from the front door. But no one had opened the store that morning. Several men who might have been on Raúl's porch any other day gathered outside the post office.

Cadie smoothed the front of the linen skirt she had borrowed from her mother's closet. She pushed open the heavy door to the middle school. Her footsteps echoed in the familiar hall where she once hid behind the lockers to spy on her seventh-grade crush.

"Cadie, it's me." Daniela had called her half an hour earlier as Cadie lay awake in bed. "Sal got suspended. The first week back at school and she gets herself fucking suspended. I can't leave the hospital. And Mom's still at the police station, trying to find out why they won't release my dad." Daniela's voice slid up a register and cracked against the background noise of her rapid, urgent footsteps.

"I can get her." Cadie fumbled to pull on her bra as she walked to her mother's closet. She pumped her throbbing fist open and closed, stretching the bruise left from punching Ryan the night before.

"Thanks." Daniela's voice broke. "I should be the one picking her up. I'm working too much. What the hell am I doing, Cadie?"

"You're taking care of your family. You're working so you can build the life you want for Sal. I can get her. It's not a problem," Cadie said. In truth, she didn't feel equipped to handle an angsty teenager who had gotten suspended, but she couldn't help feeling pleased Daniela had asked her to help.

As a student, Cadie had admired the kids who dared to step out of line enough to get suspended. Cadie graduated high school having never even served detention. What had Sal done to get herself ejected?

"I have to be somewhere, but not until three. I could always take her with me if no one's home yet," Cadie said.

"Thanks. You can leave her with my parents. If they're home." Daniela spoke quietly now. "Text me and let me know what happens. I'm working a double. If my parents don't come home—"

"I'll hang on to Sal as long as you want. It'll be fun. But why's your dad still at the station?"

"I don't know. Did he seem okay when you left last night?"

"Yeah. He was tired. We were all tired. I was with him the whole time, and then sometime after midnight they said the charges against me had been dropped. They sent me home."

"Of course they did." Daniela sighed loudly.

As she walked toward the middle school principal's office, Cadie quickened her pace. She needed to meet the fire crew in four hours to tag trees. Best case, Raúl would be released in time to take Sal. Worst case, she would drag Sal with her to the work site. She straightened her back and opened the door to the vice principal's office.

"This is totally unfair," Sal said as soon as they exited the building. "I was exercising my constitutional right to free speech."

"You don't need to convince me. I'm just taking custody of you until your mom or grandparents get home." Cadie tried to keep up with Sal's quick strides. "Do you want to talk about it?"

Sal rolled her eyes.

"What's on your leg?" Cadie pointed to a band of barbed wire with a fist rising up out of the barbs drawn in black ink on Sal's thigh.

"Resistance art. I drew it." The corners of Sal's mouth twitched, even as she tried to act tough.

Sal halted at the edge of the sidewalk. Her indignance melted as she absorbed the message painted on her grandfather's store.

Go Home.

"No, no, no!" Sal broke into a run. A pickup truck slammed on its brakes as she darted across the street without looking. Cadie waved an apology to the driver, who scowled at her and drove away. Cadie caught up with Sal on the porch of the store, staring at the graffiti. Cadie put a hesitant hand on Sal's shoulder. Sal pushed her off.

"Why's the store closed? Where are my grandparents? Where are they?" she shouted, looking up and down the street. Ryan and two other guys sitting in front of the fire station stood up from their lawn chairs to watch them. Ryan half waved. Cadie gave him the finger.

Sal looked at Cadie, then flipped him off too. "Fuck him," Sal said. "Fuck all of them."

"Your grandmother's over at the police station now, trying to find out why they haven't let him leave yet."

"They let you leave last night."

"I know. It's not fair."

"Figures. Look at you." Sal kicked the white clapboard under the graffiti so hard Cadie worried she would hurt her foot. "And look at my grandfather."

"Let's clean this up before your grandparents see it. We can go back to my place and get some buckets and supplies."

Cadie started down the steps, but Sal did not follow. "We can get stuff from inside the store. It'll be faster."

"It's locked."

"I know all their hiding spots. I'll get the key."

Cadie followed Sal around back to a wire cage stacked with refillable propane tanks.

Sal stuck her hand through the fence and reached behind a tank leaning against the back of the store. She triumphantly retrieved a fake rock with a key inside and unlocked the back door.

The air inside the store hung heavy with memories trapped in the accumulation of color, sound, humidity. Sensory echoes not tethered to a specific time or event. The same air, the same molecules she and Daniela had shared as kids still circulated in this room. She inhaled the myth of her own childhood. It tasted like turpentine.

Familiar fishing tackle lay under the glass counter, as if untouched for the past thirty years. Rows of spray paint lined up like tin soldiers. The vandals who sprayed the store had probably bought the paint here. Raúl probably knew them.

"Here, put it in your bag. Quick." Daniela had tossed a can of gold spray paint to Cadie after they dropped their blueberries off at Angie's one afternoon. "It matches your bike. We can patch the rust spots."

"I don't have any money."

"I won't tell if you don't." Daniela had taken the can from Cadie's hand and put it in Cadie's backpack. "Who's going to know?"

Nearly three decades later, as Cadie ran her finger along the dusty cans, she remembered the precise shade they stole. Summer sunset. Cadie picked up a matchbook from the basket by the counter and slipped it in her pocket.

Four dented metal lockers lined the back wall of the storeroom. Across the tops of the lockers, names spelled out in reflective mailbox letters read *Raúl, Dolores, Agnes,* and *Fernando.* One of those lockers had probably belonged Juan once.

Sal grabbed two mop buckets from the corner and took two new scrub brushes from a display aisle. Sal clenched her jaw as they filled the buckets with warm, soapy water and carried them outside.

Cadie and Sal scrubbed the graffiti while on full display for the entire town. Morning sun slid across the porch. Cadie worked on the front edge of the paint, racing the sun to remove the hateful words before the light hit them. She tried not to think about Clyde, if maybe he was watching them too.

They had scrubbed and smeared two letters each when heavy footsteps sounded on the wooden stairs around the side of the porch, out of their line of vision. Clutching her scrub brush as the only weapon within reach, Cadie leapt between Sal and the on-coming footsteps.

28

"Grampa!" Sal barreled past Cadie to hug Raúl as he rounded the corner of the hardware store porch. "They let you go."

His disheveled hair and wrinkled clothes made him appear older than he had the day before. He looked as if he hadn't slept all night.

"You're okay?" Cadie said.

"I'm fine." Raúl's eyes flickered from Cadie's defensive stance to her aggressively poised scrub brush. "Were you planning to scrub me to death?"

"I hadn't really thought it through." Cadie lowered the brush. "Who would do this? We should call the police."

"We don't need to call them. They can see it just fine." Raúl looked down the street at the police station. He hitched his pants up and scuffed his shoe over the floorboards. "Besides, I don't want to know who did it."

Years of smiling had carved deep lines around Raúl's eyes, leaving light tan lines that erupted from the corners when he did not smile. Cadie had never noticed them before because he almost always smiled. Standing there in front of the empty store, his eyes looked rounder and deeper, framed by a starburst of used-up smiles.

"Shouldn't you be in school?" Raúl asked Sal.

"I had to pick her up early today. Daniela was at—"

"I got suspended," Sal interrupted. "They were picking on this kid whose dad works at the farm. They kept calling him Pedro. Like every Latinx kid is named Pedro. So, I had to stop them, right?"

"You got in a fight?" Raúl said.

"Geez, no. Peaceful protest. You should read about Gandhi," Sal said. "I told them his name was Jaime, so they should call him

Jaime. Everybody deserves to be called by their name, right? But the teacher didn't even do anything about it."

"You got suspended for that?" Day-old sweat and stale coffee clung to the wrinkled clothes Raúl still wore from the night before.

"Well, I might have been standing on the teacher's desk yelling about it." Sal's shoulders drooped. "And I might have refused to get down. I pulled a bunch of other kids up on the desk to protest with me. We broke the teacher's paperweight and a mug."

Raúl smiled down at his feet. "Maybe Cadie and I could learn from your peaceful protests.

"Let me see your hand." Raúl extended an open hand to Cadie.

Cadie placed her right hand on Raúl's leathery palm. He examined her swollen knuckles. "Nothing looks broken. Does it hurt?"

"I'm fine." Cadie bit on the inside of her cheek to hold back a smile. She'd never hit anyone in her entire life. Her hand didn't hurt. It felt powerful.

Raúl stood with feet at shoulder width apart. He looked immovable, as if anchored in the granite ledge that held the entire town in place. Raúl was the rock, the boulder glaciers had deposited, a weathered stone riddled with fissures that refused to crack open.

"I hope the store never catches fire." Raúl looked in the direction of the fire station. "I'm not sure they'd put it out."

"Are we in trouble?" Sal said.

Raúl pulled Sal into his chest, smashing her cheek against the barrel of his torso. Sal closed her eyes. "I shouldn't have hit anyone. Neither should Cadie. I'm proud you stood up for that boy, but we need to be careful."

He released Sal from the bear hug. "Can you get three Cokes from the fridge?"

As she passed Cadie, Sal sprang up on her tiptoes to whisper in her ear. "I don't care what he says. You and me, we're badass."

Sal let the door slam.

"Did they charge you?" Cadie said.

Raúl nodded. "You?"

"Apparently I don't hit hard enough."

Raúl touched Cadie's bruised cheek where she'd hit her head on the pavement. "You don't need to protect me." He cupped her chin in his hand as if she were a child.

Sal came out with three old-fashioned glass Coke bottles. Raúl gripped the metal caps with the bottom of his T-shirt and twisted them open with long, slow hisses. The sharp bubbles burst against Cadie's tongue. She longed to be a carefree child sipping a Coke while twirling on Angie's bar stool.

Cars slowed as they passed the store. Drivers craned their necks to read the graffiti.

"I planned to open the store, but I don't think anyone is coming," Raúl said. It was almost noon.

A car drove by and a man in a baseball cap hurled a rock toward the store, smashing a window. Raúl ducked and covered his head with his arms as glass shards sprayed inside the store.

"Gramps!" Sal ran to Raúl's side.

"I'm fine." He straightened up slowly.

Sal pushed away from him when he tried to hug her. She stomped her foot hard on the loose boards. "I wish everyone would stop lying to me."

"About what?" Raúl said.

"About everything. Things are not fine. *You* are not fine."

Raúl nodded slowly. He embodied a calmness, a steadiness that had always put Cadie at ease. His ready smile and the way he stood with his shoulders back gave the impression he was in control without ever appearing controlling. Even now, he did not appear flustered. Raúl had been waiting for Sal's challenge.

"Okay," he said.

"Okay what?"

"I'll tell you everything," Raúl said. Another car drove by and Raúl stared down the driver. "They kept me at the station all night because they identified the man buried in the woods, and they wanted to talk to me about it."

Don't say his name. Please don't say his name, Cadie pleaded silently.

"It's Juan Hernández, like everyone suspected." Raúl blinked hard and continued. "They're opening a formal murder investigation. Witnesses saw us arguing right before he disappeared twenty-seven years ago. I was the last person to see him."

No. Clyde was.

"At least we can finally put Juan to rest," he said.

They were supposed to have one more day. Garrett had promised the report would not come back for at least one more day. The men in front of the fire station paced on the sidewalk watching Cadie, Sal, and Raúl. What were they talking about? What were they planning? Maybe Daniela had been right. Maybe they shouldn't have trusted Garrett to protect Raúl.

"Does everyone know about the ID?" Cadie asked.

"I don't know. Garrett argued with the chief that making the information public during all this mess would make things worse," Raúl said. "But I don't know what they decided."

"Just because you were the last one who saw that guy doesn't mean you killed him. That's totally circumstantial evidence," Sal said. "What were you arguing about anyway?"

"Nothing important. Juan added hours to his time card, and I told him I wouldn't pay the extra time. He was furious at me for not believing him. I overreacted." Raúl pinched the bridge of his nose and squeezed his eyes shut. "Dolores called me later. That woman can yell. She had given Juan the extra hours to help clean out the storeroom. I never got the chance to apologize to him. I should have trusted him."

"Police can't charge you if they don't have evidence. It's unconstitutional." Sal's face was red and splotchy. She wiped her nose on the shoulder of her shirt.

"But they can deport me."

"They can't deport citizens," Sal said.

Raúl drew his eyebrows together. "I'm not a citizen. I never have been."

Basketballs bouncing on the courts behind the rec center echoed through the sleepy streets.

"Yes, you are. You have to be." Sal's lower lip trembled.

Raúl shook his head.

"Mom lied to me. Again." Sal clenched her teeth and narrowed her teary eyes. "She keeps so many secrets."

"Sal," Raúl said.

"Did they ask you about your immigration status last night?" Cadie said.

Raúl shook his head and cast a glance down the street.

"I'm the only person in this family who's proud to be Salvadoran," Sal said. "You and Mom and Gram, you pretend we're *sooo* American all the time, like that's the only respectable thing anyone can be. No one even taught me Spanish, and all the kids who speak Spanish call me coconut because I'm white on the inside. But guess what? All the white kids here think I should go back to where I came from. And I don't even know where I come from." Sal threw her scrub brush at the smeared letters. *Go Home.*

Cadie's tongue stuck to the top of her dry mouth. She did not belong there with Raúl and Sal. But she could not make herself walk away.

"You're right." Raúl's voice remained calm and quiet. The air around them stopped moving. "But there is a reason I never talk about El Salvador."

"What?" Sal said sharply, as if no answer could satisfy her.

"I love my country. When I grew up we had a wonderful home. It was small, but—" Raúl paused and smiled to himself. "I used to chase my brothers in our yard. We had these goats—"

"You have brothers?" Sal interrupted.

"I had two older brothers, but they both died during the civil war. Your grandmother lived in our same village. She and her sister used to sell pupusas in the market. That's where I first met her."

"I love Gram's pupusas," Sal whispered.

"I joined the army after we got married." Raúl's voice was so low Cadie became conscious of the sound of her own breathing. "The government controlled the army, and during the war," he paused and wiped sweat from his brow, "they used the army to do horrible things. They sent the military into villages with orders to kill people, civilians who did nothing wrong other than oppose the government."

"Did you kill people?" Sal whispered.

"I didn't know what they sent us to do. I was new and didn't know better. We were a weapon used to quiet anyone who challenged the government." Raúl's voice gained strength. He straightened his back.

"Why didn't you quit?" Sal narrowed her eyes.

"I would have been thrown in prison, or worse. Right after I joined, they sent us into a village. We were told to kill everyone there. But when we arrived, it was mostly civilians, women, and children in the village. They were unarmed. But we had our orders."

"No, I don't want to hear it." Sal put her hands over her ears, but Raúl pulled them down and clasped them in his.

"I refused. My commanding officer pointed a rifle at me and told me to follow orders or he would shoot me for treason." Raúl shifted his gaze far off in the distance. Cadie followed his eyes, but they were fixed on something she would never be able to see. "I raised my weapon and aimed it at a young boy, about your age, but at the last second, I turned and shot my officer instead. I shot my own commanding officer so I wouldn't have to kill those people." Raúl's voice cracked. "But they all died that day anyway. It didn't even matter."

"Did the officer die?" Sal said.

"I don't know for sure. I ran off and hid for days. If they had found me, I would have been killed."

Gooseflesh crawled up Cadie's neck as she imagined Raúl hiding, fearing for his life. Raúl never had the luxury of choosing jail, like her own father had when he refused to fight in Vietnam.

"At that point, I had no choice but to run, to leave El Salvador. It was more dangerous than simply getting to the border. So many people went missing during those years. When I asked Dolores to take Daniela and meet me at the border, I was asking her to risk her life and Daniela's. They could have stayed and let me run alone. But that woman." Raúl smiled. "That is one stubborn woman. I found out later that soldiers went to our home and burned it to the ground."

"How did Gram get to the border?" Sal leaned close to her grandfather.

"She carried your mom on foot for three days. They slept under bridges and on the side of the road on the way to meet me. She is the strongest, bravest woman I've ever known."

"Gram," Sal whispered.

"But that is not the El Salvador I want you to know. That is not my El Salvador." He shook his head.

More people had gathered in front of the fire station. Raúl watched them cluster together, looking back at the hardware store every so often.

"We walked for so long. I don't even know how long. Many people did not survive that journey."

"Just the three of you?" Sal asked.

"We met up with a group of young men and teenagers and they let us walk with them. We felt safer in a group." Raúl smiled faintly as he spoke. "The boys took turns carrying your mother on their shoulders. I don't think we could have made it alone.

"When we got to the US, we couldn't seek asylum as refugees because, at the time, the US government supported the Salvadoran army because they saw the Salvadoran government as Cold War allies against the communists. They would have sent me back to face a military trial and probably execution. We used all our money to buy fake papers. Fake Social Security numbers. Fake names."

"Fake names?" Sal said.

"My parents called me Juan." Raúl's voice cracked as he said his birth name out loud. "My name is Juan."

"Like that man they found in the woods," Sal said.

"Exactly like Juan Hernández." Raúl's voice hitched again. "Your grandmother's name was Irís. We called your mother Luisa, after my mother, who was an artist, like you."

"Wait. Mom? If Mom doesn't have real papers . . ." Sal's eyes stormed. "So you all lied to me. My whole life."

"Yes, I guess we did."

"If you get sent back to El Salvador, what will they do to you?" Sal said.

"The military does not act kindly to deserters. Especially ones who shot an officer. But it was a long time ago, a different government. I don't know what would happen now."

"Can't you explain all that to our government now? Wouldn't they understand?" Sal said.

"I've been using a false Social Security number, false name. I've paid taxes every year, never been in trouble. But I've been living under a false identity the entire time." Raúl put his arm around Sal's shoulders. This time, she did not fight him. She leaned into his chest and wiped her face on his shirt. "Laws are laws, and a lie is still a lie."

They sat silently for a few minutes. Cadie's pulse ratcheted up with every car that drove by. Cadie had been so afraid of exposing Dolores. But Raúl's revelation changed everything. His vulnerability presented an even more dangerous threat than Dolores's.

"And if they figure out you don't have papers, they'll know about Gram and Mom," Sal said, her voice barely above a whisper. "What would happen to me?"

"Nothing will happen to any of us," Raúl said, but he didn't look convinced or convincing.

"I can't just sit here anymore." Sal jumped up and threw a scrub brush into the bucket. Milky blue water splashed the wall. "I'm getting a Popsicle."

"Don't tell your mother," Raúl said.

"About what? That she has a fake name? That you're wanted for murder? What don't you want me to tell her?" Tears rolled down Sal's cheeks.

"Don't tell her about the ice cream bar. We'll talk to her together about everything else, okay?"

"She doesn't know?"

"She knows most of it. But not about why we left. I never wanted any of you to know what I'd done. But I think it's time to stop keeping so many secrets," Raúl said.

Sal's eyes softened. "You're the best man I've ever known." Sal pecked him on the cheek before walking inside. "I won't tell Mom about the sweets."

Raúl arched his back and cracked his neck.

The group of men in front of the fire station had grown to ten. Stripped of its quaint veneer, Maple Crest looked ugly, gray.

Raúl wiped his brow with his sleeve. "I've spent most of my life trying to hide who I am. What if someone finds out? What if I go to jail? Or worse, what if they send us back? But there are always consequences for our choices, even when we don't think they are fair."

"If you could go back, would you have done anything differently?"

"That is a pointless question."

"No, it's not. Given the choices you had, I think you should be proud. Your family is safe, healthy, and thriving because you and Dolores made a difficult, brave decision."

Ryan's sister Claire, pushing a baby stroller, approached the hardware store. She waved and pulled a brown paper bag out from under the carriage.

"I saw what happened last night." Claire stayed back at an awkward distance, too far away for a comfortable conversation, but too close to be ignored. She looked over Cadie's shoulder at Raúl, then at the broken window.

"The store's closed today," Raúl said.

"I'm dropping off some tomatoes and corn from my garden. I promised Dolores I'd bring them by." She held up the paper sack. "I put in a couple of zucchini and onions, too."

Raúl walked toward her and took the bag. "That's very thoughtful."

"It's the least I could do. Dolores babysat a few times this month and she won't let me pay her." Claire looked behind Raúl to the smeared but legible words on the wall. "Do you need any help cleaning up?"

"We have it under control," he said. "But I appreciate the offer."

Claire looked down the street at Ryan, then turned back to Raúl.

"He didn't do this. I know he can be an ass when he drinks, but he wouldn't do this."

"I know he didn't," Raúl said. "We spent the night at the police station together."

"He feels really bad."

"He should feel bad," Cadie said.

"I'm sorry, too," Claire said.

"You didn't do anything," Raúl said.

"That's what I'm sorry about." Claire dragged her foot in the dust, forming a small cloud around her feet. "This isn't our town. You know that, right? With the farms going under and this god-awful heat, everyone's on edge, not themselves."

Raúl shrugged. "Thank you for the vegetables."

Claire walked past the fire station without acknowledging her brother.

"Do you have any white paint?" Cadie asked Raúl. She pressed the bristles of her scrub brush into the clapboard until they bent. Flecks of blue-tinted paint fell to the porch floor. Her shoulders ached as she bore down. But no matter how hard she scrubbed, the blurred words remained. *Go Home.*

"What kind of hardware store do you think I run? Of course I have white paint. But the rest of the clapboard is so dirty. Fresh paint will stand out too much."

"Then let's paint the whole store." Cadie stepped back and leaned on the deck railing. "If you step away, the blurred letters look kind of like a cloud."

"Excellent idea." Raúl clapped his hands.

"What?"

"Paint a cloud. We'll take their mess and make it beautiful. Make sure you put a silver lining on it."

"I'm a terrible artist. You should let Daniela do it."

"She's working a double shift. She won't be home until late. I want to fix this now." He leaned against the railing next to her. "You fight off the vandals while I go get your paint and check on Sal."

"Tío," Cadie called to him before he went inside. "When I was eleven, Daniela and I stole a can of spray paint from your store to touch up my bike."

"If you made it this far in life and that's the worst thing weighing on your conscience, then I envy you."

A blister was forming on her right hand where she squeezed the brush. She scrubbed harder. Through the broken window, Cadie could see Sal slouched in a lawn chair, a Popsicle stick hanging out of her mouth as she tapped away on her phone.

"You can work off your debt by painting that cloud." Raúl returned with an opened can of sky blue paint and a brush.

"A blue cloud?"

"Why not?"

"Why did you put yourself in the middle of the fight last night?" Cadie asked Raúl as he stirred the paint with a stick.

"Why did you?" He waited for a response Cadie could not give.

"Not speaking up against injustice is just as bad as being complicit. I've been quiet too long." Raúl bent over to pick up a piece of broken glass. "How can I ever hope for forgiveness if I can't stand up for other people?"

Cadie would have given up any chance at her own redemption to ease the pain she saw in Raúl's eyes.

"Thanks for looking after Sal. I can take it from here if you have somewhere to be."

"I have to work off my debt, remember?" She pointed to the blue smear on the wall. If she worked quickly, she would make it to meet the fire crew with plenty of time.

Raúl nodded and went back inside, leaving Cadie alone on the porch. Cadie watched through the window as he walked past Sal and ruffled her spiky hair. Sal grabbed his hand and kissed it without looking up from her phone.

Cadie sketched the outline of her imperfect cloud on the wall, filled it in with pale blue paint, and edged it with a thin silver lining. She stepped back to survey her work. It looked like an eight-year-old's painting. Daniela would have created a masterpiece. She could make art out of anything.

"I brought stuff to make a map." Daniela had burst into Cadie's house one rainy morning that was too blustery to take their boat out. She had unfolded a piece of plain white paper with a light pencil outline of the cove and the islands.

Daniela had unrolled another paper with clusters of blueberries painted in a thick, shiny ink. "I boiled a bunch of berries down last night and strained it through a pair of my mom's pantyhose. She's going to kill me." Daniela pulled a small plastic container out of her backpack. She pried off the top to reveal the velvety, viscous ink.

Cadie swirled the liquid, watching it coat the sides of the container and slide back down.

"I'm going to trace the whole map in blueberry ink," Daniela said.

They spread the paper out on the damp floor of Cadie's unfinished basement, the humidity softening the paper as they pressed it against the cold cement. The purple lines made Cadie's mouth water. The scratch of the metal tip on the paper carved the indelible image into her memory.

They would never get lost again.

Cadie had dipped her finger into the leftover ink and licked it. Concentrated summer tingled on her tongue with a tease of adventure that made her teeth chatter.

Weeks after Daniela had drawn the map, Cadie added directions to the beech tree where they hid the gun in case she ever needed to find it. Cadie had laminated the map and The Poachers' Code at the library.

"Very nice," Raúl said, admiring Cadie's painted cloud from the doorway. "Feel better?"

"About what?"

"I absolve you of your guilt."

"If only it were that easy, huh?" Cadie watched his smile fade. "What you did mattered. You stood up against a corrupt government."

"It doesn't seem to have made a difference, does it?" Dark circles hung under his eyes.

"It matters to me. It matters to your family."

He smiled weakly.

"Look at Sal. She's exactly like you. She started a protest today to protect a kid from being bullied. Your granddaughter."

"Ahhh." Raúl nodded. "My granddaughter who got suspended from school today."

"You're proud of what she did, and you know it." Cadie threw her arms around Raúl's barrel chest.

"Very, very proud," he whispered in her ear.

A car drove by and honked repeatedly. "Go back where you came from," an occupant shouted.

Raúl flinched in Cadie's embrace, but he didn't let go.

29

I absolve you of your guilt. Raúl's words played over in Cadie's mind as she drove to meet the fire crew and tag trees. Blue and silver paint speckled her hands and forearms from painting Raúl's cloud. Her swollen knuckles ached from the fight and from gripping the scrub brush.

She parked her car at the trailhead in a lot surrounded by singed trees. The fire on the slope of Mount Griffin, which she had witnessed from the top of Mount Steady days earlier, had melted the macadam, which now lay bubbled and warped. She followed the trail into the charred husk of a forest. Deep tire tracks from timber crews had already broken through the sooty crust. A sweet, smoky aroma kicked up around her.

Beauty she had not anticipated saturated the light and air. The fire had rendered the woods a negative X-ray of itself, stripped down to its most elemental and raw form, like a cast of dancers frozen in position. The absence of color quieted her mind like a drug as she walked through the stark, silent landscape.

Air moved without the buffer of branches and leaves overhead. No one could hide in this scorched graveyard. It wasn't a forest anymore. It wasn't a fire, a refuge, or a home. In this half-place, Cadie's burdens felt lighter, as if the gravity drawing them against her heart had been diminished.

Chalky debris swirling in the air caught rays of sunlight. Cadie blew into the cloud of particles and watched the ash dance. Vertical lines of the snag forest drew her eyes upward to the shocking blue of the sky. The sky she had left behind in Maple Crest had not seemed as blue.

Cadie walked toward a petite woman bent over examining a tree trunk. When she heard Cadie's footsteps she stood up. Cadie recognized the shock of purple hair from outside the ethics committee meeting.

"You're Piper?"

"Cadence Kessler!" The woman dropped her bag and a compact chain saw to run toward Cadie. "I'm so happy to finally meet you, like for real meet you." The smell of patchouli nearly gagged Cadie as Piper pulled her into a hug.

"Everyone is talking about you. Have you seen the CadenceUnderFire hashtag?"

"Did you start that?"

"I won't confirm or deny that. I'm the one who e-mailed you about the Bicknell's thrush. Do you remember?"

"I read the material you sent. It was well researched."

Piper beamed. She picked up her chain saw. "The university's going to take a lot of heat, because of what you did, you know." She swung the chain saw back and forth as she talked. "The government can sue the school and it would set in motion a series of other challenges. You could end up in the Supreme Court."

"I don't think so." Cadie swallowed down the stomach acid creeping up her throat. "It's not that big a deal. I just collected a few dead beetles."

"You could be the reason they open federal lands back up." Piper paused.

"Or I could go to jail and never work again." Cadie did not want to be a test case for environmental law. She wanted to prove her thesis about the beetles, publish a paper, and prevent a few fires.

"It's about so much more than your bark beetle research," Piper said, seeming to read Cadie's mind. "It's about my thrush and tons of other research being cut off. Because of what you did, I took a chance and turned my research in, including the dates and locations of the samples I took. I figured I'd get kicked out of my program, but my department's backing me. My research director cited your project. This is uncharted territory, but if the science community sticks together, we can ride this out until we can reverse the ban."

"You can't count on that happening." Cadie tried not to show the pride blooming in her chest.

"It'll happen. We're screwed if it doesn't, and I refuse to give up hope."

"Well, we're legally on public land now. Maybe we should take advantage and get some work done," Cadie said, and walked away from Piper. The towering pines looked like etchings against the blue sky, their spines straight and proud.

Cadie froze at the rapid-fire trill of a single Bicknell's thrush. A different sound than the night call, but in the same key. Unlike its somber night song, the thrush's morning call always ended on an up note, a question. Cadie's heart flipped as a rush of memory washed over her. Lying in the hammock with her father as he taught her bird calls. The giddy thrill of hearing the night call as the birds prepared to migrate south.

It took half a second to realize the call was not a Bicknell's, but Piper's impressive imitation.

Cadie replied with her own less-convincing call.

"Cadence Kessler, you have many talents." Piper bounced up next to Cadie and tilted her head to look up at the treetops. "They could come back here, you know. They often show up after fires and help rebuild. They're industrious critters. There's still a population of them around here. But they're coming back from the Caribbean in smaller and smaller numbers every spring because of all the hurricanes and deforestation there. And our temps are getting higher, driving them north into Canada."

The hollow space in Cadie's chest pressed against her lungs, a loneliness left behind by the tiny bird and everything else that had vanished from Cadie's life. She bit her lower lip to quiet the unexpected quiver.

"I miss them too," Piper whispered, her melodic voice taking on a gentle rasp as she readjusted the chain saw slung over her shoulder.

Cadie cleared her throat and walked ahead of Piper. Her foot-steps crunched in the silence, but Piper did not follow.

"Timber!" Piper shouted from twenty feet behind Cadie. "Timber, timber."

Cadie instinctively threw her arms up to protect her head and spun around, scanning the woods for the falling tree. But the woods stood motionless. Silent.

"What the hell?" Cadie yelled at Piper, who now had her back to Cadie.

"Timber!" A floppy Bernese mountain dog bound through the forest and tackled Piper. The hulking animal looked like it had been rolling in soot. "Where've you been, girl?"

"That's a terrible name for a dog." Cadie made a mental note to tell Daniela about the dog in the forest named Timber. "You scared the shit out of me. If you lived on the beach you wouldn't name your dog Shark, would you?"

"I probably would do exactly that." Piper buried her head in the dog's thick neck fur.

"I'm going to go tag some trees. Good luck with your research," Cadie said, trying to calm her pulse, still racing from the "timber" scare. "Nice meeting you. And, thanks, by the way, for showing up at the hearing. I think it helped."

"There's something I want to talk to you about." Piper followed Cadie with Timber at her heels. "I think we should let the fires burn."

Piper let her pronouncement hang in the air, waiting for Cadie to rebut her, but Cadie did not respond.

"It's not like I don't care about the houses or businesses that might burn. But we can't hold back the inevitable. Forests will burn, levies will break, seawalls will fail, and it's going to be catastrophic. Everyone's going to ask, 'Why didn't anyone warn us?' I'll throw my hands up and say, 'I did, but no one got out of the way.'"

"And all the people in the path of the fires?" Cadie said, annoyed at the way Piper ended each sentence on a high note, as if asking a question. "We have a responsibility to try to save their homes."

"I mean, I don't want anyone to lose a house or a life. But if your home is in the inevitable path of a wildfire, get the hell out of the house," Piper said.

"So just let everything burn?"

"Basically, there are two mindsets: First, thin the trees and buy some time. Build the levies and storm walls. And the farmers, they're like, 'I grow wheat and corn and that's what I grow, dammit.' When climate conditions make that challenging, they suck more water from the aquifers, dump more fertilizers, pour on the chemicals so they can keep growing that same crop.

"But there's a second mindset," Piper continued. "Accept that the climate is already shifting. It's not some looming monster that will bring eighty-foot waves crashing into New York City. It's already arriving in inches of sea level rise, in fractions of a degree of temperature increases. I mean look what's happening in the Caribbean and Central America."

Piper scrambled to keep pace with Cadie as they stepped over fallen branches and slid down rocky inclines. She wished Piper would stop talking so loudly. It felt disrespectful to the wounded forest.

"Do I want to reverse climate change? Sure," Piper continued. Cadie clenched her jaw. "But guess what, it isn't an option. I don't give a shit if your grandfather and his grandfather grew some spectacular variety of corn on this same piece of land. If that corn won't grow anymore because of altered climate conditions, maybe it's time to grow something else. If the fire's coming, get the hell out of the way. Don't just stand there wringing your hands and crying, 'It's not fair.'"

"There's a middle ground, for now." Cadie had the feeling Piper had given this speech many times before.

"There's no middle ground."

"Edgerton's on the other side of that ridge." Cadie pointed to a mountain ahead. "Driving here I could see patches of dead pines spotting the mountainsides. At least eight thousand people live there. You can't just say, 'Oh well, we're going to let your town burn. Move along now.'"

Piper snapped a burnt branch with her hands and examined the interior of the wood, blackened all the way through.

"What if it was your hometown?" Cadie asked.

"It will be one day. And I'll be devastated."

Cadie wanted to admire the purity of Piper's motives, but her naiveté was dangerous.

"I'm here to teach the crews how to tag infested trees today," Cadie said, brushing her hands off. "This is something productive I can actually do. Maybe we can reduce the fire threat for Edgerton, at least for now."

"Good luck with that." Piper's resolve did not seem shaken, but she looked genuinely sad. "I've read that researchers in Nova Scotia are seeing Bicknell's moving in after fires and helping rebuild the habitat. Maybe they haven't given up on us completely."

Cadie kept walking.

"And they love beetles, you know. If the fires don't lure the Bicknell's home, maybe the beetle buffet will." Piper turned to Cadie as if waiting for a response.

Cadie didn't want to talk. She wanted to get her work done and go back to Maple Crest, a thought that struck her as ironic after spending most of her life avoiding her hometown. But she wanted to talk to Garrett about how the police were responding to the graffiti at the hardware store. Her pulse quickened as she thought of the linger of cinnamon on Garrett's lips.

"I know you don't exactly agree with me, but maybe we can share data. I mean ultimately, we want the same things, right?" Piper said.

"I'll think about it." Cadie had been studying the mountain pine beetle for years. She had tracked it across the country and warned everyone it was coming to New England. Finally, people were listening to her, paying attention to her. She wasn't ready to hand over her research to a grad student.

"I've been reading this study from Colorado," Piper continued. "They've been monitoring forests that burned as a result of the mountain pine beetles there. It's a small study, but it's pretty cool."

"Does it offer ideas on how to prevent the fires?"

"The answer isn't always to *stop* the fires." Piper sounded exasperated. "The study compares these forests to other forests that were *not* affected by pine beetles, but also burned."

"And?"

Piper's eyes widened with enthusiasm. "So, the forests affected by pine beetles grew back stronger and more resilient than forests that burned, but were *not* affected by beetles." Piper paused for a reaction from Cadie, then continued when Cadie didn't respond. "Don't you see? What if the pine beetles know what's coming? I mean, not consciously, or anything. But they just *know*. They're clearing the way for a forest that will adapt to the new climate. Maybe the thrushes are helping by returning after the fires? It's like, Nature can't repair itself, but it's making plans for the future. Maybe we're getting in the way of those plans."

Piper stopped walking and yanked on the cord of her chain saw.

Cadie jumped as it roared to life.

Piper sliced into a blackened pine trunk, carving out a thick wedge to expose the wood underneath. She proceeded to cut a wedge out of another tree nearby.

"Look at the difference. This one is still alive." She held out the wedge for Cadie to take. Cadie smelled the wood and scraped her fingernail across the pulpy surface. The bark and the first layer of cambium were dry and brittle. But underneath, the yellow wood remained damp and healthy. Piper handed her a second piece. The tree had been dead or dying before the fire hit. The interior was almost as dry as the outer ring. The parched pulp flaked under her nail.

"Don't you see? The first tree is alive. Not all of the strong ones will survive the fire, but the ones that do are the heartiest, the ones that put up a fight and said 'fuck you' to the drought. *And* to the beetles. This is the tree that will repopulate the forest now that the beetles are dead and the fire has passed. And it won't have any competition from weaker trees, because the fire and the beetles wiped them out. Survival of the fittest."

Cadie almost pointed out that Piper had damaged a resilient tree by carving a wedge out of the trunk, but decided against it.

"It's like the beetles are coming in and preparing the forests to burn. The species that survive the fires are the climate warriors. This forest right here—" Piper held her arms over her head and spun in a circle. "This will be the forest of the future. The Earth is spinning one thousand miles an hour. Things are going to shift, things are going to burn. Nature will select trees better able to adapt."

"So the bark beetles will save us?" Cadie couldn't help smiling at Piper's optimism, even though her theories did not convince Cadie.

"Well, maybe they aren't the heroes of the story, but they aren't the villain either."

"Send me the research and I'll look at it."

"Awesome," Piper said. "You'll find the crew over the ridge. They're expecting you."

"Thanks." Cadie extended her hand, but Piper pulled her into a hug instead.

"Cadence under fire. We've got your back."

"Right." Cadie grimaced at Piper, but smiled as soon as she turned her back.

The forestry department would never intentionally allow wide swaths of forest in this area to burn. Voters would blame politicians. Politicians would do whatever it took to get reelected, and no one would look at the big picture.

Yet Piper's pure belief in science stirred a softness in Cadie's chest, allowing her to breathe more deeply and taste a clarity in the air that she had missed earlier. She attempted another bird call, but no answer came.

Ashen twigs and scorched ground cover crumbled under her boots as Cadie trudged on. When she stopped moving, silence surrounded her. An aimless breeze rose up every few minutes, strong enough to sway the crisp branches, but not enough to make them chatter.

When Cadie was in a crowded mall, at a conference, or even

on campus, she craved silence and stillness. She longed for space to hear her breath and feel her heartbeat without the competition of the rest of the world. Silence lived at the top of mountains and deep in the woods, where the nuances of worms under soil, insects in the air, trees exhaling, and animals wooing gave dimension to the quiet.

But the utter silence of the burnt-out woods burrowed into her head, creating an echo chamber where all her thoughts bounced against each other without compassion.

Layers upon layers of blackened tree trunks extended to the limits of her vision. Surveying fire damage from maps or from samples in a lab gave Cadie the tools to evaluate the damage. But standing in the middle of the wasteland, feeling the crush of burnt branches under her feet, Cadie felt their loss in her bones.

The deeper Cadie walked into the X-ray of a forest, the more adrift she felt.

The rumble of a truck engine and the hum of chain saws encroached on the silence. Over the ridge, a barren rocky terrain had created a natural firebreak. Crews below the ridge line had already cut down dozens of live pines, many showing signs of the telltale rust. Behind her, the charred landscape. In front of her, the intentional devastation of a living forest.

She made her way down the slope and approached the crew chief.

"I'm Cadie Kessler, I'm supposed to meet someone here to look at the trees you're tagging."

"Cadence under fire." He extended a hand. "I'm Joe. I'll show you around."

That hashtag was going to haunt her.

After walking the site and showing the team how to identify infested pines, Cadie broke away to collect her own samples before heading back to the cottage.

"I'd like about eight to ten unburnt, heavily infested trees from the periphery of the fire line," Cadie told Joe before she left. "As intact as possible."

"No problem," he said. "I'll have them delivered to the lot behind the research trailer."

"Mostly older growth. And a couple of younger ones." Cadie only needed three trees for her research. She would negotiate with Thea to let her keep the rest to mill into floorboards. They had plenty of space behind the lab, and once she had the boards milled, she could store them in the garage at the cottage until she was ready to build. Although where, when, and how she would build a house were not questions she could answer yet.

Her home would not be constructed out of polished marble or gleaming pine boards. It would be built of obstacles. Rocks from her hikes. New Hampshire granite. Boards marred by beetles. The intricate lace carved by the beetles would remind her every day how magnificent her adversary had been. How beautiful destruction could be.

As she left the crew, heading toward the trailhead, Cadie heard Piper whistling. She wanted to leave without talking to her. She didn't have the strength or the time for another lecture. The bird chirp of Cadie's cell phone shattered the quiet, and Piper looked up with a broad smile and a wave. Cadie waved and answered Garrett's call, grateful for the excuse to walk by without talking to Piper.

"Hey, I'm sorry about last night, about ditching you in the middle of all that mess," Garrett said. "I needed to get Tino away from the fight. I didn't want Ryan provoking him to do something stupid."

"Ryan provoked Raúl instead." Wind hissed in the bare branches overhead. "I heard the body was ID'd. You said it wouldn't come out until tomorrow. You know it's going to leak out," she said. "And, hey, what are you doing about the graffiti on the hardware store?"

"Raúl refused to make a statement. He wants it all to go away. Can I come over so we can talk about all this?" Garrett said.

"It's been a long day and I have a bunch of research to go over." She longed to curl up on the couch with Garrett and have a glass of wine. But her past tenderness toward Garrett had driven her to put the Garcias at risk and destroyed her friendship with Daniela. She couldn't risk doing it again. She needed to focus.

"A few more small fires started up. A couple were close by, but it sounds like they've been contained. At least they're finally listening to you."

"How close?" Cadie said.

"They caught a small brush fire about twenty miles north. Sounds like it started from a cigarette butt tossed out a car window," Garrett said. "If it would just fucking rain."

"That's way too close. I'm heading back now."

"You're going back to Concord?" Garrett said.

Cadie liked the disappointment in his voice.

"No. I want to stay close by in case Daniela needs me." Cadie could rummage through her mother's clothes closet for another day before going back to her apartment.

"Right. So, can I call tomorrow?"

"Yeah, but call sooner if anything changes."

Cadie held the phone to her ear a few seconds after Garret hung up. She almost called him back to say she had changed her mind, that she wanted him to come over. Fuck the fires, the beetles. Didn't she deserve a little happiness?

Bony trees seemed to be pointing at her as she walked back to her car. She wanted to throw herself down in front of the trees and beg forgiveness. For cutting them down. For craving the recognition of her colleagues. For resenting Piper's contrarian views. For always asking the forest to protect her secrets. And for not keeping the secrets she had vowed to keep herself.

She dialed Daniela's number, but it went straight to voicemail.

A logging truck rolled into the parking lot near Cadie's car. The hiss of the air brakes and the grinding gears made her shudder. The truck would be piled high with pine trees when it pulled out. It would take a hundred trucks to make a dent. The engine continued growling at her even after the driver had parked. A puff of thick black smoke belched out of the exhaust.

"Turn off the fucking engine," Cadie yelled to the driver, knowing he couldn't hear her. No one could hear her.

30

She ran a bath with her mother's lavender-scented bubbles and poured a few splashes of her father's bourbon over ice. The stiff alcohol warmed her throat, coating the scratchiness left behind from her walk in the ashy woods.

While the tub filled, she puttered around, looking at objects her family had left behind when they moved to Boston. It occurred to Cadie that her most prized possession was a pile of rocks. She had nothing else to show for her life's work, other than a degree and perpetually dirty fingernails. And now Piper's questions nagged at her, forcing her to reconsider her own scientific theories. What if she was approaching the fires from the wrong angle? What if the answer was to let everything burn?

She went into her parents' room to find a shirt to sleep in. The earthy clay, the malleable perfume of her mother, clung to every surface in the room. Her father's comforting scent of ChapStick and Halls Mentho-Lyptus, mixed with the traces of his oil paint, surrounded her.

She picked up a ChapStick her father had left by his bed and spread it on her dry lips.

Footsteps crunched on the gravel driveway. She hadn't heard a car approach over the sound of running water. She pressed her body against the wall next to the window. Boots clunked on the deck stairs. They continued around the side porch, rattling the loose boards. She hadn't locked the door. Her joints felt rusted in position.

She could hide under the bed or in the closet, but if anyone wanted to find her—if Clyde wanted to find her—it wouldn't take long. She gnawed on her thumb as he paused. Water heading to the bathtub coursed through the pipes in the walls, splashing into the half-full basin.

Cadie flinched as the kitchen door slammed shut. Without the rusty spring, she hadn't heard it open. The uninvited footsteps entered the cottage. The house no longer had a landline. Her cell phone was in her bedroom. Her parents had replaced the old, warped windows with narrow louvered panels. She couldn't escape without running down the hall and through the kitchen.

The pipes trembled inside the walls. The water level rose in the tub down the hall. She swallowed the last of the bourbon in a gulp that burned her throat and heated her belly with a slow roar. Cadie had been hiding from Clyde her entire life, making excuses to leave public events early because she convinced herself she had seen him in the crowd. He had taken too many years from her, robbed her of too much.

Floorboards in the kitchen creaked under the intruder's weight.

She picked up a large blue vase. She placed her thumb in the imprint of her mother's thumb on the bottom, the signature on every piece she made. The thick ceramic base felt heavy enough to crack a skull. She could stop it all. Right now.

Her hands stopped shaking as she lifted the vase over her head and waited by the bedroom door.

The footsteps paused in the kitchen. The creak of the floor told her he stood in front of the refrigerator. Muscles in her shoulders twitched. She raised the vase higher, ready to smash it down with the force of three decades of compressed rage.

She imagined his hot breath in her ear. *You want your friend to disappear?*

The heightening pitch of the water told her that the tub was about to overflow, but she didn't care. She wanted him to come. She wanted to rip her chest open and unleash the fear and guilt that gnawed at her in the middle of the night.

She adjusted her grip on the vase and prepared to open the door. She would startle him, smash him on the head, and run outside.

Footsteps moved down the hallway. A shadow slid under the gap between the bedroom door and the floor.

"Cadie?" Garrett called. "Are you here?"

Relief, or maybe disappointment, made her steady hands tremble.

"What the hell? You scared the shit out of me." She pushed open the bedroom door.

"I didn't mean to scare you." He looked sheepish, standing in the hallway. "I should have called."

"Or maybe knock?"

"Are you redecorating?" He gestured toward the vase she clutched with white knuckles.

"I was about to smash it over your head. I thought you were . . ." Cadie walked into the kitchen and put the vase on the counter. "I thought you were Clyde."

"Why would you think that?"

"Who else would break into my house and try to kill me?"

"No one's trying to kill you."

"Wait here." Cadie sprinted down the hall and closed the tap just as the water was about to crest over the lip of the tub. The bubbles rose almost a foot above the water.

"You smell like smoke." He lifted a fistful of her curls to his face.

"I spent the afternoon surveying a snag forest left behind after that fire on Mount Griffin."

"How'd it go?"

"Well enough." She tried to calm her breath and her heart rate.

"God, you're shaking," Garrett said. "I should've knocked. But really, there's nothing to be afraid of."

"Besides Clyde? Or that everyone will know I covered up a murder?" She didn't mention the bigger fear that consumed her: that she would never be brave enough to own her past.

Garrett walked to the window overlooking the lake. The sun hung low in the sky. An impatient crescent moon peered through the haze.

He sat on the edge of the kitchen table, his knee bouncing.

"Do you want to go for a walk?" Cadie needed to calm her own jitters. The oppressiveness of steamy lavender made the house feel stuffy. The air felt thick. She needed to get outside.

"Now?"

"Now." She put a bottle of red wine, the one her mother had been saving, two plastic cups, and a wine opener in her backpack. Garrett followed her into the woods.

"This is where Daniela and I met up every day." She guided him down the overgrown path between her house and the Garcias'.

She gulped at the air, trying to saturate her body from the inside with the earthy smell, but even the fragrance of the forest seemed off-balance. Instead of the mushroomy aroma of decay, the premature scent of crumbling leaves and broken pine needles hovered in the stagnant air.

Cadie paused at a pair of thick pine trunks, both dotted with resin tubes that had not been there two days earlier. They shouldn't be here, not at this elevation. The beetles were moving faster than Cadie thought.

She walked farther down the overgrown path, stopped in the clearing, and spread her arms wide. "And this is where I stashed your boat." She pointed to the shape of the boat outlined in watermelon-sized stones Cadie had painstakingly arranged to elevate the up-ended boat over the winter. Cadie had dragged it through the woods by herself that October, not wanting to call Daniela for help.

To passersby, the patina of moss, pine needles, tree sap, and time covering the stones might have camouflaged the shape of the rowboat. But to Cadie's eye, the outline remained sharp.

A plush pad of moss grew in the center of the boat skeleton.

Garrett stepped inside the frame and tilted his face up to catch the day's remaining light. He extended his hand to her, and she joined him.

He sat cross-legged in the middle of the ghost ship and opened the wine.

A chorus of bullfrogs bellowed from the water's edge, gulping air. Crickets filled in the spaces between the frogs' pleadings. She felt more like herself in the woods than she did indoors, closer to some undefinable, wild place she longed to inhabit.

He handed her a cup of wine and she took two swallows.

"I'm really sorry I scared you," he whispered.

She crawled closer until her nose was inches from his. "Call first next time?" She kissed him and pulled back to study his face. She tried not to see Clyde in his features. His hairline and posture mimicked Clyde's, but the smoother line of Garrett's jaw and his gentle smile erased his uncle's harsh edges.

He touched both hands to her face, tracing the contour of her cheekbones and down the nape of her neck and arms until they came to rest on her hips. She inched closer; residual adrenaline coursed through her, heating the wine that lingered on her tongue. The unresolved edge of fear amplified the woodlands night orchestra, the smell of moss, and patterns of waning light.

His fingers inched under the edge of her shirt, caressing the bare skin of her lower back.

Cadie held Garrett's gaze as she eased off her button-down shirt and pulled her tank top over her head. She unbuttoned his shirt and pressed her palms against his warm chest.

Under the canopy of branches, the clicks of the woods blended with Garrett's breath in her ear, in her mouth. She wrapped herself around his body, under his body, slipping deeper into the forest floor, becoming part of the muscular decay and renewal of the forest as they made love with the intimacy of a first kiss and the fierceness of unrecoverable time.

The crowns of oak trees framed a window straight up to the sky, where starlings billowed like lace. Cadie inhaled Garrett's exhale. Mineral iridescence tingled on her tongue. Garrett tasted like the lake. Or maybe the lake had always tasted like him.

Cadie lay with her head on his chest, floating in the ghost of a ship that had been the foundation of her greatest joy and deepest wound. She traced the contour of a lichen-covered stone next to Garrett's shoulder on the port side of the boat skeleton.

"It feels like a different lifetime," she said. "A wayward boat, secret love letters from a mysterious stranger. Daniela and I even drew treasure maps. But they're all gone. Like none of it ever happened."

The forest soaked up her words, her sweat, her regret.

"But if it hadn't happened," he said, as he pulled a leaf from her hair, "we wouldn't be here now. How do I reconcile that?"

Evening sun shone through gaps in the pine trees, casting a shadow over Garrett's face and backlighting the messy outline of his hair. He traced the shadow of a tree branch across her arm, sending a chill over her skin.

"None of what happened was your fault, Cadie. If you never found the boat, if I never set it loose, Clyde still would have robbed that store. Juan would still be gone," Garrett said.

"But we should have turned Clyde in. You can't make that part okay."

Garrett propped himself up on his elbow and kissed her shoulder. "I wish I had known about your illicit business, your maps, your secrets."

"I'd show it to you, the map, but it's gone."

"What was on it?"

An eerie calm settled in the forest. The birds quieted. The wind stilled itself.

"The cove, these woods." Cadie swallowed twice. "And where we hid the gun."

Garrett turned his head to one side as if he didn't understand her words. "I thought you threw it in the lake."

"I didn't."

"Where is it?" Garrett's eyes widened in that same expression Cadie had seen in the Summer Kid's eyes whenever they paddled too close. A blue vein pulsed against his temple.

"We hid it in a hollow tree in the woods back along the easement, but it's gone. Neither of us ever told anyone. I think Clyde found it."

"Why didn't you get rid of it like I asked?"

"I don't know. I was scared. I was eleven."

"But you never showed anyone or told anyone?"

"I told you, no one else knew, not even Dolores."

"Cadie, this is a big problem. If whoever has the gun links it to Juan's death . . ." Garrett paused and looked around the clearing, as if making sure no one could hear them. "That gun is registered to Clyde. It could all come back on us."

"I'm pretty sure Clyde's the one who found it." She fumbled to reach her pants to get the note she found in the tree. "Who else would have left this in my hiding spot?"

Garrett grabbed the note and stared at it for a few seconds. "This isn't Clyde's handwriting."

"So maybe he disguised his handwriting. It's him. I know it." Cadie felt less certain as she watched the perplexed look on Garrett's face.

"Clyde thinks the gun's at the bottom of the lake. I did too, until just now. He wouldn't have gone looking for it, and even if he had, how could he have found your exact hiding spot in this giant expanse of woods?" Garrett said. "Clyde isn't this monster you make him out to be."

"In case you forgot, he's a murderer. I get it that he thought he was being noble by getting Juan's money back from that racist shopkeeper who stole it. It was stupid, but I can maybe believe he had noble intentions. But Juan? I was there. I heard them fighting."

"I know, but—"

"Stop. Even if shooting him *was* an accident, Juan was his friend. He just let him die. He didn't even try to get help." Cadie felt Garrett's heart rate accelerating as she spoke. "We left him there too. Clyde isn't the only one who needs to atone. I've spent my whole life running away from this. All of us have."

The noises lingering at the edge of evening—the waning warbles of birds, crickets tuning up their evening chorus—filled in the emptiness around them. The woodland chatter usually calmed her, but lying in the outline of the rowboat with Garrett, the pitch of the crickets' wings rubbing together seemed off-key, the harmony of chirrups, out of sync.

"Cadie." He took a deep breath. "I haven't told you everything, either."

His pager buzzed from his pants pocket behind him. Garrett reached over to read the message. "Shit. There's a fire." He let out a long stream of air as if grateful for the distraction.

"No kidding, that's what I've been trying to tell everyone," Cadie said. "What didn't you tell me?"

"No, I mean the fire's *here*. Or close, anyway. I have to go."

"You're not a firefighter. Why do you have to go?"

"We need to start evacuations in some parts of town, just in case." Garrett fumbled for his clothes.

"How far away is it?" The evening air chilled Cadie's skin where Garrett had been pressed against her. She reached for her shirt. "Where's the evacuation zone?"

"I don't have all the details. But you might want to get anything important out of your house. It's probably fine, but just to be safe. They're setting up a shelter at the rec center. I'll find you there later."

"Wait, what were you going to tell me?" Cadie grabbed his arm as he buttoned his shirt. "What don't I know?"

"I'll explain later. I promise. And we need to figure out who wrote that note. Clyde didn't do it. I'm sure of that." He leaned over and kissed her, letting his lips linger on hers a few seconds, then abruptly jumped up and disappeared into the shadows.

31

By the time Cadie got dressed and back to the cottage, Garrett's truck was gone. The small house felt empty. A seeping loneliness filled the kitchen and spilled down the hall toward her bedroom. She grabbed her backpack and sprinted to her car. If a fire was coming, maybe she could help.

At the fire station Cadie found three middle-aged men bent over a desk, looking at maps. "We already dug firebreaks here, here, and here," Chester said to the other firefighters.

"Have you seen any of those dying pines I told you about? If you have, those are the areas you should be most worried about." Cadie walked up to the men and looked at the maps.

"I think we've got this covered, young lady," Chester said.

"No, you don't. Will you listen for one fucking minute?"

"Whoa there, settle down."

"I will, if you do your goddamn job," Cadie said.

"Exactly. It's *our* job. Not yours. Aren't you Ryan's friend?" The man turned to the other two firemen, who had pulled back from the maps. "Ryan bet me ten bucks he could get her number. I'm no fool, I figured there's no way a cute thing like that's giving her number to Ryan, so I took the bet. Damn if he didn't come back with her number in less than two minutes."

"What areas are you evacuating?" Cadie ran her hand over the large map of the state on the wall. Four different fires, most of them far north of Maple Crest, appeared to be burning. "Wait, these are all active fires?"

"They're all small. Most started in the last several hours. One of them's already contained. One's near us, and we've got crews from all over the state on their way," a firefighter said.

"The fire won't make it past this ridge, will it?" Cadie pointed to a natural barrier ridgeline.

"Maybe you should be packing up your belongings if you're so worried," a firefighter said.

"The woods between here and here." She pointed to the range just outside of town and the forest that edged close to the lake. "This whole forest is at risk if it gets past the ridge. There's too much dead wood, and with dried-up marsh in there, there's no way you can stop a fire once it hits this line." Cadie drew a slash across a stretch of forest dangerously close to the base of the Hook. "These woods are already infested with that beetle I told you about. And that means dead wood."

"Like I said, Forest Service firefighters are on their way. At least it's not anywhere near the town center."

The firefighters looked at the map, no longer teasing Cadie.

"How do you know all of this?" The older man's voice no longer sounded confrontational.

"This is what I do. I'm an entomologist with the forestry department." Cadie paced the floor in the small office. "We needed to thin trees days ago. It's too late now."

Cadie's phone buzzed.

I won't be a part of your lies anymore. I'm putting it back, read a message from Sal's phone number.

"Is that Ryan calling to ask you out?" Chester laughed, although even he no longer appeared amused by his jokes.

Putting what back? Cadie wrote back. A chill ran up her spine.

Whatever you did, you keep my mom and my family out of it.

"Shit," Cadie said out loud. Sal had the map. Of course Sal had the map. She'd all but told Cadie that night they met at the Garcias'. *I read The Poachers' Code*, she had whispered, but Cadie had assumed Sal found it on the underside of the bedroom shelf.

The Code had been hidden with the map. And the map led directly to the gun.

Sal was going to put the gun back into the hollow tree.

"Shit, shit, shit." Cadie fumbled to dial Sal's number, but it went straight to voicemail.

"Don't get so worked up. Ryan won't answer right away. He's out warning folks to evacuate." Chester hiked his pants up. "We need to head out."

Don't go into the woods. There's a fire evacuation order. Where are you? I'll come get you. Cadie waited for confirmation that Sal had received her text, but the message remained unread.

Cadie ran out of the fire station without acknowledging the heckling of the firefighters.

She tried calling Daniela, but it went straight to voicemail again. Dolores answered when Cadie called the Garcias'. "Have you heard from Sal?"

"No." Dolores's voice sounded tight. "We've been looking for her. There's a voluntary evacuation order. I think we should leave. But I can't find her."

"I think Sal's in the woods. It's a long story. I'm going to go look for her. My phone's about to die. I need you to call Garrett and tell him I'm looking for Sal. Tell him to go to the place where I used to winter the boat. Do you understand? Tell Garrett to meet me in the place where I wintered the boat to help me find Sal. Tell him it's an emergency."

"What's she doing in the woods?"

"I can't explain now. You and Raúl need to evacuate."

"Raúl's at the store. I told him I'd meet him at the evacuation shelter. But I'm not leaving without Sal. What if she comes back here?"

"Leave her a note. I'll go to the house and look for her if I can't find her in the woods."

"I'll tell Daniela." Dolores's voice sounded calmer than Cadie would have expected.

"If my phone dies, I'll text you from Sal's phone. We'll meet you at the shelter. Call Garrett right now."

Cadie sprinted toward her car, parked in front of the hardware store. A thirteen-year-old girl in the woods with a gun. The fire shouldn't move as far as their woods, even according to the models in the fire station. But she could already smell it.

What if Sal got trapped in the woods? Did she know about the fire or the evacuation?

"Answer the phone, Sal," she said out loud, hitting redial again and again. She stopped as she approached her car. A man leaned on the hood. He shifted his weight from one leg to the other.

Clyde looked up at her.

Cadie thought about running back to the fire station a few blocks away, but Clyde's voice all those years ago echoed in her head. *Don't be an idiot. You know I can catch you.*

"Raúl didn't shoot anybody and we both know it," Clyde yelled, slurring his words. He took a few wobbly steps toward her.

Cadie backed up. She wrapped her hand around the stone in her pocket, the one she'd picked up outside the post office two days earlier. She held the flat side against her palm, a sharp, jagged point facing out as he approached her.

Clyde moved toward her and leaned so close the alcohol on his breath formed a mist in front of her face. "I tried to take care of him. I even threatened a little girl to protect him." Spittle sprayed the side of Cadie's face.

Clyde's eyes looked wet and far away. He straightened his back.

Cadie pulled the stone from her pocket and squeezed it. They both stood motionless for stretched-out seconds. She could smash him in the head and run back to the fire station. In his drunken haze, he wouldn't be able to catch her. The cool granite felt powerful in her fist. She raised her arm to hit him.

"I was supposed to keep him safe." Clyde stepped back from her reach and smashed his beer bottle on the ground.

"We both know what you did." Cadie readjusted her grip and held the stone in the air above her shoulder.

"I'm not letting Raúl go down for this," Clyde said. His face looked so much like Garrett's. The same asymmetrical droop to his eye. But the opposite eye. As if they were mirror images of each other.

Cadie eased her grip on the rock, but held it in striking position.

Clyde turned his back to Cadie and shuffled over the gravel. Without turning to face her, he yelled, "He'll do anything to protect his secrets."

"Raúl isn't hiding anything," Cadie yelled.

He swatted his hand at her and shook his head. "I promised my sister I'd take care of her kid," Clyde muttered to the ground as if he'd forgotten Cadie was there.

The street was quiet, too quiet, even for Maple Crest.

"There's a fire moving this way," Cadie called to Clyde. He swatted his hand back at her again, as if he didn't care, and continued down the center of the empty street, his hands stuffed deep in his pants pockets.

With less than an hour of light remaining, the woods would fall dark quickly.

As she unlocked her car, another vehicle skidded into the parking lot and pulled in behind her, blocking her in.

"Cadie, thank God." Daniela jumped out of the car. "No one can find Sal. The fire's getting close."

"She just texted me." Cadie showed Daniela Sal's message. "I think she's got the gun, but I'm not sure. She won't answer me. I'm headed to the woods between our houses to look for her."

"Fuck, fuck, fuck!" Daniela thrust both hands into her thick hair and dug her fingernails into her scalp.

"You go back to the house and get your mom." Cadie put both hands on Daniela's shoulders. Daniela's whole body trembled. Daniela had always been the strong one, the brave one. Her fear sent a chill through Cadie.

Daniela pressed her lips into a tight white line the exact way Dolores did when she was scared. She pulled Cadie into a tight embrace. "I'll find my parents. Call me when you have Sal and we'll meet up at the rec center."

Cadie remembered that feeling of floating in the lake, head to head with Daniela, clinging to each other's fingers. Holding Daniela now in the parking lot, Cadie felt the surge of her friend's desperation pulsing inside her.

"We're going to find her." Cadie tried to sound more confident than she felt.

Gravel sprayed as Daniela sped out of the parking lot.

Green-gray smoke from the mountains made it feel like dusk, although the sun still hovered above the horizon line. Cadie couldn't help but marvel at the colors nature created when it was about to lose control.

32

Cadie spent the two years following Juan's death trying to reclaim the control she lost that day. She learned to suppress the reflex to jump when she heard a car backfire, but couldn't quash the impulse to hide when she imagined she saw Clyde at the movies, at the grocery store, everywhere she went.

The night before the movers arrived, Cadie sat in the only bedroom she had ever known. She looked at the sad drape of her Girl Scout sash slung over the hutch above her desk, where it had drooped, untouched, for two years.

She ached to leave this place.

When her father had approached her with news of his job teaching art in Boston, his eyes looked guilty, as if he expected her to beg him to stay. But she had thrown her arms around his neck and nuzzled into his scratchy whiskers.

"I'm so proud of you," she had whispered.

"But we'll have to move."

"Boston will be fun."

Her father had pulled back from her embrace and stared at Cadie.

"When did you grow up?"

Cadie shrugged. She knew exactly when she had grown up, and she couldn't wait to leave every reminder of it behind.

She hadn't packed anything with her but clothes and a few books. All the evidence of her childhood—the trinkets, the favorite toys, the unopened bike seat she could never bring herself to put on her bike—would stay in the house that they planned to use as a summer retreat. She had not informed her parents, but Cadie vowed never to return.

That final night before the move, Cadie curled up into a tight knot in bed, trying to conjure a flicker of nostalgia. But all she felt was relief. The oak branches outside her window cast shadows of spindly spiders on her ceiling and down the wall toward the foot of her bed. The stone in her gut had grown to a boulder. It slowed her down as she walked and resisted when she tried to get up. It rolled around, taking up space and crushing her appetite.

She spent her nights waiting. Waiting for sleep to come. Waiting for the nightmares to wake her. Waiting for the sun to rise.

A rustling of footsteps outside crunched over twigs and brush near the edge of the woods. The heavy paws were too big to be a skunk or raccoon. Cadie froze as the deliberate steps moved closer to the house, tromping over the gravel. She pressed into the corner where her bed tucked against a sloping wall, her pillow tight across her lap. She wished she could disappear into the shadow world on the walls. The steps approached her windowsill and stopped, sniffing for Cadie.

The beast outside her window snuffled and exhaled with a slight vocalization no animal could make. The footsteps, the breath, were human. If she tried to get to the door, the person at her window would see her. If she tried to crawl under the bed, he would hear her.

The distinct outline of a person stood against the shifting shadow branches on her wall. An arm rose toward her open window. Cadie ducked under her quilt as knuckles hit the window frame.

"Cadie, it's me," Daniela whispered. "Are you awake?"

"It's one in the morning." Cadie crawled down to the foot of the bed to look out the window.

"I can't sleep," Daniela said. "You're leaving tomorrow, aren't you?"

The purple circles under her eyes and unbrushed hair made Daniela look as vulnerable as Cadie felt. When their hands touched, palm to palm through the screen, Cadie saw that the same stone crushing her from the inside weighed on Daniela too. Cadie popped the screen out and helped Daniela climb over the window-sill. Flakes of dirty white paint from the exterior clung to her shirt as she shimmied over the edge.

"I was afraid Friar would bark and wake everyone up." Daniela held a folded towel under one arm.

"Friar's gone," Cadie whispered. "We buried him in the woods a month ago."

"Oh, God, Cadie. I'm sorry." Daniela's wide eyes did not convey sympathy or a requisite gesture to console. Daniela appeared heart-broken for her own sake. Tears welled in her eyes. "I loved that dog."

"I put a stone in that clearing near where I stashed the boat," Cadie said. They both looked out the window into the darkness. "I hate leaving him here."

"I could check on him every now and then, if you want."

Cadie nodded, not trusting herself to speak without crying. Knowing someone else missed Friar, that someone else might visit the stone, felt important. An ache not relieved, but shared.

She wanted to tell Daniela how much she'd missed her and tell her she was sorry. Sorry for not keeping her promise. Sorry for get-ting Dolores involved. Sorry for putting Daniela's family in danger. Regret and fear stabbed Cadie in her gut every time she had seen Daniela after that summer. Losing her best friend had been the price she paid to keep the guilt away.

But Cadie said nothing. As much as she missed her friend, she wanted to let go. Too many dark memories haunted these woods. She would be better off with nothing to miss when the moving truck drove away in the morning.

"I brought you a going-away present, but you need to be quiet." Daniela sat next to Cadie on the edge of the bed and unfolded the towel as if she were handling fine crystal. Inside lay one of the small wooden tambourines from Daniela's bedroom wall. The tiny stacks of cymbals caught the moonlight and cast faint glimmers, like wan-ing stars, onto the tree limbs on her wall.

"It's to keep the bears away. I don't want you to be scared any-more."

"But you love this thing." Cadie fingered the smooth wooden circle the diameter of a salad plate. The delicate shimmering discs made a muted chime, diffused by the towel.

"Shhhh!" Daniela whispered as Cadie turned the jingling instrument over in her hands. "I still have the other one."

"Thanks." Cadie rewrapped the towel around the tambourine and placed it on her nightstand. "I'll never worry about bears again."

"I'll always have your back, Cadie Braidy." Daniela held her thumb up to Cadie so the scar on her thumb faced out. Phantom pain shot through Cadie's thumb as she pressed her own scar against Daniela's. She felt the rush of their blood pulsing against each other. Scooting backward toward the corner of her bed, she made room for Daniela next to her. Daniela put her head on Cadie's shoulder and they sat silently in the stillness.

"I'll never tell," Cadie whispered.

"I know."

The minor key of a Bicknell's thrush cut through in the forest. They were preparing to head south soon too. Cadie sat up straight and put a finger to her lips. She strained her ears, hoping to hear the call one last time.

"Why do you love that bird so much?" Daniela whispered.

"Because no one else notices it. You hear the day song all the time. Most people don't even know it sings at night sometimes," Cadie said.

"Maybe it only sings for you. Maybe no one will ever hear it again after you leave."

The tiny thrush was never meant to live in that forest. Maybe Cadie no longer belonged there either.

Cadie slipped off her paracord bracelet and fastened it around Daniela's wrist. "In case of emergency."

"Thanks," Daniela said. "I feel safer already."

Cadie was as tall as Daniela now. Sitting next to her felt different, yet familiar, as if the cells in her body remembered Daniela's heartbeat. They watched the shadows without speaking. Moonlight skimmed Cadie's feet, glancing the tips of Daniela's toes next to hers. The stone settled into a stationary place in Cadie's gut, where, over time, she would learn to ignore the weight.

The following morning before her parents woke, Cadie snuck into the woods carrying the tambourine. The rhythmic trill against her thigh gave her courage as she walked. She imagined the sound forming a protective force field around her. A bouquet of ferns and Queen Anne's lace lay in front of Friar's grave. Daniela must have picked them on her way home the previous night.

Cadie knelt on the ground to arrange the ferns in a fan over Friar's grave. She would miss the individual pieces of this forest. The oaks, beech, and hemlock. Rotting logs, moss, and the dew on spiderwebs. Bird calls she knew by heart. But the forest itself and the secrets it enshrined, she could walk away from.

"I'll never forget you're here," she whispered.

She did not want that ache back. She had mourned Friar. She had let go of Daniela. She had let go of everything. Or at least she had tried.

Cadie collected four rocks from the periphery of the clearing and added them to the stone outline of the rowboat. Over the past two years she had made a habit of adding stones to fill in the gaps. She could tell Daniela had been adding stones too, although Cadie had never seen her do it. Larger rocks had settled into the soil and become a permanent feature of the forest floor. The outline had grown sharper and more defined. Cadie wondered if Daniela would continue adding stones after Cadie moved.

The white speckle of waterlilies, their broad petals already open to the morning sun, greeted her as she pushed through the curtain of dew-covered hemlock branches to step out onto the rock where she and Daniela used to meet.

Her tambourine rang out in a crystalline shimmer above the morning mist on the lake.

Cadie sat so her toes dipped into the water and untied the stiff, sandy rope tethering the rowboat to the birch tree. She wound the rope into a neat coil on the bottom of the boat and straightened the oars, exactly the way she had found them two years earlier.

Cadie tilted her face up to the sun and stuck her tongue out. She focused on the air, but the lemon fizz was gone. She scooped up a mouthful of lake water. The water tasted mossy, the way she imagined lake water had always tasted to everyone else. She swished it around her teeth and spit it out in a stream. Instead of feeling emboldened by the minerals in her lake and the smell of her forest, she felt tied, like a ball to a chain, to the land and stone that underscored every step she had ever taken.

She pushed the boat into the same gentle current that had brought it to her. It twisted until it found its path and slipped away, as if it had never been there. For a moment, she panicked and almost dove in after it. It was her boat. But then again, it had never really belonged to her.

33

Still shaking from her encounter with Clyde, Cadie skidded into her driveway and ran inside to find a flashlight. She rummaged through kitchen drawers.

She had to find Sal before the fire did.

It felt as if time had stopped in those kitchen drawers. Marbles mixed in with grimy pennies, paper clips, and keys that no longer had locks. No flashlights. She dumped the contents of the next drawer on the kitchen counter. Three nickels spun like tops on the butcher block.

As the last coin collapsed on the counter, the lights went out. The hum of electricity fell silent in the walls. No birds outside. No crickets.

The power went out frequently, she told herself. Nothing to worry about.

She grabbed her backpack. The tambourine rattled inside the canvas bag, a sound that had accompanied her up and down mountains. A sound meant to warn wild creatures. A noise that might alert a thirteen-year-old who did not want to be found. Cadie set the tambourine on the counter.

A vehicle with red flashing lights pulled up her driveway. When Cadie got to the door, she found Ryan in full fire gear.

"What do you want?" Cadie said.

"We're asking residents of the Hook to voluntarily evacuate." He spoke to her as if they were strangers.

His ugly words at the Deer Park rang in her mind. Pale purple bruises edged in yellow marred Ryan's cheek and jawline from

Cadie's and Raúl's fists. Ryan touched his jaw when he noticed Cadie inspecting his injuries.

"You have twenty minutes to gather up any important belongings. If you need a place to sleep, there's a shelter at the rec center. Can we have your word that you will clear out within twenty minutes so we can check the house off as evacuated?"

"Yes." Cadie grabbed a coffee mug her mother had made and stuffed it in her open pack.

"Is anyone else here? Does anyone else live here?"

"No. You know no one lives here." She scanned the shadow-filled cottage. Would this be the last time she saw it?

"I'm following protocol." He looked at Cadie's foot tapping against the floor. "It's going to be okay, as long as the wind doesn't turn. But we aren't taking any chances."

"Got it. I'm leaving." Cadie walked toward the door. Ryan didn't move.

"Is Garrett here?"

"I told you I'm alone. Not that it's any of your business. Why?"

"Nothing, I thought—" Ryan looked embarrassed. "Never mind."

He took a few steps toward the driveway and stopped. "I'm sorry about last night. Things got out of hand. I got out of hand. I said some stuff."

"Don't you have fires to put out?" Cadie pushed past him.

"I didn't mean anything. I just . . ." Ryan looked like an over-grown child playing fireman.

"You need to go." She tapped her boot on the floor. "Besides, I'm not the one you need to apologize to."

He looked at her with his upside-down smile and backed off of the porch without breaking eye contact. "I'm sorry."

"Fuck you," she said under her breath.

Ryan loped off like a high school football player. He would always be a high school football player.

Cadie tried Sal's phone, but her own phone had no signal. She darted into the trees. It would take twenty minutes to get to the beech tree where she suspected Sal had gone to return the gun.

Cadie's feet knew where to go even if her eyes weren't yet adjusted to the dark. She could navigate these woods without a flashlight and save her cell phone battery. She could be a squirrel, a deer, like she had been as a girl.

She moved down the path, past the stones marking Friar's grave. A fern brushed against her leg, and for a moment she thought it was Friar, staying close as he always had.

As Cadie approached the clearing where she had hidden the gun in the beech tree, a feathery chill brushed across her bare arms. Dappled moonlight sifted down between the branches. Footsteps crackled in the near distance. She dropped to her knees and shimmied under a low-hanging hemlock to peer into the clearing. She crouched under the branches, waiting for her eyes to adjust.

She didn't want to startle Sal.

On the opposite side of the clearing Sal stood about twenty feet away from a man Cadie could not see clearly. Had Clyde gotten there before her?

She resisted the urge to jump out and announce herself to Sal and the man. She fingered a dry oak leaf and listened.

"Tell me why you want it," Sal said. Shadows defined the sharp bridge of her nose and the angular jawline she shared with Daniela.

"Let me have the gun and I'll explain." He took a step toward Sal. His voice sounded strained, ready to explode. "I don't want you to hurt yourself."

Cadie could almost feel his breath in her ear. On her lips.

The clouds shifted, illuminating the man's face, Garrett's face. The fear prickling up Cadie's neck melted down her back.

It was just Garrett. Dolores had called him like Cadie asked.

His familiar voice should have eased her fear. But the tension in Sal's eyes made Cadie pause. Her pulse quickened.

"Don't come any closer." Sal's eyes darted around the clearing. She lifted her arms and pointed the weapon at Garrett.

Cadie crept closer behind the low brush on the perimeter of the clearing and perched on her haunches behind a bush.

"What does this gun have to do with my mother?" Sal held both arms out straight, gripping the weapon. "Did she kill that man they found?"

Could the gun still fire after all those years sealed in layers of Ziploc bags? Was it loaded?

Cadie's stomach twisted as she tried to push back the memory of Juan's voice. *Don't point that thing at me.* She had to stop Sal, but her joints felt frozen, her lips unable to form words.

Garrett stepped closer to Sal and clawed both hands through his hair.

"I want—" He paused. Moonlight caught the stubble on his jawline. The muscles in his cheek tensed as if he were chewing his words. "You need to put the gun down before you do something you'll regret."

Stay calm, Cadie willed Garrett, willed herself. And Sal. *Please, Sal, put the gun down.*

Sal inched her feet apart and squared her shoulders.

"You don't want to have to live with shooting someone." Garrett's voice quivered like a child's. "Trust me. I know."

"Yeah, right. Who'd you shoot?" Sal challenged.

The oak leaf crumbled like dust between Cadie's fingers; only the skeleton of rigid veins clung to the stem. Cadie put the stem between her lips and sucked on the dry stubble to calm her racing heartbeat.

A twig snapped under Cadie's foot. She froze, waiting for Garrett to answer the question.

"Is someone there?" Garrett called. His eyes passed over her hiding spot in the shadows. The look of desperation on his face was like that of a scared child.

"Did my mother shoot that man?"

Garrett shook his head.

"Cadie did it, didn't she?"

Cadie sucked in a sharp breath. How could Sal think Cadie killed someone? The accusation hit the tender spot Cadie had guarded for decades. She hadn't pulled the trigger, but wasn't she just as bad for having hidden the truth for so long?

"No." His voice sounded raspy. "Cadie didn't do anything."

Tell her, Cadie pleaded silently. *Tell her it was Clyde.*

Garrett's hand moved toward his waistband where the bulge of his holster stuck out from beneath his untucked shirt. In profile, his face looked distorted. Garrett, but not Garrett. The oak stem unraveled in Cadie's mouth.

"You don't understand. I panicked." He slid his fingers under his shirt and wrapped them around his gun. His voice strained with a desperation Cadie had never heard from him, at least not from him as an adult.

There's something I didn't tell you. . . . Garrett had tried to tell her something.

No. There was nothing else to know. Clyde shot Juan. Cadie had been there. She heard it. She heard the shot. She heard it.

But she hadn't seen anything.

She spat the oak stem out, but the threads coated the inside of her mouth with bitter particles.

He'll do anything to protect his secrets, Clyde had warned her.

Garrett, with those soft blue eyes, had begged her, *Please help me.*

Cadie dug her fingernails into her palms to stop the truth from exposing itself.

Had Garrett pulled the trigger? Had Garrett killed Juan?

Her breath felt too fast, too loud. Her insides roiled as if the stones she had been carrying all these years had melted into molten rock. She wanted to reach back in time and shake the little girl with the red braids. *How could you not have seen this? How could you not have known?*

Had she known all along? Had some part of her known the truth? She reached into her pocket and rubbed her fingers over the coarse stone. The feeling of granite under her fingertips usually soothed her. Steady granite, the one thing she could always rely on. She had almost thrown the same rock at Clyde hours earlier, but maybe it had never been Clyde she needed to fear.

"Please, Sal, drop the gun," Garrett said, his voice sounding unsteady. "You don't want to shoot me. It will haunt you for the rest of your life."

"*You* shot him?" Sal's eyes widened and she tightened her grip on the weapon that had killed Juan. The weapon Garrett had fired. The weapon he had asked Cadie to dump in the lake. "You killed that guy?"

If Cadie had done what he'd asked and dumped the gun in the lake, none of this would be happening. Or if she had turned him in. But Cadie hadn't done either and now her secrets had drawn all three of them into the woods at this moment.

Garrett slid his gun from its holster without denying her accusation.

The little girl inside Cadie pleaded with herself to duck behind the bushes, to run back toward the cottage. But she was no longer a child. Sal would not pay the price for Cadie's cowardice.

Cadie stepped out with her hands over her head. "Garrett. Sal, put the guns down. It's me. It's Cadie."

"Cadie?" A little-boy smile flickered in the corners of Garrett's mouth, then disappeared. He sounded confused, mounting panic evident as his eyes flashed from Cadie to Sal and back to Cadie. "Stay back. I don't want you to get hurt."

"Why are you here, Cadie?" Sal spoke through a clenched jaw.

Cadie couldn't suppress a twinge of admiration, maybe jealousy, for the girl's boldness.

"Cadie." Garrett's voice intoned the desperation Cadie had seen in his eyes as he waved her away from his pier that long-ago, but ever-present summer.

Cadie's feet burned in her hiking boots. Her trembling knees quieted as the heat rose up her legs and filled her chest. Perspiration dripped down her neck, her back, between her breasts.

"Sal's confused. Tell her to put the gun down." Garrett shifted from one foot to the other and grabbed at his hair.

"Garrett." Cadie tried to keep her voice calm. "I think you should put yours down first."

Twenty feet separated him from Sal. As Sal looked toward Cadie,

Garrett aimed his gun at the girl. He took one step toward her. Then another.

"You don't understand," he said.

"I think I do," Cadie said.

All the nights she had lain awake reliving the sound of that gunshot, she had wrapped herself in the myth that she had protected Garrett. She had saved the Summer Kid. And she had tried to protect Daniela's family.

The muscles along his jaw twitched.

"Garrett." Cadie stepped closer. "Please lower your gun."

He ignored her and cracked his neck, never taking his eyes off of Sal. His hands trembled as he readjusted his grip on the gun.

Cadie fingered the bumpy stone in her pocket. She held time in her hand. Crystals of cooled magma from another millennium. In a vulnerable moment, under enough pressure, even granite bends.

Cadie hurled the stone toward Garrett's head just as a gunshot exploded in the night.

34

"Noooo!" Cadie felt a long wail rip from her throat and fill the clearing, although she couldn't hear her voice over the pounding of her heart and the blood rushing through her ears.

The air above Cadie's head sizzled. A bullet thunked into the tree behind her shoulder, and the smell of sulfur swirled around her.

Garrett slumped to the ground.

Sal froze with the weapon in her outstretched arms. Her eyes wide and unblinking, she stared at Garrett on the ground in front of her.

"Sal, you need to put the gun down."

Sal did not move.

"Sal, it's me, Cadie. Can you put the gun down for me?" Cadie tried to calm her voice.

"I shot him."

"I need to check on him. Okay?" She wanted to run to him, to get there before he sat up and found his gun. If he sat up. *Don't be dead.* She forced herself to move slowly so she wouldn't startle Sal. *Garrett, please don't be dead.*

He lay motionless on the ground.

Sal had not shifted her posture. Arms straight in front of her, hands locked on the gun.

Cadie touched a hand to Garrett's chest, still rising and falling with breath. He moaned, and Cadie recoiled. Part of her wanted to find a bullet wound and press into it so he would feel the pain more acutely. And part of her longed for him to open those blue eyes and reassure her everything was fine.

This had all been a misunderstanding.

A whiff of smoke sifted through the branches, clinging to Cadie's tongue. She spat in the dirt to keep down a dry heave as she ran her hands over the familiar lines of his chest, abdomen, face, and neck. And the smooth skin behind his ear. Unwelcomed tenderness edged in as she thought of pressing her lips against his neck.

"Cadie." He grabbed her wrist and held her arm.

She yanked her arm out of his grasp and continued searching for a bullet wound.

Blood trickled between Cadie's fingers when she touched the soft spot of Garrett's temple, exactly where Cadie had aimed the rock.

"You didn't hit him." She looked up at Sal, who still had not moved. "I did. I threw a rock at his head. There's no bullet wound."

Sal lowered her weapon a few inches. "Is he okay?"

"He's just stunned. But I need your shirt, quick."

Garrett tried to sit up, but Cadie shoved him back to the ground. Cadie leaned her elbow into his chest. "Don't move."

"Give me your shirt," Cadie ordered Sal. "We need to stop the bleeding."

Sal laid the gun next to her feet and peeled off her plaid button-down. She tossed it to Cadie and stood in her tank top, shivering in the warm air.

Cadie crawled past the shirt on the ground to grab the gun by Sal's feet.

She would have recognized that gun with her eyes closed. She had dreamt of the precise weight, the texture of the grip panel. She touched her fingertip to the muzzle, warm from having been fired.

She slid the barrel into the waistband of her shorts. Garrett lay flat on his back, both hands clutching his head. She couldn't find his gun in the dark mass of leaves and twigs covering the ground. Cadie needed to find his weapon before Garrett did. Before Sal did. She rustled the leaves, picked up rocks. It had to be there.

"There." Sal pointed at a glint in the leaves behind his head.

Cadie nodded at Sal and picked up Garrett's gun, smaller and sleeker than the one pressing into her hip. She tucked Garrett's weapon into her shorts next to the other one. His gun felt cold against her skin. Cadie's waistband pulled tight and cut into her stomach. Metal dug into her back with each movement.

She beckoned Sal to come closer.

"I need you to hold this." She guided Sal's hand to hold the shirt against Garrett's temple.

Sal knelt next to Cadie.

"We need to get out of here," Cadie said. "The wind could shift and bring the fire this way." She tore at the paracord bracelet on her wrist with her teeth. It tasted like the sweat and tree sap from several years' worth of *just in case.* Sal helped unwind the long cord.

She pulled her head back immediately as she caught a whiff of his vanilla soap mixed with perspiration. And maybe a hint of her own body odor on his skin.

He turned on his side and Cadie held his wrists together behind his back so Sal could tie them together.

"Don't do this. I'm not going to hurt you," Garrett said in a soft, intimate whisper that made Cadie want to lean in closer. "I never would have hurt Sal. You know that."

"Like you would never hurt Juan?"

"I was a kid. I made a mistake. I wanted to tell you."

"None of that matters." Cadie turned him roughly onto his back.

Sal sat back, pulled her arms tight around her knees, and seemed to shrink.

"Sal pointed a weapon at me. I needed to calm her down. I wouldn't have—" He stopped mid-sentence and tilted his head back to look at the sky as if waiting for an answer to the question rolling around in his mind. "Juan was going to turn Clyde in for shooting that store clerk." Garrett looked over at Sal. "I just wanted to scare him so he wouldn't turn Clyde in. I never meant . . ."

Sal looked up and held Garrett's stare. Her posture softened.

"Don't look at her," Cadie said.

"Clyde was, is, my only family." He looked to Sal for sympathy. "I had to protect my family."

Sal let her gaze fall to the leaves at her feet.

"You were protecting yourself," Cadie said.

Garrett's police radio crackled on his hip. "Tierney? Where the hell are you?" a voice shouted through the line. "Fire broke through the ridge. We need to evacuate the Hook immediately. You copy?"

"My house!" Sal jumped up.

Cadie looked up and down the creek bed separating the Garcias' property from hers. Fire crews had already widened the firebreak and hauled off the underbrush. She gave a silent thanks for the soft, muddy banks that never let trees take root. Including both sides of the creek, the firebreak spanned forty feet. In a raging forest fire, embers rising on hot air currents could breach a gap of that size with ease. But a small fire wouldn't.

Cadie, however, did not know which kind of fire approached.

"My truck's along your driveway. I need to get back to it so I can help with the evacuations."

"Don't be an idiot," Cadie said. "If it's beyond the ridge, it's not safe to go back toward my house. You have no idea how fast it's moving."

"People are counting on me." Garrett's eyes flashed with the same panic Cadie remembered seeing on the Summer Kid's face. "I'm getting my truck. You two need to get out of the woods. Can you get to the Garcias'?"

Cadie nodded.

Sal put her hand on Cadie's shoulder. Her smile and dark eyes, so much like Daniela's. Cadie wanted to grab Sal and wrap her arms around the girl. A fierce desire to protect Sal beat stronger than her fear of the fire or of Garrett.

"Let him go." Sal squeezed Cadie's shoulder.

Garrett's face took on a blue pallor in the moonlight. The blood trickling down the side of his head matted his blond hair, blackening it in the darkness. The urge to wipe it away pulsed nearly as strong as the urge to hit him the way she had Ryan. The satisfaction of physical contact, the impact surging through her fist, to her shoulder, and into her gut, had made her feel powerful. The impulse unnerved her.

She had spent years searching the foster system in New Hampshire, trying to find out what happened to that boy. She had lain awake at night as a teenager worried about him living with a killer. The little girl with the braids howled from deep inside her. She could taste the fire rising up from her lungs. Her breath felt so hot she imagined she could ignite the forest with one word.

Garrett's gaze landed on the butt of his gun sticking out from her waistband.

Cadie backed up several steps. The weapons felt heavy, pulling against her clothing and digging into her flesh. She held his stare.

She felt the fire thrumming in the earth beneath them, in the stillness of the trees, in the dry air. It was coming.

Silence hung thick in the air. Cadie's limbs felt heavy and her mind felt slurry.

Ever since she moved to Boston when she was thirteen, Cadie had clung to the tenets of The Poachers' Code as a plea with the universe to keep the truth buried. But that truth had always been a lie. Who had Cadie been protecting all these years? Garrett, Daniela, Raúl, Dolores, or herself? How would she explain it to her parents? To Thea?

Breath from the approaching fire thickened the sticky air. There was no holding it back. None of it. The heat, the beetles, the fire, the truth. They were all closing in.

Cadie didn't move. She didn't want to release Garrett, but what did she hope to accomplish by keeping him tied up?

"I risked so much for you," he whispered, looking over Cadie's shoulder at Sal to see if the girl could hear them. Sal hugged her knees to her chest and buried her face in her knees.

"What have you *ever* done for me?" Cadie said.

"It's a pretty big coincidence that a fire broke out in Hobson the night after you warned your boss that exact thing might happen," Garrett whispered so Sal wouldn't hear.

"That was because of the beetles and a campfire." Cadie tried to sound confident. Her arms and fingers felt cold as her blood rushed to her torso.

"Sometimes nature needs a nudge," Garrett said.

"People could have died." Cadie pumped her fist, trying to reignite the pain in her bruised knuckles, digging for a spike of pain to drown out the roar escalating in her mind.

"But they didn't." Garrett smiled at her expectantly. "You broke the rules because you had a greater purpose. You know you're right about the beetles, the fires that are coming. I took a careful calculated risk too. Close to a firebreak, far from residential areas. No campers in the area and near a fire station."

"I would never put people at risk just to prove a point."

"Didn't you? What if you had gotten trapped up on Mount Steady and the fire had closed in? Would you have called for help? Would you have put firefighters' lives at risk to come rescue you?"

"It's not the same thing and you know it."

"I did it for you, because I believe in you," Garrett whispered in a soothing voice that caused gooseflesh to rise on her skin. He scooted toward Cadie until his knee touched her leg. "I know how much this forest means to you. Now you have a platform to do something to effect real change. Use it."

Cadie resisted the flicker of solidarity. Garrett saw her in a way no one else did. But, no, not like this. She pushed the comfort away and dug deeper for the rage, the fire inside her. Her seething hatred of Clyde, as much a part of her as her heart and lungs, now floated above her, disembodied. Her desire for Garrett's breath on her neck morphed into revulsion, leaving Cadie spinning like a compass with no true north.

She felt sick. Would the ethics committee have been so forgiving if the Hobson fire hadn't happened? Would they have reinstated her based purely on the strength of her research and projections? Or had they been scared into it by the fire? The exact fire she had predicted.

"I've always been waiting for you," Garrett whispered.

"I was waiting too." Heat in her chest burned as she spoke. She moved farther away from him. "But not for you."

The foundation of all her childhood dreams and nightmares

shifted beneath her, new truths displacing the stories she had told herself for decades. All she had worked for might be stripped away from her if the university found out the man she had been sleeping with started a fire based on information Cadie had given him.

"How could you think I wanted this?" she hissed. Heat rushed back to her numb limbs. "My goal is to prevent fires, not start them."

"Sometimes you have to start a small fire to stop a big one," Garrett said.

"I smell smoke," Sal called to Cadie.

Cadie pulled her pocketknife from her backpack and flicked the blade open. She met Garrett's eyes. The amber specks glittered like stars against the blue she had held in her mind since that first time she saw him on his pier. He seemed unnaturally calm, resigned, focused.

"This fire. You didn't . . ." Cadie squeezed the grip on the knife.

"God, no. Of course not."

She cut through the cord around his wrists, but he did not move. Her fingers lingered on his skin.

"Go," Cadie yelled at him.

"I can't leave my weapon with you, you know that."

"How do I know you aren't going to turn it on Sal and me?"

"Cadie, I'd never—"

"Just give it to him," Sal said.

Cadie pulled both weapons from her waistband. She lay Garrett's gun on the ground and held the old one in her hands, arm stretched out straight, her finger around the trigger.

"What are you doing?" Sal tried to pull Cadie's arms down so the weapon didn't point at Garrett. Cadie shrugged her off. She kicked Garrett's weapon toward him and backed several steps away from him.

"Put it in your holster and walk away with your hands in the air so I know you aren't going to turn it on us."

"Cadie, please don't be like this," he said, but followed her instructions.

He disappeared into the woods, sprinting toward his truck in Cadie's driveway.

Cadie turned back to Sal, who sat with her back against the beech tree that once hid the gun Cadie now carried. Tears streaked Sal's cheeks, but she no longer cried. "You and Mom didn't kill that guy?"

"No." Sal deserved more than a one-syllable answer. Cadie had spent a lifetime deconstructing Juan's death and what her role in the story had been. She took cover in the looming fire to avoid putting the story back together. "Come on, we need to get out of here."

Sal kept pace with Cadie as she moved in the direction of the creek and the Garcias' home.

"Did you leave that note in the tree?" Cadie asked.

"Yeah."

"But why would you threaten your own family?"

"I didn't." Sal looked up.

"'Go Home. Or someone will get hurt.'" Cadie quoted the note she found in the tree.

"I was threatening *you*. I wanted *you* to go home and let the past be before my family got hurt."

"Oh." *Go Home.* She had assumed the note was meant for the Garcias. Her own arrogance burned.

Cadie folded a pine needle, green and waxy, between her fingers. Even with the drought and the dead wood, most of the trees in this forest still had life. They would not give in easily to the flames. Without wind to carry it, the fire would move slowly.

Cadie had time. But not much.

They ducked under a low-hanging branch and emerged on Cadie's bank of Silas Creek.

Cadie surveyed the wide berth on her side of the water and on the Garcias' side. Fire crews—the crews that had discovered Juan's remains—had already cleared the brush on both sides. Mounting heat warmed her neck like a lover's breath as she unzipped her backpack and rummaged in the bottom for the matches she had taken from the hardware store. Adrenaline surged and her fingers trembled as she tore a matchstick from the cardboard book.

"I'm going to try to save your house. But you have to do everything I say, okay?"

Sal nodded.

"I'm going to light a back burn on my side of the creek. If the wind remains calm, the fire will consume everything on this side of the water, and it will move into the woods, away from us. When the big fire catches up to it, there won't be any fuel left to burn between the fire line and the creek. It won't be able to jump to your side."

"But your house." Sal's eyebrows arched high and her dark eyes widened with alarm.

"It's just wood and stone." Cadie tried to sound as if she didn't care, but her voice quivered. If the fire had already broken past the ridge, her home was directly in its path. Even if, by some miracle, the main fire didn't make it to her cottage, the fire she was about to ignite definitely would.

Cadie licked her finger and held it in the air. Barely a breeze, for now.

Be still, she begged the wind, and struck a match.

The match erupted in the darkness. The stick burned slowly, the warmth edging closer to her skin. She cupped her other hand around the flame, letting the heat rise under her chin. The tiny flicker sucked oxygen out of the air, out of Cadie's own lungs.

I stop fires. I don't light them.

Cadie had spent three decades standing with her back to a precipice, her arms open wide to hold back everything she feared, beating down truths that were always meant to rise, like stones in the New Hampshire forest. Pressing back against new species that threatened to throw the woodlands off-balance. Stopping fires that needed to rage. Swallowing words that needed to be spoken.

Now, standing on the edge of Silas Creek with a lit match, she imagined her forest the way it would look the following day. Charred. Barren. Dead. But not really dead.

Piper was right. This forest would rise up stronger.

Under it all, beneath the matted leaves, the rocky soil, and the tangled tree roots, the story of Juan Hernández was scratching its way to the surface. Cadie no longer wanted to stop any of it.

When the flame touched her skin, she dropped the match.

It fell slowly, leaving a streak of light like the tail of a comet as it landed in a nest of crisp beech leaves. Cadie dropped to her knees and blew into the kindling. The fire inhaled her breath and crackled with life.

Her nemesis. Her partner.

Two things could happen. If the wind kicked up, embers, even from a fledgling fire, could sail the expanse over the creek toward the Garcias' house. But if the wind remained calm long enough, the fire would stay on Cadie's side of the creek, retreat into the woods toward her cottage, and spare Daniela's home. She closed her eyes, trying to remember the firefighting training the forestry department required her to take part in. How many feet did a firebreak require?

Wisps of flame climbed the parched branches of a shrub, instinctively clawing its way toward the dry wood in the direction of her home. Cadie dropped another match twenty feet downstream, and another, until the bank alit with a string of tiny, hungry flames.

She handed Sal a lit match and gestured upstream. Protecting the flame with a cupped hand, Sal ran beyond the edge of the small fires Cadie had lit and looked back. Cadie nodded at her and Sal let the match drop into a pile of dried leaves.

Flickering flames drew Cadie's eye to beech nuts scattered on the ground. If this forest was going to burn, she would take part of it with her. She slipped them into her pocket.

A scream rose above the hissing flames. Cadie thought she'd imagined it until Sal jumped up.

"Sal," the voice called from the other side of the back burn Cadie had lit.

"Mom!" Sal shouted.

Daniela was in the fire gap, wedged between two fires moving toward each other.

Sal started running toward Daniela's voice, but Cadie grabbed her arm.

"Wade through the creek. See that path? It's overgrown, but it goes to your house. Get the canoe out and wait for me on the beach for ten minutes. I'll be back with your mom."

"I'm not leaving until I see her."

Cadie squeezed Sal's arm hard. "Do what I tell you. We'll be right there. It will take me longer to find your mom if you're with me. Do you want me to find her?"

Sal nodded. Tears glistened in her eyes.

"If we aren't there in ten minutes, take the boat and row to the marina, then walk to the rec center. Your grandparents are waiting for you there." Cadie pointed to the path. Sal splashed through the water and stopped midway to look back at Cadie.

"Go. Run!" Cadie yelled. Sal climbed the opposite bank and disappeared into the trees.

35

"Daniela?" Cadie shouted as she surveyed the back burn she had started. She could circumvent the fire by running downstream. But she had to get back before the entire bank caught or she would be trapped between firewalls with Daniela.

Cadie ran downstream twenty yards and into the woods.

"Daniela?" she shouted. She pulled her tank top up to cover her face against the smoke. "Where are you?"

"Over here."

Cadie crashed through underbrush, half blind in the dark. *Don't lose your bearings. Stay focused.*

"We're here," Daniela called.

"Keep yelling," Cadie shouted. "I'm coming."

Cadie followed Daniela's voice, imagining her younger self chasing Daniela through these same woods, breathless just for the sake of being breathless.

Cadie found Daniela standing with Dolores.

"Where's Sal?" Daniela grabbed Cadie's arm. "Garrett said she was with you."

"You saw Garrett?"

"He went back for his truck," Daniela said. "Where's Sal?"

"She's safe. I sent her through the path to your house. To the water. She's getting the canoe ready. There's a small fire ahead. We need to hurry so we can get around it."

If the gap between the small fires she had started merged, they wouldn't be able to break through to the creek, to Sal.

Half running, half walking, Daniela led them toward the creek.

Cadie ached to swirl her arms and conjure the wind as Garrett once had from the end of his pier. She closed her eyes and imagined sucking the breath out of the fire, saving them the way the wind had carried the cyclone of dust and leaves to save Cadie when Clyde cornered her behind the library.

A loud pop erupted as vaporized water cracked a tree in the distance. Five hundred and seventy-two degrees—the flashpoint at which wood bursts into flames. If she could hear the fire, it was near her cottage, maybe beyond it. She swallowed and tried to focus. Did Garrett make it to his truck? Would he be able to get out of her driveway to the main road?

So much had transpired in that patch of forest which, by morning, would likely be char and ash. A new beginning. Or another attempt to erase the past.

Dolores touched Cadie's arm in silent acknowledgment that both of them were thinking about the last time they had been together in the woods. The anger Cadie had felt toward Garrett minutes earlier now turned on Dolores. Anger felt better than the storm of betrayal tearing at her insides. She pulled her arm away from Dolores.

"I had no right to put you in that position," Dolores whispered so Daniela couldn't hear her. "You were a child."

"Don't. Not now." Cadie wiped her face and headed toward the back burn. *Find Sal. Find Sal,* she repeated over and over in her mind.

"We need to go downstream to get around the other fire." Cadie walked faster to catch up to Daniela. "Why are you and your mom out here? I thought you were going to the rec center."

"We tracked Sal's cell with an app on her phone," Daniela said as they navigated the rocky forest floor. "I tried to call you, but we lost our cell signal. We knew she was out here, this side of the creek, but we didn't know where. Garrett heard us shouting for Sal and told us where you were."

They ran downstream to evade the back burn and broke into the clearing to find Sal still standing in the opening to the pathway toward the Garcias' house on the opposite bank.

"Mom!" Sal shouted.

"Why didn't you go to the beach like I told you?" Cadie yelled.

"I knew you'd come back. You're Cadie Braidy."

Sal and Daniela ran toward each other, meeting in the middle of the creek. Daniela pulled Sal close and rocked her against her chest.

"I couldn't leave without you," Sal said.

"It's okay. I'm here." Daniela cupped Sal's face in her hands, kissed her daughter's forehead, and fingered the sweaty hair framing her face.

The creeping fire was gaining momentum more quickly than Cadie had expected. The back burn raged with purpose as it scrambled to engage the bigger fire. Flames consumed the flash fuels of moss and leaves and twigs. Tongues hissed and writhed with hunger for the trees Cadie used to climb as a little girl. Her fort in the holly trees. The hammock where she and her father used to practice bird calls.

Upstream, Cadie noticed the rusty remnants of the barbed-wire fence crawling across the water. Dead vines, leaves, and debris wound around the metal, creating a flammable bridge over the creek to the Garcias' property.

Flames slithered less than thirty yards from the fence.

Cadie had effectively lit a fuse that would set the Garcias' home on fire.

Cadie ran toward the fence. She tugged at the wires, trying to break them loose from the posts, but they wouldn't give.

"What did I do?" she said under her breath.

"It's going to jump the creek across the fence," Cadie yelled as she tore at the vines, gnawed them with her teeth. A barb pierced her palm. She pulled harder. Sal stepped in behind her and did the same.

"Don't let the rusty metal cut you," Cadie said.

Sal rolled her eyes.

Daniela and Dolores splashed through the water and began yanking on the vines. Cold water swirled around their legs. Smoke thickened the air.

"We got this, Cadie Braidy." Daniela smiled at her.

Cadie's body pulsed with power. All the fear that had coiled up inside her, protecting her from memories she wanted to forget, exploded with purpose. She wiped the blood from cuts on her palm against her thighs and dug her heels against the slippery rocks. She let the barbs tear into the flesh as she squeezed the wire. With a snap, she fell backward. The rusted wire broke free from a staple binding it to the post, unfurling on top of Cadie. A jagged wire sliced into her calf, splaying her skin open.

"You did it!" Sal's dirt-smeared, tear-stained cheeks glowed. Dolores and Daniela unwound the tangle of wire and vines from on top of Cadie and piled it on the Garcias' side of the creek.

Dolores looked like she could be thirty years old. Only a quarter mile up that creek, on the other side of that fence, lay the grave they had dug together. Her hands bled as they had bled all those years ago. But this day, she and Dolores fought to save something. Dolores put a hand on Cadie's shoulder and squeezed.

"Your leg." Sal knelt in the water next to Cadie. The cut was long and open. But it had missed the major blood vessels.

"Yeah. We're all going to need tetanus shots." Cadie took Sal's hand and examined the cuts on her palms.

Daniela pulled Cadie up from the water and together they walked toward the Garcias' side. Cadie mounted the incline on the bank and rooted her feet into the soil.

Motionless clouds hovered next to the slip of a moon.

The fire would not cross this creek.

Across the water, sparks danced like notes in a symphony, layers and colors, harmony and melody thrashing with unrestrained grace. Embers shot up like the fireworks she and her parents used to watch lying on their backs on the beach in front of the cottage.

A flutter in the low bushes, a rustle in the leaves, caught Cadie's attention. Something lingered in the clearing, formed out of dust and time, held together by shame. A memory so heavy that gravity lent it shape and dimension. Cadie—young Cadie—lingered in those woods, her arm still itching from bug bites. The little girl who believed in magic and adventure. She had stayed in those woods with Juan Hernández.

Cadie wanted to run back across the creek to rescue her younger self. She longed to rub the young girl's back as she pushed the fear of Clyde into that dark place in her gut every night while she lay awake in bed. She wanted to whisper in her ear, *It was never Clyde you needed to be afraid of.*

The back burn inhaled Cadie's breath and roared, leaving her empty and small in the night. Smoke draped over the woods like a tattered shawl.

A loon called out, guiding them toward the lake.

"Let's go," Dolores said. She held up the light of her cell phone as they ran through the forest toward the Garcias' beach. Sal leapt like a deer from rock to rock. Cadie tried to keep up, but the gash in her leg burned with every step. Lockjaw, she thought, mocking the fears she'd clung to as a girl.

Daniela slipped her arm around Cadie's waist to support her limp. Daniela's arm pressed against the gun on Cadie's hip.

"Is that—?" Daniela pulled her arm back.

"Sal had it. She's had it the whole time."

"Jesus, what did we do?" Daniela said.

Cadie wasn't ready to tell Daniela that Sal had fired the gun at Garrett. If Sal had killed him, would Cadie have covered it up to protect Sal the way Clyde had for Garrett? How close had they come to repeating history?

Sal reached the house first and stopped abruptly as she stepped out of the woods. The house stood intact. Silhouetted against the purple sky, Sal raised both arms up overhead and howled a long "Yes!" into the night.

Water lapped against the pylons with the hush of delicate breaking glass, beckoning Cadie to be the mermaid she once believed herself to be.

Her calf throbbed. Blood soaked her sock and shoe.

Dolores ducked inside the shed and pulled down a curtain. She tore the fabric with her teeth and ripped it into strips.

Sal watched the orange swell above the trees in the distance. "The fire could still get across the creek, couldn't it?" she said.

"It's possible. But nothing inside that house matters," Dolores said. She knelt next to Cadie and bound the strips around Cadie's wound so tightly it took Cadie's breath.

Daniela slipped into the captain's seat in the rear of the canoe. Sal and Dolores huddled in the middle. Cadie lowered herself to her knees in the front of the canoe with slow, fluid motions so the gun didn't jab into her hip. She pulled her shirt down to keep the weapon out of sight.

Maybe none of it had been real. She had not set a fire. She had never helped bury Juan Hernández. If she could close her eyes, none of it would have happened.

But she couldn't close her eyes.

The lake shimmered like an expanse of fluttering silk covered in sequins. Cadie dragged her hand through the water to soothe the cuts on her fingers and palm from the barbed wire. The lake felt like a cup of tea left to sit too long, barely warmer than the air, yet still comforting.

The songs of frogs and crickets Cadie heard through her bedroom window traveled from across the water. Bats skimmed the surface of the lake, feasting on the night bugs skittering across it.

As they rounded the Hook toward Cadie's cottage, a torch rose from her wood-shingled roof. Cadie's childhood painted the sky the way a sunset ignites the horizon with its remorseful palette. The glaze on her mother's ceramics and her father's oil paintings peeled away. The embers of A Wrinkle in Time and Tuck Everlasting burst up into the sky alongside Garrett's furtive, adolescent love notes.

The cottage, with all its dark places and painful memories, had always held that point of center in her heart, even when she didn't want it to. Boston had never been home, as she and her parents moved from apartment to apartment until she graduated high school. College in Vermont, a stint in Colorado, and more recently, the tiny apartment in Concord, none of which had ever become home.

She had spent so much energy distancing herself from Maple Crest, yet she always relied on the tug that pulled her back like an anchor.

She thought of Sal's note. *Go Home.*

If this place no longer claimed her, where was home?

The main fire and the back burn had already merged, consuming everything in the space between. Swooning flames stretched up, flicking embers skyward, where Cadie lost them among the stars. She stopped paddling and let the boat drift. They were nowhere. Sound could barely find them. Maybe time would not stomp forward if they just drifted, drifted, drifted, and hid. She rubbed the blister the match had left on the tip of her thumb.

This open water had been the backdrop for all the secrets that haunted her. But it had also been her playground, like Tom and Huck's Mississippi, the Swiss Family Robinson's island. She wanted to love the lake again.

As they passed Garrett's pier, Cadie could almost make out the profile of the Summer Kid in his slung-back lawn chair, sitting among the shadows. The specter nodded at Cadie, but she turned away. Her belief that she had saved Garrett had been her armor. Stripped of that mythology, her story had no hero, no quest, no righteous sacrifice, no happily ever after.

36

The four women walked from the marina to town against the backdrop of a stubbled cornfield. They could have been anywhere. No features defined the lonely strip except the company with whom they walked. If they looked straight ahead, the fires and secrets remained behind them.

Cadie tried to suppress the pain throbbing up her leg, through her chest, and pounding in her skull. *Walk. Don't think. Just walk.* She allowed the rhythm to lull her into a trance.

Daniela slowed her pace to wait for Cadie. Dolores and Sal, about twenty yards ahead of them, looked over their shoulders, each of them wondering if Cadie would keep their secrets, Cadie imagined.

"I need to tell you something. Actually, there's a lot I need to tell you," Cadie said to Daniela. She swallowed hard and cleared her throat of ash. She tasted the truth before she spoke it. The words coated her tongue like warm maple syrup. "I knew where to find the grave that day because I was there the whole time."

Daniela stopped walking, but did not look at Cadie.

"After I left your house, after your mom got that emergency phone call and rushed out, I ran into the woods like I told you. I heard something, so I hid. But I didn't really run away. I stayed."

"You watched? You saw them bury Juan?" Daniela's voice softened. She put her hand on Cadie's forearm. "Shit. You lived with that image in your head all this time?"

"I wish that was it." If she said it out loud she could never take it back. Ahead of them, Dolores and Sal kept walking. "I didn't watch. I helped them bury Juan."

"What? Did Clyde force you to do it? Did he threaten you?"

"Clyde wasn't there."

"So, wait, you and Garrett buried him alone? You and your Summer Kid are keeping this quiet to cover your own asses?"

"I helped Garrett—and your mother. Your mom, Garrett, and I buried Juan together."

"What are you talking about? She wasn't there."

"She was. And what your mom did that day is considered being an accessory after the fact to a murder. She was an adult and there's no statute of limitations. It can carry the same sentence as actually committing a murder. That's what Garrett was trying to explain to me when we were in his office the other day."

Daniela refused to look at Cadie.

"The reason Garrett and I didn't want to come forward with the truth to protect your dad is that it would put your mom at risk. Raúl didn't do anything. There's no evidence, no witnesses that can put him at the scene. It would be awful for your dad to go through, but in the end, he wouldn't get convicted, or even charged." Cadie left out her new fear of what awaited Raúl if he were deported back to El Salvador.

"But my mom," Daniela whispered.

"That call your mom got, that emergency at the store? That was Clyde calling for your dad. He freaked out about what happened to Juan. He called your dad for help, but your mom answered. Your mom didn't go to the store. She went to Clyde's house."

"How could you keep that from me?"

"I was afraid to tell you. It was my fault she went to Clyde's in the first place. When he called, Clyde was ranting about needing to keep Garrett safe. And I had *just* told your mother that a kid named Garrett was in trouble. How many Garretts do you know in Maple Crest? That's why she went. Because I broke our promise."

"So, you and Garrett decided amongst yourselves to keep this from me and come up with a plan that impacts my family without telling me any of this?"

"I wanted to tell you. Your mom's the one who made us promise not to tell anyone, including you. I kept the secret for her. Not for Garrett."

"You should have told me. You were my best friend."

"Your mom made us swear to never speak of that day again. Not to each other, my parents, you, or even Raúl. If no one talked about it, it never happened. No one else could ever find out."

"You really buried him?" Daniela whispered.

"The three of us dragged him through the woods. I helped dig the grave and bury him." Cadie pressed the heels of her hands against her eyes to push out the images in her mind. The misaligned buttons, the sliver of white between his eyelids. "I wanted to make all of that go away. I didn't want to think about it ever again."

"God, Cadie." Daniela's eyes filled with tears. "You never told anyone, ever? Not your park ranger or your parents?"

"It never happened. I locked it away and tried to forget. Until I got your text message the other day. Now it's the only thing I can think about." The feel of his flesh as she gripped him under his arm. The crack of his skull hitting the rock when Dolores lost her grip and dropped him.

Daniela pulled Cadie's hands away from her face and wrapped her arms around her friend. Daniela's breath stuttered as she held back a sob.

"Don't worry, I'm not going to tell anyone," Cadie whispered.

"That's not what I'm worried about."

"Then what?"

"My God. You carried that alone? All these years?"

Chush, thud. Chush, thud. Ever since she had received Daniela's message at the top of the mountain, the past had been pressing closer and closer, surrounding her. *Chush, thud. Chush, thud.*

"You kept that secret to protect my family."

Cadie couldn't speak.

"It must have been killing you."

Cadie buried her face in Daniela's hair and tried to calm her breath. Slow and even. In, out. In, out. His soft face, floppy hair. He could have been sleeping.

"Are you okay?" Daniela pulled back and tucked Cadie's hair behind her ear.

"I will be. But right now, that's not what we need to focus on. We need to protect your parents."

Cadie felt dizzy and hot. The road seemed to sway like a mirage ahead of her. She needed to tell Daniela about Sal pulling the gun on Garrett and Garrett aiming his gun at Sal. That Garrett was the one who killed Juan, not Clyde. But it all felt too big to give words to yet. Every step sent pain shooting up her leg, which felt almost too heavy to drag. *Just walk.*

Daniela slipped an arm around Cadie's waist to take some pressure off her injured leg. Daniela's hair smelled of smoke and a trace of floral perfume that reminded her of Daniela's childhood room.

"Sal found The Poachers' Code and the map. That's how she ended up with the gun," Cadie said.

"The Poachers' Code." Daniela looked up at the sky as they walked. "We were such goddamn idiots."

"After the fire, when everything calms down, I'll tell you everything. We can decide together what we want to do." Cadie stumbled; the throbbing in her leg had moved up her torso and her head pounded so that the light from the moon seemed to pulse in sync with her heartbeat. In the darkness, the cheerful gingham curtain had turned black with blood.

"For now, we need to get you to a doctor." Daniela threaded her arm tighter around Cadie's waist.

Sal broke into a sprint as they approached the rec center, which had been transformed into an evacuation shelter. Vehicles stuffed with possessions crammed the parking lot and spilled over onto the grass. Disoriented children with sleeping bags under arms, a small boy with a worn stuffed monkey clasped to his chest, trailed behind falsely cheerful parents. People ran to embrace friends, shouting names across the parking lot. Music blared over the chug of a generator. Other than the minimal lighting inside the rec center, the town remained dark from the power outage.

"Dolores," Raúl shouted as he ran toward them. Sal ran into his open arms. His chest heaved with silent sobs as he opened his arms to Dolores and Daniela. Daniela pulled Cadie in with her. The flood of relief in the knot of bodies made Cadie feel simultaneously safe and entirely alone.

"¿Estas herida?" Raúl examined the cuts on Sal's hands and guided her toward the rec center.

Sal smiled weakly and leaned against her grandfather as they walked toward the building.

Dolores hung back with Cadie.

"You need medical attention," Dolores said while staring across the parking lot. She waved to friends and smiled. But her smile faded when her friends looked away.

After a few seconds Dolores let a heavy sigh slip through her lips and tilted her chin toward the sky. "His name was Carlos."

"Who?" Cadie said.

"There was no Juan Hernández. He took that name after we crossed the border together. He was fourteen." Dolores folded her arms across her chest. "He carried Daniela on his shoulders like she was a doll. He sang to her."

Moonlight caught the tears sliding down Dolores's cheeks.

"You knew him? From before?"

Dolores nodded. "We traveled together for weeks. When Raúl bought papers for us, they took his given name—Juan—from him. He argued with them for a way to keep his name. It was his father's name. And his grandfather's. But they wiped it all away. All the history. When he became Raúl, that young boy Carlos took up the name Juan to honor my husband's family. We went our separate ways, and didn't hear from him for seven years.

"When he contacted us years later looking for work, Raúl convinced Clyde to give him a job on the farm and he moved here. By then, Daniela did not remember him. We thought it best not to stir those memories. Maybe we shielded her from too much."

All the air in Cadie's lungs felt trapped. She couldn't breathe in. She couldn't breathe out.

"After I went to their house and saw what Garrett had done, I became a witness. The police would want to talk to me, maybe talk to Raúl. It was too late to help Juan, so I made a choice." Dolores paused. "And I've had to live with it. We both have. He carried my daughter for weeks. I don't know how we would have made it here without him. And I left that poor boy alone in the woods. It's unforgivable."

People milled around them, some crying at having lost their homes, others looking for loved ones, and clinging to the ones they found. Cadie felt like a stranger in her hometown. She longed to get in her car, drive back to Concord, and pretend none of this had happened.

"I should have taken care of you. You were a little girl. I abandoned you when you needed me so I could protect my family," Dolores said. "But no one protected you."

"I just told Daniela what we did." Cadie braced herself for Dolores to be angry. "I thought you should know."

"I suspected that's what you were talking about."

"You need to talk to her. I'm going inside." Cadie needed to sit down.

"Wait." Dolores grabbed Cadie's wrist. Her fingers dug into her skin with desperation. "Let me tell Raúl. He doesn't know any of this. He had enough regret of his own. I kept this one for myself. Let me tell him."

Cadie nodded.

Dolores's back looked so rigid, so strong.

"I'm sorry for all the pain I know you endured." Dolores stroked Cadie's face.

Cadie leaned her cheek into Dolores's hand and closed her eyes. The warmth of Dolores's touch grounded Cadie. For the first time in hours she wasn't rushing to something or running from something. She didn't want to open her eyes and face what came next.

Cadie limped through the clusters of people in the lobby of the rec center. She was so thirsty. So tired.

Ryan sat in a chair while another firefighter cleaned a burn on his face. He jumped up when he saw Cadie.

"Geez. You okay? What happened to your leg?" Ryan pointed to the bloody curtain wrapped around her calf. His sweaty hair spiked up, and dirt smudged his neck. "I thought you were evacuating."

"I had to find someone first," Cadie said.

Bandages wrapped around Ryan's forearms. Raw blisters covered the side of his forehead and his hair was singed above one ear.

Fluorescent lights buzzed above her head. The floor felt spongy, unstable. She grabbed the back of a metal folding chair for support.

"Jesus, what the hell happened to you?" Ryan looked her up and down. His eyes rested on the hilt sticking out of her waistband. Cadie pulled the shirt tight around her.

The dim emergency lights flickered every few minutes as the generator struggled to keep the power on.

"Have you seen Garrett?" Her own voice sounded far away, as if coming out of someone else's mouth. The fluorescent bulb sizzled in an irregular rhythm then, without warning, changed to a different pitch that screeched in Cadie's teeth.

"Garrett's fine. I saw him, like, two hours ago. He's helping with evacuations." Ryan kneeled on the floor to look at the cut on Cadie's leg.

The fabric, stiff with dried blood, stuck to the cut as Ryan peeled it back. Cadie's vision frayed at the edges and her knees buckled at the pain. Ryan caught her elbow and guided her into a cold metal chair. She shivered despite the heat.

"Hey, I need a blanket over here," he shouted.

Cadie watched her hands shaking in her lap. Tacky blood clung to her fingers and forearms.

Ryan wrapped a blanket around her. "I'm going to go wash my hands so I can dress your wound until we can get you to the hospital."

"I'm fine." Cadie shrugged the blanket off.

Ryan pulled the blanket back around Cadie's shoulders.

A wave of nausea rose. She swallowed hard.

What if Pip and Pippi went on a date? Garrett had coded into the pages of *Tuck Everlasting* that long-ago summer. In the years that followed, Cadie had spent hours poring over *Great Expectations* and *Pippi Longstocking*, trying to determine whether Garrett had been posing a hypothetical literary question or asking her out. A week after he proposed that Pip and Pippi go out on a date, Cadie heard the gunshot, and she never responded to his question.

Someone knocked over a metal chair with a crash behind Cadie. She jumped. Ryan put a slow hand on her shoulder.

"Sit tight for a minute. We need to take care of your leg." Ryan leaned close to her ear and whispered, "But first, I need to take that firearm. I'm not going to ask why you have it, but you can't walk around with that in here."

Cadie pulled her shirt tight around her waist to shield the gun.

Ryan held both hands up in front of Cadie, as if surrendering. He looked around to make sure no one watched them. Cadie slid the gun out of her shorts. Room-temperature air hit Cadie's exposed skin with a chill.

Ryan folded a plastic bag around the gun and eased it toward his lap. Cadie put her hand on it to stop him. She had never wanted to see that gun again. But there it was. Evidence. Proof of what had transpired.

She imagined the fury in Clyde's chest the day he pulled that gun on the shopkeeper for insulting Juan and stealing his money. *That guy sits on his white ass all day while you work hard. He can't just take your fucking money.* Clyde had reasoned with Juan while Cadie had clung to the rock ledge below them. She imagined Clyde's face red with passion. And Clyde had covered it all up, letting Cadie believe he shot Juan, all to protect Garrett.

She felt Garrett's fear of losing Clyde emblazoned in the steel. His entire world at stake as he aimed it at Juan. And Sal. The near miss that could have changed everything. Cadie's stomach lurched at the thought of what could have happened if that bullet had hit Garrett. Or Cadie.

The gun grew heavy in her lap, burdened with fear, hate, and regret. The pressure on her thighs became unbearable.

"Take it," she said.

"Is it loaded?" Ryan asked.

"I think so."

"Are you in trouble?" Ryan unloaded it under the tent of the plastic bag and put two bullets in his pants pocket.

"I don't know." Cadie waited for Ryan to ask for details. He stared at her with quiet eyes. His lack of judgment or interrogation felt like a kindness she did not deserve. She wanted him to accuse her of something, to get angry with her so she could yell back.

"I'm taking your gun out to my truck. Just for now. We can talk about it later." He put a hand on her shoulder as he stood up. "And I'm going to find you an EMT for your leg. Don't go anywhere."

People gathered in clusters around the room, hugging each other, consoling each other over lost homes and farms. Cadie sat alone on the flimsy metal chair.

Ryan returned with a bottle of water.

Cadie drank the entire bottle without stopping. The water soothed her scratchy throat and washed down the ash that clung to her teeth.

"You lit the back burn, didn't you?" Ryan's voice maintained a gentle tone that made Cadie feel slightly drunk. "I'm not going to tell anyone."

"Why not? Arson's a crime." She imagined the fire she had started swooping through the forest.

"You saved the Garcias' house and a bunch of other homes on that side of the Hook."

She imagined the flames consuming her books.

The room felt so crowded all of a sudden. Or maybe it had been crowded the whole time. She couldn't remember. Loud music pulsed in her ears. Two babies screamed from opposite corners of the room. The thud of her perfectly aimed stone smashing against Garrett's skull reverberated in her mind.

37

"You sure you want to do this without anesthesia?" a young doctor asked as she cleaned the gash on Cadie's leg in the triage station set up in the rec center. "If you go to the ER, they can give you lidocaine. You won't feel the stitches."

"I'm not going to the hospital."

Sleeping families on cots and on the floor filled the back half of the room. Small clusters of adults sat in chairs, talking in hushed tones. They would all wake up to an altered Maple Crest.

"Cadie, don't do this. It's going to hurt." Daniela sat in a folding chair next to her.

"Just stitch it up," Cadie told the doctor. Her body felt too heavy to walk to a car, too exhausted to endure a hospital waiting room. With the cottage and her car lost in the fire, she didn't know where to go or how to get there.

Daniela ripped the top off of a pizza box from the table behind her and folded the cardboard quadruple thick. "Here, bite on this."

"Don't be so dramatic. It's stitches." Cadie accepted the cardboard.

"You got this, Cadie Braidy." Daniela took Cadie's hand in hers.

Cadie sank her teeth into the cardboard and squeezed Daniela's hand. The needle stung with less ferocity than she expected. She breathed through it the way she imagined someone would breathe through labor.

"Ready?" The doctor looked more nervous than Cadie felt. "The subcutaneous stitches are going to hurt more."

"Just do it," she said through the mouthful of pizza box.

Cadie felt almost grateful for the sharp pain that wiped everything else from her mind. Nothing but pain for a few graceful seconds.

The metal doors at the front of the rec center slammed open with a clatter. "The hardware store's on fire!" someone yelled. "All the fire trucks are already out at other fires. We need help!"

Later, Cadie would not remember if it had been a man, a woman, or a child who announced the fire. She would remember the half second of utter silence followed by a synchronized wave of people rushing toward the door.

Daniela's hand went limp in Cadie's grip. The doctor froze in the middle of a stitch.

"Go help your parents. I'm fine. I'll find you later," Cadie said.

Daniela kissed Cadie on the cheek and ran for the door. Cadie watched Dolores and Raúl follow her.

"Don't move." The doctor's hand seemed to move in slow motion as she pulled the thread through Cadie's skin. About a dozen adults and handfuls of children remained in the room where at least a hundred people had been minutes earlier.

"Can you hurry?" Cadie spit the cardboard to the floor. The pain grew more acute with each stitch. She ground her teeth and rocked her torso in the chair to absorb the waves of pain.

"No running or jumping or anything that could disrupt the stitches, okay?" The doctor tied off the final stitch and dressed the wound. "Try to keep it elevated. If you see any redness or . . ."

Cadie tried sprinting to the door, but the pain held her to a steady limp.

A crowd had already gathered around the burning hardware store when Cadie arrived. The faint outline of Cadie's cloud with a silver lining shone through the char on the wood siding. Shards of broken glass glistened on the stairs as water rained through the porch rafters.

Neighbors formed a bucket brigade, throwing water on railings and the side wall. Teenagers with shovels dug around the sides of the building, tossing dirt on patches of burning grass. Cars lined up with headlights aimed at the hardware store.

Ryan and Tino lugged coiled fire hoses from the fire station to a hydrant half a block from the store. Cadie watched Tino struggle to loosen the valve while Ryan directed him with his good arm how to connect the hose, the injured arm strapped to his chest in a sling.

Someone dragged a cooler filled with beer and water bottles toward the bucket brigade. The hum in the air, punctuated by occasional laughter and blaring country music, felt more like a street party than the scene of a fire.

The air crackled with an untamed static.

The horizon line in the direction of the lake glowed red-orange like a stubborn sunset against the dark sky. But instead of west, the incandescence rose from the south, disorienting Cadie, who already felt slightly dizzy. The color danced and rolled, sending up a shroud of smoke to mute its glow.

Tino dug his feet into the gravel and aimed the stream at the porch roof. Ryan backed across the hardware store parking lot, unwinding a garden hose attached to the post office spigot. Ryan's posture looked different in the moonlight. He didn't stutter step with his approval-seeking half smile. He moved with purpose and confidence. Cadie hardly recognized him.

Raúl sprinted toward Ryan to help with the hose. The bruise Raúl had left on Ryan's cheek disappeared in the smoke-filled air.

Cadie turned in a circle, watching the scene. Daniela paced next to Sal, who squatted on her haunches, like a ball of kinetic energy about to burst. The young girl rocked back and forth, chewing on her lip as a reflection of the flames burned in her dark eyes. Soot smeared Daniela's face, and half of her hair had fallen out of her ponytail.

Behind the swarm of bodies moving around the fire, a figure ran toward them from the direction of the rec center. Even at a distance, the distinctive flop of Garrett's hair gave him away. A flood of relief that he had made it out of the woods smacked up against Cadie's roiling anger.

Something inside the store exploded. Camp stove fuel, maybe a propane tank. A ball of fire swelled inside, and a window on the porch exploded outward. In a matter of seconds the seemingly tame fire morphed into a monster.

Dolores walked up and stood beside Cadie. The flicker of the fire made the silver in her hair shimmer.

"It'll be okay." Cadie kept her eyes on Garrett.

Neighbors spun around them, carrying buckets, passing hoses, shoveling dirt. The fire appeared to have started on the porch near the graffiti, near the boarded-up window a vandal had smashed with a rock days earlier. Cadie surveyed the street. No other buildings in town had caught fire. The creeping forest fire burned miles from town.

"Someone did this on purpose, didn't they?" Cadie said.

"One person lit the fire, but the rest of the town is putting it out." Dolores's furrowed brow and wringing hands did not match the optimism of her words. "Our papers are inside."

Dolores did not need to explain. The forged papers could not be replaced.

"I know exactly where they are. I'm going in the back door." Dolores wasn't asking for approval or permission. "I'll be back out in minutes."

"You can't." Cadie scrutinized the fire, which now consumed the entire left side of the building. She grabbed Dolores's small hand, in part to reassure her that everything would be okay, and in part to hold on to her in case she tried to run toward the fire. "It's too dangerous."

"You don't get to decide what risk is acceptable for my family." Dolores twisted her necklace around her finger and took a slow step backward toward the fire. Cadie saw the woman Raúl saw. *The strongest, bravest woman I've ever known.* All the risk and sacrifice. The fear and joys of living in this imperfect place. It had always been a risk. Every day.

Cadie released her grip on Dolores's hand.

Garrett had stopped to help Raúl and Ryan with the hoses. No one watched Cadie and Dolores.

"Let's go before anyone sees us." Cadie took a hesitant step forward, pain shooting up her injured leg.

"You can barely walk. I'll be right out." Dolores looked at Cadie with the same conviction as she had that day in the woods. *We will never speak of this again. Ever.* Dolores ran around the side of the burning building.

"Tía, no!" Cadie shouted, and hobbled after her, but Dolores disappeared inside. Cadie looked up and she locked eyes with Sal, still sitting on her haunches, coiled like a trap about to spring. Sal looked toward the door where her grandmother had disappeared and shot forward like a bullet out of a gun before Daniela could grab her.

Sound blurred into a cloud around Cadie. Ryan dropped the garden hose, which twisted like an angry snake as water spewed in all directions. Raúl wrapped his arms around Daniela, holding her back as she thrashed to break free. Daniela's lips moved, and her face contorted as she shouted for Sal.

Cadie heard nothing but a roar that seemed to be coming from inside herself.

It felt like hours, although only minutes passed before Dolores burst out of the side door carrying a fireproof document box under her arm. Cadie felt the whoosh of air as Maple Crest sucked in a collective, smoke-filled breath and watched the door.

"Where's Sal?" The words ripped themselves from Daniela's throat as she fought to escape Raúl's grip. "She followed you in the back door."

Dolores's eyes widened as she looked back at the blazing building.

"The back door's blocked. The fire—" she yelled. The metal box clattered to the ground by Dolores's feet. The tight coil of her hair had loosened into a precarious knot sagging above her collar, escaped strands flailing in hot currents of air. "There's no way out through the back door."

A series of small explosions burst from the back of the store. Cadie imagined all the cans of spray paint lined up like soldiers exploding one after another as the heat became unbearable.

Garrett's eyes darted from Dolores to Daniela and Raúl, finally landing on Cadie. Fear moved between them the way it had when they were kids. Both of them children. Just children. Scared, making the best decisions they knew how to protect the people they loved. The muscles in Garrett's face hardened, shifting from a look of fear to determination. He nodded at Cadie as if they shared a secret plan. She nodded back in agreement. Later, she would wonder if the slight tilt of her chin had given him permission, courage. Maybe hope.

Garrett sprinted toward the side door Dolores had exited from and disappeared into the smoke. Cadie raised her arms to calm the flames, to tame the wind with the same conviction Garrett had summoned when they were kids.

Heat warped her vision and seared her eyes as she squinted to see through the smoke. Two windows on the far side of the building exploded outward. A fire truck pulled up, casting fragments of red light against the curtains of smoke.

Garrett pushed the porch door open, one arm looped around Sal's waist. She appeared semi-conscious, overcome by smoke, but not visibly injured. Cheers rose up from onlookers as he stumbled forward. The support beam on the porch sagged and groaned threateningly. Garrett pushed Sal forward off the porch, just as a thick crossbeam dropped like a lit match, hitting Garrett's lower back with a crack that split through the growl of fire.

He seemed to hang suspended in midair as he lurched forward, the beam pushing him toward the ground. He looked at Cadie, his eyes clear blue, for what felt like an impossibly long moment before time sped up and he landed, motionless, a few feet from Sal.

The roof of the hardware store collapsed in a riot of sparks. Embers floated in the purple air like fireflies.

It could have been so beautiful.

"Don't move him!" Ryan threw off the sling supporting his burnt arm. He grimaced and heaved the smoldering beam off of Garrett with bare fingers. Cadie crawled forward, gagging on the singe of Ryan's burning skin.

Cadie touched Garrett's face, hot from the fire, remembering the flush that rushed up her arm the first time he kissed her so many years ago. Wispy hair fell away from his sweaty neck, revealing the cigarette burns below his hairline. The thirty-year-old wounds looked raw in the flickering of the firelight.

She placed her hand on Garrett's back, waiting for the rise and fall of breath that did not come.

EMTs pushed Cadie aside. They immobilized his neck and back, strapped him to a board, flipped him over, and dragged him clear of the fire. CPR, and a flurry of hands. *Clear!* Garrett's body arched with an electric current that failed to restart his heart. Again. And once more.

Sizzling embers rose up and turned to ash above their heads.

Cadie felt as if her own chest had been cracked open, exposing her most guarded feelings. Her rage at Garrett's deception felt bigger, more volatile, like it might consume her. He had lied. Over and over he had allowed her to believe that Clyde had killed Juan. Cadie tried to hold on to the anger. Rage, with its unpredictable writhing, gave her cover against the wave she felt coming.

Sal sat up a few feet away from the EMTs working on Garrett, her eyes wild like a confused animal's. Her mouth hung wide open as if she were screaming, but no sound emerged.

Cadie's tongue felt thick. Her eyes stung. The bitter taste of charcoal filled her mouth. The heat on her cheeks and arms made her skin feel tight as if it might burst and peel away so she could wriggle out of it, toss her molted form into the fire, and slither back to the woods.

The more she tried to focus on physical sensations, the harder it became to breathe. It wasn't the smoke that choked her, but her own muscles, which felt too short, too tight to pull enough air into her lungs. The weight of granite blocks piled on her chest, one stone at a time, pressing the air out of her.

"He was a good man," Dolores whispered in Cadie's ear as EMTs carried Garrett toward an ambulance without any pretense of urgency.

"No he wasn't." Cadie gulped in air and tried to calm the spasms of coughing. She would not cry for Garrett. "You know that better than anyone."

"One moment doesn't define a person's life. It's what you choose to do after that determines who you are." Dolores's red-rimmed eyes looked calm as she clutched the box of documents to her chest.

Heat from the fire burned on Cadie's neck. She swatted away the tenderness of Garrett's lips on her skin. She wanted to chase the ambulance and beat her fists on his quiet chest and howl at him, curse him.

She wanted to hold him.

Her breath burned like fire in her mouth.

Daniela and Raúl huddled around Sal as an EMT held an oxygen mask to the girl's face and another checked her vitals. Daniela stroked her daughter's hair.

Despite the heat of the fire, a chill gripped Cadie and she began to tremble. First her hands, then her arms, legs, and entire body. She stood up on wobbly legs to inch toward the heat of the blaze, but the only heat she felt came from Clyde's eyes as he watched her. She tried not to look at him, but couldn't help herself. He stood alone under an unlit streetlight, his cheeks wet in the moonlight. An uninvited solidarity pulled her toward him.

She curled her shaking fists tight. Her leg throbbed with every step. How could he have allowed two children and a young mother to bury Juan? His mistreatment of that small, helpless boy, his inability to take responsibility for his actions had set it all in motion.

Clyde held her stare as she limped toward him. His body shook and he swallowed down the sobs that erupted in wet gasps. He plowed his fingers through his hair. She wanted to channel all her fear and anger into him. But her loathing slid off him no matter how deep she dug for the familiar repulsion.

He looked like he wanted her to yell at him, to curse him, to hit him. The slump of his shoulders seemed to beg her to cast blame so he wouldn't have to look at his nephew's dead body being loaded into the ambulance. She didn't want to acknowledge the weight of Clyde's loss, but it stood in front of her, raw and aching.

Cadie had always felt the gravity of that moment in the woods as the center point of her life. All of her experiences and memories were either before or after the gunshot. The moment that challenged her to make better decisions, to be a worthy person. The guilt she carried became a constant reminder to make choices she could live with, to hold stories that didn't add to the weight she already carried.

But Garrett had snatched that coarse touchstone from her, robbing her of her one steady guiding principle.

Cadie felt unmoored without her fear of Clyde or her hatred of him.

She sped up the last few steps toward him, ignoring the pain in her leg. She lunged at Clyde. He stiffened as she threw her arms around his thick chest and refused to let go. She held him fiercely, forcing him to sob in her arms as she allowed herself to unravel.

Clyde knew nothing about Raúl's past in El Salvador. Dolores did not know Clyde had threatened Cadie all those years ago. Sal did not know about Clyde's role in the first shooting in the convenience store. Daniela did not know Sal had fired a gun at Garrett. Raúl did not know Garrett had killed Juan or that his wife had buried him.

Only Cadie knew all the pieces. She carried all their stories, the combined weight a burden and a privilege.

One moment doesn't define a person's life.

If each of them could be released of that one moment. If only they could wipe the slate clean.

It's what you choose to do after that determines who you are.

But there had to be consequences. If they continued burying each other's truths the chain would never end. Someone in that crowd had set the hardware store on fire. And someone else knew who did it. How far would they go to hide that truth? How many people would this new secret tear apart?

Cadie wanted to know everything, to tell everything, and start again. She waited until Clyde's breathing calmed, until the spastic gasps, both hers and his, subsided, and she let him go.

A wave moved through the gathering crowd, like a low-frequency signal, as news of Garrett's death spread. A group of middle school boys stood in a cluster with Tino, their bodies limp with grief over the loss of a friend, a mentor. Cadie recognized the boys from the basketball court the day she had stopped to talk to Garrett.

"No way. He's not dead. This is fucked up." Fernando's words rose above the smoke. His mouth twisted and the muscles alongside his jaw tightened.

Sal stood with her head buried in the shoulder of a girl her age. Sal looked up and trapped Cadie in a dense stare. Cadie recognized the shadow that would follow Sal down dark alleys for the rest of her life, no matter how many times Cadie and Daniela told her it was not her fault. Sal would always wonder. What if she had not taken the gun? What if she had not gone into the woods to put it back? What if she had never aimed it at Garrett? What if she hadn't run into the burning building after Dolores?

For a moment Cadie felt like that little girl with the long red braids surrounded by neighbors taking care of each other. In the morning, those who still had homes would start making casseroles to feed their displaced neighbors. That was how Maple Crest handled disaster.

Sal stepped back from the circle of grieving teens.

Cadie tightened both hands into fists, pressing the tender cuts on her palms. It would be different for Sal. Daniela, Raúl, Dolores, and Cadie would be there for her. She wouldn't have to bury her secrets. She wouldn't have to cry alone.

The lines in Sal's forehead deepened as she furrowed her brow, just like Dolores, and curled her shoulders forward.

Cadie dug her fingernails into her palms, reopening a gash cut by the barbed wire. Blood trickled down her hand, but she didn't wipe it away. No matter how closely they circled around Sal, no one would be able to chase the inevitable nightmares or the anguish she would feel as she lay in bed wondering *what if?*

Cadie willed the ache in Sal's chest to come to her.

She already had a home for it.

38

Cadie's body reacted to the sight of Clyde before her mind had a chance to calm herself. Sweat dripped down her neck as he walked across the police station parking lot toward her. She wiped her damp palms on her jeans.

Three days had passed since the fire, but the town still smoldered with grief and disbelief. No matter how many times she had washed her hair, Cadie couldn't rinse away the smell of smoke.

She swallowed down her fear as Clyde came closer. How could she make peace with the monster who had tormented her dreams her whole life? Although, it hadn't really been Clyde, but a beast she had created in her mind, formed out of lies and fears and secrets. She knew she should meet him halfway, but she couldn't make her body move.

He stopped a couple feet away from Cadie and extended his hand without looking her in the eye. He looked haggard, as if he hadn't slept in days. His messy hair gathered in greasy clumps. A food stain that looked days old marred his wrinkled shirt.

Cadie stared at his calloused palm, hesitant to touch him as she remembered his weight pressing her against the maple tree, the smell of his breath. Clyde let his hand hang in the air a few seconds too long before finally letting it drop to his side.

"You're sure you're ready to do this?" Cadie said, trying to sound in control of her emotions.

"You can't outrun consequences forever," Clyde said.

"I know why you did it. You were sticking up for Juan when no one else would. I know there was three hundred dollars in the drawer, but you only took fifty because that's exactly how much that guy stole from Juan. You could have taken all three hundred, but you didn't. I'm not absolving you. It was a stupid plan, but in a warped way, you meant well."

Clyde huffed a wheezy laugh and shook his head. "I didn't end up helping Juan at all. I killed him."

"No, you didn't. Garrett did." Garrett's name felt clumsy in her mouth, the way a word repeated over and over loses its meaning. Garrett. Garrett. The Summer Kid. Garrett. Maybe if she allowed herself to revisit all the prickly memories, she could dull the edge of anguish his name conjured. Her anger toward him battled with the ache he left behind. Let the anger win, she pleaded. The sharpness of fear had consumed her for so long, but the dull beat of sorrow weighed so much more than fear. Let the anger win, she pleaded.

Clyde bristled at Garrett's name too. He sniffed and looked up at the treetops surrounding the police station.

"I'm an accessory no matter what. It was my gun. I covered it up. It's not like I'm taking blame that doesn't belong to me. No point in bringing the Garcias down with me. By convincing me to go in to work and not attract attention, then helping Garrett, you know, in the woods, Dolores made it possible for me to raise him instead of sending him to foster care. I didn't deserve that kindness, neither did Garrett. I know that. But I tried to do better after that. Not that it makes anything okay."

Clyde plowed a hand through his scraggly hair and Cadie flinched at the familiar gesture.

"Dolores was afraid for her family and I put her in that position by dragging her into my mess. I never should have called the Garcias for help. I panicked. Raúl was the only person I knew I could trust. Dolores intercepted the phone call. I don't even know how she knew to come over, though. I was crying and blabbering on about finding Raúl. But I never told her what happened. She just showed up."

"I was with Dolores when you called," Cadie said. "Even though we swore we wouldn't tell anyone what happened, I lost it. Dolores could tell something was wrong and I told her someone got shot. I mentioned a boy named Garrett. Daniela tried to shut me up. God, she was so mad at me."

"Dolores knew I had custody of a nephew named Garrett." Clyde nodded as the missing pieces of the story fell into place. "Sometimes when I got off work at the hardware store, when Raúl wasn't looking, she'd toss me a pack of KitKat bars to take home for him. I used to eat them myself most of the time. He would've been so much better off if I let the state take him."

Clyde blinked hard several times and pinched the bridge of his nose. "Once Dolores showed up and saw the body, she was trapped. If she reported me, she'd get called as a witness in a murder, potentially exposing her family. And if it was discovered later that she had been there, she would have been an accessory after the fact."

"We all made bad choices that day," Cadie said.

"But Jesus, I never should have allowed Dolores to bury him. I let a twelve-year-old boy and an old lady bury a body to protect me." Clyde's eyes widened as if the magnitude of what he did was only now crystalizing. "What the hell is wrong with me?"

"I helped them, you know," Cadie said.

"Helped who?"

"Dolores and Garrett. I helped them drag Juan through the woods, dig the grave, and bury him. I'm not blameless in this."

"I didn't know that." Clyde clutched at his hair again. "I'm so goddamn sorry. She told me to go to work, act normal so no one would question me about where I'd been that day. Just go to work and act normal. I should have argued with her. None of this will fall on the Garcias, or you, or anyone else."

This was Clyde. An imperfect uncle. A reckless but loyal friend. A man willing to face the consequences of his actions.

"I'll testify I threatened to hurt you if you told anyone," he said. "I mean, it's true."

A ghost of that fear spiked in her chest, as she remembered the terrors, the nightmares she suffered her entire life reliving Clyde's threat.

"I swear, scaring you, saying I'd turn the Garcias in if you talked, that's haunted me my whole life. I never would have done any of that. Never. As soon as I said it, I felt sick. That's why I ran off so quickly. I ran into the woods and vomited until there was nothing left of me. I don't even know how long I sat there on that rock cursing myself."

Clyde wiped his eyes.

Cadie remembered the swirl of dust and leaves that had swooped across the parking lot. She had imagined Garrett conjuring the wind to scare Clyde and save her. But Clyde hadn't been choking on dust from a conjured specter. He had been gagging on his own guilt and fear.

The colors in her carefully curated memory shifted, the sepia images turned sharp and bright, and, for the first time, Cadie could see the fear that had been in Clyde's eyes that day. Fear of going to jail, fear of losing custody of Garrett, fear of failing his dead sister. And a deep fear that his actions would expose the Garcias if Cadie told anyone what had happened. The memory sharpened as she turned it over and over in her mind.

"Juan was my friend," Clyde said.

"I know."

"You're going to take a hit too, you know. I mean, you were just a kid, you'll be okay. But still. People will know."

"I'll be fine." Her stomach turned. She hoped she would be fine.

"You were out on the lake and heard the shot. That's all. But you and Dolores were never in the woods. It was me and Garrett who buried the body. No one else."

"I thought we were done lying."

"It's one thing to not report *hearing* a gunshot. It's another to admit to burying a body. And putting you in the woods might stir questions about Daniela. It's easier this way. And safer. I started this. I'm prepared to face the consequences. I don't want to derail your life any more than I already have. And I don't want to get in the way of your work. It's important."

"You know what I do?"

"I don't live under a rock." Clyde tried to force a smile. "I follow #CadenceUnderFire."

"Wait. How do you know about that?" It had never occurred to her that all these years she had been avoiding Clyde, Clyde might have been keeping tabs on her.

"The Internet?" Clyde shook his head. "I'm not a stalker. I just try to stay informed, you know, about climate change. I think it's bullshit, by the way, what they're doing. They can't lock scientists out of public lands like that."

"I have one suggestion before we go inside," Cadie said. "Do not call Dolores an old lady on the record. She will destroy you."

"Good advice." Clyde drew in a deep breath and held it for a few seconds before releasing it in a forceful stream.

"Okay then?" Cadie took a few steps toward the station door, but Clyde did not follow.

"Garrett was so proud of being a police officer, even if it was just in this small town. He made a difference here."

"I know." Cadie took another step toward the door. Clyde did not follow.

Cadie searched Clyde's watery eyes for the monster she loathed, but he had dissipated, evaporated in the hot August air.

"He lived his whole life trying to make up for that one day. You believe that, don't you?" Clyde said.

Cadie nodded.

The boy on the pier in the ratty lawn chair. The kid who cherished her books as much as she did. The author of her first love letters. Cadie pushed down the ache swelling in her chest as they walked up the stairs to the police station side by side.

This is where it ends, Cadie told herself as a blast of cold air hit her face.

39

"I knew you'd be here." Daniela sat down next to Cadie on the blackened remains of Cadie's fireplace after she had left the police station.

Scaly soot lifted off the stone like barnacles, crunching under Cadie's thighs as she scooted over to make room for Daniela. The defiant chimney rose out of the charred remains of her childhood home. A few erect wooden beams marked where the walls used to keep the woods from creeping into the house. Those creaky walls her parents had filled, over and over, with caulk and insulation.

It was that golden hour when the sky bends forward and breathes the honey glow of evening across the treetops on the other side of the lake. The trees absorbed the warmth and shot the light back from the surface of every amber-washed leaf.

On Cadie's side of the lake, a whistling breeze searched the naked trees for leaves to rustle. A branch crashed to the ground in the distance. Straggler honeybees should have been making their final trek back to the hive, their haunches loaded with pollen. But there was no pollen here. No hive to go home to.

"Are your parents going to rebuild?" Daniela rested her head on Cadie's shoulder.

The soot kicked up a smell like the hickory bacon on Cadie's father's breath as they read together on Sundays after breakfast. Fleeting images of sleepovers with Daniela on her bedroom floor bumped up against flashes of bony shadows dancing on the walls, pointing at her accusingly.

"They want *me* to rebuild here. They're giving it to me." She imagined the stones from her cairn rooting into this piece of land, the roughly hewn floorboards marred with beetle etchings under her feet as she looked out over the lake every morning.

"Is that what you want?" Daniela asked.

"I don't know."

"You could put up a yurt instead, and cook over an open fire." Daniela reached out to rub her hands over an imaginary flame in the hearth, revealing an ink drawing on her upper arm. "You can finally live out all your survivalist fantasies."

"Is that a tattoo?"

Daniela ran her hand over a colorful bird with a green back and blue head. "Sal drew it last night. She wants to be a tattoo artist. It's her new thing. Resistance art."

"Why the bird?"

"It's the Torogoz, the national symbol of El Salvador. I kind of wish it was real ink." Daniela traced the outline of the bird's tail with her finger and flexed her bicep. "Are we too old to be badass?"

"Never." Cadie laughed and thought of Dolores standing next to her in the creek, yanking at the vines and the barbed-wire fence. "Your mom's still a badass."

Daniela blew out a long stream of air that disrupted the ash swirling in front of them.

The mountains on the other side of the lake looked the same as they always had. Bald granite jutting above the tree line, forever oblivious to fires, gunshots, and the movement of time. The Earth would not record this fire in its geologic memory. The ash of this moment would be compressed so tightly it would disappear in time.

"I'm glad everyone will know what happened to Juan," Daniela said.

Cadie's stomach tightened.

"We left him to rot in the woods as if it never mattered that he existed," Daniela said. "My whole life, it made me feel like I never mattered either. If Juan was disposable, unwanted, then so was I. So was my family."

How had Cadie run through the woods with Daniela, day after

day, picked buckets of berries right next to her, and not understood the weight of her constant fear?

"I've spent so much of my life desperate for people to see me— yet not wanting to be seen. I don't want Sal to feel that way," Daniela said. "Hiding is exhausting."

Cadie had been hiding from Clyde all these years. Looking for him in grocery stores and airports. Misplaced anger and fear had etched lines into her forehead and robbed her of sleep. But Daniela's fear had carved lines on the inside of her. Permanent lines no one could see.

"I remember him now," Daniela said.

"Who?"

"Juan. I remember riding on his shoulders when we left El Salvador. It's fuzzy. But I even remember a song he used to sing to me. I've always remembered it. I just didn't know where the memory came from." Daniela whistled a few bars. Cadie recognized it as the melody Daniela used to play on her wooden flute when they were kids.

"Now I'll remember, too," Cadie said.

"I brought you something." Daniela pulled a small tambourine out of her purse, the partner to the one she'd given Cadie the night before she moved to Boston. "If you insist on traipsing through the woods alone, chasing those goddamn bugs, you're going to need this."

The varnish on the lightweight wooden hoop felt slippery. She had long ago worn the gloss off the old tambourine, the water-warped instrument that had bounced against her backpack up and down so many mountains.

Cadie shook the hoop over her head for several seconds. The gentle clatter filled the empty spaces between the blackened timbers, between Cadie's bones. The woods, the fire, the earth had reclaimed the tambourine's sister, now a crumble somewhere in the ash pile. The shiny discs sparkled, catching the sun and tossing shimmers of light against the ground, the blackened tree trunks, and the sooty hearth.

"Your dad gave this to you." Cadie extended the instrument back toward Daniela. The familiar weight felt satisfying in her hand. "Sal should have it."

"Sal's not afraid of bears." Daniela raised one eyebrow and half smiled.

Cadie thought of the wet nose of the bear she had watched die on the highway. The heave of its chest under her hand, the humidity of its last sigh. She felt the bear's breath inside her now.

"I'm not afraid anymore." She didn't realize that she meant the words until after they had passed through her lips. She worried for Raúl and Dolores, for Sal and Daniela, for herself. But concern occupied a different space than fear had. Worry prodded at her, but it left room for something else. For breath, for hope, maybe.

"I want you to have it." Daniela pushed the tambourine back toward Cadie.

Charcoal-tinged air tickled Cadie's sinuses with microscopic bits of her books, her father's art, and the sister to the tambourine she now held in her hands. "I'll take good care of it."

"I know."

"A team from Vermont found evidence of the beetles near the Canadian border after reading my research. This is just the beginning. With changing temps there'll be more. Not just here. Not just beetles. And a few more research institutions have stepped forward to openly defy the research ban."

"Then why are you sitting here?" Daniela pushed her hair behind her ears. "Don't you have some research to get on? Fires to stop?"

"I missed you, you know. So much." Cadie closed her eyes and imagined floating head to head in the lake, her fingers curled around Daniela's. Drifting as the sun poured down on their faces.

Daniela appeared somehow at ease as she ground the char to dust under her foot. The woods creaked like an old rocking chair.

The warm stones of the fireplace radiated a sense of calm that penetrated Cadie's jeans and her skin, through to her bones until the stillness saturated her marrow. Cadie hoped Daniela could feel it too. Cadie rubbed greasy soot between her fingers and thumb and smeared a thick black stripe under each eye. She did the same on Daniela's cheeks. The residual char filled in the scar on her thumb where years ago she had carved a promise out of her own flesh. And Daniela's. The black etching looked like the silhouette of a burnt tree.

"My parents hired a lawyer."

"Why? They aren't implicated in anything, are they?"

"No, it was Sal. I don't know if you've noticed, but she has a lot of opinions."

"Sal? No way."

"Now that she knows my parents and I are technically undocumented, she's obsessed with immigration laws. She's been talking about it nonstop. We were at dinner and Sal gets all mad and says, 'So if you, who have a business, jobs, friends, pay taxes, volunteer, can't even come forward, then who can? If we can't fight for our rights—for their rights—then who will do it?'"

"Geez. What did your father say?"

"He cried," Daniela said. "He actually cried. Then he got mad. I mean, he went from tears rolling down his cheeks, to steam-coming-out-of-his-ears mad in seconds.

"Enough!" Daniela shouted and slapped her knees, breaking the silence in the chalky forest. "He bangs the table and yells 'Enough!' At first, I thought he was mad at Sal, but Sal looks at him and grins. 'Enough!' she yells, and slams down on the table. And Dad smiles.

"And that was it. They hired a lawyer. We're going to move slowly, but she thinks we have a strong case. She already located the arrest warrant for my father for disobeying orders, shooting an officer, and abandoning his unit. She even found a record of their house being burnt down days later. They had a perfect case for asylum status when we first got here, but it was too risky because the US was in bed with the Salvadoran government."

"This isn't exactly a great moment in US history to be undocumented either."

"Even more reason to stand up and fight."

"You sound like Sal."

"Why, thank you."

"If they hadn't been so afraid of being exposed, none of this would have happened. I wouldn't have been afraid to tell the truth about what we heard that day. My mom wouldn't have been scared enough to cover up Juan's murder. And Clyde wouldn't have been able to scare you by threatening my family. All because we were so damned afraid."

"I wish I'd understood all that back then."

"We can't look backward. Just forward." Daniela shrugged.

"Why are you so calm? Aren't you scared?"

"I'm terrified, actually," she said. "But my parents are so optimistic. It's kind of contagious. It turns out there weren't many witnesses to the attack in the village my father told us about. Not many first-person accounts about what actually happened. My father's never been able to tell his story, and now that they are looking back at history differently, his story is important. If things go well, my parents might actually go home to El Salvador for the first time."

"I thought that's what they were trying to avoid?"

"If they can get papers, they might be able to go visit. Sal could go with them. It would mean the world to her. The lawyer thinks it's possible. But nothing's for sure, especially in this anti-immigration climate. It could be a long time, or it might never happen."

"What about you? Do you have a case?"

"The lawyer's going to take on all of our cases. She's optimistic," Daniela said. "But there's a lot of risk. I wanted to believe marrying a US citizen made me safe. But even then, I was still using false papers. They might go easier on me because I was only three. It's not like I bought the papers myself. It's all I've ever known. The lawyer says we have a lot of reasons to hope."

"But no guarantees?"

"No guarantees."

"I don't get why you're doing this." Cadie didn't want to ask what would happen to Sal if their petition failed.

"We're tired of hiding." Daniela straightened her back and clapped her hands to change the subject. "I've been following your hashtag. There's, like, thirty universities signed on your petition."

"It's not my petition. This woman, Piper, she studies endangered birds. She started it. Somehow my name became the hashtag. But, yeah, it's kind of incredible."

"I always knew you'd change the world," Daniela said. "But couldn't you get arrested? Maybe try a more low-profile, no-hashtag approach?"

"Nope. I'm going to fight. Just like you."

"Will you come back for Juan's memorial service?"

"Yeah." Cadie thought back to the silent prayer she'd attempted while clinging to Dolores's hand after they buried Juan, and about the desperate eulogy Daniela had offered at his graveside so many years ago. He deserved so much more than words scraped together in secret.

As the truth about Juan's murder and the cover-up emerged, Cadie's guilt had not subsided, but intensified. The secrets about Garrett, the Garcias, and Clyde, about the gun, the boat, and the beech tree, all those secrets had linked arms to create a shield protecting Cadie from her deepest shame, the one that gutted her now as she forced herself to confront it.

Cadie had been complicit in erasing Juan Hernández. His name, his body, his history. She stared into the black gash that had been ripped into this small community, the wound she had been averting her eyes from for decades, and she allowed it to hurt. She didn't dig her fingernails into her thighs to distract her thoughts. She didn't mentally recite the periodic table as she had trained herself to do in college as a diversion. She needed it to hurt.

"It sounds like there's going to be a big crowd. My parents volunteered to pay for the service, and Chester Talbot, of all people, offered to host a reception at the sugarhouse," Daniela said.

"Chester Talbot?"

"People can surprise you, I guess." Daniela brushed the ash from her scrubs and stood up. "I have to get to the hospital."

A small mound of loose dirt at the base of the fireplace indicated that ants were already back, turning the soil, resuscitating the land with tiny breaths.

Daniela extended both hands to Cadie, dragging her up off the hearth and into a tight embrace. Daniela rocked from foot to foot, swaying Cadie's body with hers.

"I'm sorry about Garrett."

"He wasn't the person I wanted him to be." Cadie stepped back from Daniela and wrapped her arms around her own waist, squeezing her elbows tight to her ribs. She didn't want to acknowledge the hopes she had hung on Garrett. "But I guess I understand him now. He was scared, just like we were. One moment doesn't define a person's life."

"I don't know. He saved Sal's life. I'm going to let that define how I remember him," Daniela said. "It's okay to be angry and sad at the same time, you know."

"I thought for a minute maybe we had a chance together." Cadie's breath stuttered as if she had already cried the tears she refused to release. "I thought maybe he really was the storybook character I imagined him to be when we were kids. We believed in a lot of things that weren't real, didn't we?"

"I guess it's time we grew up." Daniela raised her eyebrows high.

"I wouldn't go that far."

Daniela laughed. A real laugh, the way she did when they were kids. "I missed you, too."

They walked to Daniela's car, charred earth shattering with every step.

"I'll be here when you come back, Cadie Braidy. We don't need to do this alone anymore." Daniela waved out the window as her car crept down the blackened path of the driveway.

Cadie didn't like the loneliness Garrett's presence—and his absence—had carved out inside her. Without the tightly bound secrets filling her up, she felt hollow. But lighter. She inhaled deeply. Primordial particles that had been her forest hit the back of her throat and filled her lungs.

Cadie thought of Piper and her commitment to letting the fires burn to give rise to a super-species of pine that would repopulate the woods. Would it be possible to restrict forest fires to unpopulated areas, then harvest surviving specimens from those areas to replace trees in more populated areas? On a smaller and much slower scale, it would allow the forest to adapt to the changing climate while protecting populated areas from fires.

It seemed too easy. Or implausibly difficult. But Cadie suspected Thea might buy into this idea. Maybe she could even get Piper on board. Everything was shifting, changing, and Cadie no longer wanted to ignore it. She wanted to stare the future in the face without blinking.

Cadie scooped the beechnuts she had rescued before the fire out of her pocket. She dug three shallow holes about twenty feet apart from each other and placed a seed in each hole. She rubbed the pebbly soil between her fingers. The truth lived in those tiny stones. It held fast in the dust left behind when time eroded rock into soil, in the flecks of gold suspended in shafts of underwater light, and in microscopic particles that coursed through Cadie's veins.

She pressed sooty earth over the seeds and looked up at the clouds brewing overhead.

The truth can be buried, crushed, or burnt, but it will always rise.

She rubbed a pebble between her fingers then pushed it deep into the blackened earth. One last truth she would hold on to for herself, for Garrett. *It only took one match.* Garrett's words settled into the nest in her gut where she knew their sharpness would dull over time. She would tend them and cover them with soft stories. But this new truth would fester in her, just as the old secrets had, until one day it, too, would rise up and free her.

Who-hoooo. An owl broke the silence.

She picked up her backpack and followed the call. The blackened forest floor crumbled under her feet.

Who-hoooo.

All the other creatures had fled. The mice, spiders, crickets, squirrels. The silence they left behind hurt. The owl sat on a charred branch. Its home had been in these woods. Its mottled brown and amber stood out in stark contrast to the black and gray backdrop. Exposed without camouflage, the great bird blinked at Cadie and pulled its square head lower into its shoulders. Its whole body shuddered, as if shaking off a bad memory.

The owl launched itself into the air. Time to start over. The only sounds in the entire forest were the slow flap of wild wings and the pounding of Cadie's heart.

She pulled *Kidnapped* out of her bag. Musty cinnamon rose from its pages. The book opened to the pressed maple leaves she once believed had saved her from Clyde.

A high-pitched, erratic flute spiraled down from the charred limbs above her. The melody rolled like water cascading over rocks only to swoop upward at the last second, asking a question that needed no words.

A Bicknell's thrush. Cadie choked on the ashy air and wiped her wet eyes.

The maple leaves lay flat, perfectly preserved, the serrated edges sharp and precise. Cadie lifted the lacy ghosts out by the stems. All the vigor, the turgor, the mass, long evaporated. She crumbled the leaves in her fist, their only resistance a papery hush. Leaf fragments grabbed the wind and rose above her, catching in her hair, sticking to her lips. She rubbed her hands together over her head as the dusty particles swirled and dispersed in every direction until they were gone, carried away on the breath of a forest ready to be reborn.

ACKNOWLEDGMENTS

My journey to publication has been long and bumpy, but every rejection, each obstacle, brought new and wonderful people into my life. I have a lot to be grateful for.

Publishing my debut during the COVID-19 pandemic makes me part of a club I never wanted to join. But in the midst of uncertainty, fear, and grief, I found community. To the many 2020 and 2021 debut writers who walked this unpaved path to publication with me—especially Nancy Johnson, Elizabeth Shelburne, Desmond Hall, Alison Hammer, Lainey Cameron, Michael Zapata, Ava Homa, Denny S. Bryce, Lauren Ho, Christine Clancy, Suzanne Park, Natalie Jenner, and Nguyễn Phan Quế Mai'—we share the unwanted but permanent bond of having launched our first novels during a global pandemic. We cried, cursed, commiserated. We pivoted. We lifted each other up and rewrote the book on how to launch a book. And we did it together. I am grateful and proud to have had you all at my side.

To Eve Bridburg, GrubStreet's founder and executive director, thank you for the home you have created for the writing community of Boston. I'm incredibly grateful for your friendship, leadership, and dedication to justice and equity in the writing world and beyond.

Thank you to GrubStreet's Novel Incubator and Novel Generator programs, with a special shout-out to Season Six of the Incubator—Milo Todd, Desmond Hall, Sarah Penner, Rose Himber Howse, David Goldstein, Laura Roper, Ashley Weckbacher, Julia Rold, Leslie Teel, and Pam Loring. Your fingerprints are all over my book. I owe so much to GrubStreet writing instructors Michelle Hoover and Lisa Borders for guiding me through all the suspenseful plot points along my writing path. You have both served me well as the "Captain Happens" of my literary journey.

I'm incredibly grateful to the many folks who have read drafts and offered feedback and encouragement, especially Jennifer Dardzinski, Angela Alvarez, Hank Phillippi Ryan, Omar El Akkad, JM Cools, Ashley Shelby, Louise Miller, Michael Zapata, Lise Gordon, Eileen Marks, Tina Fox, Kim Michelle Richardson, Louise Miller, Kate Moretti, Julie Abbott Clark, Erin Bartels, Sherrill Bounnell, Carrie Dunn Clarke, Kate Racculia, Kathleen Barber, Kim Savage, Kelli Estes, Erin Harris, Donald Maass, and Amaryah Orenstein. A special shout-out to firefighter Chad Stamps, Dr. Ginger Barrow, and Caroline Reilley, PNP, for offering their professional expertise. I'm forever grateful to Carol Reid, my high school English teacher and Margie Hodor, my middle school English teacher, who both taught me to love words, think in metaphor, and honor grammar, and to Lawrence Zoller, my middle school science teacher who instilled in me an abiding love of ecology, and of birds in particular.

Thank you to my many writing mentors: Peter Geye, who mentored me through that first finished draft and the querying process; Paul Lisicky, my Tin House mentor; Victoria Griffin, my RevPit mentor; and Rachel Barenbaum, my Novel Incubator mentor.

Thank you to the booksellers who read early galleys of my book, especially to Kathy Crowley and Miriam Lapson, my early champions at Belmont Books, and Pamela Klinger-Horn at Excelsior Bay Books. I'm grateful for the support of several writing communities, including GrubStreet, the Women's Fiction Writers Association, the Women's National Book Association Boston Chapter, Tin House, and the community at The Writer Unboxed, especially Therese Walsh and Heather Webb.

A huge thanks to Amy Brady, editor in chief of the *Chicago Review of Books* and creator of the Burning Worlds newsletter, whose passion for literature that engages climate science inspired me to believe there might be an audience for this book. Amy, you are my literary superhero.

To my critique partner Milo Todd, you are a talented writer, editor, and advisor, but more importantly, you are a brilliant friend, a wise, kind soul with an infinitely generous spirit. (And your gingerbread-baking skills are legend.) I can't wait for the world to read your books.

To Nancy Johnson, my writing soulmate, I'm so grateful to have been walking this path with you in almost perfectly synchronized lock-step. One of the greatest treasures of my writing journey has been finding you. Your talent, kindness, wisdom, and friendship inspire me daily. Celebrating our debut launches together is the cherry on this amazing publishing cake.

To my film agent, Addison Duffy of United Talent Agency, thank you for jumping on this project right from the start, before I even had a book contract.

I am incredibly grateful to have landed at Forge Books. The entire team—especially Alexis Saarela, Sarah Reidy, Eileen Lawrence, Lucille Rettino, Linda Quinton, Jennifer McClelland-Smith, Patrick Canfield, and Sara Pannenberg—has championed *Waiting for the Night Song* with the enthusiasm every writer dreams of. To Katie Klimowicz, my cover designer, thank you for envisioning my book with elegance and style.

To Kristin Sevick, my editor at Forge, thank you, thank you, thank you for believing in me enough to buy this book. Your keen editorial mind elevated my story and strengthened my characters. I trust in your judgment and vision, and I love working with you.

I could write pages extolling all the reasons I'm grateful for my agent, Stacy Testa of Writers House. Stacy called me on Halloween, just as early trick-or-treaters were hitting the streets. I was staring at a pumpkin-shaped bowl full of Kit Kats when she offered me representation and changed the course of my literary life. Stacy is a sharp, insightful editor and a savvy businesswoman with an uncanny ability to answer every message immediately. She is funny, brilliant, kind, and fiercely devoted to her writers. Thank you for believing me, Stacy. And know that I think of you and smile every time I see a Kit Kat.

To my power team of amazing women—Betsy Walsh, Eileen

Marks, Jenny Rappole, Ginger Barrow, Julie Mays Sudduth, Christy Hartmann, Heather Chadwick Ramirez, Darian Neckermann, Clara McEleney, Lauren Gibson, Heather Klinkhamer, Rita Tomaz, and Nicole Schaefer, thank you for always asking when—not if—my book would be published. And a special thanks to Jennifer Dardzinski, who has been by my side since we were kids. Everyone should be so lucky to have such a steadfast and loyal friend who is willing to read endless drafts and give honest, helpful feedback.

To my childhood friend Stephanie Zerhusen, who spent never-ending summers climbing trees, building forts, splashing in creeks, running through the woods, and concocting outlandish plots with me, thank you for being the Daniela to my Cadie (but without the murdery parts).

A huge thanks to my in-laws Pat and Rich Dalton for their un-wavering optimism about my book and their cheerful willingness to entertain my kids at "Camp Dalton" so I could write.

To my parents, Ross and Barbara Carrick, I am so fortunate to have grown up in a home full of love and books and writing and inspiration. My father has published three genealogy books, and my mother ran a puppet theater, for which she wrote all the scripts. Thank you for the endless stories you read to me, and especially for the ones you made up on the spot. I feel like the luckiest girl in the world to have had you both as my parents. To my sister Susan Jarecha, you may be younger than me, but I have always looked up to you. Thanks for always being available to share a long-distance glass of phone wine and a good long talk—and for putting up with me that awful year when I was thirteen.

To my four kids—Mikaela, Bronte, Chaney, and Everett—you are by far the most compelling, complicated, brilliant characters I have ever created. You push me to be better, do better, try harder, learn more, and take risks. With your giant hearts and mighty spir-its, you have become my role models. Also, I sincerely apologize for all the missed calls and text messages, and for all the times I said, "I'll be right there. I juuuust need to finish this one paragraph." The good news: I finally finished the last paragraph! The bad news: I started another book.

I never could have written this book without the love, support, and infinite patience of my husband, Sean Dalton. That first day we met, when you saw me asleep with my head in a chemistry textbook, you woke me up with the nerdiest pick-up line in history: *"Studying by osmosis?"* Thirty-two years and four kids later, our nerdy chemistry is still going strong. Although I never included your thoughtful suggestions about adding aliens or dragons in my book, I appreciate the custom cocktails you invented to match the themes in my writing. Thank you for always believing in me and this book, even when (especially when) I doubted myself. I love you.

And, lastly, to the real-life Summer Kid—the boy who sat alone on the end of his pier reading, fishing, and daydreaming—I have no idea who you are or what your name is, but as I paddled by your pier, summer after summer, you inspired a story in my mind that took on a life of its own. I hope your world is rich and full of the adventure I imagined you to be dreaming of.

Look for Julie Carrick Dalton's
next novel

The Last Beekeeper

Available Winter 2023